GETTING OUT OF THE HOUSE

As   . It
was   the
hea   she
pre   Tho
wou   ght,
bea   hy,
awl   awl

No   ner
sub   ter.
She   she
can   s a
fibl   hen
Ma   k it
obv   es.
No

Dri   ays
bra   by
sto   ing
cor   she
lea   ove
the

GETTING OUT OF THE HOUSE

Isla Dewar

WINDSOR
PARAGON

First published 2005
by
Review
This Large Print edition published 2006
by
BBC Audiobooks Ltd by arrangement with
Headline Book Publishing
ISBN 1 4056 1344 0   (Windsor Hardcover)
ISBN 1 4056 1345 9   (Paragon Softcover)

British Library Cataloguing in Publication Data available

Printed and bound in Great Britain by
Antony Rowe Ltd., Chippenham, Wiltshire

For Nick, Sri, Adam and Kate

Mangoes

Things were different, then. Children had their own lives, marched to the beat of their own drums. Evenings, there were calls in the street as they played outside, footballs skiffing over pavements, the rattle of sticks dragged against railings. They were all sent outdoors so their mothers could get on with things. It would have been unthinkable, anyway, to stay indoors when there was so much world out there to explore.

It was a time, Nora remembered, of small gangs, best friends—hers was Julie Richards, though that closeness hadn't lasted long, Julie moved away; then there was Karen McClusky, but that was a different kind of friendship. There were exciting finds, treasures—a bird's egg, a really good stick. Children spoke two languages, playground and living room. You got a smack on the head for speaking playground in the living room. Nora's mother, Maisie, would recoil at the sound of slang. 'We don't have words like that in this home.'

Mostly, though, when Nora looked back, her childhood was a blank. A kind of inner darkness, with small cracks of daylight seeping through here and there. Memories. Things that had stayed with her—a scolding, a holiday in Devon, books she loved, the time her Aunt May took her to the cinema to see *Mary Poppins*, and mangoes. The mangoes had changed everything. She could divide her small childhood into two, before mangoes and after mangoes.

In November 1964, at the age of nine, Nora was

sent to do the family shop, an important mission. In the pocket of her blue corduroy trousers, elastic-waisted, was the shopping list her mother had written, and her small brown leather purse containing the folded pound notes she'd been given. She carried an old red canvas shopping bag, fraying at the seams.

The shopping list was not necessary, as Nora knew it by heart. Every Saturday morning, Maisie sat at the kitchen table and wrote on her Basildon Bond notepad what supplies she needed. As the list never varied from week to week, Nora could recite it as easily as she could recite Wordsworth's 'Composed Upon Westminster Bridge' which she was learning at school. She chanted the two as she went, tiptoeing, skipping, keeping her eye out for cracks and lines. She was superstitious about pavements.

'Earth has not anything to show more fair,' she sang to herself, 'three quarters mince, three quarters stewing steak. Dull would he be of soul, half-pound bacon, piece meat for roasting, who could pass by, three pounds potatoes, pound cooking apples, four eating apples, half-pound tomatoes, half-pound cheddar cheese, packet ginger biscuits, packet tea, small tin instant coffee, a sight so touching in its majesty . . .'

Maisie, Nora's mother, was ill, chronic bronchitis. Nobody in the family knew if it really was chronic, or, indeed, if it was bronchitis. She'd self-diagnosed, and taken to her bed. It being Saturday, Dr Buchan hadn't been summoned as he usually was to tend to Maisie when she was unwell, which was often. She was, as Nora was to remark later in her life, fond of a good illness, a devout hypochondriac.

Anticipating a long stay in bed, Maisie had on the cabinet at her side a pack of cigarettes, matches, ashtray, a box of Quality Street chocolates, a selection of books that Nora had picked out for her on her Saturday-morning trip to the library (she chose the ones with the most vivid covers) and the transistor radio that normally sat on the kitchen windowsill. She was an emotional soul. Books, films, music, sad stories in the newspapers about abandoned pets, and sick children who triumphed over debilitating diseases regularly moved her to tears.

Today it had been music. Maisie had been listening, as she coughed and slowly sucked a caramel, to Rachmaninov's second piano concerto. Her head ached, breathing was painful, she was contemplating death. Tears flowed. Nora, passing her mother's bedroom door, heard sobbing and burst in to see what was wrong. A person would have to be in excruciating pain to cry that hard.

Maisie, who had been fantasising about her own funeral, hadn't been glad to see her. As farewell ceremonies went, the one that had drifted into Maisie's mind wasn't heartening. Hardly anybody had bothered to come. But there, in the front pew of the church, were her husband, Alex, her older daughter, Cathryn, her sister, May, who lived round the corner, all stricken with grief, weeping. Nora was also there, wearing her school uniform, her hat rammed on to her head, almost covering her eyes, badge at the back as she never checked it before she put it on. She was looking confused.

In Maisie's imaginings, her coffin was laden with white lilies, and somewhere an organ was playing.

Her family had mouthed a leaden, fumbling rendition of 'Abide With Me'. It seemed to her, as she watched the fantasy unreel in her head, that nobody really cared she was gone.

Making up stories, watching them like movies of the mind, was her favourite thing to do. She was a little ashamed of it, thinking it was something she should have long grown out of. But she felt she had no control over them, they arrived in her head. She'd stop whatever she was doing, stand unnervingly still and let them flow, lips moving slightly as she played her part. Sometimes her mind movies were wonderful: she was a star, everybody loved her, everything went her way. Sometimes they were awful: things went wrong, people were rude, nobody understood her. Sometimes, like this one, they were just lonely and sad.

'What's up?' said Nora, startled and concerned at her bedside.

Maisie, horrified at being interrupted in the middle of her daydream, said, 'Get out.' It was a hiss, not at all pleasant.

Nora had slunk from the room and gone downstairs, where Cathryn was preparing lunch. Cathryn was six years older than Nora, and was experimenting with beans on toast, the usual Saturday lunchtime fare. Maisie claimed that since Saturday was a holiday for everyone else, it should be a holiday for her too. 'No cooking,' she said. 'Beans on toast for lunch. And cold meat salad for tea.' Cathryn was adding curry powder and chopped tomatoes to make the beans more exotic.

'Mum's crying,' Nora told her.

Cathryn shrugged, said that Mum was always

4

crying these days, and carried on with her experiment. Adding curry, tasting. Looking a little dismayed.

'Mum's crying,' Nora told her dad.

Alex pretended he hadn't heard her. He went out to his garden shed to sort out his tools. He was used to Maisie's fluctuating emotions, but never knew what to do about them.

Inside, Cathryn handed Nora a tray, on which lay a plate of beans on toast, a slice of buttered bread, a cup of tea, a fork and knife, and a plastic daffodil in a glass egg cup, and told her to take it upstairs. 'Mum's lunch.'

'You take it,' Nora said. 'I'm not going up there. She's crying.'

But Cathryn insisted. 'I'm serving up. You're just hanging about.'

Nora took the tray and stamped up the stairs. Fearing she might be rejected once more, she started to shout, to let her mother know she'd soon be entering her room. 'Lunch coming. Lunch coming.' And got carried away. She kicked open the bedroom door and marched round the room. 'Lunch coming. Lunch coming.'

The noise, the movement shifted Maisie from her doldrums. She felt cheered. She smiled, a weak smile. The smile of an invalid trying to hide her pain. 'You're daft,' she told Nora. It was said scoldingly, but not without affection.

She looked at the tray. 'Now, isn't this beautiful? A wee flower and everything. Cathryn's so thoughtful.' She took a mouthful, and frowned, trying to discern exactly what she was tasting.

Nora told her about the curry powder.

'See,' said Maisie. 'That's clever. I'd never've

5

thought of doing that.'

Nora thought glumly that she'd never have thought of adding curry to the beans either, or of a plastic daffodil in an egg cup. She wished she was clever and thoughtful, like Cathryn.

Cheered by the attention, the thoughtful little plastic flower, Maisie said, 'How would you like to be a big girl this afternoon? Make up for your daftness. You can do the shopping.'

An hour later, Nora was walking to the shops, Cathryn's exotic beans lying leaden in her stomach, reciting her list and Wordsworth. 'This City now doth, like a garment, wear, tin corned beef, tin spam, the beauty of the morning, tin peaches, tin floor polish . . .'

She was prone to drifting off into her own world, reciting favourite poems such as Robert Louis Stevenson's *Travel*: 'I should like to rise and go, Where the golden apples grow; Where below another sky, Parrot islands anchored lie,' she'd say to herself as she climbed the stairs at school, or sat at home doing her homework. Or she'd sing songs in her head; her most recent favourite was 'Please Please Me', which hummed round and round in her mind blotting out all the ordinary, mundane and boring things.

This had happened during a maths test a week ago. Nora had scored nothing out of fifty. It took five men seven hours to dig a ditch fifty-six yards long and three feet deep; how long would it take three men? Nora had read this, and wondered. What sort of men? Were they wearing overalls and big boots? Did they stop for lunch? Nothing about that in the question. Did they have sandwiches wrapped in greaseproof paper, and if so, what was in the sandwiches? She hoped it wasn't spam, which she hated. It was slippy in your mouth. She'd written, *I think it would be about twelve hours, but more if they had a break for a cup of tea and a bite to eat. Also, the weather could be freezing, in which case it would be hard to dig, or boiling hot, and the men would be tired and sweaty. Then it would take more than twelve hours. So, they'd have to stop working and go home for tea. This question is impossible to answer.*

The teacher had marked this with a red cross, meaning, wrong. And there were the dire words, *See me*, at the bottom of the page.

There had been a gasp when the teacher had read out Nora's nothing out of fifty. In unison forty little people inhaled loudly. Nobody got nothing out of fifty. You always got one, at least, for spelling your name properly. But Nora hadn't even done that. Dreaming, singing her song in her head, she'd carelessly written Noar Marshell.

Nora had not mentioned the shame of her nothing out of fifty at home. But word had spread through the school. In the playground she'd experienced mockery, pointing, derision and laughter. She'd been called names—thicko, beanbrain—and discovered that singing songs in your head can be a great comfort in times of misery.

The shops, this Saturday, were busy. Lit against the grey November afternoon, windows were filled with fascinating goodies. The Beatles blasted out from the record shop on the corner; there was a poster of the Fab Four to gaze at. She longed to buy a record, but she was nine, and the price of a single was three weeks' pocket money.

Teenagers gathered at the café, drinking frothy coffee, playing the jukebox. Cathryn spent Saturday afternoons there, talking heatedly about hairstyles, clothes, boys, and the possibility of being killed by a nuclear bomb. She drank Coca-Cola with ice cubes chinking against the glass, and a slice of lemon bobbing just below the surface fizz. Nora sighed. Such sophistication was beyond her.

First stop was the butcher's, a busy place. Hectic on a Saturday. Mr Hopeton was small and round, red of face and jolly. 'It's all the meat,' Maisie said. 'Makes people optimistic.'

'Well, young Nora,' he said. Huge voice. 'On your own? Where's Mum today?'

'She's ill. In bed.'

'Nothing serious, I hope.'

'It's very serious,' said Nora. 'It's chronic.'

'Has she seen the doctor?'

Nora remembered Maisie saying that she couldn't call Dr Buchan, it was Saturday. She should have phoned him yesterday. 'Too late to get him now. I'll have to wait till Monday.'

'It's too late for the doctor,' Nora told Mr Hopeton, shaking her head, looking forlorn.

'Oh, my,' said Mr Hopeton. 'I'm sorry to hear that.' He exchanged a dismayed look with the people standing behind Nora waiting to be served. He liked Maisie, who was sociable away from the house.

Nora had noticed there were two Maisies. The outside one spoke with her outside voice, which was slightly higher and louder than her inside voice, and with more rounded vowels. Her inside voice was her natural Scottish brogue. Maisie

8

always sounded different from the rest of the family. She had a Celtic twang, a lilt. Alex, Cathryn and Nora all had the same London accent.

In this shop Maisie laughed and flirted and spoke in her outside voice. She was quite the star of the butcher's queue.

Nora asked for the stewing steak and mince. When Mr Hopeton had brought her that, she asked for a piece of meat for roasting. He held his large knife on a rolled cut of beef. 'This much?' Nora nodded. Then he moved the knife along an extra three inches. 'Bit of extra for the invalid.' He did the same with the bacon, letting the slicing machine whirr and the slices pile up.

The gammon steaks caught Nora's eye. Thick and juicy and a beautiful pink-red colour. What a treat for the family, she thought, if for a change— and Maisie often said she liked a bit of a change now and then—they had gammon steaks with a browned slice of pineapple on top. She'd seen this in her mother's *Woman's Own*, a colourful plateful, steaks, mashed potatoes and vividly green peas. *Rustle up a Mid-week Miracle*, the article had said. She bought four of them, and left.

She was pleased by this adventurous buy. It would be a welcome break from the usual food rota.

Life at Nora's home was routine. Routines that moved into other routines, routines within routines. There was the food routine. Roast beef on Sunday, leftover roast on Monday. Tuesday stew, Wednesday leftover stew. Thursday mince, Friday fish, and on Saturday Maisie had her no-cook day. Even the eating of meals had a fixed routine. At teatime they had to finish their main course—fish and chips on a good day, cod's roe on a bad, along with a slice of bread and butter—then, perhaps, there'd be a slice of chocolate cake. It was a sin punishable by being dismissed from the table and banished to your room to sit alone for the rest of the evening to eat a piece of cake before finishing the boring things.

There was a bath routine. Wash face and hands before feet, which would be the dirtiest bit of your body. Anyone using the lavatory was strictly instructed to use two, and only two, sheets of toilet paper.

There was the ironing routine—one week Nora did it, the next Cathryn. They were instructed to do the little things first, before the iron got hot. Then the sheets, then the shirts. Nora found it all a bit wearing, and thought the gammon steaks would be a relief for everyone.

It was two minutes' walk from the butcher's to the fruit shop. But Nora dawdled. She watched people in the street, cars on the road, and people on buses, who stared back at her. She got caught up in the whirl of Saturday afternoon bustle, and the magic of being alone, unchaperoned, in the midst of it.

She watched two women in the street sharing a long gossip. One was wearing a red skirt and a yellow blouse that barely buttoned across her bust. She was small and wide, very wide. Vast bum. She was black, and had a gloriously healthy sheen. She was laughing. Laughing and laughing and laughing. It seemed to start in her stomach and come bursting out of her throat, that laughter. It was joyous. 'Ooooh-ha-ha-ha,' she went. And she couldn't stop. She wiped her eyes, still laughing.

Nora wanted to laugh like that. She wanted to be with someone who laughed like that. She wanted to go home with that gorgeous woman, and share the strange fruits in the basket she carried over her arm. She stared.

The woman, sensing the intense look, turned. 'You lost, honey?'

Nora was shaken by this. She'd been wrapped up in her daydreams, thoughts of going home with the laughing woman, being drawn into her huge happy family, sitting round the table joking and chatting. In fact her imaginings had become so vivid, so real, she had, for a moment, forgotten she was standing in the street, staring. She shook her head. 'No.' And turned, walked away, blushing.

The fruit shop was Nora's favourite. Mrs Firth, who owned it, was small and fragile. Her hair was wiry, thick like a scouring pad, and beneath it was a thin face, long nose, and lips coloured with a smear of red lipstick that overlapped the edges. That was all the make-up she wore. Nora could see the lines round her eyes, and the scattering of freckles on the top of her cheeks, across her nose. She had what Nora thought of as twittery hands, that flitted over the fruit and veg as she selected them, and gently squeezed tomatoes to check they were firm. She wore a green overall.

'Where's Mrs Marshall today?' she asked. Maisie was known here, but didn't project very much. She wasn't a star in the fruit shop. She considered vegetables to be necessary but boring.

'Ill,' said Nora. 'Chronic.'

'Goodness,' said Mrs Firth. 'What does the doctor say?'

'Too late for the doctor, I'm afraid,' said Nora.

11

If Mrs Firth didn't much like Maisie, she was fond of Nora. She popped a small bunch of grapes into a bag and said they were for the invalid, and gave Nora a banana, 'For being a good brave girl.'

Nora was drawn by the lure of the colours of the fruit and vegetables packed into boxes that lay open on the shelves. Along with the things on her mother's list, she bought a red pepper, too shiny to resist. And two mangoes: she liked the word and longed to know what they were like beneath their dull green skin. These were the sort of things the gleaming, laughing woman in the bright billowing clothes would buy.

By now the bag was getting heavy. And by the time she left the grocer's, where she'd bought a tin of pineapple rings for the gammon, and had been given a tin of mandarins, a small tin of orange juice and a lollipop for herself, it was too heavy for her to lift. She had to drag it to the bus stop.

She'd been told to walk to the shops but take the bus back. Even Maisie, who regularly overestimated what children could and couldn't do, realised Nora wouldn't be strong enough to carry a whole week's shop all the way home.

Once off the bus, though, she still had to walk the length of the street to her house. She found that if she lifted the bag with both hands and walked sideways, she could manage two or three steps before she had to put it down again. It took a while, but puffing and wheezing, and with sweat running down her back, she made it to the front door. Then down the hall and into the kitchen. She dumped the bag, went through to the living room and threw herself on to the sofa, declaring herself to be knackered.

'Don't say that. It's common.' Maisie had risen from her bed and come down, wrapped in her worn red dressing gown, to inspect the purchases.

'Gammon steaks,' she called as she hauled things from the bag. 'They weren't on the list.'

'I thought it would make a change to have gammon steaks,' said Nora from her prone position on the sofa. 'You like a bit of a change.'

'This is a huge bit of meat for roasting, and how much bacon is this?'

'Butcher gave me extra on account of you being ill,' said Nora.

'Grapes,' said Maisie. 'Mandarins. What's all this?'

'Stuff from people to help you get better.'

'What have you been saying about me?' said Maisie.

'Nothing,' said Nora. 'Just you weren't feeling well.'

The pineapple rings passed without comment. It was the mangoes that brought on the outburst. 'What the hell's this?'

'Mangoes,' said Nora.

'Mangoes? Mangoes? Who told you to buy mangoes? We don't eat mangoes. That's foreign food.'

'I thought they'd make us happy. It's a happy word. Mango. We could eat them and chat.'

'Mangoes?' It seemed to be all Maisie could say. A strange fury had taken hold of her. 'We are *not* the sort of people who have mangoes. How dare you spend our good money on muck like that?'

She came barging into the living room, one in each hand, and thrust them under Nora's nose.

'We don't eat this foreign tripe. For crying out

loud, I send you to do a simple thing like the shopping and you come home with a load of rubbish. How much did all this cost? Where's my change?'

Nora got up and made to leave the room. She had no change.

'Don't you go running away,' said Maisie. 'You're going to have to take them back. Mangoes, I'll bloody mango you.'

Nora panicked. She bolted. Out the door, down the path and round the corner to her Aunt May, who was her friend and who could be relied on for advice and chocolate biscuits.

Auntie May was sitting by the fire knitting when Nora arrived, sweaty and gasping for breath after her sprint from the house.

May was the family fixer, the sorter-out of dilemmas—like the arrival of weird fruit in a household. An outspoken bustler, she could best Maisie in any argument, and was an excellent person to have on your side when physical punishment threatened.

Fifteen years ago, her husband, Ronald, had died, and now she kept herself busy visiting other members of her family, playing bridge with her friends, swimming at the local baths twice a week, having coffee with Maisie on Tuesday mornings, and knitting. Her needles clacked, balls of wool unravelled, and misshapen garments, dubiously coloured, that nobody wanted to wear, emerged.

'Mangoes?' she said. 'You're telling me your mother's got in a state over a couple of mangoes?'

Nora nodded. 'She says she's going to mango me.'

'Oh dear,' said May. 'How much did they cost,

14

by the way?'

'Quite a lot,' Nora told her. She wasn't going to admit to an actual sum.

'How much is quite a lot?' asked May.

'A lot.'

'Does Maisie know how much they cost?'

'We haven't got round to that yet,' said Nora.

'And what were you doing in the fruit shop anyway?'

'The shopping.'

'Where was your mother?'

'In bed. She's poorly.'

May said, 'Ah.' Now she could understand the purpose of the visit. 'Maisie will be looking for her change. And you haven't any because of the mangoes.'

She jabbed her knitting needles into the ball of wool and heaved herself, grunting, from her chair. Fetching her purse from her handbag, she shoved five shillings into Nora's pocket. 'There you go.'

She put on her brown coat and wrapped a silk scarf round her neck. 'Let's get going. I'm not a great fruit person, but I want a taste.'

Like most families, the Marshalls spent time together. But this was usually a matter of them all being in the same room at the same time— eating a meal, perhaps, or watching a television programme. In everything, Maisie always took centre stage. The others didn't say much. At mealtimes, Maisie would recount her day. In front of the television, the choice of programme would be hers. They rarely discussed anything. Major catastrophes could unfold on the small screen in front of them; they'd look at them in the same silence in which they viewed dramas, comedies and

15

game shows. They never went on family outings to the cinema or the theatre. They never played games.

The tasting of the mangoes, then, was one of the first family events Nora had experienced. It was the first time in her memory that they had all gathered round to try something new together. There was a sense of joining in.

The fruit were on the draining board in the kitchen. Cathryn said they looked like green turds, and she wasn't having anything to do with them.

May fetched a knife from the drawer in the cabinet. Maisie laid out five plates, each with dessert fork placed on top. May cut with surgeon's delicacy into the fruit. 'Got a big stone in it.' Everyone clustered round and peered. May gave a commentary on the proceedings. 'Juicy. Kind of pale yellow inside.'

'Like sick,' said Cathryn.

'Hard to slice,' said May. But she managed. A pulpy dollop was placed on each plate. She was the first to taste. 'I like that. I'm not a fruit person, as you know. But that I could take to. I could be partial to a mango.'

Maisie agreed. 'Lovely,' she said. 'A bit peachy. But nicer. You don't have that bum-fluff skin. Sweet.'

Alex said it was the best fruit he'd ever eaten. 'Not that I eat fruit. Well, an apple, sometimes, when I'm stuck for something to eat.'

Even Cathryn was won over. 'This is really good,' she said with surprise. 'This could be the fruit of the future.'

'Y'know,' said May, slurping and pointing to the diminishing dollop on her plate. 'This would be very nice with one of them gammon steaks. Better than pineapple rings. I'm partial to a gammon steak.'

Nora smirked. She was dipping her finger into the juices left on the draining board, and licking. Mangoes were wonderful. No wonder the woman in the billowing multicoloured clothes was laughing. She must have mangoes all the time.

She was sent to wash her hands. She lingered outside the kitchen, eavesdropping.

'What got into you, sending a child to do the shopping?' said May. 'There's all sorts out there. You never know what could have happened to her.'

'Nora's fine,' said Maisie. 'Who'd do anything to Nora? She's no beauty. Cathryn I'd worry about.'

'How did she carry all that stuff home? You should have got me to do it.'

'She's going to have to get used to all that. What else is there for her but to settle down with some decent hard-working man? She's got no brains at all. Her school reports are dreadful. She doesn't know I know, but she got nothing in one of her tests. Nothing at all, out of fifty. She even spelt her name wrong. She's not stupid, but it's hard to know what's going on in her head.'

'She may surprise you yet,' said May.

'I doubt it,' said Maisie. 'I worry. What's going to become of her? Can you see Nora holding down a job? What sort of job would that be? A doctor? Lawyer? I don't think so. A secretary? Nora? Can you imagine her sitting all day behind a typewriter, doing shorthand, taking phone calls?'

Auntie May said she couldn't.

'She's up one minute, down the next. Found her

17

last week standing in the middle of the kitchen, when she was meant to be doing the dishes, conducting the Berlin Philharmonic Orchestra on the radio with a wooden spoon, splattering the place with soapy water. Then she was making a fuss and crying because I was going to kill a spider. Said it might have babies at home waiting for it to bring in food. You just don't know what she'll come up with next. And she's a scruff. Goes out in the morning neat as a pin. Comes home with her school tie halfway round her neck, if she hasn't tied it round her head. Shoelaces undone, socks round her ankles, pockets stuffed with rubbish. I know she's my own, and I shouldn't put her down. But she's clueless. And she tells lies.'

Nora's heart numbed. This was true. She was a fibber. Didn't know why she did it. She seemed to open her mouth and out they came, lies. Had she not told her teacher the family was moving to Canada? Why had she done that? She didn't know. Of course, the teacher told the headmistress, who'd phoned Maisie and said the school needed to be properly informed if children were going to be removed. Big scolding, sore bum, and a night in her room with no tea.

Her favourite fibs were the ones she told Julie, her best friend. Maisie had once overheard a conversation between the two.

'My dad's a lion tamer,' Nora had said.

'Well mine's the man on the flying trapeze,' said Julie.

'Mine gets fired out of a cannon. He wears a helmet and he lands in a net fifty feet away,' said Nora.

'Mine tap-dances on the stage.' Julie.

'Mine once kissed Brigitte Bardot.' Nora.

Then they'd giggled. 'Stop that, you two.' Maisie, horrified at the fib-upmanship. 'Telling lies about your fathers. I'll take the back of my hand to the both of you.'

'Why can't she be like Cathryn, clever and, well, good-looking?' said Maisie now to Aunt May. 'Cathryn's a grand lass. She'll go far.'

Nora had often wondered herself why she couldn't be more like her sister. She'd always been slightly in awe of Cathryn, who had been a beautiful infant and had grown into a beautiful child. By the time she was fifteen, going on sixteen, it was obvious she was going to be a beautiful woman. She had lustrous dark hair, high cheekbones, brown eyes. She moved easily through her adolescence, untroubled by rollercoaster emotions or acne. Her very hormones were kind to her.

People would stare at her, as if wanting to get hold of or be part of her loveliness. They would want to know what she was thinking, believing that behind such an exquisite face there could only be exquisite thoughts of landscapes or poetry, or, perhaps, some rare profundity that was quite beyond ordinary-looking mortals.

In fact, though Cathryn was passionate about nuclear disarmament and regularly sent money to Barnardo's, she was as prone to young thoughts as any teenager. She enjoyed her popularity. Mostly when the phone rang it was some lovestruck boy wanting a date. On Valentine's Day a pile of cards addressed to her tumbled through the letter box. Nora only ever got one if she sent it to herself.

Cathryn was an excellent scholar, studying for

O-level Greek, Latin, German and French as well as advanced mathematics, history and English. She rarely got less than an A in anything. She was, Maisie crowed, the perfect daughter.

Nora, on the other hand, was average at everything except sports. Here she dipped below average and sank into complete failure. Her teachers would shake their heads sadly and say, 'You're not your sister, are you?'

Nora would say that indeed she wasn't her sister, she was Nora, a completely different person. This would be taken as cheek and she'd be given lines to write at home. Many an evening was spent in her bedroom writing *I must not express my impudent thoughts to my superiors* two hundred times.

At home, visitors would admire Cathryn and tell Maisie how proud she must be to have such a beautiful and clever daughter. Maisie would smile and agree. Then they'd turn to Nora. They didn't mean to be rude. But compared to her sister, Nora was plain and unaccomplished. 'And who's this?' the visitor might say, smiling. Looking her up and down, searching for some attribute they might compliment Nora on. But they could never find anything.

Nora would strike a geeky pose, pressing her arms to her sides, sucking in her cheeks and crossing her eyes, and say, 'I'm Nora, the geeky little sister.'

Mostly, visitors would say, 'Oh, surely not.'

But there were a few who smiled and nodded. There would be a look of mixed amusement and sympathy. A fellow geek, Nora would think.

It was a relief to discover that she was not alone.

There were other people in the world who marched to the beat of their own drum, even if they did it clumsily without knowing the tune they were trying to keep in time to. People who were out of kilter with everyone around them, who said the wrong things at gatherings, started singing in church a couple of bars ahead of the rest of the congregation, absent-mindedly put on mismatching socks in the morning, and, from time to time, walked around with their eyes shut to find out what it would be like to be blind.

Nora had done this once and had crashed into a table, knocking a vase of flowers to the floor. She'd paused a moment, considering the damage, debating if she should confess to her crime. Then, deciding against it, she had fled the house. When she returned she said it had nothing to do with her, she'd been out all morning. Maisie had declared that the broken vase and ruined flowers were a mystery. 'We must have a ghost.'

'I wish she was more like Cathryn,' said Maisie now. 'I understand her. I'll never understand Nora.'

Eavesdropping behind the door, Nora shrugged. At nine, she was just about old enough to get some perverse gratification out of being misunderstood. It gave her a slight thrill, which she didn't understand at all.

The Preferred One

By Thursday, Maisie decided she was well enough to leave her sick bed and go to the shops. There were a few things she needed. Bananas, as she did a rather good bananas in custard drenched in brown sugar for a quick pudding; eggs, as she hadn't trusted Nora to bring half a dozen home in one piece. And, most of all, tonic wine.

Maisie was amazed at the wondrous qualities of tonic wine. She sang its praises. 'It fair gives me a lift,' she told Alex. 'It's all the minerals and vitamins. I can feel it doing me good. A wee glass in the afternoon sets me up for the rest of the day.'

Alex suspected the lift she got had more to do with the tonic wine's surprising alcohol content than the minerals and vitamins, but never said so.

In the butcher's shop, Maisie was greeted with surprise. Seeing her standing before him asking for half a dozen eggs, Mr Hopeton's eyes widened. 'What are you doing here? Thought you were on the brink of death.'

Maisie said, 'Good heavens, whatever made you think that?' Even as she spoke, the answer was creeping into the recesses of her mind. Nora.

'Young Nora,' said Mr Hopeton. 'According to her, you were chronic. It was too late for the doctor.'

Maisie said, 'Ah.' Then, 'A touch of bronchitis, I'm afraid. And it was too late for the doctor. It being Saturday, and him being on the golf course probably. Nora got it wrong.'

'Ah,' said Mr Hopeton in turn.

22

But Maisie could see her appearance had caused him more than astonishment. He'd been angered by it. He'd spent some time on Saturday thinking how sad it was that Nora was about to lose her mother. He'd sympathised with poor Mr Marshall left without his wife, who was such a sociable woman, and with two girls to bring up. He'd grieved a little for Maisie, who he liked. He'd donated a large section of beef and several slices of bacon to the stricken family. He felt duped. He was grumpy. He sullenly handed Maisie her eggs, took her money and bade her goodbye.

Maisie was, of course, mortified.

And the horror continued as the episode at the butcher's was repeated in the other shops she went to. Shock that she was still alive. Resentment that the small donations to the family—grapes, a tin of mandarin oranges—had been extracted under false pretences.

Maisie hurried home, head down. Her recent encounters had made her cringe. Indeed, it would be years before she saw it as funny. She could not understand that her daughter's only mistake had been, while on an adult mission, to try to talk to the adults she met in adult fashion. Giving people the impression her mother was at home, breathing her last.

Maisie could hardly wait for Nora to return home from school.

'You made a mockery of me,' she said as soon as Nora came through the front door.

Nora, standing in the hallway at the door of her bedroom, school blazer slipping from her shoulders, tie askew and socks crumpled round her ankles, threw her school bag on to her bed,

23

then came into the living room and said, 'How?'

'You told everybody that I was dying,' said Maisie.

'Did not,' said Nora.

'Did too,' said Maisie. 'When you were doing the shopping, you told everyone I was dying. You said it was too late for the doctor.'

'It *was* too late for the doctor,' said Nora. 'You said so.'

'When you tell people it's too late for the doctor, it means there's no point him looking at you because there's nothing he can do. You're going to die. When I said it was too late for the doctor, I meant it was Saturday and the surgery would be shut. It wasn't like I was an emergency or anything.'

Nora said, 'Oh.'

Cathryn came home. She slipped in the front door and, hearing raised voices, snuck upstairs. There was a scolding going on, and she didn't want to become embroiled in it. She'd be expected to take sides. Maisie always expected other family members to back her against the admonished one.

'You made people think I was about to pop off, and they gave you things. They were shocked to see me alive. I felt like a scrounger. I was back affronted,' said Maisie.

'Shouldn't that be black affronted?' asked Nora.

This stopped Maisie's flow. She thought about it. At the top of the stairs, Cathryn paused to listen.

'It's never black affronted,' said Maisie. 'It's back affronted. It means you're so embarrassed and ashamed you wish your front was at your back so's nobody can see how mortified you are.'

24

On the stairs, Cathryn sniggered.

Nora said, 'Oh.'

'It'll be years before I can put my face in at the butcher's again,' said Maisie. This grieved her. She believed it important to maintain good relations with the local shopkeepers. A butcher you were friendly with was more likely to sell you succulent lamb chops and stewing steak that would turn tender when cooked.

She turned on Nora. 'How could you be so stupid? And look at you. You're a mess. What sort of state is that to come home in? Do you ever see Cathryn like that? Sometimes I think you're brainless. You just don't think. Look at Cathryn, she never just opens her mouth and spills out rubbish. She's clever. She thinks. Why can't you be like Cathryn? I by far prefer her to you.'

At the top of the stairs, Cathryn drew her breath and felt a thrill. It was good to be the preferred one. Still, she suspected Maisie had just said something dreadful. She felt for Nora. And more, she did not really want to be Maisie's favourite; she had a notion even then, young as she was, that a lot was expected of the favoured one. No, she did not like what she was hearing at all.

Nora felt a glitch, a small bump in time. It was as if everything stopped. A pained expression froze on her face. She slipped away. Backing slowly, silently down the hall, she tiptoed to her room, where she sat on the bed, hands folded, placed on her lap, staring at the wall. Grief and shame swept through her. But she did not cry, she was too shocked for that.

Her mother preferred Cathryn. All the things her mother did, and all the time she did them, she

25

preferred Cathryn. And when Nora came home from school, dumped her bag in her room and shouted, 'Hello, Mum, I'm home,' her mother would rather it was Cathryn. It was a heart-stopping revelation. But then, Nora thought, I prefer her to me too.

It was perplexing. Nora had never thought about her sister as the favourite child. She'd never thought her mother would prefer one person to another. In fact, she hadn't thought her mother had opinions. She was just there.

Cathryn, the favourite child, in her room, was trying a new hairstyle. Her radio played. A song she liked came on and she turned up the volume. Ray Charles sang 'Georgia On My Mind'. Nora heard it. For a few minutes, everything stopped. It was beautiful. *Georgia, oh Georgia* . . . Such longing, such sadness. She wanted to go there, wherever it was, she didn't know. But she imagined a lush, green place. Exquisite buildings on streets lined with high trees, the air heavy with orange blossom. For now, and for the rest of her life, this would be her favourite song.

She decided that she preferred her sister to her mother, her father to her mother, indeed anybody in the world to her mother. She vowed she would never become a doctor, a lawyer or a secretary. She would never get married.

She would be a tramp when she grew up, she'd wander the highways and byways living off the land. Then again, she might learn to play the guitar and become a rock star. A millionaire, then Maisie would be sorry.

She declared a secret war on her mother, making faces behind her back, stealing coins from her purse, hiding her cigarettes. When Maisie wasn't looking, Nora poured salt on her food, put spoonfuls of sugar in her tea. She would hide one of Maisie's shoes, so whenever Maisie wanted to go out she'd hop about the house shouting, 'Has anybody seen my shoe?'

Nora filled a private notebook with stories of the Purple Princess and the Scone Witch. Nora was the virtuous, devilishly clever and beautiful Purple Princess, who could fly, and who had been stolen at birth by an evil crone, the hideously ugly Scone Witch (Maisie), who planned to poison all the children in the world with her scones. It was the Purple Princess's mission to ruin the witch's scones. Whenever Maisie was baking, Nora would sneak into the kitchen and turn the oven down or up. The food inside either burned or came out lumpen and half-cooked. *Saved the world from another batch*, she'd write in her notebook. *The planet will sleep tonight.*

Sensing the hostility, and feeling awful for having in a moment of fury told her that she preferred her sister, Maisie would, every now and then, look at Nora and say, 'Ach, mangoes.'

Nora would look smug and reply, 'Mangoes are lovely.'

She knew Maisie would not argue; she knew something about her mother. Two weeks after the shopping incident, Nora had been handed a damp parcel of potato peelings wrapped in newspaper and told to put them in the dustbin outside the back door. She'd opened the lid, and instead of tossing in her damp parcel, had peered inside. There, beside an empty bottle of Maisie's Sanatogen tonic wine, was a newspaper-wrapped parcel someone had thrown in earlier in the day. It had spilt open, laying bare its contents unto the fields and sky: the peel and stones of exotic fruit. Nora stared at them, amazed. Her mother had been secretly feasting on mangoes.

A Bit of Colour

The house where Nora and her family lived was in a long, long row of identical houses, built not long before the war on the outskirts of London. Walk along the street, turn the corner, more houses, all the same. Walk along that street, turn the corner, rows of houses. All the same.

If the exterior was uninspiring, the interior was overwhelming.

Inside, Nora's home was frugally furnished. Each room contained what it was expected to contain, nothing more. Nothing to indicate to a visitor any family quirks or hobbies: no musical instruments, no ice skates, no tennis rackets, hula-hoops, records, car manuals, walking boots, telescopes for star-gazing, sketchpads, drawings, exotic plants, magazines. Nothing. Nothing to suggest that anything other than humdrum routine living took place within these walls.

Frugal it was. But not drab, never that. There was one picture in the house. It hung over the fireplace in the living room, and was of a carnival, perhaps in Spain or New Orleans. It showed a pierrot dancing with a woman in a long blue dress, holding a mask over her eyes. The crowd behind them was multicoloured and blurred; fireworks splashed the night sky above them. The carpet in the living room was blue and yellow, the three-piece suite red and black, the curtains striped red, white and green with strings of yellow and pink flowers running down between them. The sitting room at the front of the house and the bedrooms were similarly lively.

Maisie always said that she liked a bit of colour. But not being able to decide which colour she liked, she used them all.

The only room in the house that wasn't ablaze with patterns was Nora's. This was because, technically, Nora's bedroom wasn't a room, but a box room. A large box room, certainly, big enough to take a single bed and a chest of drawers, but still not a room. It was, therefore, painted white. Maisie, who considered herself to be a woman of taste, thought it common to wallpaper a box room. It was, then, a small space, but Nora loved it. She always felt safe there. And for the rest of her life, though she enjoyed living in big, airy rooms, she preferred to sleep in small spaces.

Her sister Cathryn had one of the three upstairs bedrooms, a riot of many shades of pink. The others were Maisie and Alex's room, and the guest room, which was used when relatives, part of Maisie's sprawling family, came to stay. It would have been unthinkable for them to sleep in the box room. Guests, Maisie said, should be treated with courtesy. So the best room in the house was, then, the guest bedroom, which was kept shut. For Nora and Cathryn it was forbidden territory.

Maisie and Alex had moved into that house when they moved to London from Edinburgh, two years after they married. It was the backdrop of

Nora's childhood. All her life, though she could not recall events in detail, she would remember every inch of where they had taken place. The cupboard in the kitchen, for example, where Maisie kept her crockery and pots. Cups lined up, hanging from hooks; pots on a stand, the huge black chip pan at the bottom, the small aluminium pot at the top. She could recall the smell of that kitchen: a strange mix of fat and room spray.

She could bring to mind the sounds of water in the pipes when she ran a bath; the old, thin blue-and-white-striped towels that hung on the bathroom rail; and the contents of the cabinet on the wall: iron pills, aspirin, her father's razor and shaving cream, a spare bar of Camay. She could remember, too, the way her bed creaked when she climbed into it, the shapes that she saw when she stared too long at the pattern on the living room wallpaper. All that, and more.

They always ate breakfast at seven thirty in the morning. Her father had bacon and egg: one egg, two slices of bacon. Nora and Cathryn had toast. Maisie thought it absurd to give children a cooked breakfast. 'Kids don't need anything like that.'

Maisie's cooking wasn't so much frugal as economical. Meals were prepared on a tight budget. And her food wasn't loveless, just made to fill, cooked without passion. Indeed, Maisie was a passionate woman, she just never found anything to be passionate about. From time to time, her frustrated emotions would boil up, and she'd rage.

When in these furies she'd stamp about the house, tight-lipped, waving her arms about, and anyone caught in her path would be berated. It was usually Nora. 'You, madam, can just clean the windows. It isn't up to me. You look out of them every bit as much as I do.'

Probably Maisie should have gone out to work. But at the time, it was accepted that a woman should stay home and concern herself with her house and family. So most of her days were spent alone at home with her imagination, feeling duty-bound to clean, tidy, and provide three meals a day. She knew four was the cliché. She did breakfast, lunch and supper in the evening. Where the fourth came in, she didn't know. Anyone wanting anything over and above the regular food provided had to make it for themselves.

Weekdays, between eight in the morning and four in the afternoon, was women's time in the neighbourhood. With husbands at work and children at school, they'd often gather in one another's kitchens to drink tea and gossip—usually about their absent husbands and children. Maisie was part of this, but preferred to stay home. She'd clean slowly, and daydream. Between chores she'd sit by the fire listening to the radio or reading one of the books Nora selected for her from the local library on Saturday mornings.

The business of setting out routines for everything released her. She knew what she had to do every day, and once her work was done, she was free to slip into her imaginings. Things she'd like to happen, things she dreaded happening.

She could invent a scenario, then convince herself it was true. Hearing a siren howl a couple of streets away, she'd think perhaps something had happened to one of her children or her husband. Though it might be two in the afternoon and all of the people in her life were busy in other places,

31

she could persuade herself that one of them had been killed. She would spend the next few hours envisioning every moment of her life from the moment the police rang her doorbell, bearing terrible news, to the funeral, where she'd be bent double with grief. She thought that if it was Alex who had met his end, cruelly mowed down by some irresponsible driver, she'd wear his wedding ring on a gold chain round her neck, next to her heart, for the rest of her life. Times would be hard without him. She imagined herself having to add to her miserable widow's pension by taking a low-paid job in a shop or a factory. She'd be uncomplaining and noble. By the time Nora or Cathryn arrived home, Maisie would have worked herself into a state of nervous apprehension.

Then again, had she whiled away her post-chore hours dreaming up a scenario where she came into a load of money, or where she was the star of a West End show, or where it was her and not Ingrid Bergman who led a horde of children to safety in *The Inn of the Sixth Happiness*, she'd be full of joy and singing when her own offspring came home. Maisie's moods were usually a result of where her imagination took her.

Nora's father ate his evening meal alone when he returned from work. Sometimes Maisie would join him, drinking a cup of tea as he ate and regaling him with the adventures of her day. Maisie was an expert chatterer, and could effortlessly make a drama out of the mundane. Alex would listen, nodding and smiling. He loved this prattle and rarely said anything about the sort of day he'd had.

He was an insurance assessor. Nora, as a child,

didn't know what this meant. What she did know was that her father went out of the house at eight in the morning, and came home at six in the evening. He always wore a hat.

In Nora's early memories, Maisie sang. The radio played all day. She'd join in with the record selections on *Housewives' Choice*, and then with the jolly songs on *Music While You Work*. She'd sing as she cooked, sing as she vacuumed and dusted. Her repertoire was mostly show songs. She didn't favour torrid love songs, or mournful melodies about lost romance. Frank Sinatra was out. Maisie declared she didn't like him. He was a boozer and a womaniser, and untrustworthy. She liked Doris Day, Bing Crosby and Rosemary Clooney. Good, clean-living, salt-of-the-earth folks.

Once a week, Thursdays, Maisie went to an amateur operatic society. When a performance was looming, she went almost every night. Sometimes, in the evenings, when she was at home, she'd put on shows for Alex. Cathryn and Nora would have small parts; Maisie was the director and star. She'd sing 'The Sound of Music' twirling round and round, arms spread. Cathryn would do 'Sixteen Going On Seventeen', and Nora did 'My Favourite Things', but usually had to be helped out, as she never sounded quite enthusiastic enough about brown paper packages tied up with string. Maisie was a demanding director. 'Put your heart into it,' she'd say. 'Let us feel your joy and pain.' Both sisters hated these family operatic evenings and eventually looked for excuses to get out of the house when Maisie called, 'It's showtime, everybody.' They both grew up to hate musicals.

Alex would sit by the fire, paper in hand, cigarette burning slowly in his fingers, watching. Smiling. Maisie would laugh, and dance, till, panting, she'd drop on to the sofa, legs spread out before her. 'Oh me, I'm getting too old for all of this.'

Nora couldn't remember exactly when the singing and dancing stopped. But it was about the time when her mother first threw all her possessions out into the garden. And that had been a few weeks after the mango incident. Maisie would have been in her late forties at the time.

The thing about Maisie was her moods, which were all to do with the daily scenarios she drifted into. Nobody quite knew what they were coming home to, but they could tell if she was happy, friendly, miserable or sulky the minute she said hello.

Still, Maisie was a doomster. Not for her the silver lining to every cloud. She claimed this was the legacy of her impoverished Scottish childhood. She'd been raised in an Edinburgh slum, she said. There had been no laughter, and barely enough food to feed her and her three brothers and three sisters. 'Hard times,' she said. 'And my father was a drunk, which gave me a healthy respect for alcohol.'

When, some years later, Nora moved to Edinburgh, she visited the slum—MacDonald Road—and was surprised to find it to be wide, pleasant, tree-lined: not in the least bit slummy. There was, however, a certain perverse pleasure in discovering that her mother had lied. It was good for Nora to know she was not the only one in the

34

family who made up stories.

On the day of the first assault on her room, Nora had come home from school and, as always, shouted, 'Hello.' Silence. Nora stood, wondering. This was new. She went to her little room to dump her bag and change into her playing clothes—corduroy trousers and sloppy joe. Her heart stopped, and a slow terror grew in her stomach.

The room was empty. A bed, a mattress, a chest of drawers. Nothing else. She looked under her bed. Nothing. Opened all the drawers, peeked in. Nothing. She went through to the kitchen, where her mother, wrestling with a new scone recipe, didn't look at her, but continued stirring the mixture in her bowl.

'Where's my stuff?' said Nora.

'Threw it out,' said her mother. 'Damn mess. Threw it all out.' She jerked her floury thumb towards the window.

Nora looked out at the garden. What she saw confused and unhinged her.

The garden was an immaculate quarter-acre. Lawn mown every Sunday afternoon into perfect Wimbledon stripes, borders sparingly planted with military rows of daffodils and tulips in spring, dahlias, lupins and campanula in summer. A couple of rose bushes. A small vegetable patch with cabbages, sprouts and a neat row of lettuces behind a trim box hedge. The earth was vigorously hoed, friable and almost breathtakingly free of weeds.

It was only years later that Nora discovered how lush and bountiful gardens could be; the plants here seemed cowed, dutiful. They grew, they flowered, but in the Marshalls' patch of ground they seemed joyless about it. Anything that had the effrontery to arrive in the borders through self-seeding, a horticultural gatecrasher, was whipped out, and almost scolded for its cheek.

Now the garden looked devastated. But politely so. If there was such a thing as genteel ravaging, then that was what had happened in Nora's back garden. It was strewn with books, toys (though Nora never had many), clothes. The sheets lay in crumpled heaps on the lawn. The bedspread (a mix of red and yellow flowers) was caught in a rose bush; pillows had come to earth down by the lupins. Pens, pencils, pyjamas (her very favourite blue and white polka-dot ones) were scattered amongst pansies and forget-me-nots. Knickers, vests and other clothes were draped here and there, over the pristine box hedge, on the ground between flowers, on the grass. Shoes had travelled furthest and had made it to the vegetable patch. Her shiny patent leather Sunday-best pair with the silver buckles on the side were among the cabbages; her playing shoes, black plimsolls, were nearby; her Wellington boots had got as far as the compost heap.

In later years, Nora was to wonder about that. It must have been a mighty throw that sent a welly hurtling such a distance. She'd imagine her mother standing at the back door, Wellington boot in hand, going through the pre-throw warm-up practised by baseball pitchers, slapping the boot from hand to hand, eyeing the compost heap, then hoisting the boot high over her head as she heaved back, one leg bent, the other off the ground. Deep breath, then pitch forward, boot taking to the air and flying. She wondered if her mother had been wearing her curlers (as she was apt to do in the mornings) at the time. She could definitely have been a contender in any welly-tossing competition. If she had actually done it. In time, Nora decided she hadn't. The boots must have been carried down the garden, then thrown on to the compost heap.

It was the books that horrified Nora. They had been thrown out heartlessly. Coming back to earth after their brief flight from the back door had hurt them. Spines were broken, pages crumpled and stained with grass and earth. They'd crushed plants as they thumped down. *Black Beauty* had been snapped in two, both halves lying side by side on top of a ruined campanula. Nora retrieved this, and the other books, first.

It took eight trips to bring everything back into her room. And until well past teatime to make up her bed, with the same sheets as it was not a bed-changing day. That was Monday. In fact every third Monday, since Maisie did the beds in rotation.

Nora wondered if her mother had made eight trips to the back door. And how long this had taken her. Did the fury deepen as she emptied drawers, hauled linen off the bed, gathered books, toys and other childish paraphernalia and lugged it to the door, then sent it all spinning through the air, and away out of her sight? It certainly must have disrupted her routine, which, since it was Friday, was cleaning the bath and shoving Domestos down the loo. That, and chatting to the fish man, who arrived with his van at about two o'clock in the afternoon.

'That'll learn you,' said Maisie calmly. She still

didn't look at Nora. She scattered a dusting of flour on her work surface, removed the dough from her bowl, and started to flatten it with her rolling pin.

There was no fish for tea that night. 'All her fault,' Maisie said, pointing a stiff finger at Nora. 'I missed the fish man because I was too busy with her room.'

They had boiled eggs. Though Nora didn't have anything. She was too busy sorting out her room, making the bed, folding her clothes and putting them back in their drawers. This she did with a mix of deep humiliation, confusion and anger. She was the filthy one, the family shame who had brought the horror of disgusting boiled eggs (Maisie's were either brick hard, slightly greenish in the area where the yolk stopped and the white began, or disgustingly undercooked, whites transparent and runny) for tea instead of fish, crispy bright orange in its ruskoline coating, and chips with tomato sauce. She would never be able to look her sister in the eye again. She'd be hated for ever. A biting consternation juddered in her tummy. Her mother loathed her, that was for sure.

Then again, there was a certain rage. Nobody should throw *Black Beauty* into the garden, nobody. *Pilgrim's Progress*, maybe. But *Black Beauty* was lovely.

Nora thought she might run away. She could live in woods somewhere. There weren't any nearby, but she could find a dense forest and build a house out of branches and leaves and live on berries and roots. She'd seen trappers do that in films on television. She could make clothes out of deer skins, and maybe catch fish. It was possible. It would definitely be better than sleeping in a box room that you had to keep tidy.

She heard her father come home. He didn't have boiled eggs; Maisie cooked him a steak, which she always braised with onions. Nora heard the clatter of crockery as it was served up, and the sound of Maisie telling him stories of her day, her voice lifting at the exciting bits.

'So I threw everything out. Right out, into the garden it went. I won't have a mess in my house. That'll learn her.'

Alex said nothing. He never did.

Later, Nora went into the kitchen and washed the dishes. She and Cathryn did them on alternate days, and today was her turn. She dried them, then put them away. Wiped the sink and draining board as was expected. Then went to bed. No television, and no Quality Streets, which was the Friday family treat. She lamented the toffee that was flat as a penny and came wrapped in yellow paper which, when she held it to her eyes, tinted the world.

She was ostracised for three days. Every time Maisie saw her she would tighten her lips, and disapprove. Nobody could disapprove like Maisie. She sent out waves of rejection that silenced the family, made the air leaden.

Of all Nora's memories, the lights in the darkness, this was the most vivid. She could see it all. Herself standing at the back door, looking out at the garden with everything she owned scattered across it. The slow beating of wooden spoon against mixing bowl behind her. There were other feelings, but she was too young then to put them into words. Everything that was precious to her

39

had been taken and tossed out. Her privacy had been usurped. She'd been cruelly reminded that the small room she occupied wasn't hers at all, and that nothing she owned mattered. With that came the thought that was to haunt her for years—*she* didn't matter either.

She found a new friend, Karen McClusky. Karen was tall, dark-haired, her parents were rich. She had a pony and took piano lessons. Nora told her mother that Karen's dad drove a big red Jaguar.

'Going to Karen's house after school,' Nora would say. Maisie would only complain that Karen never came to their house.

That would have been difficult. Karen didn't exist. It wasn't that Nora had invented an imaginary friend; she'd just come up with an excuse to stay out of the house for as long as possible. After school, on the pretext of being with her new best friend, Nora would wander. She walked for miles, stared into shop windows, watched men digging the road, anything. She tiptoed and skipped, watching for lines and cracks, still superstitious about pavements. On good days, she'd sit in the park, reading. She did anything rather than go home.

The Thereness of Nora

Seventeen years later, standing in Edinburgh's Grassmarket, Nora told Brendan about her mother preferring her sister.

Brendan sighed, and said, 'Well, mothers. Who

can explain them?'

'I could have been permanently damaged. What a terrible thing to say about your own child. It'll haunt me for the rest of my life.'

Brendan shrugged, and opened his mouth. But whatever he was about to say was interrupted by Nora. 'Don't you dare say move on, or get over it. I won't. I refuse to. I've been emotionally crippled by my mother. She was appalling.'

Brendan said that everybody's mother was appalling from time to time.

'Not as bad as mine. Nobody's was as bad as mine.'

It was a Saturday in September; the street was busy, a milling mass of tourists, shoppers and students. Brendan took her by the shoulders and turned her round and round.

'Look,' he said, 'all these people, and they all have mothers. And all their mothers were at some time appalling. They were probably in league with your mother, some sort of sisterhood.'

'You think?' she said.

'Definitely, the sisterhood of appalling mothers.'

'Well, I won't be one of them,' said Nora. 'My child will never be treated like that. Except that I am not going to have a child. Not ever. Absolutely not.'

'Not ever? How do you know that?'

'I just know it. Some things you know. Right from the beginning of *me*, the real me, the me I am now, I knew I'd never have children.'

This surprised Brendan. He envied Nora her conviction. He had no convictions at all. He was known for his lack of ambition, and thought of himself as an ambler. Someone who pottered through life, taking pleasure in small things. Waking up next to Jen, his wife, every morning. Though he had to admit that if it had been left up to him, he wouldn't be doing this. He'd only got married because she insisted on it. Still, now he *was* married, he enjoyed it.

Other pleasures were making tea—the perfect cup—listening to music, buying music, watching films, and talking. Of all these pleasures, talking was his favourite. He loved to chat. Which was what had attracted him to Nora. She was a fellow chatterer.

The thing about Nora and Brendan was that they rarely touched each other. Even at New Year, when people flung their arms round strangers' necks and kissed them, wishing them everything they could hope for, a dazzling new twelve months of success and joy. Amidst the tears, laughter and sudden bursts of song, Brendan would only catch Nora's eye from somewhere across the room, raise his glass of dry ginger towards her—he never drank—and smile. But it would be a good smile; his eyes would light up, his whole face seemed to open to her. He meant that smile. If relationships could be consummated with words, with long, meandering conversations, with admitting self-doubts, confessions and shared tastes in daydreams, then Nora and Brendan had done that. Definitely that. Even so, Jen, Brendan's wife, had nothing to worry about: he adored her.

There was something about the way Nora walked: long, delicate strides, almost a lope, on tiptoe, too. And there was something about the way she held herself, shoulders slightly rounded, head bowed, body at a little tilt, that said shy, insecure. It was a hushed movement. And it was, though Brendan didn't realise this till he'd known her for some time, the walk of someone who wanted to move through the world discreetly, to walk across rooms without disturbing the air. Though Nora always claimed it was the walk of a woman who in the past had been superstitious about pavements. Lines and cracks.

Then again, there was something about the way she engaged people she was talking to, an almost disconcerting eye contact that suggested she was not quite as insecure as she seemed. People fascinated her, she wanted to know all about them: where they lived, what they did, what they thought about this and that, what they loved to eat, what their mothers were like. But since she was shy, and prone to self-deprecation, she rarely asked all the questions she longed to ask, and tended to invent lives for most of the people she met. And since she rarely volunteered information about herself, people invented a life for her based on what they'd gathered about quiet people from films they'd seen, books they'd read. They said she was interesting, which surprised her. She didn't think she was interesting at all.

Brendan would watch her moving along the corridors of the building where they both worked, which were long, and, when the sun shone, splashed with morning light from the row of east-facing windows, and swore she shut her eyes and held her breath as she went. Her hair would fall over her face, and the sheets of script she carried from the balloonists to the sticky-up girl flapped at her side. If she encountered someone she knew, she'd say, 'Hi,' in a voice that was soft as air. You had to strain to hear it.

He liked her face. It had a quietness. Not plain; certainly not beautiful. It was a face you could get attached to. She had brown hair that fell straight to her shoulders. And though she prided herself on having mastered the art of not being noticed, she always got a second glance. It was that second glance that earned her approval. Perhaps it was the way she dressed. She had her own style; not outrageous, just her own way of putting things together, browns and blacks, browns and blues. A shirt hanging below a waistcoat; sometimes she wore braces with her jeans, or a black velvet skirt with a full-length grey cardigan. All this, too, was a second-glance sort of thing. People noticed when they looked again.

Another thing about Nora was the very thereness of her. That was how Brendan put it. She was always quietly *there* when you needed her. Never critical, just gently watching your face, listening to what you had to say. He thought her more than pleasant company; she was comforting company. Easy to be with, quick to take up a notion or speculation and add to it, take it to a higher level. She was witty. Oh, she was obsessive, prone to absurd rages, secretive, sulky, annoyingly superstitious, all that and more. Who didn't have their faults? But still, of all the people he knew, if Brendan had to choose one person to spend time with, to sit with, just walk along the street with, he would pick Nora. Though that was something he kept from his wife, Jen.

Nora found Brendan's friendship reassuring. It was a relief, after years of being solitary, to come across someone she could talk to. And talk they did, walking for miles through Edinburgh's streets, exchanging confessions, doubts, observations, notions, till they'd stop, look about and he'd say, 'Where the hell are we?'

Nora would say she didn't know. She was following him.

'But I was following you,' he'd say.

They'd look at one another, shrug, turn and retrace their steps till they came across a familiar landmark, and make their way home from there.

William Martinetti also noticed Nora. At least, when he interviewed her for a position with his company, Martinetti and McBride, he was amused by her. He said to Hugh Randall, his managing editor, that he'd found her quite engaging.

Nora had seen the advert in the *Evening Standard*, and had applied in desperation, after trying for sixteen jobs and being turned down for all of them. She had been invited for an interview at their offices in Edinburgh. She was twenty-six, had dropped out of university after a bout of glandular fever, and had in the past few years been employed in several office jobs where she filed, typed, answered the phone and made tea.

William Martinetti was the most elegant man Nora had ever met. Bespoke from head to foot, everything from his shoes to his tie was handmade. He sat apart from Hugh Randall, watching Nora as she answered his questions. On the desk in front of him was darkly bitter coffee in a tiny cup, and a glass of iced water. From time to time he'd look at his immaculately manicured fingernails, then at Nora. He didn't say much, something Nora found unnerving. But then William Martinetti knew that.

He seemed too stylish for this cramped place.

The room, the official Martinetti interview room, was small and brown. There was a desk, behind it two chairs, in front one more chair, where Nora sat. She could see through a glass partition into the room beyond where people seemed to be busy sorting mail.

William Martinetti had inherited the company from his father, Ernest, who had inherited it from *his* father, Paul. Paul had gone into business with Alistair McBride, who'd owned a print company producing menus and circulars. It was Paul's idea to print pamphlets instructing people on such matters as vegetable growing, French polishing, and bike maintenance that he'd sold to newsagents, going on foot from shop to shop.

A keen reader of whodunits, he'd added a detective series, Tales from the Lawrence Cole Casebook, that he'd written himself. After that came Tales from the Wild West, which were told in comic-strip form, written by Alistair McBride's father and drawn by his wife. By now, the firm had employed an editor and a small army of freelance writers who contributed small specialist paperback books on such subjects as bee-keeping, knitting, carpentry and keeping fit. They occupied an office in Edinburgh's High Street.

Paul's son, Ernest, took over the business in 1934. He expanded it to include comics about superheroes, and turned the paperbacks into a list of specialist magazines about fishing, cycling, gardening, aquarium management, bread-making, bee-keeping, and health and beauty. William joined the firm in the fifties, when he was sixteen. He'd started in the print room, done a short spell in accounts, then moved to work on magazines.

By now the organisation had moved to a new building on an industrial site on Edinburgh's outskirts and was producing books as well as comics and magazines. Alistair McBride had died leaving no heirs, and now the company was solely in Martinetti hands. All that remained of Alistair was a glowering portrait in the foyer.

It was rumoured that William had wanted to add works of high literature to the company output, but his father had objected. There were whispers of a huge fight, a feud between the two, that the elder Martinetti had won. He'd said the company did not and would never publish works of literature. They produced magazines that offered handy hints on hobbies and escapist comics for good down-to-earth folk. There was no money in literature.

Nobody who was employed at Martinetti and McBride knew how rich the Martinettis were. But it was accepted they were not as wealthy as they used to be. Still, William was immaculately and expensively dressed and came to work every day in a Bentley, though it was over fifteen years old. The word was that after his furious row with his father, now dead and also subject of a glowering portrait in the foyer, he'd removed himself from the day-to-day workings of the business, leaving decisions to Hugh Randall, managing editor, magazines, and Farrell Greyson, managing editor, comics. Now William came and went; he sat at his desk phoning friends, reading Russian classics. It was said he only attended interviews because he needed to remind himself, from time to time, what ordinary people were like.

He did, however, consider himself to be an

excellent judge of character. Looking at Nora, listening to her replies to Hugh Randall's questions about how she might fit into a team, and what she read in her own time, he thought she'd do. Hugh Randall, however, had decided she wouldn't do. He didn't like her clothes, he didn't like her answers to his questions, he didn't like her at all.

Hugh was a small man, compact. As if he'd been meant to be taller, but all the extra inches had gone out rather than up. He looked bullish. What anybody looking at him immediately noticed was his hair. Thick, black, growing enthusiastically wild, it seemed to have a life of its own. It matched his thick-rimmed black glasses. He looked like a stocky Groucho Marx, without the moustache.

When he'd asked Nora which Martinetti magazine was her favourite, she'd stared at him and said, 'Um.' And when he'd asked her if she enjoyed their comics, she'd said, 'No. I never read any of them. I prefer books.'

William had smiled. He liked her honesty. He preferred books, too.

'So why did you drop out of university?' asked Hugh Randall.

'I caught glandular fever,' said Nora. Which was true.

'But you could have returned to your course once you recovered,' said Hugh.

'I'd been off for weeks. It would have been hard to catch up.'

Hugh said, 'Hmm.'

William said, 'I don't quite believe that.'

Nora said, 'What?'

'Nonsense,' said William. 'What you told us was

nonsense.'

Nora blushed, and broke down. 'You're right. I was doing philosophy, but I was rubbish at it. I thought it would be a lot of people talking about the meaning of life. But there was maths. I really can't do maths. I'd have done something else if I'd known. I didn't find out anything about why we are here, and the meaning of life. I just kept failing the exams.'

At this, Hugh had been about to say he'd let her know. But William said, 'Excellent. Just what we want to hear. We don't want philosophers in the Martinetti organisation. We don't do the meaning of life. It's all practical here. Bread-making, bee-keeping, bike maintenance. Glad to hear you dropped out. Can you start next month?'

Nora said she could. Then, thanking both men profusely, she left, relieved that at last she could leave home, and her mother, for ever, she hoped.

When she'd gone, Hugh told William that he didn't consider Nora to be Martinetti material. 'She said she never read our publications.'

'Excellent,' said William. 'I'm rather with Groucho Marx on that one. Just as he wouldn't want to join any club that would have him as a member, I wouldn't employ someone to write for our publications who actually reads them.'

Skylines and Car Parks

Brendan's first conversation with Nora was when he came across her standing in the corridor staring out of the window. She'd been thinking about her mother, and what Maisie had said when Nora had told her she was working on a cycling magazine and would, in time, be making up features for it.

'Well, thank goodness you can make things up. You've never owned a bike in your life, can't even ride one. You know as much about cycling as I do about brain surgery.'

Nora had winced. It was true, she was expert at making things up. Had she not once filled notebooks with stories of the Purple Princess's battles with the Scone Witch? And convinced one of her early, and disappointingly gullible, boyfriends that Maisie had been parachuted into France during the war, then captured and tortured by the Nazis? Yes, stories, or lies, downright stupid lies, as Maisie called them, were what Nora, in her dreamy way, did rather well. Of course they weren't lies, Nora thought, they were just elaborations, a little gingering up of boring, ordinary, day-to-day life.

Brendan had come to stand beside her, and join her in her gaze at the world beyond the window—the Edinburgh skyline.

'Bloody awful, isn't it?' he'd said. 'Probably the most depressing sight in the world.'

'I think it's rather lovely,' she'd said.

'What are you looking at?' he'd wanted to know.

'The skyline, the castle in the distance,' she'd

told him.

'I was looking at the car park.'

She said, 'Ah.'

He'd told her that once she'd been working here for a couple of years, the car park would be what she looked at. 'It'll suit your mood.'

'No,' she'd said. 'I will always look up.'

He'd smiled. He knew this was never going to be true, but why tread on her aspirations? She was young, ambitious and a dreamer. It wouldn't last.

'I will be staring at the stars, while you look at muck and grubbiness and gravel,' she'd said, and stuck out her tongue at him. This had made him laugh.

The Martinetti building where both Nora and Brendan worked, where they'd met, was an apologetic assembly of bricks. There was nothing to it. It seemed to sulk at the far end of the industrial estate at Sighthill where it had been built shortly after the war, all four bland storeys of it. A fifth floor—the penthouse suite—had been added sometime in the late sixties, but this was only at the far end, giving the whole place an odd, stubby L-shape. Once it had been white; now it was a shabby shade of pale grey.

In time Nora mastered the art of not looking at the building as she walked across the car park. It was surrounded by a wire fence that had briars rooted in the ground at its base. Stray chocolate wrappers and faded, crumpled pages of newspaper were trapped in their sprawling thorny branches. The ground beneath her feet as she moved towards the front door was pot-holed and gritty.

In summer, cars coming and going sent up clouds of dust that hung in the hot air, swirled in

51

the wind. For there was always a wind there. Thistles, nettles and dandelions had settled and flourished in the cracks in the tarmac. Swallows swooped and skimmed overhead, or cruised the thermals higher up. There was always a crow strutting between the parked cars. But really, there was nothing nature could do to soften the desolation of this place. It was depressing in summer, and worse in winter.

Nora wondered why nothing was ever done to make it less formidable, more pleasing on the eye. It was so awful, she had a suspicion it was deliberate. There was a keep-the-peasants-down atmosphere; don't let them get ideas above their station. Make the approach to their place of employment grim.

Inside it wasn't so bad. In the foyer, the grimness gave way to blandness. Pale beige walls, semi-circular desk behind which sat the doorman, a strict man in a black suit and peaked cap. On the desk was the visitor's book; all people who were not actual Martinetti employees were obliged to sign in, and out again. Sometimes, someone would enter the building and head straight for the stairs without bothering to announce themselves at the desk. Shocked at such effrontery, the doorman would stop the rebel by shouting, 'Oi, you, sign the book.'

The interesting thing about the doorman was that he seemed to have no discernible face beneath the peaked cap. Obviously, Nora knew there had to be the same eyes, nose and mouth as everyone else. But it was hard to conjure them up when you tried to describe him. The hat was all you saw. Perhaps, Nora thought, his face comes off with the cap, and leaves a featureless blank. Perhaps his face without the cap was naked, the way the faces of spectacle-wearers are when the spectacles are removed. They appear suddenly pale and vulnerable.

But the real thing about the doorman, and it was a thing Nora didn't like to think about, was that for the first five months she worked at Martinetti and McBride, she had said, 'Good morning, Alistair,' when she arrived, and, 'Goodnight, Alistair,' when she went away. This was because on her first day, someone had flicked a finger at the grim portrait on the wall and told her that was Alistair. Not following the direction of the finger, she had assumed they'd been talking about the doorman. One day Brendan told her the man was actually called Edward. Why hadn't *Edward* told her? Indeed, why hadn't anybody told her till now?

'That sums up everything about this place,' she said. 'Complacency. Complacency and absurdity.'

The first floor of the Martinetti building was its saving grace. It had a shabby opulence. The offices were mahogany-panelled, book-lined; there were button-back leather sofas, ancient, rarely polished. The floors were carpeted, dark brown. Paintings, mostly of Italian landscapes, hung along the corridor walls. This floor was the Martinetti showcase. It was here that their books were produced.

There was no doubt that those who worked here on the first floor considered themselves a cut above those who worked on the second and third floors. They kept to themselves. Except for George Henry, but he was considered a rebel, though he had impeccable manners, even if he was a little clumsy and prone to making unsuitable remarks. Somebody had called him, behind his back, of course, a genteel oaf. He didn't wear a suit. And he was known to go drinking with people from magazines and comics. He was tolerated, but never favoured. He would never become a senior editor.

The books themselves were all non-fiction and mostly about cats, gardening, motoring, travel and health. *Garden Cats*, Nora was astonished to discover, had sold since its publication ten years ago over six million copies. It was a collection of pictures of cats in gardens, beneath each picture the names of both cat and flowers, and a short verse.

'Who would buy this?' she'd asked Brendan.

'People with cats and gardens,' he'd said. 'Plenty of them about.'

Another title was *Weeds, You Ought to Love Them*. It was a history of weeds, and their culinary and medicinal uses. *The Cheese-Lover's Guide to Europe, Camping for Beginners, The Importance of Grief, One Hundred Things to Make You Happy* and *What's Up There, The Heavens Explained* were all reliable sellers. *The Complete Guide to Root Vegetables*, however, had not sold well.

All in all, they were books that people bought because they might come in handy one day. It might be handy to know the names of the constellations, stars and planets. Handy to know the history of weeds, and what they might be used for. Handy to consult a pocket-sized book and find one hundred things to make you happy. They were books for people who did not read books, and they sold very well indeed.

The magazines were produced on the second floor. There was no opulence here. Only long corridors painted a nondescript pea-soup colour, overhead fluorescent lighting, on the floor endless brown linoleum.

These corridors were the daily stamping ground of editors, subs, artists, writers, colourists, balloonists and sticky-up girls. They all, on account of the lighting and the green paint, looked slightly seasick.

Nora worked on *Cycling for Ladies*, which had been established sometime in the forties and of which Brendan was deputy editor. It featured articles on suggested bike rides, bike maintenance, new bikes on the market, and cycling gadgets, along with adverts for cycling wear and obscure brands of embrocation.

It was officially aimed at women of all ages who enjoyed outdoor activities. And it was dated. Sales were low, and getting lower by the week.

Nora had spent her first days reading through the last six months' back copies. 'Just to get the feel of what we do here,' Brendan had told her.

'How are you getting on?' he'd asked at the end of her second week.

Nora said she was becoming strangely expert in a subject she knew nothing about. 'I can't ride a bike,' she confessed.

'Cool,' said Brendan. 'I haven't been on a bike since I was thirteen.'

Her studies of the back issues of *Cycling for Ladies* were constantly interrupted by being asked to run errands. As office junior, she was the official messenger. At her age she thought this a little demeaning but, hey, she was in a new town, in

55

a job she liked. It was the first step in what she imagined would be a dazzling career. Mostly she went along the corridor to the balloonists.

'Balloonists?' she'd said.

'Along the corridor,' said Maureen, who edited the letters page, flapping a dismissive hand at the door.

Nora realised, of course, that the balloonists were simply the people who typed the speech in scripts into blocks.

The magazine had two strips. In one, 'Cyril the Cyclist Tells You How', Cyril, an old cycling buff, explained in chatty language, frame by frame, simple repair techniques—mending a puncture, changing a tyre, replacing wheels, saddles or handlebars. The other was six frames featuring the comical adventures of Bertha the Biker.

Nora would take the scripts to the balloonists, then, later, pick up the sheets of typed-up speeches and bring them back to the office to Mags, who was the sticky-up girl. Mags would cut out the speeches and stick them on to the finished artwork, then she'd draw an immaculate oval, complete with a tail leading to the lips of whoever was doing the talking, round each one.

Sometimes she'd get carried away talking about the flat she and her boyfriend had bought and the decor they were planning, or what had been on television the night before, and in that moment of lost concentration, Cyril the Cyclist, an endearing white-haired chap who owned a repair shop, would say, 'Oh dear, the chain on my brand-new ten-gear racing bike has come off. I can't fix it. I just don't understand these things.'

And the one with the dilemma would reply,

'There's nothing to it. Even a young lass like you can put a chain back on.'

The interesting thing was, nobody reading the magazine ever noticed these slips. Or if they did, they never wrote in to point them out. They had, Nora hoped, better things to do.

Still, contemplating balloonists, Nora considered a career change. It was such a good word—balloonist. It would look impressive on her passport. It would be a grand thing at parties, when people asked her what she did, to say, 'Actually, I'm a balloonist.' But in a matter-of-fact kind of way. She'd be humble about giving people the notion she earned her living floating high above the ground navigating thermals in a large basket that hung wonderfully beneath a multicoloured balloon, rather than sitting in a small overheated office typing up speeches for comic strips.

As the weeks passed and wading through back copies began to bore her, Nora started to take long routes round the building on her way to and from the balloonists. She'd go down the back stairs to the book floor, walk the length of the long corridor, then up the main stairs to the magazine department. Or she might go up the back stairs to the comics floor and walk along that to the main staircase, then down to where she worked.

There was an air of contained anarchy on the comics floor. In one room somebody played the tuba, and it was rumoured there was an office nobody could enter unless they could answer a set of questions on Bob Dylan.

The comic characters were all superheroes whose adventures appeared monthly. They were

wholesome, down-to-earth chaps, in honest jobs—
a postman, a watchmaker, a piano tuner, a coal
miner. But when danger threatened, or the planet
was in peril, they would cast off their everyday
clothes and appear, muscles bulging, in
extraordinary colourful, tight-fitting outfits, purple
and green, silver and gold, lilac and yellow, and
take to the sky. On the third floor, everybody could
fly. Nora had little empathy with any of it. She had
never liked superhero stories. But flying might be
fun.

This was all overseen by Farrell Greyson, a man
as legendary as the heroes in the comic books,
some of whom he'd created. It was said he
occupied a huge carpeted office, wore outlandish
ties, loved art, and knew, somehow, everything that
went on in the building. Nora, in her wanderings,
never, ever saw him.

She'd dawdle, looking into offices as she went.
But she never dared to go as far as Bax did. Alan
Baxter, her editor, and editor of titles about boot
sale finds, crosswords and furniture restoration,
had an office to himself across the hall from the
large room where all the other *Cycling for Ladies*
workers busied themselves. He arrived every
morning, draped his jacket over the back of his
chair, and went out again. Where to? Nobody
really knew. He had been spotted sitting at a table
in a tearoom on the Corstorphine road, reading a
newspaper, silver teapot and plate of scones in
front of him. He'd been looking very content.

There were other sightings of Bax—emerging
from the George IV Bridge Library, standing at
the bar in the Doric, strolling through Princes
Street Gardens with a woman who wasn't his wife

but might have been his daughter, eating a peach and gazing into shop windows in St Stephen's Street. The man got around.

He got around so much that there was a map of Edinburgh on the wall with spots where he'd been sighted marked in red. It was known as the SOB (sightings of Bax) chart. On the rare occasions when the man came into the office, he would stand considering this map, hands in pockets. If he knew what it was about, he never mentioned it. Nor did he ever ask what all the bright red spots across the city meant.

Once, when Nora had been at Martinetti and McBride for six weeks, Bax came into the office. 'And who is this?' he said, pointing at her.

'Nora,' Brendan told him. 'The new junior.'

'Excellent,' said Bax. 'And are you enjoying being one of us?'

'Yes,' said Nora.

Bax said, 'Excellent,' again. And that, more or less, was all the communication Nora had with her boss. Whenever she needed advice, she asked Brendan.

It was accepted by everyone, except Brendan himself, that he would never become an editor. It was a jacket thing. He never wore one. Instead, he wore a large, comfortable crew-neck jersey over a shirt, and jeans. He had a selection of jumpers, mostly grey, black or dark blue. He swore he didn't own a jacket, and had no need of one as he spent very little time out of doors. He also claimed that jackets cramped his style. 'They're too tight at the arms,' he'd say, making movements demonstrating how restraining a jacket was. 'And if I wear one, I spend all my time waiting for the moment I can take it off.' When it rained, he carried an umbrella.

He was a tall man, over six feet to Nora's five foot two. He wasn't fat, but was, he admitted, heading that way. 'There's a lot of me,' he'd say. 'More than is necessary, and most of it is roast beef and potatoes.' His favourite meal.

He had long hair that scraped past his collar. His manner was gentle. Life and people, he told Nora, confused him. 'I never know what to say when folk tell me their guilty secrets.' This was something that was always happening to him; he was that sort of person. 'People think I'm understanding,' he said. 'But it's not true. Mostly, I'm bewildered.'

He sat at the main desk in the office, at the window, facing the room. Nora was in the corner across from him, with a window to her left that she spent a great deal of her time staring out of. She could see across the rooftops to Edinburgh castle in the distance. It was ideal for daydreaming, which was her favourite occupation, especially at work, when the endless reading of back copies slipped from being boring to being tedious.

Jason, who did a column about racing events, sat in the opposite corner. Actually his name was Brian, but he'd changed it.

'Not so much a name change,' he told Nora. 'More a creative career move.'

Jason was what Bax called a gangly youth, with a skin problem. He was not fazed by this; he was a man on the make. He had his eye on the main chance, but worried he might not recognise it when it came along. He was rarely in the office; he said he was far too busy to waste time sitting behind a desk. There were people to meet and interview and shirts to buy. Still, every week an article appeared with his face at the top. In the pieces he wrote, he was always catching up with someone famous in the cycling world.

He was also the only member of staff who actually owned and rode a bike. He cycled to the office every morning, carried his expensive racer up the stairs, and parked it just outside the door, in the corridor. He changed into a suit and pristine shirt in the lavatory.

Seeking to avoid the heaving morning traffic, he came in early and was always at his desk at least an hour before anyone else arrived. This was noted and taken for enthusiasm and diligence by Hugh Randall, who also liked to come into work early.

In time, Nora decided that Jason had the formula for being popular. It's simple, she thought. How to be popular: just don't let it ever cross your mind that people don't like you.

At the other side of the room sat Maureen, Sasha and Carol, who did the features pages, the letters page, and the pages reviewing new bikes and accessories. Mags, the sticky-up girl, who also helped with the layout, had a drawing board slightly in front of them. The four of them had formed a clique, and spent their days thumbing through magazines that were a lot glossier than *Cycling for Ladies*. They discussed interiors, holidays, clothes, television programmes, the lives of celebrities and their own families with a passion that made the others in the office feel they were missing something.

'They terrify me,' Brendan told Nora. 'They are the cause of my bewilderment.'

After a month, Nora was given her first actual

job.

'A bit of trousering,' Brendan said.

Nora said nothing. Trousering sounded vaguely filthy, unless they were expecting her to take up hems.

Brendan gave her a stack of Cyril the Cyclist strips, dating back to the fifties. They were caked with small, crumbling mounds of white paint, where things had been whited out so an alteration could be made.

'Go through them,' said Brendan. 'Mark the trousers and cycling gear and have John Mackay in the art department white them out and redraw them to bring them up to date. Then change the dialogue so people don't say things like gee whizz or stone me. Change it to whatever. I don't know. Make it more rock 'n' roll.'

It took some time for Nora to mark up all the trousers with turn-ups to be replaced with jeans. Twin sets were turned into T-shirts. Mid-calf skirts became shorts, and all shoes were transformed into trainers. People said, 'Cool, Cyril. Thanks a lot.'

She still had to make several trips a day to the balloonists. Each time she walked across the office, Brendan would watch her go. The walk interested him.

'I love the way you walk,' he said one day.

'It's the walk of someone who is wary of pavements,' she told him.

'What?' he said.

'You know, stand on a line you break your spine. Stand on a crack you break your back. I watch where I put my feet.'

'You believe all that?'

'When I was nine, I believed in all sorts of things: shooting stars, black cats, wishbones, anything that would bring me luck. I believed if I shut my eyes and seriously willed it, I could fly. Didn't work. I never did.'

It was a Friday. Nora had been working with Brendan for almost two months, and he asked if she'd like to come along to the pub and meet the gang.

'Gang?' she said, scorn in her tone. She wasn't a gang sort of person.

Brendan was impressed. Nobody in the gang was a gang sort of person. In fact, had any of them heard him saying this, they'd have got up and walked out of the Black Barrel, which was where the gang met.

'I have to get back to my digs,' said Nora.

'No you don't,' said Brendan. 'Nobody wants to get back to their digs.'

Nora had to admit this was true. She was staying at the time in Mrs Robertson's guest house in Portobello.

Mrs Robertson, Edna, was an old school friend of Maisie's. As soon as she'd heard that Nora was moving to her native city, Maisie had phoned her up. They'd kept in touch through Christmas cards, but hadn't spoken in years. Nora had listened as arrangements were made for her to stay at the guest house Edna had started up after her husband died. Then there had been a stream of reminiscences: how was so-and-so doing? What ever happened to Grace Withers, who'd been so uppity and had refused to take part in school sports? Remember old Pasty Watts, the maths teacher, who'd picked his nose? 'Oh, happy times,' said Maisie. 'We must get together and have a proper chat.'

Nora hoped that when Maisie and Edna Robertson met for a proper chat, she wouldn't be there. The phone conversation had lasted for over two hours. The room Edna offered Nora was on the top floor. 'Shared toilet,' said Edna. 'Bed, breakfast and evening meal served at six. Doors close prompt at half past ten.'

'Now I'll know where you are,' said Maisie. 'I won't be keeping myself awake worrying about you.'

'Have you been there?' asked Nora.

'No,' said Maisie. 'But you'll be with Edna. And I know Edna. She'll see you all right.'

And so she did. She was a tall, friendly woman who remembered Maisie fondly. The house was large and comfortable, the meals plentiful and good. The real problem was that it was on the wrong side of town, over an hour's bus journey from the Martinetti and McBride building, which meant Nora had to leave just as breakfast was being served, and the evening meal was well underway by the time she got back. Edna fed her, but plainly wasn't happy about her time-keeping.

'We have set meal times,' she said.

Nora explained about her working hours. But Edna said her other guests managed to come and go according to the rules.

As the other guests were mostly tourists, people on holiday who did not have to observe a nine-to-five routine, Nora thought this a little unfair.

Edna's house was on the promenade, overlooking the sea. Every morning Nora woke to the sound of water, and she'd think it was raining.

She loved the view from her window, the sparkle of sun on water, and the smell of ozone. Her room was tiny, its walls decorated with a cluttered turquoise and gold paper. The duvet on the bed had a pink and yellow cover. Mrs Robertson claimed it was cheery. Nora wondered if she'd found it easy to settle in because the alarming decor reminded her of home. But, tempted by an evening away from it, she agreed to go and meet the gang.

The gang were sitting at a table by the fire. This was their table, and they all had their regular seats. Brendan told her who everyone was. Mona at the far corner, George Henry next to her, Nathan across from them. Brendan, when he sat down, would be next to Nathan.

It was a small place. Looking round, the words 'seedy' and 'peeling' sprang to Nora's mind. The wood-panelled walls had been painted ages ago, and now the paint was coming away in long curling strips. The seats were old wooden benches; a fire burbled in the grate winter and summer. There were paintings of hunt scenes here and there, and a pock-marked dartboard.

'What'll you have?' asked Brendan.

Nora paused. This was a problem. She didn't know what to have. She didn't drink, really. She didn't like the taste. But she thought she'd have more kudos if she asked for something alcoholic rather than an orange juice or a Coke.

'Gin and tonic,' she said. That was a proper drink, the sort of drink drinkers asked for.

He brought her a pint of beer. 'You may want a gin and tonic, but this is what you're getting.'

As they walked towards the gang, Nora heard

Mona whisper to George, 'Oh God, Brendan's brought one of his waifs again.'

Her heart sank. Mona was right, she was a waif. She was thin. Her hair was straight and very fine. She was wearing a long, faded denim skirt and a purple T-shirt with flared sleeves that had seen better days. She thought she should leave, slip away, get out of here, but didn't know what to do with her drink. Hand it to Brendan? Only he was carrying his drink, orange juice, and his briefcase. He didn't have a hand free to take it. So she continued across the bar to the table and sat down.

'We were discussing,' said Mona, not waiting for an introduction, 'why we came to work for Martinetti in the first place. What were we thinking of? I thought that within a month I'd be doing my own column, saying witty and slightly anarchic things and making people sit up and notice what was going on in the world.'

'So,' said George, 'we're talking about the usual thing—work.'

'Sex and work,' said Nathan, 'is what we always talk about. Surely we ought to be able to discuss something else.'

Mona said, 'So what about you . . . er . . .'

'Nora,' said Brendan.

'What about you, Nora?' said Mona.

Nora knew it was a test. She knew she had to say something dynamic, innovative and downright witty. But her brain emptied.

She thought. She considered the matter, sipped the beer, which tasted horrible. Though it wasn't so bad on the second sip. And on the third she thought she might get used to it.

Why had she come here? She'd wanted to get

away from her mother. Her mother's temper, her erratic moods, her sulks, her thick disapproving silences, her voice that drilled through Nora's daydreams, interrupted her reading, cut into the tunes she was listening to on the radio.

'I just needed to get out of the house,' she said.

They all nodded. They considered this a very fine answer indeed. They sympathised, knew the feeling. There was a short bonding silence as they all remembered moments of escape, houses they'd had to get out of at some time or other.

'Yeah,' said Nathan. 'There's that.' He smiled at her.

That was all it took. An honest answer. She was in, part of the gang that didn't like to be called a gang. They would become the family she'd never really had.

A Mobile Handbag and a Comfort Blanket

They left the pub at about half past seven and went their separate ways. George would, as soon as he arrived at his flat, switch on the television in the living room and the small hi-fi in the kitchen. He found the silence the worst thing about living alone. He'd listen to opera as he perused his Elizabeth David cookbooks for something he could make from the contents of his fridge and cupboards.

Nathan, at forty-one the oldest of the group, would walk to Royal Circus, where he lived, stopping on the way for some Italian food. After that, he'd buy a bottle of wine, which he would drink as he sat in his darkened living room, pondering his life—the job he hated, head of the art department, and the loneliness he was just beginning to admit to six months after his divorce from Lorna had come through.

Tonight, though, he would think about Nora and her getting-out-of-the-house remark. It had amused him at the time, but alone in his flat, he would think that if he hadn't spent so much of his time out of the house, his wife wouldn't have started to find comfort with another man, and he would still be living there with the woman he loved.

For a few moments before they dispersed, they'd all stood on the pavement outside the pub, watching Mona go. It was that easy time in the evening, the lull time when the day has ended, but the night hasn't yet begun.

Mona said she had a date, and set off along the street, heels clicking on the pavement, to the main thoroughfare. She was small; somehow even six-inch stilettos didn't make her seem taller. In fact, they intensified her smallness. They were an indicator of Mona's attitude: extremely small but doing something about it. She claimed that the fact that she wasn't all that well endowed, vertically speaking, didn't matter as long as there were good shoes available. 'A woman can always buy an extra few inches in any high street, anywhere.'

Her hair was cut in a cropped bob. Eyebrows carefully plucked into a precise line. Her lips were painted red; her skin was pale, almost deathly. She avoided the sun. She claimed to hate summer, declaring it hot, dusty and a time of empty desks because people disappeared on holiday. She preferred to take a fortnight off in late October, when she went to Italy, though not for the buildings, the art or the food. She went for the shoes.

'There she goes,' said Brendan. 'She'll be up when the night turns into night proper. The time of darkness, when souls are bared and people reach out to other people to prove they aren't lonely.'

'Which is when?' asked Nora.

'About two or three in the morning,' said Brendan. 'She has a sex life.'

'And you don't?'

'Not like Mona's I don't.'

Nora turned, and saw that George and Nathan were also watching Mona go. Admiring her small strides, the vigorously swinging left arm, the determined way she forged forward. She rounded the corner, and even after she was no longer in view, they still stared.

Brendan broke the spell. He opened the door of his car, a Saab which was about fifteen years old and had once been red, but was now a faded rose-pink colour, and unreliable. He and Nora had come in it from work to the pub, which was on the Southside, the opposite side of Edinburgh, and conveniently close to where Mona, George and Brendan lived.

'Coming?' he said to Nora.

'Where to?'

'Home. You've got to meet Jen. She'll like you.'

Nora said, 'OK,' and got in.

The car coughed and wheezed, and after a few coaxings started up. And the radio came on; he never switched it off.

'It's temperamental,' Brendan said. Something he found endearing in a car. He said he had empathy with a vehicle that didn't always start up; he felt that way himself, a lot. 'Days when I get ensconced and just want to sit and be where I am. I don't want to move.' He patted the steering wheel. 'Great car, really. Well, it's got a fantastic radio. That's what I look for in a car. Driving with the radio on is one of life's pleasures, don't you think?'

Nora said she'd let him know if she ever got a car.

Inside, the car was heaped with things. Stuff. Books, cups, chocolate wrappers, newspapers, and records that he'd lent out, got back, thrown on to the back seat and never bothered to take into the house. The glove box and the pockets in the car's doors all overflowed with receipts.

'All this junk you take with you everywhere in your car, it reminds me of my handbag,' said Nora. 'That's what you have, a mobile handbag.'

Thinking of the useless things he'd spotted in Jen's handbag, Brendan thought this might be true.

Certainly, the comments Mona had made about his briefcase were true. He'd once told her that he didn't really know why he carried it to and from work every day, because he never opened it. In fact, he could no longer recall what was in it. 'I just don't feel right without it,' he'd said. 'I need it. My arm feels empty without it tucked underneath.'

'It brings you comfort,' Mona had suggested.

'Yes,' he agreed. 'It's falling to bits, but very comforting.'

'It's your comfort blanket, then,' said Mona. 'You need it for security.'

Brendan found this embarrassingly demeaning. But he had to admit the accuracy of both Nora's and Mona's observations. He had a mobile handbag and a comfort blanket. He wondered if women carried handbags as a kind of solace, something to hold tight in moments of awkwardness, despair, bewilderment or mortification. Or maybe they just liked to have something to hang on to. That was what he did with his briefcase. He didn't feel complete without it.

He crunched the car into first gear, and took off without signalling or looking in his rear-view mirror. In time, his driving was to worry Nora.

'This house you had to get out of,' he said. 'Was it terrible?'

'It wasn't a bad house,' Nora said. 'It was fine from the outside. Inside it was a bit overwhelming. My mother always said she liked a bit of colour. But she kind of overdid it.'

'So,' said Brendan now as they swished through the evening streets. 'What about your ma and pa? What were they like?'

He was the worst driver Nora had ever encountered. He whizzed up to traffic lights, hoping to get through before they turned red. And when he couldn't, he slammed on the brakes, shooting Nora forward in her seat. He screamed suddenly round corners, never, ever signalling. And now they were thundering the wrong way up a one-way street.

'Isn't this one-way?' said Nora.

'Yes,' said Brendan. 'But it's well after seven o'clock. And I'm local.'

71

'The one-way rule doesn't get enforced after seven, then?' said Nora.

'Of course it does. But there's nobody about to enforce it. And, like I said, I live here.'

'In this street?'

'No. In Edinburgh. I was born here.'

'Traffic laws don't apply to Edinburgh locals?'

'Well, technically. But really they're only for tourists,' said Brendan. 'That's my opinion, anyway.'

Nora said, 'Ah.' Then, because she couldn't think of anything to say about his interpretation of traffic laws, she answered his question. 'My dad was fine. He was quiet. Never really said much. He must have had opinions, only I never heard any of them. My mother, however, was nuts.'

Brendan didn't take Nora's remark about her mother being nuts seriously. He figured that all parents were nuts. It was part of the job. He knew many sane, easy-going people who'd had children and had become, overnight, it seemed, nuts.

'Ah, mothers. Where would we be without them? Well, nowhere really. We wouldn't have been born,' he said. Then he raised his hand. 'Sssh.' The DJ on the radio was playing a song he liked, Talking Heads' 'Once in a Lifetime'. 'A radio moment,' he said. When it was over, he asked, 'Do you have radio moments?'

'I remember the first time I heard Ray Charles singing "Georgia On My Mind". Every time I hear that song, I'm right back in the moment when I first heard it.'

'That's it, a radio moment. When something comes out at you, and it's wonderful, stops you in your tracks. You think your life is about to change.

Though it doesn't. The Clash, the Stranglers, Pink Floyd, all radio moments. I remember the first time I heard Dylan sing "Visions of Johanna". I was seventeen. I was in my bedroom at home, pulling on my Chelsea boots, which I loved, and there it was filling the room and everything stopped. Great radio moment.' He stopped the car, but kept the engine running, so he could keep the radio on. He was greedy for music. 'This is it. Home.'

They were in the driveway of a large Victorian house, bay windows, neglected front garden. The lights were on, curtains still open. Nora could see into the living room: a huge rubber plant, walls of albums.

'We'll have to go on a Talking Heads mission tomorrow,' said Brendan.

Nora said, 'Fine. I'd like that.'

He sat, thinking. 'What were we talking about before that song came on?'

'My mother being nuts,' said Nora.

'Oh yes, why was that, then?'

'She used to throw my stuff out.'

He stared at her. 'She did what?'

'She'd go to my room, gather my stuff and throw it all out into the garden. Then I'd come home from school, pick it all up and take it back to my room.'

Brendan said, 'Weird. Why did she do that?'

'She said I was messy.'

'Were you? Are you?'

'Yeah. But no more than any other kid. I just had stuff lying around.'

Brendan said, 'Weird,' again. Then asked Nora if she liked being in Edinburgh.

She told him she loved Edinburgh. Which was true. But in fact she was lonely. She hadn't made any friends, and sometimes with Edna Robertson's strict meal routine, she missed her supper. She was hungry.

Maisie hadn't wanted her to come. 'What are you going all the way up there for?'

'I got a job,' said Nora.

'And you can't get one here?'

'I can,' said Nora. 'But not like this one. This job will prepare me for a career. I'll learn a skill I can use to get a job here in London in a couple of years.'

'Well,' said Maisie. 'You'll be miserable. It's freezing up there and the food's muck.'

In fact the food had been fine, and the weather too.

Still, Nora had been lonely. She'd had nobody to talk to at weekends. She'd been constipated, had bad dreams that often featured bicycles, and had, on several occasions, cried herself to sleep. She'd phoned home often, but never confessed how miserable she felt. She'd gone to find her mother's old home, and the school she'd attended, and had stood on the pavement staring at it, trying to imagine Maisie, the child, going in through the huge iron gates. But couldn't.

At the guest house, people disappeared to their rooms early and rarely lingered in the main sitting room to chat. At work her colleagues rushed home at five o'clock on the dot.

Nora was lonely, but didn't mention this to Brendan when he asked if she liked being in Edinburgh. She said, 'I'm starting to love it here.'

He switched off the engine, got out of the car,

said, 'It grows on you. You'll never want to leave. Let's go find Jen.'

Waiting for Mona

Some time between three and four in the morning, George heard Mona climb the stairs to her flat. He lived in the same building, one floor down from her, and monitored her comings and goings.

'Creepy,' Brendan had said when George confessed this to him.

'No,' said George. 'It's not.'

'Yes it is,' said Brendan. 'Creepy. Like those lonely disturbed men in the movies who spy on their neighbours and build up fantasies about them. 'Then one day they burst out of their apartments and kill everybody they meet.'

'I'm not like that,' said George. 'Christ, I just worry about her being out there in the city streets alone at night. She could get mugged. So I wait listening for her to come home, then I can fall asleep.'

Brendan had said that Mona was very rarely alone out there in the city streets. She usually had a person with her, a male person. Furthermore, he added, he doubted anybody would dare mug Mona, and God help anyone who did. 'She'd set about them with her handbag, resulting in a trip to hospital.'

'She would,' agreed George. 'I don't know why I do it. But if she's out late, I don't relax till I hear her coming up the stairs.'

'It's motherly,' said Brendan.

George glared at him.

'OK, fatherly, then,' said Brendan. 'Does she know about this?'

'No,' said George.

'Do you fancy her? Have you ever slept with her?'

At this, George had walked away saying that he wished he'd never mentioned it. In fact, George and Mona *had* slept together. It had happened a year ago, when Mona's mother died, and neither of them had mentioned it since.

George was a man who liked to cook and hated to shop. He enjoyed visits to the delicatessen, and spent contented hours browsing the shelves there, buying tins and jars of things he had no actual use for, but liked the labels. Supermarkets, however, appalled him. They were too brightly lit, too busy, too noisy, stocked far too many things that reminded him of what he ought to do—wipe surfaces, clean the sink—and not enough things with interesting, natty labels he could turn over in his hands and contemplate. In fact, that was his main complaint about supermarkets: they were not places where he could comfortably muse and ponder. Consequently he rarely visited them. So he rarely had the vital ingredients for the dishes he liked to make—garlic, onions, lemons, limes and ginger—and had to borrow them from Mona.

Two or three times a week he would knock on her door, and ask if she happened to have whatever it was he needed. In time, Mona got so used to this, she stocked up on things George might come asking for whenever she went to the supermarket.

As more time passed, the relationship became

76

more casual. George would knock on Mona's door, then open it and call out that he'd come for some garlic, 'Just a couple of cloves will do. I'll get it.' He'd go to the kitchen, help himself to what he needed, and leave, shouting, 'Thanks.' In return for this, suspecting she didn't eat properly, he regularly brought Mona bowls of soup—spicy lentil, or onion with Gruyère cheese—and casseroles of lamb or chicken, or pasta dishes he'd concocted.

When Mona's mother died suddenly, he left her alone, not wanting to intrude on her grief. Three weeks after the funeral, however, he decided it might be all right to make borrowing contact again. Mona would be in control of her emotions by now, surely.

But Mona had been too busy organising the funeral to bother with emotions. It had been a huge affair, with vast arrangements of flowers, and her mother's favourite songs—'Somewhere Over the Rainbow' (which went down well) and 'C'est Si Bon' (which caused a few raised eyebrows)—followed by a gathering at a local hotel, more flowers, and caterers to nag. Then there had been notes of thanks to all the senders of wreaths and sympathy cards. And, as executor of the will, the estate to sort out. So Mona hadn't yet fully registered that her mother had gone. Would never again be at the other end of the phone. And they'd chatted often, they were close.

Then, three weeks after the funeral, Mona had been on her way home after a soulless day at work. She had organised a fashion photo shoot. The staff photographer, Willie, was past sixty and a man of few words. He diligently snapped whatever Mona wanted, but she had to suggest poses, and arrange the model to look interesting and slightly sexy. The model, Katey, worked in the art department (there was no budget for professionals), and complained that she had to get back to her drawing board as she had to do an illustration of a chocolate cake.

It being November, they were working on the spring issue. So the clothes were skimpy, and the weather was chilly. Katey, wearing a pair of striped cotton shorts, flip-flops, a straw hat and a T-shirt that stopped short of her belly button, was covered with goosebumps and near to tears.

Mona knew they should have done this indoors, but had thought, it being sunny, nobody looking at the photos would realise how bitter it was. So they were in the car park, using George Henry's ancient convertible Beetle, roof down, as a prop.

By three o'clock the light was fading, and they gave up.

Willie was saying, 'I don't know why you bother. Nobody's going to go about wearing them clothes. And nobody reads your magazine anyway.'

Katey was crying by now, and her hands were so numb she knew she'd never be able to hold a pen. She told Mona she was a bossy, jumped-up, tasteless bitch.

And Mona, carrying a pile of clothes, had sunk into a depression. Her feet were cold. Her heart was heavy. She knew, too, that Willie was not a photographer cunning enough to disguise the failings of their surroundings. She'd end up with shots of a miserable girl, looking not in the least summery, standing beside a rusting car amidst gravel and weeds with a huge, prison-like fence in the background. When Hugh Randall, the managing editor saw them, as he surely would, he'd say, 'You used up your budget on this crap?'

And she'd say, 'What budget? There was no budget. There never is. We beg for clothes, use Willie, who couldn't take a decent holiday snap, and a cheeky arse from the art department for a model. This is what you get.' She decided to go home.

She was cold. She was miserable. It was four o'clock and the afternoon was grey. The street she was driving through was also grey. And empty, except for a small child, a girl, who was standing on the pavement alone. She must have been five, maybe six. Her hair was tumbling red, face scattered with freckles. She wore a grey school uniform. Her feet were drowning in a pair of lurid pink high heels, her mother's probably. Mona smiled. She thought it must have been her first smile for weeks.

She leaned into the window, watching the girl. As her car swished past, she waved and the child waved back. Mona glanced in her rear-view mirror. The girl's mother emerged from a building with tiny angry steps, scooped up her daughter, tucked her under her arm, removed the shoes, and carried child and pink high heels indoors.

Once home, Mona ran a bath, put *Madam Butterfly* on the hi-fi and, leaving the living-room and bathroom doors open, lay soaking, listening, feeling the chill easing away and trying not to think. Half an hour later, when the water was starting to cool, she got out and wrapped herself in her silk robe. In the kitchen she brewed coffee, thought about the child in the pink high heels, and remembered.

She'd been about six and loved dressing up. She would spend happy hours sitting at her mother's dressing table, daubing lipstick around her mouth, liberally patting on powder and putting clownish amounts of shadow on her eyelids. Once, when she'd done with titivating her face, she was so enamoured of how she looked, she knew she needed more. The dress, the shoes, the perfume, the jewellery. She dragged her mother's green silk evening dress from the wardrobe and put it on over her tartan trousers and red jumper, raided the jewel box for a pearl necklace, and slipped her feet into a pair of black patent leather high heels, several sizes too big. A swift glance in the mirror told her she was gorgeous; she had to let her mother see.

'Look at me,' she'd said as she swept into the kitchen, shoes clacking on the lino, dress trailing.

She hadn't known till that moment that her mother could shout so loudly. She swore in later years that the scream of 'GET THAT OFF!' actually hurt. Her eardrums throbbed. She hiked up the dress and took off. Down the hall, out the front door, her mother thundering after her. Where she was going, she did not know. Just away, out of here. She tripped over the front step, and tumbled headlong on to the drive, splitting her head.

In a second, the scenario changed. Her mother's rage melted into guilt. Mona, now howling, was scooped up and taken inside, her wounds bathed. She was fed chocolate biscuits and cocoa, and cuddled. Twenty-seven years later, she still had the scar.

Now, standing in her living room, Mona reached

up and ran the tips of her fingers over the bleached white mark on her forehead. She smiled. She had to share this memory, and the story of the pink high heels, with her mother. She picked up the phone, started to dial, and it came to her. Her mother wasn't there any more. And would never be there.

It was the start of the silence that comes to the bereaved. Mona would never hear her mother's voice again. All the emotions she had been fending off for the past three weeks flooded in. She lay face down on the sofa, and cried.

By now it was past five o'clock. Darkness had moved in, but Mona didn't notice. She wept till she could hardly breathe. She was on one of those excruciating staggered inhales, thinking she might die from crying and sudden awareness of loss, wiping her nose on the sleeve of her robe, when she realised there was someone in the room behind her. She turned.

'Oh, George,' she said.

He stood looking at her. He'd come to borrow some garlic, had fetched it from the kitchen and was on his way back down the hall when he had heard her sobs and come to investigate. She knew how embarrassed he was. Almost as embarrassed as she felt at being discovered in this state. He didn't say anything. But then, Mona thought, if she came across him lying howling on his sofa, she wouldn't know what to say either.

He sat beside her. Reached out and patted her. 'It's OK,' he said.

She told him she'd just acknowledged her mother was dead. 'I've been too busy with the death stuff to really think about it. Then today I saw something that reminded me of her. And it all welled up.' She told him about the little girl in the pink shoes.

'It's tough,' he said. 'I remember I missed my mother when I went to boarding school. I cried every night in the dorm.'

Mona said she hadn't known he'd gone to boarding school. 'Was it posh? Is your family disgustingly rich?'

'Yes, on both counts. Though I don't see my family now. They disowned me after I wouldn't join the business.'

They both floated into a long silence. She sensed he wanted to go, but she needed someone to be near her. 'Talk to me. Let me know there's someone with me,' she said.

He looked at her. Wasn't that the thing, Mona thought, when someone asked you to talk to them you never could think of a damn thing to say. He touched her shoulder and looked at her tenderly. She thought she heard him say, 'Aqaba. Aqaba.'

It sounded lovely. *Aqaba*. She wondered what it meant.

After that, they didn't say anything for a while. Though George kept his hand on her, moving it gently against her shoulder. She asked him to hold her. 'I just need some human contact.'

She moved into his arms, and they stayed locked, wrapped against one another, till he touched the top of her head with his lips. She looked up at him, put her arms round his neck, and they kissed. Then they kissed properly, passionately. Making love was easy. No garments to clumsily wriggle out of; Mona was naked under her robe. Afterwards they lay awhile, Mona draped almost on top of him. From time to time he kissed her forehead, till she fell asleep.

George slipped off the sofa, fetched her duvet from the bedroom and put it over her. Then he took his garlic and went downstairs.

In his kitchen, he prepared a risotto, thinking about what had happened. He wondered if he'd taken advantage of her. But no, she'd been as willing as him. He remembered saying, 'Aqaba,' and wished he hadn't. Only *Lawrence of Arabia* was on television tonight, and he'd been thinking about it. The long trek across the desert to take Aqaba.

He wondered if it was one of the best films ever made. And recalled reading somewhere that Albert Finney or Marlon Brando had been considered for the lead. Then he sighed and shook his head; he was thinking displacement thoughts. He was trying to get what had happened with Mona out of his head.

He decided that what had happened, the sex, was either the start of something, or the end of something. They'd be lovers. And if not, they would no longer be friends. He wanted to sit in front of the television watching the film, but needed to know how things were with Mona, so he put some of his food on to a plate, sprinkled it with Parmesan and took it up to her. 'Eat,' he said. 'Food is good when you're sad. It helps. In fact, food is good whatever mood you're in.'

So she ate, and felt better. Fearing an awkward silence, on account of what they'd done not that long ago, and fearing also that George might want to do it again, Mona put on the television. Together, side by side on her sofa, not touching, but comfortably close, they watched *Lawrence of Arabia*. When Lawrence got to the desert and hitched up with Omar Sharif, and they discussed taking Aqaba, Mona shrieked, 'Aqaba! That's what you were on about. You were worried about missing your film.'

George looked shamefaced and said he was sorry.

Mona gave him a mock punch and said he could get them both a glass of wine from the kitchen. 'You bum.' Now George knew that as far as Mona was concerned their swift act of love would change nothing. Nothing new would begin, nothing old would end. They'd still be friends.

When the film ended, he told her to go to bed and she'd be fine in the morning. He'd drive her to work if she wanted. He gathered his plates and went back to his flat.

Mona thought how odd it was that she should unburden herself to this man. Till this evening, she'd thought of him as gentle and awkward. A little bit soft. But there was more. He was thoughtful, a surprisingly good lover. He belonged, Mona thought, in a different time, a world long past. The word that came to mind was gallant. How else to describe someone who would give up the chance to watch his favourite film to comfort a woman he fed from time to time.

That was their moment of passion. Though Mona didn't think of it as passion; she called it comfort sex. It was lovely. It had done the trick, helped her through a bleak patch.

George thought about it often. These days, when Mona was out, he'd lie awake waiting to hear her return. But Brendan had been wrong. He wasn't being motherly, or fatherly. He was being normal. He'd had sex with Mona once, and he wanted more.

The Fine Art of Omelette Making

Nora followed Brendan into his house. Down the hall to the kitchen, noting the decor as she went. Not that she was being critical; she was quite taken with it. It was so different from the house she'd been brought up in. The hall was wide, a faded blue and green rug stretched the length of it. Its only furnishing was a huge hall stand that was hung with many coats, none of which, Nora was to discover, anybody in the household ever wore. Beneath it and beside it were assorted shoes. On its only shelf was an antique typewriter. On the wall between the hall stand and the kitchen door was a row of framed black-and-white photographs of the same typewriter, all taken by Brendan during his brief photographic period a couple of years ago.

Nora thought the kitchen a joy. She almost raised her hands in pleasure at the sight of it. The clutter was wonderful. Maisie would have had a glorious time chucking everything out. There was so much stuff it would have taken her all day.

There were dishes soaking in the sink, dishes on one side of the sink waiting to get soaked, and more dishes on the other side that had been soaked and washed, waiting to be put away. The units were crowded with storage jars, cereal packets and books. The fridge door was massed with magnets holding drawings, notes, bills. On the far wall were two huge framed cinema posters, *Casablanca* and *On the Waterfront*. French doors led out to the garden; through them Nora could see more clutter—a wooden table and four chairs, a rusting barbecue, a wheelbarrow, a watering can, flower pots.

Jen, Brendan's wife, was sitting reading a newspaper at a vast and obviously very old pine table. She was the thinnest person Nora had ever met. She seemed to be made of bone, and looked like she might break if she so much as bent over. Her hair was black, cropped short, framing her face. Her skin was tight, almost as if there wasn't enough of it and it had been stretched to cover her cheeks. Her eyes were large, brown and slightly protruding, but her mouth was wide and friendly. It looked like it did a lot of smiling. It was the thinness, though, that was startling. Jen could have doubled for Popeye's girlfriend, and didn't look like a woman who would age well.

She looked up from her newspaper. 'Hi. Good day?'

Brendan told her not to be silly. When did he ever have a good day? 'Days are what they are, and what they are is rarely good. You?'

She shrugged. 'Usual. Though we had twins, which was a surprise. Though not as much of a surprise to us as it was to the mother.'

Nora would have to say that of all the people she met around that time, Jen was the most remarkable. And, as Brendan's wife, she wasn't even part of what went on. She had little time for any of them, except Brendan, of course. She didn't care for their talk of music, films, books. Their speculations and musings, their confessions, guilts and observations. Yet it would be dismissive to say she was a practical soul. She was so much more than that. So much better than any of us, Nora thought. She was the good one. She was worthy. Real. Not adrift in a sea of hopes, dreams, fraying ambitions like the rest of us.

Jen was a midwife. At the heart of things, the nub of things, Nora thought. She saw fresh, wet new faces arrive in the world, almost daily. The wonder of that, a tiny whole human being coming into the world. It was hardly surprising she did not share in their intense self-examinations. She knew too much about the beauty, pain and marvellousness of things. She once told Nora that she could no longer count how many babies she'd seen born, and it still amazed her. 'I still shed a tear every single time.'

Jen never seemed to object to Nora's friendship with Brendan, and Nora admired her for that. All the hours they spent together, their walks, trips to the cinema, sharing of new discoveries—books, films, a record, a song. All the things they confessed to one another, and Jen just let them be.

'Any chance of a cup of tea?' said Brendan. Then, remembering he hadn't come home alone, 'This is Nora, by the way.'

Jen looked up at Nora, studied her briefly, smiled and said, 'Hello, Nora.'

Nora said hello back. Sat down and considered the brief look. Could someone be warm and dismissive at the same time? The look had been warmly dismissive, definitely, Nora thought. It said that Jen welcomed her, but didn't think much of her. But then, Jen didn't think much of anybody who worked for Martinetti and McBride.

'Have you met Brendan's gang?' she asked.

Nora said she had.

'And how was the fabulous Mona?'

'She was in good form,' said Nora.

'Actually,' said Jen, 'like most people I'm not so much interested in Mona as in Mona's sex life.'

'She had a date,' said Nora. 'But I don't know who with.'

Brendan was making tea, which was, for him, an important ritual. The heating of the pot, the measuring in of the exact amount of tea leaves; bags were anathema. The pouring into the pot of the exact amount of boiling water. The wait for the brew to infuse. He could not bear weak tea. He liked it strong and black and drank cup after cup all evening. He gave Nora and Jen a cup each, then sat at the table with his own and sipped. 'Ah. That's better.'

As they sat, Brendan and Jen talked comfortably of the things that filled the edges of their life together—the paying of the gas bill; the fact that Brendan was wearing second-day socks because he couldn't find a clean pair this morning; who was doing the shop tomorrow.

'Me,' said Jen. 'You come home with nonsense.' She turned to Nora. 'He'll buy a huge lump of beef for roasting, potatoes, tea and chocolate biscuits. He buys things he takes a shine to and never thinks to get washing powder, ergo, the lack of fresh socks.'

Brendan shrugged. 'That's probably true. But what the hell's the point of going to the supermarket, which is boring, and coming home with boring stuff? It's a shitty way to spend a Saturday afternoon.'

'Oh, I just love going to the supermarket,' said Jen. There was a good deal of sarcasm in her tone.

Which Brendan ignored. 'Excellent. You won't mind doing the shopping, then. Because me and Nora are going out to get a Talking Heads record, then on to the Modern Art Gallery, probably. What do you think, Nora?'

Nora said fine.

Jen looked at her and said, 'Don't be fooled. He knows nothing about art. He only goes for the cakes.'

This was a relief to Nora, who had briefly imagined she might be asked to voice knowledgeable opinions about paintings. She definitely knew a lot more about cakes.

She noted that there seemed to be no routine in this house. Nobody had leapt up to do the dishes, and though it was after eight o'clock there was no sign of either Brendan or Jen preparing a meal for themselves. All this was interesting to her. She was slowly becoming aware that though these two people were married, they chatted like people who weren't married. Until this moment, she had believed, in some distant, almost unreachable corner of her mind, that people got married and quickly settled into a life of set menus, tidiness and regular bedtimes, like Maisie and Alex.

This was not a home that Maisie would approve of. And it wasn't just the lack of routine, or the clutter. The house, though large, was terraced with a shared driveway. Maisie had very firm ideas about such things. A house must stand alone, on its own ground, however small that patch of ground might be. It was Maisie's belief that a person must be able to circumnavigate the outside of their home. Any other kind of residence just wasn't worth considering. All this made Brendan and Jen's household very appealing to Nora.

There was an undertow to the mild conversation going on. There were looks and sighs. Who was going to make the evening meal? Brendan eventually got up and said, 'All right. All right, I'll do it.' He looked at Nora. 'You make omelettes?'

'No.' She thought for a horrified moment she'd have to cook. The only thing she could make was toast.

'Excellent,' said Brendan. 'Let me demonstrate the fine art of omelette making.'

Jen said that if he was going to do his omelette demonstration, she'd go and watch television. 'Call me when it's ready,' she said.

It was a splendid demonstration, and a splendid omelette. Nora, used to Maisie's bland cooking, had never tasted anything like it. During the course of the quick lesson in omelette preparation, she revealed to Brendan that she'd never tasted a mushroom, had no idea what a salad dressing consisted of, and hadn't, before this moment, seen a pepper grinder.

As he put lettuce, tomatoes and cucumber in a bowl, Brendan had said, 'Could you get the olive oil and vinegar from the cupboard and make the salad dressing?'

Nora had fetched the oil and vinegar, put them on the kitchen unit and stared at them. In the home she'd come from, the only thing they put on salad was Heinz Salad Cream. Brendan told her what to do. Then, when he told her to add pepper,

90

she'd upended the grinder and tried to shake out its contents. He'd given her a quick lesson in pepper grinding. When he'd asked if she wanted mushrooms or cheese as a filling, she'd said she didn't like mushrooms.

'You don't like mushrooms? Why not?'

'I've never eaten one,' she said.

'So how do you know you don't like them?'

'They're slimy,' she said.

'No they're not.' He forked one from the frying pan and held it towards her. 'Try it.'

She shook her head, pressed her lips together; no mushroom was ever going to pass between them and into her mouth.

Brendan insisted. 'Try one. Then you can say you don't like mushrooms. If you don't, you'll be a food bigot.'

So she opened her mouth and let Brendan place the mushroom on her tongue. It lay there for a moment before she chewed, gingerly.

'It tastes brown and sort of earthy, like the smell of woods. It's quite nice.'

'There you go,' said Brendan. 'What made you think you didn't like them?'

She shrugged, said it was just a notion. But in truth, she knew it was more than that. The mushroom prejudice had come from her mother, who'd declared them to be fungus, and who wanted to eat that? Maisie also had an underlying belief that mushroom-eaters were rich, educated, posh people who spoke with rounded vowels, who took afternoon tea with crumpets by the fire, but absolutely never made it themselves.

Maisie knew all about this because of the love stories she read where poor heroines, often kitchen maids, found themselves cast adrift in the world of country mansions set on rolling lawns, inhabited by wealthy, titled, gentrified people who often ate mushrooms on toast as a light supper after an evening at the opera. One thing Maisie knew for sure: good-hearted, salt-of-the-earth folk who did their own dusting never ate mushrooms. They, along with spinach, broccoli, green and red peppers and garlic, were not part of life in the Marshall household.

In the end it was only a mushroom. But eating it, finding out how good it tasted, led Nora to reconsider her position on Maisie. She'd thought that perhaps her mother wasn't right about everything. But now Nora thought she wasn't right about anything.

After they'd eaten, Nora, Brendan and Jen lingered at the table drinking tea and chatting. When the yawning and looking at the clock started, it was after midnight. The last bus to Portobello was long gone, so Nora stayed the night, sleeping in the converted attic, which reminded her of the box room at home. Here, however, the walls were lined with bookshelves and the bed was huge and old, covered with a patchwork eiderdown.

In the morning when Nora came downstairs, Brendan and Jen were sitting at the kitchen table reading newspapers. They both looked up, smiled, waved her towards the teapot, and returned to their reading. Nora poured a cup of tea and joined them at the table, Brendan gave her part of his paper. They sat, sipped from their cups, scanned their papers, said nothing. The only sounds were of pages turning, and the squeals of Saturday-morning children's television coming from the living room.

Nora found all this pleasant, but couldn't help herself thinking about how Maisie treated guests. Not only did they get the best room in the house, in the morning she fussed over them. She made huge cooked breakfasts. She asked how they'd slept, if they'd been warm enough. She toasted whole loaves of bread, put out honey, marmalade and a selection of jams. She wondered what they might be planning for their day. There was never any question of them being allowed to glance at a newspaper. Reading at the table was rude. It was all exhausting.

Eventually Jen made toast, which she set on the table on top of the newspapers along with a dish of butter, a jar of marmalade and a couple of knives. Then she sat down and continued perusing her paper. They all helped themselves, though without plates, melted butter dripped on to the pages of *The Scotsman*.

'What do you usually do at the weekends, Nora?' asked Brendan.

'Not a lot. I walk along the prom. I go uptown and look round the shops. That sort of thing.' And she phoned her mother. Maisie needed weekly updates. Or rather, she needed to give Nora weekly updates on her illnesses, chats with the fish man, and how well Cathryn was doing. 'A proper lawyer, knows everything about the law.'

'Don't you know anybody?' asked Jen.

Nora shook her head. 'Not yet. I'm looking for a place of my own. I don't like the boarding house. I have to be in by half past ten.' She couldn't even go to the cinema and see the end of a film and get back before the doors were locked.

'Come here,' said Jen. 'Have the spare room You can come and go as you like.'

Nora shook her head. 'I couldn't do that.' She didn't want to be one of Brendan's waifs.

'Of course you can,' said Jen.

Nora shook her head again.

'Why not?' said Brendan.

'I'd be one of your waifs,' said Nora.

'Mona,' said Brendan. 'You shouldn't mind her.'

'If you're talking waifs, she's been one. She stayed here for a while after her huge romance ended. Didn't want to be alone. Then Nathan stayed after he and his wife split up. George when his flatmate got married and he had to move out. They've all been waifs, if that's how you put it,' said Jen.

Brendan said, 'Come and stay while you look for a flat.' He took that as settled, and went back to his paper.

Nora said, 'Thank you.' But she was confused. It had been agreed so casually, she wasn't really sure if they really meant it. Perhaps it was a joke. Then again, maybe they felt sorry for her. She never was very good at recognising friendship when it was offered. Maisie always said she lacked confidence.

Later, after Brendan had had several mugs of tea and played a few of his favourite tracks to set him up for the day, they set off for Portobello. The day was warm, balmy; they drove with the windows down. Brendan played Neil Young on the car tape deck; he was in a Neil Young-ish mood, he said. He drove with his usual nonchalance and disregard for other drivers. Nora gritted her teeth and said nothing, but she wondered if she was taking

94

politeness too far. After all, Brendan's sudden braking, his hurtling up to traffic lights, his habit of not signalling left her contemplating death. So this was how she was. She'd rather die than tell someone he was a dreadful driver.

Still, they reached Portobello unscathed. They parked at the end of John Street and walked down to the prom, where they leaned on the railings, stared at the sea and breathed the scent of warm sand.

'Used to come here as a kid,' said Brendan. 'Skinny legs, white as the inside of an apple, in maroon shorts. I used to run into the sea and come out again covered in goosebumps and shivering. Built sand castles and ate sandwiches gritty with sand. Great days.'

Nora said her mum had come here too. 'She was born in Edinburgh. Huge family but they've all gone now. Died or moved away. She came here for her holidays. They lived in MacDonald Road, fifteen minutes away.'

'Great plan, going on holiday to somewhere fifteen minutes away,' said Brendan. 'When it all goes wrong, which it inevitably does, you can get home quickly.'

Nora said she could see the sense in that. 'My mother never came back here after she left, though she always wanted to. She went to school with my landlady.'

'Ah,' said Brendan. 'She set you up with one of her old cronies so she could keep an eye on you.'

'Yep, I guess so,' said Nora. 'But I think I'm a bit old to be kept an eye on.'

'Your mother wouldn't agree. Mothers never stop keeping an eye on their young. The first thing your landlady will do after you leave will be to phone your ma.'

He was right. Mrs Robertson, not at all happy about Nora moving out, demanded a forwarding address and phone number. When Nora and Brendan arrived home after five, after spending time at the Modern Art Gallery (where they lingered longer in the café than they did looking at the paintings) and browsing through LPs in the Princes Street record shops, the phone was ringing. It was Maisie.

'You've moved,' she said.

Nora agreed she had.

'That's not very nice. After all I've done for you finding you a lovely place to live.'

Nora asked how Maisie could know it was lovely since she hadn't seen it.

'No old friend of mine would have a home that wasn't lovely,' said Maisie. 'So who's this you're staying with?'

Nora told her.

'Friends,' said Maisie. 'I suppose it's all free love and loud music. And you won't be paying rent.'

'Of course I'll be paying rent,' said Nora. Though this hadn't been negotiated yet. 'I can't freeload. And no, it's not all free love.' There was loud music. 'Brendan and Jen are married. I work with him. I can get a ride to work and won't have an hour on the bus every day.'

Maisie said, 'Hmm.'

'It's the sensible thing to do,' said Nora. She knew Maisie would have no argument against sensible.'

Maisie said, 'Hmm.'

Nora knew that Maisie thought her ungrateful,

and that she was embarrassed her daughter had moved out of her old friend's guest house after a few weeks' stay. But most of all, she knew that Maisie was upset because Nora was slipping further and further away from her. Getting as far from the house as she could, deepening the gulf between them.

Nadine, Queen of the Trails

There were meetings at Martinetti and McBride. Every week the magazine staff gathered to report on the progress of the issue about to go to press, the state of play with the issue they were working on, and ideas for the next issue. Brendan would also have a weekly meeting with Bax, and Bax had a weekly meeting with Hugh Randall. There were monthly meetings too—all the editors met with Hugh, then Hugh would report to Martinetti. In among all this there were meetings where editors met with the head of the art department or advertising or marketing or accounts.

Nora only attended the weekly staff meeting, but never had much to say and usually spent her time doodling on a notepad. She was surprised, then, to hear that her name had come up during a meeting Bax had had with Hugh Randall and Brendan.

It had been decided that what the magazine needed was a weekly piece about a woman's experiences while cycling. 'On the road,' Bax had said. 'Something gritty. Real.'

'Dust and sweat,' Hugh added.

'Ride the trails,' Brendan said.

'That's it,' said Hugh. 'A weekly report about cycling trails across the country. A queen of the trails.' Then he'd suggested the name Nadine, which he liked. He was rumoured to be a fan of country and western music: Jim Reeves, Patsy Cline and Dolly Parton all had a special place in his record collection. Bax had suggested Nora write the column since there was no budget to commission a freelance.

'Nadine, Queen of the Trails,' said Brendan. 'Hugh's idea.'

Nora, not yet astute enough to keep her opinions to herself, said, 'It's a horrible name. It's so rhinestone. Some glittery yee-ha girl who sings about lonesome nights and dead dogs.'

'So you don't like it, then?' said Brendan. 'It was Hugh's idea. You don't get to like it or dislike it. You just write it.'

'I hate it. I hate it. I hate it. It's terrible.'

'Splendid bit of passion. Exactly what we want from Nadine, Queen of the Trails. On your trusty bike, you will travel the land. Pedalling the Peak District, the Highlands, round the coasts, through leafy Dorset lanes. Who is that mystery lone woman whizzing past, pedals whirling, thighs juddering? Don't you know? It's Nadine, Queen of the Trails.'

Nora said, 'I can't ride a bike.'

'You don't have to ride a bike. You just have to write about riding a bike,' said Brendan.

'Isn't that hard? I mean, aren't you always meant to write about what you know?'

'How hard can it be to write about riding a bike?' said Brendan. 'Pedalling along, the wind on your face, the fresh smells of the countryside, the hum of tyres on tarmac.'

'When you put it like that, it sounds a snip,' said Nora. 'But somehow I suspect it won't be. I don't want to be Nadine. Get someone else.'

'It has been decreed from above. Bax and Hugh have chosen you.'

'Why?' said Nora.

'Because you are here and we can't afford a freelance.'

'But,' said Nora, 'not only can I not ride a bike, I haven't been to the Highlands, or the Peak District or Dorset, now you mention it.'

'There are books on these places in this very building. George will help you there,' said Brendan. 'And think about it, sometimes you can cycle for days, camping out under the stars.'

'I have never been camping in my life,' said Nora. 'I have to ride about with a huge load on my back, then. All the stuff I'll need to camp, plus a tent strapped to the bike. I don't fancy that.'

'The tent will be on one of your panniers. See our pannier pull-out supplement from last April for details. Anyway, you're not actually doing it, just writing about it,' said Brendan.

Nora could see there was no way out of this. She supposed she shouldn't have made such a good job of revamping Cyril. He now looked less like a cartoon watchmaker, and more like the ageing, but hip, owner of a wonderful shop tucked down a city side street that only the in bike crowd knew about. His white moustache was smaller and attached to a cropped beard. His waistcoat was patterned and worn over a T-shirt. He smiled and said things like, 'No worries. This we can do,' and his young and athletic customers said, 'Cool.' And sometimes, 'Wow.'

The actual pages of artwork were heavy with white paint, the ink lines scratchy over a rough surface, but none of this showed in the printing. All in all, everyone thought Nora had done an excellent job. 'More than just simple trousering,' said Brendan. 'You've made him a man of our times.'

So here she was about to embark on a bicycle tour of the country. Considering her inability to ride a bike, her hatred of outdoor sports, her reluctance to sleep out in a tent, it was a good thing all this was to be undertaken from the relative comfort of her desk.

'Nadine, Queen of the Trails,' she said, trying to get used to the notion. 'The Adventures of the Lone Biker. Calamity Jane on a bike.'

Brendan shrugged and said, 'That's the ticket. Now you're cooking.' And left her to it.

At first, Nora loathed writing Nadine. She hated the name, hated the whole idea, imagining a loud-mouthed, back-slapping hearty gal in rhinestone-encrusted denim mini-skirt and shirt, a large Stetson perched on top of her flouncy dyed blonde hair. But as time passed, and she wrote and wrote, and got to know her, Nora began to like her. Nadine was all the things Nora wanted to be—candid, extroverted, friendly to strangers, fearless, extraordinarily fit, and always on the lookout for new adventures.

She'd been depressed when she first mentioned the new column to the gang in the pub.

'Nadine, Queen of the Trails,' she'd said with derision and cynicism, upper lip curling.

100

But soon, as she became better acquainted with the character she was writing, Nora grew defensive if anyone mocked Nadine. 'Don't knock Nadine,' she'd say. 'She is out there riding the open road on her trusty bike Gloria, wild and feminist and free.'

'Gloria?' Mona had said.

Nora told her yes, Gloria. She'd decided someone like Nadine would give her bike a name. The bike was called Gloria, after the Van Morrison song.

Nora had put down her beer and given the gang a quick chorus. Mona had joined in. They'd both clapped their hands, then punched the air when the singing ended.

Mona had said, 'Go Nadine and Gloria.'

Nadine's first trip was across Skye. Nora described the ferry ride over to the island. A wide wake of water, the mainland fading in the distance. *Setting off along the flat, away from the ferry, cars swished past me*, she wrote, *and soon I was on my own. The air was lively, salty, fresh, the sky was blue, and there was nobody on the road but me. This is happiness.* She interspersed this with facts about cycling gleaned from the magazine. *I use a ladies' saddle, wider at the rear than men's. Us girls have bigger bums.*

She wrote about the hum of tyres on tarmac, the wind in her face, the scent of soft air and sea, and the splendid B&B which put a splash of whisky into the morning porridge.

'Excellent,' said Brendan. 'Right on the button. Just what we want. But next time, no B&Bs. Camp.'

Over the next few weeks she wrote about her adventures cycling around Gairloch, Devon and the Lake District, none of which she'd ever visited. She used tourist brochures, travel books George had given her and back copies of the magazine. Running out of things to say about bikes, she started to mention the sandwiches Nadine ate. She was fond of crab, but preferred roast beef and mustard on long trips. In lonely places she took comfort from cheese and onion.

This is cycling at its best, Nora wrote. *The quiet roads, and time to think. This is not the story of a muscled racer whizzing past fabulous scenery, head down, bum in the air, baseball hat on the wrong way round.*

In time there were letters from readers. One woman in Carlisle complained that it seemed to her that Nadine knew zip about bikes and certainly hadn't been to the Lake District in her life. Another said she'd picked up the magazine in the dentist's waiting room and it had given her a mind to go off someplace lonely and eat a good sandwich. Another suggested giving sandwich recipes at the foot of the column instead of the route map.

By now, struggling for new things to say about pedalling along leafy lanes, or up mountains, Nora started giving Nadine a life. On her way round the Fife coast, Nadine said, *I know what it's like to be rejected, I know what it's like when someone you love tells you they prefer another. It hurts. I thought the pain would last for ever. I thought the look of sorrow was etched on to my face and everyone who saw me knew I'd been abandoned. I felt worthless.* Then, remembering she was meant to be writing about biking, she mentioned the need to position the saddle so that when seated, the cyclist's patella is

102

just above the pedal spindle. *I'm after serious pedal efficiency. A smooth action with little resistance on the up-stroke.*

Somewhere north of Inverness, Nadine said she remembered all her loves. *As I ride along, their faces come to me. People I've left behind. I love being in love.* Nora was thinking about her first boyfriend, her first lover, who had broken up with her and moved to Canada. *I felt so lonesome, I stood on the hilltop and it seemed the whole world was spread below me. I knelt in the heather and cried.* Then Nadine had a lettuce, bacon and avocado sandwich and a Mars Bar, and pedalled off down the hill.

It wasn't all sorrow, though. Nadine wrote about a flirtation with another cyclist she'd met, and about her late-night conversations with her best friend, Hilly. Then, mending a puncture during a thunderstorm on a wild Yorkshire moor, she had cried. *I felt stupid, soaked through and behaving like a dumb blonde.*

Nora panned through the back pages of her life and gave her findings, her emotions and recollections to Nadine. Trawling the times in her childhood when she had wandered the streets rather than go home and face Maisie, Nora wrote, *I ride into a new town and look around at the faces. So many faces. I wonder about these people, who are they? What sort of lives do they lead? What is home like for them?*

By the time Nora wrote, *I love the open road. I love the feel of it, the smell of it. There are times when there is only the hum and whirr of tyres below me and the wind about me. My mind is clean and empty. No pain, no sorrow, no regrets—only movement*, Hugh Randall was in a fury.

He called Brendan to his office and pointed out that Nadine, Queen of the Trails was meant to be about cycling. 'Routes, a little bit of sightseeing. But mostly about riding a bike. In the last three columns there has been no mention of anything to do with biking. It was all emotions and sandwiches.'

Brendan agreed, but pointed out that the column seemed popular. 'We're getting letters,' he said. 'The readers love it.'

'It's all emotions,' said Hugh. 'It's all women and what they feel. We don't want that. Not in a cycling magazine. Tell her to stop. No bloody women's stuff, and no sandwiches. I've had Jason Pierce in here complaining about it. Quite right, too. He writes about cycling. He's our star. I don't want to lose him.'

At lunchtime Brendan suggested they go for a stroll. It was a bright chill day, a Friday; pools of unmelted frost glittered in shaded areas the sun didn't reach. Brendan wore a long red scarf, wrapped several times round his neck, and stuck his hands in his pockets for warmth. He hated gloves. Nora tripped beside him, three steps to his one. She too stuck her hands deep into her pockets. She wore a blue duffel coat, unbuttoned, a long grey scarf hanging down past its hem.

She set the pace, walking quickly, a habit from her childhood wanderings. She'd found that if she moved along pavements with purpose, nobody bothered her; only aimless dawdlers got pestered by street wanderers, religious nuts, people wanting money, and concerned old ladies asking if she was lost and where was her mummy? She may have had an interesting tiptoeing lope, but she always looked as if she knew where she was going.

The street they walked was wide and busy. Rows of similar houses fronted by winter-bare gardens, some immaculate, some not. Mostly a square of lawn and borders that were largely earth and pruned, leafless rose bushes. Every now and then a bus would howl past them, buffeting them with its backdraught, flapping Nora's coat, whipping her hair round her face. Sometimes they'd stop and face each other as they spoke, emphasising a point. Moving their arms, elbows, hands still held in their pockets to keep them warm. They were both natural gesticulators.

'Sandwiches, Nora. Not good,' said Brendan.

'Very good, I'd say.'

'You are meant to be writing about bicycling trips.'

'So, I don't know about bicycling trips. Sandwiches I know about.' She sounded defensive. 'How can I write about something I know nothing about?'

'You research,' said Brendan. 'You read. You invent. For God's sake, Surf Daddy in the magazine six doors along is seventy-eight and hasn't visited a beach in thirty years.'

'There's a seventy-eight-year-old man still working in the building?'

'He's freelance,' said Brendan. Then, 'I brought you out here to talk to you. I didn't want to say these things in front of the others in the office.'

Nora looked at her feet. She felt like a child again, scolded.

'I have to give Hugh Randall a report on you soon. I'll say you are an asset, doing well. But he's been reading your pieces and he's not happy about the food. He'd rather you concentrated on the cycling aspect.'

Nora said, 'Oh.'

'Then there's all the emotional stuff,' said Brendan. 'You've got to cut it out.'

Nora said, 'But that's what Nadine's about. All her thoughts and emotions as she rides around. Anyway, I can't cut it out. We get letters. And I mention pedalling; that's cycling.'

The magazine hadn't been getting many letters till Nadine came along. Now women wrote in about their divorces, their new boyfriends, their homes and children. They wrote to tell Nadine what they thought about as they rode along. Some didn't go cycling, but still wrote in.

'You write about kneeling in the heather and weeping. About Nadine's love life, about her best friend. The column is meant to be about good places to cycle to,' said Brendan.

Nora was adamant that women were more interested in what another woman thought and felt as she rode about on her own. 'Women are interested in other women,' she said. 'They want to know everything about them. What they eat, the colour of their living rooms, what they wear, what sex is like for them.'

'I don't care,' said Brendan. 'Just stop Nadine talking about that stuff and get back to bikes. You are making enemies. Jason Pierce hates you. You are getting more mail than him. And he writes about cycling.'

Nora shrugged. 'I write about women. Just proves women are more interested in what people think as they ride along than just riding along. The

106

thoughts rather than the ride.'

Brendan told her that Jason was starting to be bitchy about her behind her back.

Nora said, 'Not good. Men are terrible bitches. Not nearly as good as women. See,' she expounded, 'when men are bitchy it's to destroy the person they're being bitchy about. Women are bitchy so they can feel better about themselves.'

Brendan told her to take note of that. 'Hugh and Jason are bitching about you.'

Nora nodded. 'Hugh Randall is the scariest person I've ever met.'

'He's probably as scared of you as you are of him. He wants to hang on to his job. All bright young things are a threat.'

Nora denied she was a bright young thing. And asked Brendan if that was how he saw himself.

'I'm a thing that's facing middle age and lost its shine some time ago. I can't remember when,' he told her.

'Oh, Brendan. That's not you at all.'

He told her that in time everyone stopped being shiny. 'You just want to stay employed. Earning and surviving. That's it for me.'

'There has to be more than that.'

He said that there was but it seemed to have slipped to the back of his mind somewhere and he couldn't quite get hold of it. Recently, he'd been wondering if he was too old for ambition, as he was now too old for his T-shirt with the marijuana leaf on the front.

'You're ambitious, aren't you?' he said.

'Oh yes, absolutely. I'm not as crazed with aspirations as Jason Pierce; he seems stupefied with the need to get ahead. But I admit to being

107

ambitious,' said Nora.

But what exactly she was ambitious for eluded her. Fame, well, that might be nice. Wealth, that definitely would be nice. Having a huge amount of money would ease the stress of being a wastrel. But, no, that wasn't it. She didn't want to edit her own magazine, that much she knew. Yet she was ambitious. She couldn't quite define the yearning she felt. She just wanted. She wanted everything.

She wanted to live an unrestricted life, no routines. She wanted her days to be unpredictable, dangerous sometimes, wild occasionally. She never really thought about the future. She thought it was something she would discover when she got there.

She had lived, until she met Brendan, a life that was not so much sheltered as narrow. There were no adventures, just endless routines carried on, oddly, against a gaudy backdrop.

Now she had been staying with Brendan and Jen, it was as if a curtain had been raised. Not swept aside to let blinding light flood in, just gently lifted to let her see that not everyone lived in patterned rooms and ate the same thing on the same day week in week out. Though she had known this for years, experiencing it was a revelation.

Here were two people, Brendan and Jen, who spoke to each other normally, their voices a low amicable hum, almost melodic. There were no sudden histrionics, no wild tantrums—should one or the other discover there was not enough cheddar for the macaroni cheese—that made other members of the household flee to their rooms till the storm was over. Nobody was ever ostracised. There were no violent silences. People here liked one another.

'I'll show you a good time, squire, if you make me a cup of tea,' Jen might say, draping her arms round Brendan's neck.

He'd kiss the top of her head and tell her she was a tart.

Nora would watch, amazed. She hadn't known married people could be this way. Up till now, she'd stupidly thought that as soon as a woman married, she had to acquire an apron and start cooking roast beef on Sunday, leftovers on Monday. She had to do the washing on Monday, too. Brendan and Jen just shoved dirty clothes in the machine and switched it on. It didn't matter what day it was.

Life was good. She no longer dreaded going home. She was moving into each new day with enthusiasm, she was happy. That was it, she thought, she was happy. And that was her ambition, to get more of all the things that had brought this about.

'I know what my ambition is,' she said to Brendan now, stepping ahead of him, then walking backwards so she could see his face when she made her important announcement. 'I want to be happier than I am now. And I'm happy now.'

'Now at this moment? Or now as in your life generally?' he asked.

'In my life. I'm very, very happy.'

'That's the stupidest thing I've ever heard. Nobody's happy all the time. Not unless they're simple. A bit deficient intellectually speaking.'

'That's a horrible thing to say,' said Nora. 'What's wrong with being happy?'

'It's just not possible, not all the time. You

have an emotional norm. Your average mood. Sometimes you sink below it. Like when you turn into the Martinetti car park. And above it, like when you start eating your supper, when you put on your favourite record, when you get into bed at the end of the day. But happy all day, every day? You sound like a village idiot.'

'So you go around all the time feeling morose, and every now and then some little thing comes along and lifts you out of it.'

'That's me. I'm normal.'

'And I'm not?' said Nora.

'Doesn't sound like it. Actually, Nora, I didn't come walking down this long road with buses hurling past us to talk about happiness. I wanted to give you some advice. When you are writing about bike trips, write about bike trips and not the food you eat.'

'I know, I know,' said Nora. 'Advice. Don't admit to being happy. Don't go on about sandwiches.'

He shook his head, feeling hopeless. What was the point of handing out excellent advice? Nora wouldn't take it. She never did. She'd listen, quite intently, too, nod her head, then do what she wanted to do. She went her own way. She never read instructions, believing the workings of things would become obvious once you familiarised yourself with them. She formed opinions when she had only a fragment of relevant information, and refused to re-form them.

'Some of your faults,' Brendan had once told her, listing these things.

'They're never faults,' Nora said. 'They are all just part of the way I am.'

110

She was also prone to disagreeing with people.

Now, Brendan looked at his watch. 'We've come too far. We'll have to get the bus back up the road or we'll be late.'

'Can't we just be late? What's wrong with that?'

'No, we can't just be late. It would be noticed. Black marks on our records. Especially yours. You are still on probation.' He stood at the edge of the pavement, waiting for a gap in the streaming traffic so they could cross the road.

'Surely they wouldn't fire me for being late,' said Nora.

'They are watching you, assessing you. They read everything you submit.'

There was a gap, a few fleeting moments before the next approaching car got close enough to mow anyone down. Brendan seized his chance and ran.

There was something about him running that made Nora want to laugh. He was no athlete. He didn't use his arms to accelerate his speed. He kept his hands in his pockets, pointed himself towards his goal and took off, hunched and darting forward. He looked like a bumble bee.

In fact she didn't laugh. Brendan had just burst her bubble, telling her she was being watched, assessed, then dashing off at top speed before she could take issue with him. Her heart sank. In a twinkling her happiness, her blessed euphoria, disappeared. A cloud descended. She was depressed.

When she joined him on the other side of the road, she berated him. 'You've really depressed me saying that. I feel like I'm employed by the Gestapo.'

'Good,' he said. Looked at her crestfallen

expression. 'That's more like it.'

The bus arrived. They boarded, taking seats just inside the lower deck since they only had three stops to travel. They both paid their own fare. They had an unspoken financial agreement: on buses, in galleries and cinemas they each paid for themselves; in taxis, pubs, restaurants and coffee bars they split the bill. In this last case one had often spent more than the other, but both considered bickering over this to be undignified.

On buses, Brendan always sat sideways, holding the back of the seat in front. He'd be poised ready to leap to his feet and run off as soon as they arrived at his stop. Nora was calmer; no matter how short her journey, she settled in, claiming her own small space. She hated it when she couldn't get a seat at the window. 'I need room for my thoughts,' she said.

'Another thing,' said Brendan. 'You've been seen walking dreamily about the corridors. Stopping and gazing out of the window. Don't do that.'

Nora wondered if there was anything she did right.

They got off the bus at the stop across from the entrance to the building. Brendan crossed the road and went through the Martinetti gates ahead of her. Nora followed, walking purposefully, swinging her arms. 'I'm practising my corridor walk,' she said. 'No dawdling. No dreaming.'

Then she limped, hobbled. 'This is my emotional walk. Too bogged down with loneliness, pain and regret to move properly.'

She limped along, dragging her leg. She sagged. She clutched her heart. She staggered. 'I have travelled the land. I am tired and racked with pain. And lack of sandwiches.'

Brendan, not wanting to be any later than he already was, had rushed ahead. Now he turned, walking backwards, saw Nora's performance, laughed, then told her to pack it in. He knew what Nora didn't know. They were being observed from above.

Nora lurched forward.

By now Brendan had gone into the building. Hugh Randall, who had been watching the whole thing through the binoculars he kept in the left-hand drawer of his desk, could only see Nora. The girl's a fool, he thought. A clown.

He kept the binoculars specifically to spy on Martinetti employees arriving, or leaving work. He liked to know if anyone had a new car, or if they were carrying a briefcase that indicated they took their jobs seriously enough to take projects home. Or if, perhaps, someone might be stealing toilet rolls from the supply room. He kept lists of who came in early, and who arrived late.

Now he was taking note of Nora's behaviour. He decided she was acting out her feelings about Martinetti and McBride. The woman was showing how much she hated coming to work in the company he loved, the company that had employed him for over twenty-five years. He'd given his life to this place. In showing her feelings she was not only insulting the name of Martinetti, she was insulting him. The first gnawings of hatred stirred within him. That one would have to be watched.

In the pub that evening, while Brendan was at the bar getting the drinks, Nora told the others

113

that she'd been scolded for writing about sandwiches and emotions.

'Sandwiches?' said George. Here was a subject that interested him.

'I should have been writing about the bike trips of Nadine, Queen of the Trails, but instead I banged on about the things she ate. I can't ride a bike. But I can eat. I like eating. Then again, Hugh Randall doesn't like the emotions I mentioned.'

George warmed to her. 'What sort of sandwiches?'

'Cheese and onion, crab, lettuce, tomato and avocado,' said Nora. 'A woman wrote in and asked for the recipe. She didn't mention anything about cycling.'

'Excellent,' said George. He rather admired someone who could turn a cycling column into a discourse about sandwich fillings.

Nathan asked about the emotions.

'Things Nadine thought about as she rode along.'

'Well, she would think,' said Nathan. 'That's the point of it. Thinking. I go walking, take to the hills on my own, and that's what I do. Think.'

Nora shrugged, and said that was what she thought people would do. 'But Hugh Randall wants less thinking and sandwich eating and more cycling.'

In the end she was saved in the worst way possible. One morning William Martinetti came into the office. He only stayed a couple of minutes, but it was Nora he spoke to. 'Nadine, Queen of the Trails. Excellent. I love it. Keep up the good work.'

Short, sweet, but enough to make Jason and Hugh hate her even more than they did already.

Roast Beef Sundays

On Sundays Brendan cooked roast beef, and usually two or three people would turn up to help eat it. The roast beef eaters were Mona, George Henry and Nora. Nathan rarely came along. Sunday was his day with his daughter, Justine.

Brendan sometimes invited other people, but his invitations were obscure. People didn't realise they were being asked to join him in his favourite meal. 'Having roast beef on Sunday,' he might say to somebody that he thought might be interesting to get to know, who he'd come across in his wanderings in the Martinetti building, thinking this was enough. He was of the opinion that people ought to be aware he wouldn't just tell them what he was having. Surely it must be obvious they were being encouraged to come along to share what he considered to be a feast.

The roasting of the beef took a little time, as Brendan didn't consider it worth cooking a small joint. 'Small beef shrivels, big beef gets crisp on the outside, pink and juicy within,' he said.

Wearing a long blue-and-white-striped apron, he'd move between the kitchen and the living room, where he'd oversee the selection of music to be played. This would normally be whatever LPs he had bought that week.

They would be buried among the mass of albums that lined his shelves, because the money he spent on them shamed him. He didn't want Jen to know the absurd portion of his earnings he parted with weekly in record shops, so he'd keep new purchases in his car, sneaking them into the house and hiding them in between long-established items, when Jen was out.

Of course, she knew he did this but, not wanting to spoil his fun, said nothing. She suspected the sneakiness of hiding a precious newly acquired LP from her was part of the passion of it all. Of all pleasures, guilty pleasures were the best.

What worried Jen about Brendan was his appetite. Once he discovered a liking for something, he couldn't get enough of it. She'd often seen him eat an entire box of chocolate gingers on the drive from the supermarket, where he'd bought them, to the house. Ten minutes, top whack, she thought.

It was the same with music. Once he found a track he liked, he couldn't play it often enough, or loud enough. 'It passed the test,' he'd say.

'What test?' Jen would ask.

'The music test. When I hear some tracks they take me by storm. I like to imagine it's me singing or playing the guitar or the trumpet or whatever. Me. Imagine being part of some great piece of music, in the band, standing there surrounded by that sound, being one of the ones making it.'

'You just want to show off. You want the adoration of the masses.'

'Fuck, Jen. No. To be able to do something well, really, really well. And be proud of it. This is me, you'd say. This is what I can do. To like yourself, that's it. You make me sound infantile with that adoration crap.'

Jen had shrugged. 'Well pardon me. You could be really, really good at gardening or mending the upstairs tap. Instead you're starting to fritter away

116

your approaching middle age playing the air guitar.'

He told her glumly that she had just ruined one of the few pleasures left to him.

Then there was sex. They had been teenage sweethearts, conducting a chaste romance on the sofa in Jen's parents' living room, where they'd sat holding hands and kissing under the watchful eye of the Pope, whose heavily framed picture hung on the floral wallpaper. Brendan complained it didn't stop his carnal thoughts, but put paid to any carnal doings.

'That's the most alarming picture I've ever seen,' he'd said.

The relationship hadn't been consummated till they were both in their early twenties, and she was studying for her nursing exams. By then, Brendan had left home and was sharing what Jen thought must have been the filthiest flat in the world with Alan Monks, from the art department, in Edinburgh's High Street. God, she realised, he even overdid the filth.

But sex, when he'd started getting it, had seemed to be all he thought about. They had hardly gone anywhere in the evenings because all Brendan had wanted to do was go to bed. In fact, Jen had been so exhausted by his enthusiasm, she'd thought she was going to fail her exams.

So far Brendan's appetites were harmless—monogamous sex, music and tea. Jen thought that should he ever discover cigarettes and booze, they'd be quickly broke. So far, their marriage was going according to plan. They'd bought a house, had some furnishings and no children. Though this last was starting to bother Brendan.

117

'All that sex, and no babies. I fancy a couple of them, they'd fill up the empty rooms. And they'd be company, they could watch cartoons on the telly Saturday mornings with me.'

Jen was adamant. No babies till she was established, with her own ward. 'You may be in charge of the soundtrack to our lives, the roast beef and the cups of tea. But I'm in charge of the baby-making.'

Brendan had protested the unfairness of this. After all, when it came to baby-making, he had an important part to play. Jen could not do this alone. Jen had agreed she could not conceive without his help, but when it came to the carrying of the infant to term, the bringing of same infant into the world, he was a bystander.

'But,' said Brendan, 'I'd be a good bystander. I'd rub your back, I'd pamper you, pour scented oils on your feet, and bring you tasty things on a tray while you lay stretched on the sofa, watching junk TV, shouting your demands.'

Jen had said that she'd remember that when the time came; meantime, no babies. This was said with firmness, it was not negotiable. Brendan accepted it, but grudgingly, and would often return to the subject to find out if Jen had changed her mind. Or if she, at last, understood how much he longed for the stability of a proper family. How he wanted to be enmeshed in the daily turmoil of small things and small people. It seemed to him uncomplicated and ordinary. Children, he thought, would take him out of himself. He could watch them grow and learn, he could play with them, read to them. He would think about them instead of thinking about a job he'd come to dislike.

Children, he thought, might be the making of him.

But on Sundays Brendan did not talk of babies, or of any sort of longing. He played his tracks of the moment, he basted his beef, peeled potatoes for roasting, prepared a salad. He was happy.

The others would sit in the living room, reading the papers, chatting about their weekends so far, reminiscing—usually about roast-beef afternoons gone by—and, from time to time, wandering through to the kitchen to keep Brendan company, to sit at the table watching him make gravy and onion sauce.

There was a calm on Sundays. And recently there had been an undertow to that calm. Change was coming. None of them knew what it would be, but they could sense it. Maybe it had been going on too long, but they all knew that the time would arrive when they no longer met like this, so easily, casually, listening to Talking Heads or Miles Davis or Mozart or Bob Dylan. They would all move on.

Mona had, until eighteen months ago, lived with Gregory. He was a tall man, exquisitely handsome, and had what Brendan called brutish opinions. Mona took exception to this. Gregory, she maintained, was a man who said what he thought, and Brendan was a man who didn't.

Gregory didn't dislike Brendan or any of the others Mona regularly met; he disliked what they did. 'It's all trivial,' he said. 'And what use is that?'

'It isn't all trivial,' Mona would say. 'Magazines are about people. Who they are. How they got to be who they are. The things they've gone through. And they are about helping people to be better than they are. Better looking, better informed, better dressed.'

119

If only she had put that list in a different order. If she'd said, better looking, better dressed, better informed, the last one might have been what struck Gregory. He couldn't have pounced on that as cruelly as he had on the notion of helping people to be better dressed.

'Dress. What does that matter?'

'These days, a lot,' Mona had said. 'It's a shallow world. First appearances matter. You are judged the instant the person you are meeting and greeting claps eyes on you. They will decide on that first eye flick from shoes to hairstyle if you are worth getting to know.'

Gregory had said something that sounded like *pah*. He was a consultant accountant, preparing budgets for large corporations. On his say, costs were cut. People were hired, fired, made redundant, advised to take early retirement. He was paid handsomely, but the job had become too sharp, too cut and dried, too vicious for him.

Mona mocked that he was an accountant with a conscience, and the world did not need that. He mocked back that the world needed someone with a conscience more than it needed someone who had anything to do with fashion.

'Fashion,' said Mona. 'The world needs fashion. The world craves fashion. It's a reflection of the times we are living through, and a way to look at attitudes of times past. It's how individuals who have no other way of doing it can express themselves. It's who people are. It's everything.'

Gregory had told her that a gift for assembling clothes and wearing them with panache was simply a way of disguising the fact that you were brainless.

At this Mona had stormed out of the room and

into the kitchen, where she'd leaned against the sink, staring. Not knowing if she wanted to throw things at the wall in rage, or cry. In the end she did both. She threw a dishcloth in fury, but it spread out, slipped ineffectually to the floor, making the gesture useless. And that had made her weep.

The accountant with a conscience versus the brainless dandyism of the fashion slave argument happened more and more regularly in Mona's exchanges with Gregory. Once, it had bubbled up every month or so, but in time it was an everyday occurrence. And it was getting nasty.

What had started as a heated debate was getting stormier. Insults flew, and they would stand, faces red with fury, arms pressed against their sides lest they started laying into one another, fists flying. Still, Mona consoled herself, all this passion and anger made for excellent sex when they both collapsed, drained from their battles, and with nothing left but battered emotions, into bed.

Gregory's looks fascinated Mona. People stared at him across crowded rooms. Women switched, automatically, to flirt mode when they spoke to him. Sometimes, it seemed as if nobody heard what he was saying, they were so absorbed in looking at him. Not that this bothered Mona. She knew he was not the sort to indulge in casual affairs. If women flirted, Gregory rarely noticed. In fact, Mona had to point the flirting out to him. But she knew she had a rival, and one that would, in the end, win. Her adversary was his conscience. She hadn't a hope in hell against that.

And then the madness stopped. Quite suddenly, Gregory calmed down. For a while, Mona believed he had got over his fury. But no, he was living it.

He started to dress down to go to work, abandoning his selection of bespoke suits, wearing instead jeans or tracksuit bottoms and one of several hideous jumpers he had acquired. Where from? Mona never found out. His favourite was a swirling mix of purple, red and green. On his feet the training shoes he ran in every morning. They were old, muddied and tired, but he loved them. 'They make my feet happy,' he said.

He'd thought that someone would say something about the way he now dressed. This was no way to appear in board rooms to discuss budgets and projected figures for the coming year. But nobody said anything. Oh, there was surprise. He could see it—raised eyebrows, dropped jaws. But people were too polite to talk, to his face, anyway, about the inappropriateness of his clothes.

Now, he'd speak quietly about the things he hated. 'Some of them are small, but still greedy,' he said. The photocopier salesman who'd added another nought to the sum agreed on the lease he'd negotiated with a large company, after it had been signed. The company chairman who had made two people redundant, then used the money saved in wages to pay for a Bentley. 'Do you know what? I think I really hate people.'

That was the moment Mona knew she'd lost. His conscience had won. A week later Gregory quit his job. He packed his things and left to live in an old gardener's cottage in the Borders. 'I'm not leaving you,' he told Mona. 'I'm just getting away from everything and everybody else. You can come with me, if you want. If not, come see me any time.'

Mona didn't want. She couldn't imagine living,

as she put it, away from everything. No shops, pubs, restaurants, galleries, cinemas; only space and air and probably a lot of silence. 'No thanks,' she said. 'I'll visit.'

Gregory packed all his belongings in his Jaguar, and drove away. Leaving Mona to a new silence, and all his suits and hideous jumpers, which he'd left behind.

At first she'd hated being alone. The quiet in the flat unnerved her. She could hear every click and creak of the central heating pipes, and was suddenly horribly aware of the sound of her humming fridge. Sometimes, the very air around her seemed to be closing in on her. She'd gone to live with Brendan and Jen for a while. Then, realising she had to come to terns with her new circumstances, had returned home. She had to make a new life for herself. So she put on her highest heels and her bravest face and went out with friends. In wine bars and pubs she spoke too much, laughed too loudly and made jokes about her situation.

'I'm doing well,' she'd say. 'I'm fine. In fact, I'm thinking of what my replacement man will be like. I'm going to place an ad in the personals. Wanted, gentle, uncritical man, any age, who can mend things. Non-smoker, GSOH, who will be happy to stay home and fix the plumbing while I go out to play and will be glad to cuddle when I get back.'

Then she'd laugh. And look round at the laughing faces circling her. She was aware that her line of defence was fragile, a flimsy membrane between her and the rest of the world. If anyone spoke harshly or came too near, and broke it, she'd cry.

123

But slowly, slowly she began to get used to having her space to herself. Nobody made comments about her conversations with her friends on the phone. Nobody saw that she liked to eat yoghurt standing up leaning on the sink. She no longer had to discuss what to do in the evenings, or what to make for supper. She did what she wanted, ate what she wanted. She could watch any television programme she fancied. She could spend Saturday in bed reading *Vogue*. She could think. Solitary living had its merits. She was fine, she told her friends. 'Look, I'm standing up. I'm walking around. I'm getting on with things.' It was wonderful cooking for one. And who cared if she talked to herself, who was there to hear? So what if there were certain pieces of music she avoided. Rachmaninov always made her cry.

She missed Gregory, and told herself she couldn't allow herself to miss him. She had to get on with her life. In time she developed a reputation for having an interesting sex life. This was her own fault, as she talked about having dates. People assumed she was going out with a lot of different people.

This wasn't really true. She had two regular boyfriends, Ben and Richard. Ben was some years older than her, fifty-six. He was a merchant banker and took her out, usually on Thursday nights, for meals at upmarket restaurants. Richard was twenty-three and took her clubbing on Fridays. This second was an easy relationship; there was little to it other than dancing (which Mona saw as part of her exercise routine) and a few vodkas. They shared the cost of their evenings together. It wouldn't last, Mona knew that. In time she'd think she was too old for the clubs they visited, and in time, too, Richard would want to settle into a more permanent arrangement with one of the other women he saw. She thought that she would want a committed partner, too. Except that every time she thought about it, Gregory came to mind. She couldn't imagine herself long term with anyone else.

After Gregory had been away a month, Mona went to see him. She drove out of Edinburgh, past Peebles and into the border country. A vast area of empty land, strewn here and there with sheep. But mostly abandoned to its huge history.

She turned off the wide, straight main road, into a narrow side road, and then on to a track that became a grass track, then nothing. She had to walk the last quarter of a mile. Gregory lived in the house that was past the last house in the world. But it was worth the journey. It was in a clearing, surrounded by woods. It was small, three rooms. But there was a large garden bordered by beech hedges, where Gregory had already started to cultivate his vegetables. A wooden porch, heavy with blooming clematis. The air was sweet with burning wood smoke. And at the door, waiting for her, was Gregory, smiling. She'd forgotten that smile. She'd forgotten, too, how much she loved him.

Twice a month now she visited Gregory. She'd sit in the armchair in his kitchen watching him cook. While she was there, she thought the set-up charming, and indulged in fantasies of giving up her job and joining him.

The kitchen she thought inviting. It was so old-fashioned, its design was coming into favour again.

A ceramic sink, no fitted units; just a walk-in pantry in the far corner, stone-flag tiles, and overhead, exposed beams from which hung bunches of herbs and Gregory's copper pots.

In her daydream, Mona busied herself here making preserves and cakes. Though she had never baked a cake in her life, and had no intention of ever doing so in reality, in the dream, she beat eggs, sugar and flour, and later, hands shielded by a checked dishcloth, lifted from the oven a hot, perfectly rounded golden vision of a cake. But actually, she didn't like cake, and neither did Gregory. Who would eat this vision of domesticity? She didn't know.

The living room was small. An ancient and dubiously sprung sofa stood in front of a large fireplace that Gregory kept simmering with logs. It was lit, though rather dimly, by a couple of standard lamps, with matching floral shades. The sofa twanged and complained when sat upon, and once into it, the sitter had a problem getting up again. The sitter's bum seemed to slip into the bowels of the thing, and end up somewhere lower down than was truly comfortable. Not that this mattered really; the heat in the room, the pleasant tiredness she felt from her day, sitting in the garden or walking with Gregory—they walked and read a lot; there was no television—always made her snooze.

While she was there, Mona imagined herself remaining there. Quiet mornings, dew-soaked grass, and in autumn the frosted ground cracking underfoot. Geese honking overhead, the constant murmuring gossip of pigeons in the woods, the sweet smell of pine burning. The calm of it all. Oh yes, she could be happy here.

But always, driving home, she'd change her mind. As soon as she could see the city lights, she'd press harder on the accelerator, and speed towards them. There was always, too, that flood of relief when she found herself moving once more past buildings, shops, streetlights.

This is better, she'd tell herself. Driving further into town, where the buildings got higher and the smell of petrol fumes mingled with outpourings from fish and chip shops and burger joints, where the rustle and clank of traffic grew louder and louder, she'd almost weep with joy. Better and better. This is it, this is where I want to be. And if ever any of her friends asked if she was going to go live with Gregory, Mona would shake her head. 'No, too cold. Too quiet. Too muddy. I just don't do mud. It's not my thing.'

This was her line of defence. But, in fact, she didn't go and live with Gregory because he hadn't asked her again. That was the state of their relationship now. She couldn't turn up on his doorstep announcing she was here to stay. If she wanted to do that, she'd have to ask. And as Gregory was the sort of man who gave big answers to the smallest of questions, Mona shuddered to imagine what sort of unbearably huge answer he would give to a question the size of 'Can I come and live with you?'

Besides, she thought, leaving Edinburgh would make her wretched. She loved the place. Its wide sweeping streets, and its tiny alleys that often came as a surprise to her. She swore that every time she walked down the High Street, she saw a narrow close that hadn't been there the last time she passed this way.

She loved the fact that it was small enough to walk from place to place, and big enough to have restaurants and bars where interweaving cliques and friends mingled. She liked the cafés with tables on the pavement, though she had to admit that sometimes the weather was nippy, and sipping espresso al fresco wasn't as splendid as it looked to be to those passing, snug in taxis and buses. She loved it that she rarely went out without spotting a familiar face. Even if the face was only familiar enough to nod to. She loved the light. The gardens, the old squares, the buildings. She didn't even mind the grey winds that chased her down the narrow streets, whipping round her legs, ruining her hair.

Her life was here, her friends, meetings in the pub on Friday nights, roast beef Sundays at Brendan's.

George always sat in the corner seat of the sofa doing a crossword which usually took him ten minutes. This week, Mona watched him over the top of the style section of the paper she was reading, and timed him.

'How do you do that?'

'It's only words,' he said.

'Yeah, but the words you use aren't the same words us ordinary people use.'

'That's true,' said Nora.

'George uses posh words,' said Mona. 'But then you are posh, George.'

'Only someone veering towards the plebeian would say that,' said George.

Everyone said, 'Oooh.'

George smiled. He got up and went through to

the kitchen to check on the progress of the roast beef. He should open the red wine, which he always supplied. Brendan and Jen would hear him before they saw him arrive, bottles clanking in his off-licence carrier bag.

George loved the ritual of it all. Selecting the wine, he'd spend a ponderous time cruising shelves, reading labels, debating with himself what was and what was not a good year. He thought it wonderful that the same people met at the same time in the same place every week; old conversations could be recycled, intricate in-jokes developed, everybody was relaxed and helped themselves to seconds, refilled their own glasses. There was laughter.

As he left the room, he cast a small affectionate glance towards Mona, who pretended she didn't notice. But Nora noticed, and was too naive, to keep silent about it.

'I think George is secretly in love with you,' she said.

Mona lowered her paper. 'I know George is secretly in love with me. And I am very fond of him. But very fond is not enough, don't you think?'

Nora shrugged: she didn't know. She thought having someone who was very fond of her would be lovely. She could do with that. Then again, she wished she could give the short, snappy replies Mona specialised in.

Jen threw another log on the fire. The fire was hers; she lit it, tended it. There had been a time when she'd longed to spend quiet weekends with her husband, to read the papers together, perhaps go for a stroll, prepare a meal while chatting about this and that, their observations and opinions, their plans for the future. But she'd known Brendan long enough to realise that such a gregarious man would always need people around him. He needed to chat, expound, he needed an audience for his many, many theories.

But there was the private Brendan. The one she shared a bed with, who made her laugh, who spoke in the dark about things he planned to do. The children they'd have one day. The man who played the air guitar, who'd read more books than the shelves in their bedroom and attic could contain, who would wake her to read aloud some passage he thought fascinating, or just wonderful. Who would stroke her hair, her cheek and say, 'Let's make a baby.'

She'd say, 'Let's just practise.'

That man was hers. So she had come not to mind the roast beef Sundays. Especially when she alone knew the real reason for them. It was the beef. Large joints were so much more satisfying and succulent. They were more likely to turn out crisp on the outside, pink within. And if Brendan was cooking a huge piece of meat, he needed people to come help him eat it.

So she returned to the paper she was studying on postpartum depression in women after a difficult birth experience. She knew this to be a lot more worthwhile than anything anyone Brendan invited had to say, but still, she kept one ear open for anything juicy Mona might come up with.

Across the room, Nora squirmed. She'd told Mona she thought George to be secretly in love with her. What a stupid thing to say, secretly in love. It sounded so immature. What would Mona think of her? Mona was such a shiny person. She made Nora feel inept at the simple business of living everyday life.

She felt strange and fragile with these people, a newcomer in their world. She desperately wanted them all to like her. For she was having a romance with them, and with Edinburgh, and with her job. It was all achingly thrilling; every day she woke she thought of her new life in this new place, and thought nothing could be better than this, and she'd let nothing take it away from her.

She loved the way these people met and resumed old conversations, and had standard silly subjects like Mona's habit of always picking the slow queue in the bank, or Brendan's luck with parking spaces. 'Parked right outside the cinema the other night. Right at the door, came out, three steps, top whack, and there I am in the car. You could feel the envy of all the other cinema-goers and parkers.' There was, too, the matter of Brendan's dreams, which were absurd. Or the group excitement when George's grandmother sent him a fruit cake. He'd brought it to Brendan's one Sunday and they'd had to sit in anticipation of a slice till Brendan had made everyone a mug of tea. 'You can't eat it unaccompanied,' he'd said. 'You have to take a bite, then a swig, so it all gets mushy in the mouth. It is a perfect eating moment.'

She was slowly beginning to realise that it didn't matter what they all spoke about. It was the speaking that mattered, the communication. Letting the others know you were here. She wasn't used to that. At home, she'd learned to keep her mouth shut for fear her private thoughts might be ridiculed. Here they were discussed, and if they were ridiculed, it somehow made her feel more part of the group, which freed her to make fun of the others in turn. It was new to her. She'd always felt apart from other people. What she didn't grasp was that everyone else had always felt that way too.

Secrets

Every so often Maisie would say something that puzzled Alex. She'd list her ailments, then say they didn't really matter, 'As long as you're happy. That's the main thing.' And sometimes she'd look vexed and say, 'All I want in life is for everything to be all right.'

This perplexed Alex. He claimed that everything *was* all right. They nearly owned the house they lived in; a few more years would do it. They had everything they could possibly hope for—a car, second hand but serviceable, washing machine, television, fitted carpets. 'We have two weeks every year in Cornwall,' he said. 'We eat well. We're warm, especially now we've got the central heating.' Which he thought Maisie kept at too high a temperature, but never liked to mention. 'The kids are fine. Not drug addicts; as far as I know they haven't taken to drink. They are setting out on their lives. They're happy. That's as good as it gets, Maisie.'

She dismissed this. 'No it isn't. They should be in touch. They should be letting me know how they are.'

'Cathryn phones,' said Alex.

'Oh yes, Cathryn phones every week to let me

know how she's getting on. She's good, she's always been good. It's Nora I'm talking about. There hasn't been a word from her in months.'

'So she's fine. If there was anything bothering her, she'd be in touch.'

Maisie glared at him. 'That's not the point. She should be in touch anyway. It's not polite not to let people know how you are. People ask me how she is and I don't know what to say.'

Alex sighed. 'Why don't you phone her?' he said.

'I have,' said Maisie. 'Now it's her turn to phone me. That's how it should be.'

He always wondered where Maisie got her strict notions about relationships from. 'Where did you get that idea?' he said. 'Nora has a new life. She probably thinks about you, feels a little guilty about not phoning, decides to phone, then gets caught up doing something and forgets. It has always seemed to me you get your ideas about how we should behave from a washing powder advert or an old radio soap. I go out to work, come home smiling, eat a meal and watch television. You stay home, clean, and bring up the kids. These are your rules. You never asked me what I thought.'

Maisie asked what did he think, then.

'I have always thought we should do more together. You and me. You never want to go anywhere. It's just us now, no children to bother about, we can come and go as we like. But no, you want life to carry on the same all the time. And if you really want to know what I think about Nora not phoning, I think she doesn't keep in touch because you always gave her the impression you didn't really like her. That's the impression you

133

gave me.'

'How could you say such a thing?' said Maisie. 'She's my little girl. Of course I love her.'

'I didn't say love. I said like,' said Alex.

Maisie said nothing. Thick, black, filthy guilt spread through her. It was true, she didn't like Nora, never had. Nora had been impossible, she thought. Scruffy. You could dress her up all pretty in a freshly ironed dress, usually one of Cathryn's hand-me-downs, and the girl would come in from the garden ten minutes later covered in muck. And she was always asking questions. Questions, questions, questions—why is grass green? How do the birds know there's bread put out for them? Why don't the stars fall down from the sky?—when she was wanting to get on with things. The child was always daydreaming or reading. She said she wanted to work on the buses. Where did she get that notion? No daughter of Maisie's would think of such a thing. Nora had never done as she was told. Then, later, she'd gone off to school in the morning and come home late every afternoon. She was hardly ever in the house.

More than all that, Maisie had seen in Nora the child she had wanted to be. The tomboy, the reader, the asker of questions, the girl who imagined the garden was a desert island, or a prairie in the American west. She would leap out at her from behind the lupins shouting, 'No time to hang out the washing, ma'am. Them Apaches are painted up for war and headin' this way. We got to hitch up the wagons an' hightail it into town.' Maisie would say, 'Ach, stop your nonsense.' But really, in her heart, she'd wanted to join in. Imagining an Apache war party was attacking their suburban house, or that pirates had buried a chest flowing with doubloons somewhere behind the rose bushes was fun. Only women didn't do that, they had to keep the house neat as a new pin and put supper on the table. No, Maisie hadn't liked the girl, she'd been jealous of her. And she'd always felt awful about it.

Why couldn't Nora be like Cathryn? Cathryn was neat, clean, kind and more than pretty, beautiful. Cathryn phoned every week. On Thursdays, usually, not long after six in the evening.

In fact, Maisie was on Cathryn's to-do list. Having phoned, she'd put a small mental tick against it, and would be able to get on with other more important and interesting things with a clear conscience.

Cathryn had gained her law degree and now worked for a small firm of lawyers in Manchester, doing criminal cases. She shared a large house with four other people, all young and ambitious lawyers. She loved her job, she loved her life.

She had a boyfriend, Thomas Moir, a university lecturer, six years her senior. He was impetuous, handsomely dressed and loved showing her off. They were considered to be a glamorous couple and were invited to many dinner parties. During the week they lived apart but on the weekends they stayed together in his flat. Cathryn thought this arrangement perfect.

Meantime, she'd kept in touch with Clive English, who she'd dated when they were both still at school. After they'd split up, they remained friends. They went out when she came home for the odd weekend on Bank Holidays, at Easter and at Christmas. He was making his way in the world as a civil servant in the Ministry of Defence.

Clive had always been there for her, encouraged her, provided a comforting shoulder to lean on, listened to her heartaches and woes. It was an easy, joky relationship that Cathryn was proud of. She thought there couldn't be many women who were still in contact with and relaxed around the man who had been their first lover.

From time to time, Clive would drop in on Maisie and Alex to see how they were doing, and to chat about Cathryn. She thought that a bit odd, but then there had always been a homey side to Clive. Then again, both Clive and Maisie always had the same news, since she phoned both once a week. Keeping in touch was her way of keeping them all at bay. She loved her life in Manchester, and wanted to keep it separate from her home life.

Maisie loved Clive's visits. 'A lovely young man,' she said. 'I wish he and Cathryn had stayed together. They'd have made a wonderful couple.'

Alex simply said, 'Hmm. Suppose so.' He wished Maisie would let her daughters go. They were old enough to get on with their own lives.

Now, trying to hide her guilt, Maisie said, 'I think that's a terrible thing to say, that I don't like Nora.'

Alex shrugged and told her that was the impression she always gave him.

'And I don't know what you mean about me not wanting to go anywhere. I'll go places. I'll go to the cinema if you like.'

Alex told her not to bother, it was too late. And Maisie assumed that the film he wanted to see was no longer showing.

136

But Alex had meant more than that. It was too late for him to want to take Maisie anywhere. He preferred the company of Miss Winthrope. Claire, as he now called her.

Claire worked in the office along the corridor from his, in accounts. She was small, wiry, fashionably dressed, and at fifty-three, five years younger than him. She went out nights to the theatre, to the cinema; she was in a book group; she had an interesting life. And, in time, she had spoken to him—though somewhat shyly—about her ex-lover, who had left her. At that point she and Alex were becoming friends.

He had smiled and said, 'Surely not.' He couldn't imagine anyone leaving Claire Winthrope. He liked the way she dressed, scarves and beads round her neck, dark grey or black suits with pink, blue or grey silk shirts and high, high heels.

They had first spoken in the staff canteen, where one day, when there had been no other seats available, he'd asked if she minded him sitting at her table. Their conversation then had been about the awfulness of the food and the weather. It soon moved on to include favourite television programmes, old, much-loved films, holidays and longings, hopes and fears. Roundabout then, Miss Winthrope had said, 'Oh, for goodness' sake, call me Claire, please. Miss Winthrope makes me sound like an old spinster.' Which, she thought, she was, or was fast becoming. Alex said he was Alex.

By then it was summer and Claire said, 'Enough of this dire and smelly canteen, I'm taking sandwiches to the park tomorrow. I want some sunshine while it's there.'

He wasn't quite sure if this had been an invitation to join her in the park, or just a statement of intent. But he joined her. 'Thought you were right about the sunshine,' he'd said. And pulled from his briefcase a cheese and pickle sandwich, encased in its impenetrable plastic wrapping, that he'd bought at Marks and Spencer.

Soon, Claire was to say, 'No need for you to buy those plastic things. You can share mine. I always make too much.'

So Alex shared Claire's sandwiches, and brought along some grapes as a contribution. Soon the sandwiches became more and more elaborate; not just cheese and tomato, but lettuce, bacon and avocado, or prawn and mayonnaise. Alex brought along cheese, Belgian chocolate and fruit juice.

It was now that Alex bought his first new suit in ten years. Normally he picked out one in dark grey; this time he chose a paler grey and was fussy about the fit. He selected shirts to go with it, one white, one navy blue and one a slightly darker grey than the suit. He matched these with several ties. 'Just some new clothes for the office,' he told Maisie. 'Must keep up with the times.'

When it rained, he and Claire went to a small Italian restaurant nearby, where the pasta was cheap. Sometimes they bought a glass of wine. He told her about his children.

'Cathryn and Nora. Cathryn's the beauty, and brainy with it. Nora's the dreamer. I have no idea how smart she might be, she's too dreamy to even know herself. If they were standing side by side in the middle of the road and a huge jewel-encrusted bus came bearing down on them, Cathryn would jump aside. Nora would stand staring, thinking, oh, what a beautiful bus, and get crumpled.'

Claire had said, 'I rather like Nora.'

'So do I,' said Alex.

It was Christmas before they first slept together, after the firm's party. A little drunk, they'd shared a taxi home, though he lived a fair distance from her. She'd invited him in for coffee. 'Yes,' he'd said. 'I think I could do with that.'

A coffee. A kiss. Then bed. 'It's been a while,' said Alex. 'Maisie and I don't any more.'

Miss Winthrope had taken his hand. 'It's all right. I know what to do.'

Afterwards, he'd slept. Woken at four in the morning, wondering where he was. 'Oh God,' he'd said and leapt out of bed. He got home just before five. Stripped and climbed into bed with Maisie, who was in a deep sleep.

'When did you get in last night?' she asked in the morning. 'You're never usually that late.'

'Dunno,' said Alex. 'Not long after midnight. You were sound, didn't want to wake you.'

Soon he was seeing Claire twice a week. He told Maisie that the department where he worked had undergone a shake-up which meant he had to work late a couple of nights a week. He hated it, but there you go, he told her. 'It's the times we live in. People come in early, leave late.'

On the evenings he was absent from the house, Maisie missed him. Not his conversation, just his quiet presence across the room, reading the paper, watching television.

Once Maisie had looked at him as he left the house. He was wearing a soft-shouldered blue suit, a grey shirt with matching tie. 'Look at you,' she said. 'I could almost fancy you all dressed up like that.'

'I thought you would fancy me,' said Alex. 'We're married.'

'Oh, you know how it is,' said Maisie. 'All those years you forget to look at each other.'

Alex was leaving the house dressed up, smelling discreetly of cologne. He was staying out late a couple of times a week. Sometimes, on Saturdays, he disappeared for hours saying he was going to the DIY shop.

Any woman in the world, other than Maisie, would have suspected an affair. But she just thought he was dressing for the times, working to keep his place in the world. An affair? That didn't happen to people like her. That was part of the world of tabloids and people who couldn't keep a decent grip on their emotions. Good, respectable people like them never did anything like that. It was so unthinkable, it was absurd.

Maisie, also, had a secret. But hers was a harmless (or so she thought), solitary thing— sherry. For years she'd had a glass or two of tonic wine after her lunch. But some time ago she'd switched to sherry, which she thought more upmarket.

Now that her children had left home, she was alone from before eight in the morning till after six in the evening. She'd started to have a small glass of sherry after her lunch, then another before her afternoon bath, then had progressed to having one while in the bath, plus one afterwards. Then, sometimes, in the evening, if Alex had a glass of whisky, she'd have another.

It was nothing. It was a pick-me-up. It made her relax and enjoy her own company. Alex quietly noticed the dwindling bottles, but said nothing. He figured that what made her happy made him happy. Besides, it staved off those fearsome outbursts.

Over the years there had been many, so now he could tell when one was brewing. Maisie would become obsessed. He remembered the lead-up to the emptying of Nora's room, the throwing-out of all her things into the garden. Maisie would talk of nothing other than that mess. 'I see it every time I walk past the door. She's old enough now to tidy her own room.' And, 'How long does it take to put a few things away?' And, 'That's what she thinks of me. She thinks I'm some servant who cleans up after her.' Then, boom, she exploded, and Nora's possessions ended up in the garden. It happened quite a lot when Nora was growing up. Alex couldn't blame Nora if she didn't like her mother. After all, Maisie had never thrown out Cathryn's things, and her room had been as littered as Nora's.

Now, he could tell, Maisie was about to explode again. All conversational paths led to Nora, and Nora's silence. He could start talking about the garden; he'd noticed some weeds in his borders. 'If Nora was here, she could do it,' said Maisie. 'Of course you'd have to point out the weeds to her, she doesn't know a nettle from a pansy. That's if you could talk to her. There never was any talking to her when she was here. And now she's miles away in Edinburgh, it's plain she does not want to talk to us. She's forgotten all about her family, too busy having a good time.'

At first, when she'd left home, Nora had phoned often. But now, living with Brendan and Jen, her life was full. She had friends, conversations, visits to the cinema—a life. She meant to keep in touch, but kept procrastinating. She'd phone her mother tomorrow. Then tomorrow came, and she'd decide to do it the next day. Then the next. In truth, she didn't want Maisie's voice, Maisie's nagging to wreck her new and charmed existence.

Alex knew that what really annoyed Maisie was how obvious it was to the neighbours and her sister May that Nora was not in touch. They could see Cathryn on her odd visits, but so far there had been no sighting of Nora. People asked after her. 'Oh, she's fine,' Maisie would say. 'Having a grand time of it in Edinburgh. Doing well.' Sometimes she'd say that Nora had phoned. Maisie told him she thought people could tell she was lying. She felt Nora had brought disgrace on them. 'People will think we're not a happy family,' she'd said.

Alex had been right. Maisie's outburst came a week after he'd sensed it was brewing. It was March. Nora had come home for Christmas, and gone back to Edinburgh the day after Boxing Day. 'Can't you stay longer?' Maisie had said. 'It's like you can't wait to get away from us, your own family.' She'd sensed Nora's eagerness to get back to her friends.

'Mum, I told you. I've got to be back at work. I only get two days. I had to ask for this extra one.'

'If you asked for a day, why didn't you ask for two or three days? A week? You need to spend time here with us. You've become a stranger.'

Nora said that was silly. Of course she wasn't a stranger. She just had to get back to work.

They were standing in the kitchen, seven in the morning. Maisie was making Nora toast and a cup

142

of tea before she left for the station, and the train north. The house had that flat atmosphere that sometimes creeps up in the week between Christmas and New Year. The tree in the living room was starting to wilt and cast a thick spreading of needles on to the carpet; the cards on the mantelpiece kept falling over. The glitter had faded from it all. Maisie was looking forward to pulling down the decorations, declaring Christmas to be over.

She bustled, trying to hide her hurt, pulling slices of bread from the wrapped loaf and laying them out on the kitchen unit. 'I'm making you something for the journey. You don't want to be buying that food they serve on the train. Turkey sandwiches.'

She caught the dismayed look on her daughter's face. 'Well, that's Christmas. All glisten and shine and left-over bird.' She wished she had something else to offer. But the shops had been shut yesterday and there was no time to get to them now.

Not that Maisie didn't like Christmas. She did. In fact, even though she was approaching sixty, she still got excited in the days leading up to it. She eagerly decorated the house, sticking sprigs of holly on the top of all the picture frames, and when there was no room on the mantelpiece for any more cards, she stuck the extra ones on to a length of red ribbon and strung them up on the wall. She bought in far too much food, and fussed when nobody was actually eating. She'd told all the neighbours with pride that both her daughters were coming home, and wouldn't it be lovely to have them about the house again?

They had come, Cathryn and Nora, trailing their secret lives behind them. Cathryn her lover, Nora her new friends that she did not want to share with her family for fear they'd spoil everything with stories of when she was little and criticism of what she had become: a Nadine, Queen of the Trails, with a tiny salary and living in an attic room in an unkempt, noisy house. No, Maisie was not welcome in that other life.

It was, for Maisie, a bit of a let-down. Two grown-up people in her house, neither knowing quite what to do. At first it had been fine, the arrival, the welcome, kisses, hugs; both had got a gentle ticking-off for being too thin. Christmas had gone well enough, presents exchanged. But after that both Nora and Cathryn had been at something of a loose end, since Maisie wanted no help to prepare the meal. So they'd watched television. And had continued watching television after they'd all eaten, a full and hugely calorific meal, at the odd time of half past two. On Boxing Day they'd done the same. Now, Nora was anxious to get back to her real life, the one she was in love with, in Edinburgh.

'When are you going?' Maisie asked.

'As soon as I've finished this.' Nora bit into a slice of toast.' I don't want to miss the train.'

'You can't wait, can you?' said Maisie. 'You want to get back to those people you live with.'

'I'm a lodger, Mum. I pay rent.'

'Makes no difference. You want to be back there with them. I know the sort, all talk and sneering and thinking they're being funny at others' expense.'

'No, they're not like that,' said Nora. 'They are

144

nice people.'

'They're the sort of people who don't have mothers,' said Maisie.

Nora gaped at her. 'What do you mean by that? Everyone's got a mother, even if, sometimes, they don't know who they are. It's the only way to get into the world.'

'The way you behave, never getting in touch, you wouldn't think that. What I mean is, these friends of yours, they'll never talk about their families. I just bet you never mention me.'

'As a matter of fact, I do,' said Nora.

Maisie wanted to ask what Nora said about her, but didn't. 'Cathryn's staying till New Year's Eve,' she said.

'Cathryn gets more holiday than I do,' Nora told her.

Maisie said, 'Look at you. Jeans and an old black jacket and boots. Why can't you wear a nice suit like Cathryn? You always were scruffy.'

Nora sighed. 'Because I'm not Cathryn. I'm me. This is how I dress. I'm not a lawyer. I work for a small magazine with a falling circulation and I don't earn much money. But I'm happy. I thought you'd be pleased about that.'

'Happy,' said Maisie. 'What do you know about happy? You're only happy because you're miles and miles away from us. Your own family. And why couldn't you get a job in London?'

'With my qualifications I'm lucky to have got any job. I'm starting at the bottom, like most people. But who knows what boundless future awaits me? Who knows where my journey will take me as I travel life's glory road?' Nora said as she moved out of the kitchen, and down the hall to where her coat and bag lay waiting for her.

Maisie followed. 'Oh, I see you're all ready to snatch up your bag and go. But while you're travelling life's glory road, do you think you could pick up a phone from time to time and let us know how you are?'

Nora said, 'OK. I didn't realise you cared.'

'Of course I care. I'm your mother. What a dreadful thing to say. Who do you think you are?'

Nora had looked at her and said, 'I have no idea who I am.' She'd picked up her coat and bag, and walked out of the door. Then she opened it again, stuck her head round. 'But when I find out, I'll phone and let you know.'

Maisie stood in the hall, staring. She smiled, though she didn't know if Nora had been joking or not. Still, that old black, filthy guilt crept through her. She'd overdone it. That had been a nag too far.

She was jealous. She had wanted to leave home the way Nora had done. She'd wanted to walk out of that long-ago flat in MacDonald Road in Edinburgh, say goodbye to her folks, and go. And look at how Nora dressed, jeans and that old coat from some charity shop; the girl looked relaxed and comfortable. Swinging her bag on her shoulder and stepping out, taking the train back to where she was happy.

Maisie turned and saw Cathryn standing at the foot of the stairs, listening. She'd heard her berate Nora. Maisie's shame deepened. But unable to admit it, all she said to Cathryn was, 'The state of Nora. Is that any way to go back to Edinburgh? In my day, you dressed up to go on a train.'

She bustled down the hall muttering about how

she never got to be young and carefree and disappeared into the kitchen, re-emerging seconds later waving a packet wrapped in a Safeway's bag. 'And she didn't take my sandwiches. That's what Nora thinks of us.'

Nora walked along the street. She still skipped over lines and cracks in the pavement, though only here. It was a childhood thing and it pleased her. It was a frosty, bitterly cold morning, but bright enough to gladden her heart. The way she felt about home these days was that it was good to go there, but even better to go away again.

She had been quite excited about seeing her family after her time in Edinburgh. But once they'd all said hello, and talked about her journey, there didn't seem to be much to say. The place seemed so much smaller than she'd remembered, and the decor more overpowering. Maisie had coyly given her a small glass of sherry before supper on the day she arrived, and had made it seem like an initiation into adulthood. But really, back in that house she'd become the younger daughter again. The scruffy one, the oddball who didn't have a proper job. The tomboy who knew nothing about the secret art of being a woman and had no mastery of womanly things—matching handbags and shoes, the correct way to apply foundation cream, the importance of a good lip brush, how to fold a napkin and arrange flowers. Whilst she knew about them, she could not converse with Maisie about them with the same enthusiasm as Cathryn.

In the end, she and Maisie had argued. And now Nora had doubts about her parting remark. She had meant it to be a joke, a small easing of the

147

tension. But thinking about it, she realised it might have sounded rude and a bit cynical. She sighed, turned the corner heading for the bus stop. It was wonderful to be heading back to where she thought she belonged.

Now Maisie, in her kitchen, looked out over the March morning. It was a little chilly, but the promise of warmer times was there. 'It's starting to green up,' she said. She remembered standing here last March, watering the row of African violets on the windowsill, looking out and thinking the same thing. It crossed her mind that she'd been wearing the same clothes, too. Time seemed to melt away behind her, days, weeks, months. She was in this house doing the same things day in, day out. And nothing changed, nothing happened.

All she was doing these days was waiting for Nora to get in touch. It had been months now. 'Not a word from her since Christmas,' said Maisie to her plants. She thought about their parting at the door all that time ago and blamed herself. They hadn't even said goodbye properly. She hadn't said, 'Take care.' Instead she'd asked Nora who she thought she was. She re-enacted the scene in her head as it should have been. Her telling Nora to button her coat, fussing round her, making sure she had her sandwiches, telling her to look after herself. Things a proper mother does, she thought.

Every time the phone rang, she brightened, and ran to answer it. In the evenings, when Maisie was most hopeful of a call from Nora, it was usually Cathryn. 'Oh,' Maisie would say, 'it's you.' There was no hiding her disappointment; it wasn't the good daughter she was hoping to hear from.

Cathryn was always hurt by this, but would put on a show of being bright and cheerful. 'Yep. It's me. Just wondered how you were getting on.'

Maisie put her watering can away in the cupboard under the sink, wiped up the drips on the draining board. *That girl's a little madam, not getting in touch.* She went through into the living room and vigorously plumped the cushions on the sofa. *You do your best for them, you give them everything you can. Then nothing. They're off into the world and they forget about you.* She took a duster from her apron pocket and skimmed it over the television screen, then over the surface of the coffee table it stood on. *Dust. I don't know, where does it come from. That girl's living the high life up there, never thinks about her mother worrying about her, wondering how she's getting on.*

She went through to the bathroom to clean the sink and bath, though it wasn't bathroom day. That was tomorrow. *It's just me, me, me with that one. Always has been. I could be ill. I could be dead. I could be lying in hospital breathing my last, tubes hanging out of me, and would she care? Not that one.* She scrubbed round the bath where a scummy ring might have been, only she wouldn't allow such a thing to happen. *Doesn't care. Never has cared. Lives in her own world, mixes with these people she doesn't want me to meet. They probably don't even know she has a mother. Well, my girl, we'll see about that.*

She stamped upstairs, kicked off her old housework shoes, removed her tweed skirt and pink cotton shirt, her housework clothes, and put on her red wool dress and black high heels. She sat in front of her dressing table mirror and started on her make-up, painted her lips the glowing scarlet she was fond of.

Downstairs, she scribbled a swift note for Alex. *Gone to see Nora. That little madam thinks she can get away with not keeping in touch, but she's in for a shock. Love Maisie. PS There's ham in the fridge.*

A Visitor

It was only when she walked up the path to Brendan and Jen's front door that Maisie doubted herself. She hadn't expected such a big house in such a pleasant and quietly moneyed street. There was a subtle opulence here, discreet wealth. Maisie breathed it in; she could almost smell it. She imagined Nora must have worked her way into the charmed company of rich people. Still, it was terraced. The people who lived here couldn't walk round their houses like she could, rich though they may be.

Of course, she was wrong. Brendan and Jen had only managed to scrape together the deposit for their mortgage after his parents had died within three months of each other, and left him their life savings—an amount so meagre it had stopped Brendan in his tracks and made him wonder what was the point of working hard all your days when this was what you ended up with—and their flat, which hadn't been worth much. Added to that, the house had been in a diabolical state of repair when they bought it, and still was.

They'd managed, by increasing their mortgage, to have the roof replaced. But then that had been an absolute necessity; there had been holes, daylight beamed into the upper floor and attic. The woodworm had been fixed. But that was all. After an initial enthusiastic burst of decorating—the kitchen, the living room, the hall and their bedroom—Brendan and Jen had slipped into denial about their home.

They no longer noticed the purplish flock wallpaper on the upper landing, or the searing sixties orange colour some previous owner had painted the bathroom. They couldn't bring themselves to discuss the urgent need for new wiring, or the plumbing, which was temperamental and made alarming noises every time somebody flushed the lavatory or ran a bath.

Maisie rang the doorbell, and felt foolish. She shouldn't have come here. She was an interfering mother, that was what they'd think. It was getting dark; a blackbird sang its evening song. She was aware of how quiet the street was. A man walked up the path a few doors down and glanced at her as he dug into his coat pocket for his keys. His presence, the glance, made her feel alone, a stranger here and guilty about the business she was on. She was excited at the thought of seeing Nora, and at the same time dreaded the look on Nora's face when she saw her. She began to hope that there was nobody in, so she could slip away. Nora would never know she'd come, she could go home without anyone but Alex knowing. And she knew she could rely on him not to say a word, he was such a good sort.

As she turned to step away and beetle back down the path, Jen opened the door. She was still in her uniform, having got in from work not long before Maisie rang the doorbell.

'Yes,' she said, considering this overly made-up middle-aged woman in front of her.

'You'll be Jen,' said Maisie. 'Brendan's wife.'

Jen said that was indeed her.

'Thought so,' said Maisie. 'Nora said you were a nurse. I'm Maisie Marshall, Nora's mother. I've come to see her.'

Jen smiled, said hello, and let her in. 'Nora's not here at the moment. She and Brendan said they'd go to the supermarket after work. They may be a while.'

Maisie said that if Jen didn't mind, she'd wait. She was shown into the front room and offered a seat.

'Let me take your coat,' Jen said. 'Would you like a cup of tea?'

Maisie said that would be lovely, and the tea on the train hadn't been worth the drinking, it was so awful. Jen disappeared with the coat, hung it on the stand in the hall and went to put the kettle on.

Maisie could hear the chink of crockery in the distance. She took this moment of being alone in the room to steal a blatant look round. All those records, she thought. What was the point of them? You could never listen to them all. And the sofa and chairs were covered with throws; obviously they were old and bashed. They should just get new, she thought. A throw looks rumpled after you've sat on it. The floors were stripped and polished. Maisie wondered if this was a fashion thing, or maybe these people couldn't afford a carpet. I like a carpet, she thought. It's more homey. She thought a carpet softened the sounds of everyday life and was gentle underfoot.

Jen brought two steaming mugs of tea. No biscuits, Maisie noted. A biscuit was a nice thing to offer a visitor. Still, the tea was welcome. But this wasn't what she'd planned, what she'd imagined every minute of her seven-hour train journey here. In the scenario she'd dreamed up, Nora answered the door and gasped, 'Mum.' And Maisie had said, 'Yes, me. Your mother. You think you can ignore me, my girl. But you can't. I can come and check up on you any time I like.'

Jen sighed a little and settled in the chair opposite Maisie's. She knew she was about to get a revised version of Nora's life. The word according to Maisie. She glanced at her watch. Quarter to six.

'Nora and Brendan always take ages at the supermarket,' she said. 'They discuss things. Muse and speculate. I just go in, get what I want and come away again. I like to get it over with quickly.'

Maisie agreed. 'Nora was always like that. You couldn't boil her an egg but she'd wonder about the hen it came from, and if it had a happy life pecking around a farmyard.'

Jen sneaked another look at her watch. Ten to six. She listened for the sound of Brendan's car outside. Nothing.

Brendan and Nora would be wandering the aisles, picking things up, reading labels, and putting them down again. They'd be gazing into other shoppers' baskets. They'd discuss the merits of chocolate chip cookies over ginger snaps. They'd debate the lifestyle of free-range chickens.

'That sounds like Nora,' Jen said. 'I've heard her speculate on the life of oven-ready chickens.'

It had been the one time Jen had gone food shopping with Brendan and Nora. Never again,

153

she'd told herself.

'Bred in spacious barns with access to open pastures, fed organic corn,' Nora had said, turning it over in her hands.

'But was it happy?' asked Brendan. 'Was it loved? Did it frolic and play and listen to the radio in the evenings as its mummy prepared supper? Did it have a comfy bed to sleep on and a cup of cocoa and a story before it went to bed? These labels do not tell us enough.'

'I think so,' said Nora. 'From the feel of it. The weight. It feels like it had a good, fulfilling life before it ended up here.'

Brendan took it. 'Yes. I think it was called Frederick.'

'Oh no,' said Nora. 'Too much information. I don't want to know that. Vegetarians say they won't eat anything with a face. But I won't eat anything that had a name.'

Brendan had replaced Frederick and picked out another chicken. 'We'll have no-name here for supper.'

Jen sipped her tea and said to Maisie, 'Nora's like that. She stares and ponders. I think sometimes life bemuses her.'

'Do you?' said Maisie. 'You know, you're right. She never just got on with something. She had to stare, like you say. I always thought it made her seem a bit simple.'

Jen told Maisie about the time she'd gone to the supermarket with Brendan and Nora. How they'd wandered about, gazing and pondering. 'Nora wondered what it said about her, demographically and emotionally, that she picked up Weetabix rather than Rice Krispies. I just pick up the

154

Weetabix and go. Not Nora.'

Maisie nodded. 'That's right. I used to get Nora to do the shopping on Saturdays, and she never came back with what I told her to get. She'd come back with gypsy creams rather than chocolate digestives, which I'm partial to, saying she wanted to look like she came from a flamboyant family.'

Jen nodded. Actually this was quite good. Getting her irritation at Nora and Brendan's absurd psychoanalytical shopping trips off her chest. 'I've seen Nora and Brendan take half an hour to choose a pot of jam. They'll pick up the strawberry and go into a long nostalgic dialogue about their childhoods, summer days, thick slices of bread spread to the edges with butter, dripping jam. Then they're off discussing the programmes they watched on television, the games they played, books they read.'

'Really?' said Maisie. 'I don't know about that. Bread and jam? As if I fed her that. She always got a good hot meal from me.'

Jen sighed. Everything Nora and Brendan saw, anywhere they went, caused them to muse and speculate. Mona had once asked her if she worried about them. 'Oh yes,' she'd said. 'Who wouldn't?' Meaning who wouldn't worry a little about two dreamy people wandering about, talking nonsense.

'But you don't seem to object to them going places together,' said Mona.

'Of course not,' said Jen. Then, realising what Mona was actually talking about, 'I'm not bothered about them having an affair. That wouldn't happen. Brendan's too honest for that, he couldn't cope with the lies. Besides, the two of them, time they talked about it, analysed it, worked out their

155

emotions, all that stuff, the passion would be gone. Nah, they're just a couple of daydreamers. It's good he's got Nora to banter with. I'm no good at any of that.'

She smiled at Maisie. 'I just like to get on with things.'

'I never understood her,' Maisie said. 'Your own child, you'd think you would, but I never did. Once, I saw her standing across the street staring at the house. Just staring. It was five o'clock, dark, all the lights were on, and it was freezing cold. Why didn't she come in?'

Jen shrugged. 'She'd have been thinking about something.'

'That's what does it, thinking. Nora thinks too much. Thinking's dangerous.' How true that was. If she hadn't thought too much about Nora and Nora's failure to get in touch, she wouldn't have come all this way to see her. She wouldn't be sitting in this room, right now, feeling slightly embarrassed. Shouldn't think, she told herself.

It was almost seven o'clock when Maisie heard Brendan's car pull into the drive. She felt a ripple of nerves run through her. What would Nora say when she saw her? 'I shouldn't have come,' she said to Jen. 'I just wanted to know how she was, where she was living. She won't want me here.'

'She'll be delighted to see you,' said Jen.

'No she won't,' said Maisie. 'She'll be all funny and withdrawn. I know her. I was just worried. I'm past fifty, you know, and I came all this way. It's the first time in my life that I've been on a train on my own.' She looked at Jen, her eyes glistening with tears.

It was the touch that surprised her. Jen came

over to her, put her hand on her arm, said, 'It'll be fine. Really.'

Maisie realised that it had been a long time since anyone had touched her. Oh, there were small hugs at Christmas from Nora and Cathryn. But it had been a while since she and Alex had actually laid hands on one another. She looked down at Jen's long fingers and said, 'Thank you. But don't be too kind. It always makes me cry, kindness.'

Jen said she knew the feeling. She'd seen it often at work. Something awful happened, a baby died, and the mother would be stunned. Then they'd offer a bit of kindness, a smile, a word of sympathy, a touch, and tears would flow. 'Go on, cry,' Jen would say. 'Just let it out.'

She tightened her grip on Maisie. 'Don't worry,' she said. 'I'll go get Nora.'

Maisie smelled the rush of chill spring air as the front door opened. She heard Nora shout, 'Hello. We're late. But we've brought treats and goodies.'

'Ginger snaps from the Orient,' called Brendan. 'Washing powder guaranteed to whiten your whites.'

Maisie heard them rustle down the hall, the swish of carrier bags. The barge of people laden with shopping. Then Jen said, 'Your mother's here, Nora.' There was a hush, maybe Nora said, 'What?' Maisie strained, but couldn't quite hear. Somebody shut the kitchen door, and Maisie heard nothing now. This was awful, she shouldn't have come, she didn't belong. This was a strange new house, with young, sophisticated people in it. Though that Jen was very nice. But still, Maisie wished she was back at home. The fire shifted in the grate; she stared at it. She liked a room with an open fireplace; real flames were cheery. Her stomach rumbled, and it dawned on her how hungry she was.

'Mum.' Nora came into the room. 'What are you doing here?'

'I came to see you,' said Maisie. She turned in her seat, didn't get up.

Nora came and kissed her. Well, it was more of a brushing of cheeks. 'It's great to see you.' Then, a moment of doubt, 'There's nothing wrong, is there?'

'No,' said Maisie. 'Nothing wrong. It's been ages since we heard from you. So I thought, well, if you won't come to us, I'll come to you.'

Nora smiled and said that was great. This was not what Maisie wanted. In her imaginings of this meeting, she had been indignant, and she had all the best lines. Nora looked tearful and apologetic, and nobody said, 'Great.'

'You've got to come and meet Brendan,' said Nora. She led Maisie out of the room, and into the kitchen.

Brendan surprised her. She'd expected a thin, poetic and pale man, wearing something velvety, not this tall, plumpish chap with a huge blue-and-white-striped apron draped over jeans and a bright red T-shirt who smiled at her, said, 'Hello, Nora's mum.'

She smiled back, and let him take her small, cold hand into his and shake it, heartily. She was charmed, but still, wasn't it odd? Him a man and doing the shopping and the cooking, and wearing a big apron and a T-shirt, which was the sort of garment she thought only teenagers should wear.

158

In her opinion a grown man should wear a proper shirt and tie. It was smart.

The kitchen units were spread with shopping that Jen was putting away. Brendan was standing at the cooker, emptying the pulp of several cloves of garlic into the heating olive oil at the bottom of a large pot.

'You'll be staying for some pasta,' he said.

Maisie said that would be lovely. She didn't say she didn't eat pasta, and she thought garlic suspicious.

She enjoyed her spaghetti, though it wasn't her usual fare, and she had trouble getting it from the plate into her mouth without spilling sauce on her dress. 'I must make this for Alex,' she said. 'It'd be a change for him.' All through the meal she kept glancing at her watch. 'I don't want to miss my train.'

'You're going home tonight?' said Nora. 'You come all this way then turn around and go home again?'

'I just wanted to see you,' said Maisie. 'Where you are. Now I can picture you when I talk on the phone, and when I think about you.' She looked at her watch again.

'When is your train?' asked Jen.

'Eleven-ish,' said Maisie.

Nora pointed out that it was only a few minutes after eight. 'You've got hours yet.'

'I get anxious,' said Maisie. 'That's the thing about trains, they are romantic, but only at a distance when you hear them going by. When you have to get on one you worry about missing it.'

Brendan agreed with that. 'True, true. We'll drive you to the station,' he said.

159

Maisie thanked him, and asked if she could use the phone. 'I should let Alex know I'm all right, and tell him when I'm getting back in to London.'

She took her handbag with her when she went to the phone. She'd pay for the call, take a small pile of silver coins and put it on the hall stand. It didn't do to just turn up on people's doorsteps and eat their food, then make expensive calls to London without paying. But in the end there was no need, Alex didn't pick up. The phone rang and rang, and it seemed as if there was nobody there.

'He's not answering,' she told Nora.

'He'll be asleep in front of the television,' Nora said. 'Or maybe he's gone out for a takeaway, a pizza or something.'

'We never do anything like that,' said Maisie, quite shocked.

'So. You're not there. Maybe he can't be bothered cooking for himself.'

'I left him ham in the fridge,' Maisie told her. 'As if I would go off and leave the poor man with nothing to eat.'

At ten they drove Maisie to the station, which was only fifteen minutes away, but she was beginning to get flustered and the tension in the house was too much to bear. Better to be calm, and probably cold, standing on the platform waiting for the train, than warm and anxious at home.

They all stood on Platform 19 for three quarters of an hour, stamping their feet and staring now and then up the track in the direction the train would come from. Maisie was excited. 'I love stations. All the noise and the people coming and going. It's quite thrilling being in a station at night.'

'You'll be all right on the train?' said Nora, suddenly worried. She'd noticed how small her mother was. She didn't remember her being that little; she certainly hadn't seemed so back in the house in London when Nora was growing up.

'I was fine coming. I'll be fine going back. I have a book to read. I can get myself a cup of tea. I've never been on a train at night, I'm looking forward to it. Now I've done this, I'm going to do a lot more things.'

This wasn't what she'd planned, of course. The pleasant company, the meal, the laughter round the table, Brendan cooking had all been a surprise. But, really, when she thought about it, it was better than having a row, and she couldn't scold Nora in front of her friends. Nice house, she thought, bit funny inside, no carpets, and posters on the wall in the kitchen. She'd never put pictures in the kitchen, the steam would go for them. But nice people, really, really nice people. Especially Jen. Maisie felt happy and adventurous. She was thinking she should make more trips. She and Alex could go to Italy. He'd wanted to last summer, but she'd said it was too far to go, and the food would be strange. Now she'd eaten pasta, it wasn't strange at all. She could hardly wait to get home and tell Alex all about it.

When the train pulled in at last, Maisie climbed in and took a seat by the window so she could wave goodbye to Nora, Brendan and Jen.

'Have a good trip, come back soon,' they yelled.

'I will. And I'll bring Alex,' she called back.

Then the train moved away. The three of them stood watching it go.

161

'I hope she'll be all right,' said Nora. 'I should have gone with her. I don't like her being on her own all that way.'

'She'll be fine,' said Jen. 'She got here on her own. She'll get back in one piece.'

'But she's so small,' said Nora. 'Did you notice how small she is? She never used to be that small.'

Brendan said, 'Maybe you just got bigger, Nora. And didn't notice it happening.'

A Late-Night Walk Home

It had rained all day. Six o'clock in the evening, and there was no sign of it letting up. It was Friday. On their way to the pub, wipers slowly squeaking, Brendan rubbed the steamed inside of the windscreen with the back of his hand, leaned over the steering wheel, looked up at the sky, and said that it was amazing there was so much water up there.

Nora said, 'Yeah, weather. You never get used to it. Hope it isn't like this in London. My mother would have got soaked.'

'She'll be fine. Thing about London is you can go for miles and miles underground and not know what it's like in the world.'

Nora said that was true. But you had to surface sometime. 'Mum hates the tube. She hardly ever uses it. In fact, I can't remember her going out all that much after she stopped going to the operatic society. Dad takes her to the supermarket once a week. That's it, now I think about it. Last night was the first time I've seen her away from home, except

162

for family holidays. Definitely the first time I've seen her out of the house alone.'

Brendan said, 'Really? Well, maybe it'll all change now.'

Nora said, 'Yeah.'

They stopped at some traffic lights. Nora said, 'So, Bax.'

Brendan said, 'I know. Weird.'

'Weird,' Nora agreed.

Just as they were leaving work, about ten minutes ago, Brendan, on account of the rain, had offered to go and bring the car round to the front door so Nora wouldn't get wet. 'That, and I hate sharing an umbrella. You hold it over the other person, so they won't get soaked, and you get soaked yourself. Also you have to walk at the pace the other person is going. I hate that.'

Nora shrugged and said that now she thought about it, she hated sharing umbrellas too. 'It doesn't work.'

Brendan left her standing just inside the door, and went outside, opening his umbrella. 'I'll toot.'

The hall was thronged with evening people bustling to get away. Fridays were like that. There was the usual amount of people leaving the building, but somehow the urgency, the need to get away made it seem like there were more of them. All round her there were complaints about the rain, and wrestlings with waterproof coats and umbrellas. Every time the door opened damp chill air flooded in.

Nora was mesmerised by it all. The movement, the rain caught swirling in the lights outside, voices shouting, 'See ya,' and, 'Have a good weekend.' She didn't notice the face that smiled at her, then pushed through the crowd to stand in front of her. It was Bax, her editor, who, she realised, she hadn't seen for quite a long time.

'Hi,' he said. 'Have you missed me?'

'Of course,' she said. Though she was only being polite. She hadn't missed him at all; in fact she saw so little of him she hadn't even noticed his absence until now. 'Where have you been?' Thinking perhaps he'd been ill or on holiday.

'I've been downstairs,' he said. 'I got moved down to books a couple of months ago. Didn't you know? Didn't anybody mention it?'

She shook her head. 'No.'

Bax nodded and said, 'Ah.' He said it knowingly, as if the fact of Nora not being told he had been moved to another job had a deep significance that was beyond her.

'I mean,' said Nora, 'I don't want to be rude or anything, but you're so often not there, how would we know you were gone?'

Bax said that was a good point. 'In fact a very good point.'

Then there was the toot, Brendan's car outside. Nora said goodbye to Bax, and ran out the door. In the car she told Brendan about her meeting with Bax.

'He's gone,' she said. 'And we didn't know.'

Brendan said, 'Ah,' in the same way Bax had said it a few moments ago.

'What does that mean—ah?' she asked.

'Nothing,' said Brendan, and sighed.

They were caught in a stream of traffic. Nora looked across at him, saw him clench his jaw, the way he did when he was worried. He guessed he wasn't going to be made editor, which meant he

164

would probably *never* make editor. No pay rise, no bonuses. She realised that all his talk about not caring about promotion was bluff; he wanted the kudos and the extra money as much as anybody else. There was more: he was going to suffer the shame of seeing someone promoted over him.

For a second she toyed with the notion of making a joke about him getting a jacket. That would do it, if he smartened up a bit. But then she thought better of it. He was too depressed to banter.

She looked the other way, sat watching buildings go past. Brendan sighed again. Nora grasped the full depth of his disappointment. It wasn't just the lack of promotion, the not getting told about Bax's shift downstairs. He'd have to tell Jen. Confess to her that he worked for a company who didn't bother to tell him his boss had moved on. That was what they thought of him. He would have to tell her, because it would come out one way or another; someone would let it slip on a roast beef Sunday or when they dropped by to hang out, as they often did.

Jen would sympathise, she'd tell him he was too good to work where he did. He wasn't appreciated. But in some small part of her that she rarely let anyone see, there would be a bubble of triumph. This would make it easier for her to seek her own promotion in some town or city far away from here. 'Why stay?' she'd say. 'There's nothing for you here. Look how they treat you.'

Brendan would have no argument for this. They'd move away. Nora saw it all, and sighed. That was when Brendan changed the subject; he leaned over, wiped the windscreen with the back of

165

his hand and said that it was amazing there was so much water up there.

The pub was busier than usual, people sheltering from the rain. Smoke hung in the air, a thin blue film, and there was noisy chatter. The mood round the table was gloomy. Brendan was too lost in his disappointment to say much, and left early. Nora moved to go with him, but Mona kicked her under the table and shook her head. 'He needs to be alone with Jen,' she said when he'd left. Then Nathan suggested they all go for an Italian meal. He knew a place. He said they could walk.

It was about ten minutes from the pub. Mona complained most of the way, saying her shoes were getting ruined, and if she'd known it was this far, she'd have brought her car. Nathan told her to stop whining; walking in the city at night, in the rain, was one of life's real pleasures. 'You can feel the pulse of it, the swish of passing traffic, the smell of damp, the lights reflected in the gleam of wet on the road, people rushing to get into the warmth and dry. But if you just walk slowly along empty streets, you can take stock of things, your life, your worries, and they don't seem so bad. You feel alive.'

Mona minced on, little steps, high heels clicking, and said, 'Crap. You feel wet. I can think of things that make me feel alive, and they all take place indoors, usually lying down.'

It was a conversation that bedazzled Nora. She was impressed by Nathan's enthusiasm for walking in the rain in the city, and more impressed by Mona's description of what made her feel alive. It sounded wonderfully interesting.

Not that Nora hadn't had lovers, she just felt she hadn't had any that were as fascinating as Mona's. Indeed, she felt her sex life, so far, was dull compared to Mona's. Nora's dealings in sex had been quick bursts of passion in bedsits and small cramped flats. There had been gropes and fumbles in taxis and cinemas and at parties. She'd had, over the years, many boyfriends, but only four of them had become lovers. Love, for Nora, then, had been quick thrills. The quick bit she didn't like, but the thrills were good and she wanted more. She wanted a sex life like the one she imagined Mona to have which was complicated and fulfilling. Mona would, Nora was sure, enjoy long, passionate, complicated nights of pleasure with complicated men. They would love and love again, sleep a little, smoke a cigarette, talk in quiet throaty voices about life and love and literature, and make love slowly, relishing every touch, every kiss. They'd sleep some more, then, in the morning, share fresh orange juice and some other breakfasty thing—Nora hadn't quite imagined what—then they would make love. Nora would sigh over this fantasy.

She had spent a great deal of her young life looking for the secret of happiness. Now she was convinced it was good sex and plenty of it. Prior to this, until she was about sixteen, she'd thought it was Christmas.

The place that Nathan knew was tiny, and down an alley leading off from Nicholson Street. It looked fascinating, but Nora agreed with Mona when she said it was not the sort of place she normally went into. From the outside, at least, it had a certain unsettling seediness. Inside it was warm, and anyone could tell, from the aromas that didn't so much waft as ooze from the kitchen, that the food was good. The decor was sparse: a couple of Italian flags draped the far wall; large framed pictures of famous Italians, mostly Sophia Loren and Gina Lollobrigida, with a scattering of tenors, were on the other three.

Mona looked at the pictures grimly and remarked that at least they didn't include Mussolini. Then she ordered a bottle of house red and a bottle of house white, before they'd even been given menus.

Nathan was obviously a regular. The waiter asked if he wanted his usual, wild mushroom risotto. And Nathan said yes.

So Mona said she'd have what Nathan was having, and George did so too. Nora ordered gnocchi, mostly because she didn't know what it was, and wanted to seem adventurous. She glowed when Nathan said, 'Good choice.'

This was what she'd wanted for years. To be part of a crowd sitting round a candlelit table, laughing, drinking wine, in a restaurant when it was raining outside. Especially that, raining outside. She hoped to see someone standing at the window looking in, feeling sad, lonely, cold and envious. Something she had done often on her wanderings about her old neighbourhood in London and later here in Edinburgh before Brendan took her under his wing. Though she hoped the loner on the outside wouldn't be too sad, lonely, cold or envious; that would be a shame.

She told them about her mother's visit yesterday. 'It was the first time she's been out of the house alone for ages. And the first time in her life she's been on a train alone. That's amazing when you think of it.' She asked about the others' families.

Nathan said his mother was eighty and lived in Dorset. She swam eight lengths of the local pool every Tuesday and Thursday and cycled six miles to the local shops and back several times a week. 'She just keeps going and going,' he said. 'Puts me to shame.'

Mona said her mother was dead, and looked down into her glass, remembering, with some embarrassment, the details of the comfort she had taken from George when her sorrow snuck up and overwhelmed her. 'George has an interesting family,' she said, shifting the attention from herself. 'He ran away from them.'

'Hardly,' said George.

'Oh, you did,' said Mona. 'You couldn't wait to leave home. Then they disowned you.'

'Goodness,' said Nora.

'They own a paper mill,' George told her.

'They're fabulously rich,' Mona added.

'And they wanted me to take over the business when my father retired. Me being the eldest son, it was the way they imagined things would go. I'd run the business, get married, have a son who would then run the business, and on and on. Only I didn't want to do it. There was a big row, and I left in the middle of it. I packed my things, and left. My younger sister took over in my place.'

'His mother came to see him once. Chauffeur-driven car and everything. Her in a fur coat, and lots of lipstick. She told him if he didn't come home, he'd be cut out of the will. And now he is, disowned and abandoned and no inheritance.'

George shrugged. 'That's the way of it.'

'Families are fascinating,' said Nora. When everyone looked at her, she added, 'Especially at a distance.'

The rain had stopped by the time they left the restaurant. Mona and George headed home; Nathan said he'd walk with Nora, despite her protests that she'd be fine. She liked walking alone in cities.

'Nonsense,' said Nathan. 'If something happened to you, we'd all seize up with guilt.'

They walked, slightly apart, and spoke about work, books and films they had in common. Nothing special.

'What do you think Brendan will do?' Nora asked.

'Same as we all do,' said Nathan. 'Complain, curse and carry on.'

'You think?' said Nora. 'I think Jen will find a job, some promotion, away from Edinburgh. And he'll go with her.'

Nathan said there was that. 'If Jen went, he'd go with her. There's no doubt of that.'

Nora sighed, shoved her hands deep into her coat. 'Bloody cold.'

Nathan agreed and took off his scarf, wrapped it round her neck. 'There. We'll have to get you mitts to go with it. Tie them with elastic to go up one sleeve and down the other.'

After that, they didn't say much. But Nora thought it one of life's joys to walk along quiet, empty streets, after the rain had stopped and the moon had slid from behind the clouds, with a companion you didn't have to make conversation with. Such a simple pleasure. A Brahms tape that had been on Brendan's tape deck played in her head. From time to time, she and Nathan looked at one another, and smiled.

When they reached the gate of Brendan's house, Nora asked if he'd like to come in for coffee. 'Brendan won't mind.'

Nathan said, 'Think I'll just make my way home. See you Monday.' He was thinking how pleasant this had been, just walking with someone companionable when the rain had stopped. It was time, he told himself, to look for a new relationship. After he and his wife had split up, he'd slipped into a depression that had become a habit. He ate alone, went to the pub round the corner from his flat alone. He always slept alone. It was time to move on.

He leaned over and kissed Nora, nothing passionate, just a light brushing of lips on cheek. But it took her by surprise. He smiled when he saw her put her hand to the slightly damp place on her face where the kiss had landed, and stare at him.

'Sorry,' he said. 'Didn't know I was going to do that, till I did.'

Nora said that it was fine, she enjoyed it. 'I don't get kissed much these days.'

Nathan said neither did he, and would she like to come for a meal sometime? 'Just the two of us, somewhere quiet where we can chat.'

She shrugged and said, 'Why not? Yes, I'd like that.'

He said he'd see her at work and fix up a date. And Nora said, 'Fine,' again. She turned and walked up to the front door, and forgot to give him back his scarf.

Inside, Brendan was waiting for her. 'Where the hell have you been?'

'Out,' said Nora. 'We went for a meal. Mona, George, Nathan and me.'

'Your sister has been on the phone,' said Brendan.

'Cathryn? What did she want?'

'I don't know, she wouldn't say. But she's been phoning all night. She wants you to phone home. It's urgent.'

'Has somebody died?' said Nora.

Brendan said she'd better phone and find out, but he didn't think so. 'It's after midnight, Nora. You might have let us know where you were going, we were worried.'

'That's very fatherly of you,' said Nora. 'But I'm allowed out at night.' She picked up the phone and dialled the number.

'For God's sake,' said Cathryn. 'Where have you been? I've been calling and calling. You have to come home. Dad's left Mum. He's gone off with another woman.'

Nora didn't say anything for a while. She tried to take in what Cathryn had said, but couldn't. 'Don't be silly.'

'He has,' said Cathryn. 'Turns out he's been seeing her for ages.'

'Dad? Our dad? With another woman. I don't believe you. He's not like that.'

Cathryn sighed. 'It's true. You better get down here as soon as possible.'

Nora said she wanted to speak to Maisie.

'You can't,' said Cathryn. 'She's sleeping. Actually, she's passed out drunk.'

Nora laughed. 'You're kidding.'

172

'No, Nora, I'm not kidding.'

Nora said she didn't believe her. 'Our folks don't do things like that. They're ordinary.'

'Well, they just have,' said Cathryn. 'And you have to come home.'

Nora went silent, considering this. 'Why?'

'Because something has happened, and we need you here,' said Cathryn.

'But if it has happened, if he has left her, what can I do about it? Why do you need me?'

Up until this moment, whenever there was a family crisis, Nora had been told to get out of the way. Admittedly, family crises had been nothing much, really—the car wouldn't start, a pot of paint got spilled on the kitchen floor, a crazed wasp was trapped in the living room, buzzing viciously about. On these occasions, Nora had been told to keep back and let the grown-ups handle the situation. This had led her to believe in the very depths of her soul that she was useless in an emergency, a duffer, hopeless. So why would they want her there now?

'Because we're a family and we have an emergency,' said Cathryn, 'and when families have emergencies, they get together. It's what they do.'

Nora said, 'But . . .'

Cathryn said, 'Nora, just get your arse on a train tomorrow morning, and get down here.' Then she put down the phone.

Nora replaced the receiver and went through to the kitchen to talk to Brendan and Jen.

'It seems my dad has left my mum for another woman. And my mum has got drunk out of her brains and has passed out. Do you think that's true?'

173

Jen asked why it shouldn't be true.

'Because my mother and father don't do things like that,' said Nora. 'My father with another woman? I don't think so. They've been together for over thirty years. How could they split up now? I don't mean to sound rude, but my dad's dull. He never says much, he comes and goes to work. He pays the bills. He's so dull, he has turned dull into an art form.'

Even as she spoke, it occurred to Nora that nobody was that dull. Her father must have had thoughts and feelings as he came and went and paid the bills. All sorts of resentments and loneliness must have been bubbling inside him, maybe for years. She realised that she didn't know him at all. 'I have to go home,' she said.

Silk Underpants

Maisie had arrived home sometime just before nine. The train had been late, then she'd got a little confused on the tube, standing in the midst of the morning rush, tracing her route on the underground map. So the journey had taken longer than she'd thought—she'd been hoping Alex wouldn't have left for work before she got in.

But he wasn't there. Fair enough, she thought, he has to work. He can't go taking a day off just because I upped and went to Edinburgh.

Her note was still on the table. Maisie didn't look at it. She made a cup of tea and took it upstairs to the bathroom, drank it as she filled the tub. A long soak was what she needed. After that, she went to the bedroom. She'd thought she was just going to get some fresh clothes from the wardrobe, but the bed looked so tempting. She was tired. The journey on the train had been long. She hadn't slept much, though she'd tried, pulling her coat round her and scrunching into the corner, head on the back of her seat. But there had been some soldiers a little way behind her; they'd drunk, sung and shouted all the way from Edinburgh to London. Seven hours of revelry.

She slipped between the sheets, noting that the bed was made. How considerate of Alex to do that before he left for work, and the kitchen was tidy, too. She was so lucky to have such a wonderful man.

It was one o'clock before she woke. Her first instinct was to leap from bed, dress, and busy herself with all her usual day's doings. But she thought, what doings? Everything is done, the house is clean and tidy, and there is no need to start cooking. Alex won't be home till after six.

She lay awhile, then thought she'd get up, make herself something to eat, and watch afternoon television. There might be a good film on.

In the kitchen, she picked up the note she'd left for Alex the previous morning. At the bottom he'd added, *Dear Maisie, I came home to find you gone. You have taken yourself off to Edinburgh to check up on Nora. Just like that. You didn't think to phone me at work and let me know. Maisie, you think too much, you obsess. You think yourself into a rage, get angrier and angrier, and, well, explode. And you dump it all on me. I want more than all this. I have gone to live with Claire, if she'll have me. I've been seeing her for some time now. Will be in touch to sort*

175

out details. Your ham is still in the fridge. Alex.

Maisie couldn't believe what she'd read. This couldn't be, this sort of thing happened to other people, not to her. Not in this family. It was the sort of thing you read about in the newspapers, or saw on soaps on the television. She put the note down, and took a pack of lamb chops from the freezer. Alex liked a lamb chop when he came home.

She switched on the radio and peeled some potatoes. She'd leave them in a bowl of cold water till it was time to cook them. And she'd do some peas, too. With a spot of butter. When she opened the fridge, looking for some tomatoes for a sandwich, she noticed the ham. He hadn't touched it.

He hadn't eaten here last night. She thought about the bed. Alex hadn't slept here last night. It was true, he had left her. Everything stopped. It was as if the truth hit her from the inside. It seemed to rise from her stomach and shake her whole being, a rush of nerves and panic. She was holding a tomato. Johnny Mathis was singing 'The Twelfth of Never' on the radio, and she was staring at the wall, mouth open.

Cathryn was always to wonder what would have happened if she hadn't answered the phone that afternoon. She'd been on her way out of her office when her direct line rang, and had hovered a moment, holding the door knob, wondering if she should just go, leaving the caller to her answering machine. Thinking it might be something important, or one of the friends she was going to meet tonight, she decided to answer it. For years she would imagine how her life would have been if she'd shut the door and left it to ring.

It was Maisie.

'Mum,' said Cathryn. 'How are you?'

Maisie didn't bother with that. 'He's left me. Just like that, after all these years. All I've done for him. Given him my life. Kept this house spotless. He's gone off with another woman.'

'Who?' asked Cathryn. Stupidly. Well, it couldn't be her father. He didn't do things like that. He wasn't like that. He came and went. He sat at the kitchen table and wrote out cheques for all the bills. He mowed the lawn. He didn't have a secret lover. Men like that didn't.

'Your father, who do you think?'

'Dad?'

'Yes.'

'Dad's been having an affair?'

'Yes.'

'He's gone to live with the woman he's been seeing?'

'Yes.'

'When?'

'Last night. I got back this morning from Edinburgh. Obviously, he wasn't here. I thought he'd gone to work. But—'

Cathryn said, 'Edinburgh?'

'Yes,' said Maisie. 'I was thinking about Nora. Thinking and thinking, how she never gets in touch. So I thought, right, madam, if you don't come to see me, I'll go and see you. She's fine, by the way, sends her love. Anyway, I got back this morning, and right enough the note I left him was still lying on the kitchen table, but I thought nothing of it. Well, you don't. He's left me for some Claire person.'

Cathryn said, 'Oh my God.'

Maisie said, 'Exactly. I don't know what to do. And there's the chops. I don't expect he'll be eating them now. And I've got a whole huge pack of them in the freezer. They were on offer down the supermarket last week. I thought they'd be handy. Alex always liked a chop.'

'Have you told Nora?' Cathryn interrupted.

'No,' said Maisie. 'I phoned you first.'

Cathryn said, 'OK, I'll get on the first train to London. I'll be there as soon as I can. Keep calm.'

'I am calm,' said Maisie. 'Never been calmer. I thought you ought to know about your father. Soon everybody will know, but at least you'll know before they do.'

Cathryn thanked her for that and said she'd be there soon. 'Hang on.'

Maisie put down the phone. Hang on? What else was there to do but hang on? She stood and listened to the house, quiet now since she'd switched off the radio. The fridge hummed, water gurgled in the central heating pipes, a blackbird called in the garden, cars swished past on the road outside, the clock ticked. Behind all that was a deep and terrible silence that matched the hopelessness she felt. She thought it was the sound of the rest of her life.

Cathryn arrived just before seven o'clock. She walked down the hall carrying her case, and came into the living room. The electric fire was burning, two bars; the room was stifling hot. Maisie was sitting in her armchair. When she saw Cathryn, she smiled and said, 'Put the kettle on. Make us a cup of tea. There's a love.'

Cathryn brought two cups on a tray. 'Have you

178

eaten?'

'No,' said Maisie. 'Can't face food.'

'So,' said Cathryn, 'what's going on? Haven't you and Dad been getting on?'

Maisie said of course they had. 'I've been getting along with him just fine. He hasn't been getting on with me, but I didn't know about it.'

'So who is Claire?'

Maisie said she didn't know. 'Don't know where she lives. Don't know her last name, so I can't look her up in the phone book.'

'No doubt Dad will be in touch.'

Maisie said that if he was, she didn't want to speak to him.

'You have to speak to him. You have to sort this out. It's Dad.'

'Your dad, my husband. But not any more. I don't want to talk to him.'

'You don't know about any of this. It might be nothing. He might have been feeling down. It might have been a swift, reckless thing he did. Mid-life crisis. Don't you want to find out?'

Maisie said there was nothing to find out. He'd gone. 'I just want to sit here, that's all.'

Cathryn considered her mother. She was slumped sideways, head rolling slightly against the back of her chair.

'I gave him everything,' Maisie said. 'All of me. There was not a day in his life when he did not sit down to a good hot meal at the end of the day. Beds made, clean sheets, shirts ironed. I must have ironed thousands of shirts for him. Thousands and thousands.'

Cathryn said, 'I know.'

'Of course, I was stupid. Stupid to do all that.

179

Stupid not to look out for myself. And stupid not to notice what was going on. He had all those new clothes. He was coming home late from work. Going out smelling of cologne. He even bought himself a pair of silk underpants. All the signs were there. Any woman in the world would have suspected something, except me. All the signs were there. I'm a fool.'

Lulled, a bit stupefied, by the heat in the room, and tired after her journey, Cathryn again said, 'I know.'

Maisie looked at her sharply.

Cathryn said sorry, that wasn't what she meant. She said it was getting late, and, really, she ought to make them something to eat.

Maisie said that was fine, as long as it wasn't the lamb chops.

Cathryn was putting rashers of bacon under the grill when her father phoned. He wanted to come round to talk, and to pick up some things he'd left behind. He sounded nervous. Cathryn asked him to wait while she asked her mum.

'He's not coming here,' said Maisie. 'Not ever. He's made his bed, he can lie on it. He's not getting back into this house again. Even if that other woman throws him out.'

'He wants to pick up some stuff he left behind,' said Cathryn.

'No point in him coming to do that. It's all gone, every scrap of it in the bin.'

Cathryn returned to the phone and told him what Maisie had said. 'Is it true? Have you really left her?'

Alex said he had. He'd been seeing Claire for some time. He knew he'd done a terrible thing.

He'd fallen for someone else, he'd broken up the family. He wanted some happiness for himself, and there it was. 'Sorry. I don't expect you'll like me very much at the moment.' Then he gave her his address so she could come and see him. 'Sort out the details,' he said. And rang off.

Cathryn went outside. She took the lid off the dustbin and peered into it. Inside were a couple of Alex's suits. Pre-other woman, from the looks of them, she thought. There were ties, some underwear and shaving things; on top of all that, bewilderingly, was a supermarket pack of eight lamb chops, fifty per cent extra. Special price.

Back in the kitchen, she laid the table, finished making bacon and eggs and went through to tell her mother there was some food ready. Maisie was sleeping, head to one side, snoring slightly. There was, Cathryn noticed, an almost empty bottle of sherry and a glass on the floor beside her chair. Maisie was drunk.

Cathryn shook Maisie, who said, 'Don't do that. I want to sleep. Or die. I don't want to be awake.'

Cathryn heaved her mother out of her chair, draped her arm over her shoulder, gripped her waist and helped her out of the room and up the stairs. It wasn't easy. Maisie was moaning and crying and not up to walking. Upstairs, Cathryn undressed her mother, trying to avert her eyes. She wasn't prepared for this intimacy and, without thinking, really, slipped into the childish language Maisie had used, years ago, when the situation had been reversed. When Maisie was putting Cathryn to bed. 'Over the head,' Cathryn said, then, putting Maisie's arms into the sleeves of her nightdress, 'Now one hand in, and two hands in. That's the way. And into bed.'

Maisie slid under her duvet. Head on the pillow, she looked up at her daughter. 'You're a good lass. You've always been good.'

Cathryn sat on the side of the bed, holding Maisie's hand, waiting for her to sleep. It didn't take long, and when she heard the rhythmic breathing, she went back downstairs. She scraped the bacon and eggs into the bin. The food was too cold to eat; besides, she wasn't hungry. She washed up, stood by the sink staring out into the garden and the gardens beyond. Everything was quiet, still, suburban. The very breeze shifting through the fuchsia bush beside the hedge seemed respectable. You'd think to look at it that nothing could happen here.

But things did happen, they happened everywhere. And nothing—no serious clipping of hedges, mowing of lawns, dusting, wiping and vacuuming—could stop them. Dirty dogs, death disease, disgrace snapping at our heels, she thought.

She sighed, wiped her hands dry, and thought, But Time coming. She'd seen it often. It happened when ordinary people who'd assumed they were living enjoyably normal but somewhat dull lives suddenly stepped into a nightmare, usually brought about by a family member who'd been discovered, often by the police, to be naughty, absurd, thieving, drunken and sometimes even despicable. 'But,' the normal, respectable person would say, 'this cannot be.' The But Time was that gap in reality when shock and denial turned into acceptance.

Cathryn had seen mothers standing in police

182

stations having been told that their favourite child had been caught shoplifting or dealing drugs. 'But,' they would say, 'I always gave him a good breakfast. How can this be? I made sure he had clean underwear every day. Are you sure you've got the right person?'

She had been with a woman whose husband had been arrested after picking up a sixteen-year-old prostitute. 'But,' the woman had said, 'he's a chiropodist. This can't be right. You've got the wrong man.'

And a man whose wife had been caught by a store detective with unpaid-for goods worth over two thousand pounds in her bag. 'But,' he'd said, 'my wife is at home looking after our son. Last week she made twenty jars of raspberry jam. No, no, there's been a mix-up.'

Now it was her turn to enter the But Time. But it's my dad. Last time I visited he was polishing his car. At Christmas he was sitting in that chair by the fire watching a Bond film. When I was little, he used to pretend to take off my nose and show me the end of his thumb between two fingers. He carried me on his shoulders. He likes crosswords and comedy programmes. He has hardly ever been sick. He goes to work at eight and comes home just after six. He can't be having an affair.

And that's my mother upstairs sleeping off a huge amount of sherry. She used to sing to me, she cooked three meals a day except on Saturday, which she said was her day off, too. She reads historical romances. She can't be drunk.

She realised she was standing alone in the kitchen, spreading her palms, going through all this, seeking an explanation for her parents' behaviour. She needed to talk to somebody, and phoned Nora. But Nora was out, so Cathryn phoned Clive and told him what had happened. He told her he'd be there in half an hour.

He arrived smelling discreetly of Armani cologne and wearing his best weekend outfit, designer jeans and a crewneck cashmere sweater. He hugged her and said, 'What's all this, then?'

Cathryn told him once more about her father and his affair, and her mother and her sherry. For two hours she paced the living room floor, spreading her palms and saying, 'But.' He sat, sipping instant coffee, listening.

'But,' Cathryn said, 'I saw Dad a few weeks ago. He'd been doing things in the garden. I don't know what. Gardening's a mystery to me. He was wearing his old trousers, you know, the beige ones from Marks and Spencer, he was digging and stuff. Then he mowed the lawn. And all the time he was having an affair. He was thinking about that Claire woman. Can that be true? My dad?'

Clive said that you never knew about people, even people close to you. 'People will be people.'

'And my mother,' said Cathryn. 'Slumped drunk and saying she wants to die. What's going on?'

Clive came to her, put his arms round her. 'It's life, Cathryn. C'mon. You're a lawyer, you've seen this sort of thing before.'

'I have,' she agreed. 'But not in my family.'

Next day Nora arrived. She'd spent her time on the train trying to come to terms with Cathryn's news and decided that if it was true, it would all be over by the time she got there. Her father would have returned home, and everyone would be sitting round the kitchen table drinking tea and trying not to talk about it. They'd act as if it hadn't happened, and carry on with the rest of their lives without ever mentioning it. That was what her family was like.

She dropped her bag in her room, took off her coat and went through to the living room to see what was happening. Maisie smiled at her from her armchair by the fire, but didn't get up to say hello. Her face was puffy, swollen and pale—too many tears. The sleeves of her cardigan bulged with screwed-up tissues. Nora kissed her cheek, and asked how she was.

'Not so good,' said Maisie. 'It's all a bit shocking, isn't it? What do you think of your terrible father?'

Nora said she couldn't quite believe it. 'Has he really left? Are you sure he isn't coming back?'

'Oh yes,' said Maisie. 'He's not coming back. He's done what he's done. He can suffer the consequences.'

Cathryn was in the kitchen with Clive. He had left late last night, but had returned to be by Cathryn's side. They spent most of their time talking in low voices, wondering what to do about the Maisie situation. It was plain to Cathryn that her mother should not be left alone.

Nora joined them and put on the kettle. It was all so unreal, and she didn't know what to do or what to say. When she'd made herself a cup of coffee, she lingered with Cathryn and Clive.

She'd read about dramatic situations of loss and bereavement in the newspapers. *The victim is at home being comforted by loved ones*, they said. Was this what it was like? The victim sat alone in a chair, staring ahead, stunned. And the loved ones gathered in the kitchen making cups of tea and coffee, whispering among themselves. Debating the victim's future. She didn't really know, never having been a loved one before. But she thought, if she was now a loved one, she wasn't very good at it.

'What's happening,' she said to Cathryn. 'Have you heard from Dad? He's coming back, isn't he?'

Cathryn told her that Alex had phoned last night. 'He gave me his address so we can make arrangements to meet. There's a lot to sort out.'

'But,' said Nora, 'he has to come back. He can't have just gone off to another woman. He and Mum have been married for years and years. This is just a little hiccup, a misunderstanding. They'll be back together in a few days.'

Cathryn shrugged; she didn't know. 'Mum says she won't have him back. I don't know if she means it. There's a lot to be worked out. And she's in no state to be left on her own.'

Nora thought, well, I'm not staying here with her. She looked at Cathryn and saw she was thinking the same thing. For a moment they eyed each other defiantly. They both decided the other was going to stick around to look after their mother.

Maisie, in the armchair, contemplated how things would be now Alex was gone. She was thinking she wouldn't have to make regular meals any more. She'd live on tinned soup and the occasional baked potato. That was fine, she'd get by.

But it would be lonely, and she didn't know if she'd ever get used to that. She saw herself in the kitchen, wearing her grey skirt and her pink shirt with the rounded collar, her red slippers with the fur inside on her feet. She was opening a small can of tomato soup, emptying it into a pot, taking a slice of bread from the loaf and putting it on a plate. She'd eat the soup sitting at the kitchen table; the radio would be on, but it wouldn't kill the silence. She was thinking how sad this was, feeling sorry for herself.

Images of how things used to be kept drifting, uninvited, into her head. Alex, when they'd first met, at a dance hall in Edinburgh in 1944. She'd gone with May, and they'd had a gin and tonic at a bar before they went in, something that, at the time, had been almost outrageous. They'd both been hoping to meet someone new. It was something of a failure to go out dancing and come home alone.

He'd been in uniform, on leave from the army, and up from London with a friend. They'd danced, though he'd said he wasn't very good. Dancing was proper dancing then, she thought, the quickstep and the foxtrot. But they'd also jived. She'd loved that. He'd walked her home, to MacDonald Road. He'd kissed her goodnight. But he'd asked permission. 'Do you mind if I kiss you?' 'No,' she'd said. 'I don't mind at all. In fact, I was hoping you would.' Oh, that had been a lovely kiss. No more kisses for me now, she thought.

It had been cold that night. She'd shivered, only a thin party dress under her coat, and silly shoes on her feet. He'd opened his army coat and let her in, folded it round them both, held her close. She thought it the most exciting thing that had ever happened to her. Next day he was going back south to his regiment. But he would write. And he had, almost every day, long letters about his life and how he was going to be posted to Germany. Then there would be things about how he missed her, and how he wished he could see her. Love and kisses at the bottom.

He hadn't gone to Germany because he'd broken his ankle playing football. Maisie had been over the moon about that, but Alex had been upset. It would have been his first time abroad. A year after that, they'd married. At first they'd lived in Edinburgh, in a small flat near the Meadows. Then Alex had got a job in London, and they'd moved here, to this house. Their own home. They'd walked about it opening doors, turning on taps, looking out the window at the garden. They'd been proud. It had been five years before their first daughter, Cathryn, was born. But they'd been good years. They went out a lot, dancing, to the cinema, walking home hand in hand, sometimes eating fish and chips. Simple pleasures, the best pleasures, she thought.

She remembered how she'd cried every month when her period came, and he'd held her, saying it was all right. There was time. Then, at last, when she got pregnant, he'd been so happy, so bursting with pride. He'd bought her a huge bunch of roses. She'd pressed one in her *Book of Household Management*. Now, she reminded herself to get that rose and throw it out. It meant nothing now.

Then there were the children years. Watching them grow. One Christmas, when they'd thought they wouldn't be able to afford much, Alex had got a bonus on Christmas Eve, and had come home laden. Presents, food, and a tree which they'd decorated together after the girls werc in bed, to surprise them in the morning. That had been her favourite night of all, the best night of her life.

All those memories ruined now. She couldn't cherish them; he'd spoiled everything going off with that woman.

The thing that really depressed her was the shame she felt. Everyone would know that he had left her. They'd wonder about her, think that she was a bad wife, quarrelsome, nagging. A shrew, she thought. Face it, she told herself. It's sex. People will think I never let him do it. And it's true. I didn't. The trouble with sex is the minute you start thinking about how silly it looks, the two of you heaving and sweating, you go right off it.

If you don't give a man his way, she thought, he'll look around for someone who will. She'd read this in a magazine, and hadn't paid much attention to it. At the time, she'd considered herself and Alex too old and set in their ways for any such goings-on. She cursed her stupidity. She should have known he was seeing someone the minute he brought those silk underpants into the house. They were lovely, too. So soft to the touch. But you couldn't put them in the washing machine with the normal wash, they'd shrink. Had to be done by hand, in the sink. Things he'd done in those underpants, she thought, and I washed and ironed them. Cheek of it.

'It was the silk underpants,' she said aloud. 'I should have suspected something as soon as I clapped eyes on them.'

In the kitchen, Cathryn turned and raised her eyebrows to Nora and Clive.

Nora said, 'Dad must have got himself some silk underpants to make himself sexy for his fancy

189

woman. God, it's hard thinking about your old man having it off with a strange woman.' Then she said, 'Actually, I don't like to think about him having it off with anyone. Even Mum.'

Maisie overheard. 'That's just like you, Nora Marshall. Open your big mouth and say the first filthy thing that comes into your head. At a time like this, too. You have not one ounce of decency and tact in you.'

Nora blushed deeply and stared at the floor.

'Oh yes,' said Maisie. 'You've got it right. It's all about sex. And your father found someone who did it better than me. He moved beds. Deal with that. You young ones think you invented sex. It's always the same, young ones discover it, and think nobody past thirty does it. But it's been the cause of misery for centuries. You'll find out, soon enough. We'd all be a lot happier without it.'

'We wouldn't be here without it,' said Nora.

Maisie said, 'Ach. That's enough from you.'

Nora looked sheepishly at Cathryn and Clive, who were staring at her in horror. How could she talk about her father's underpants at a time like this?

Nora was having a beam-me-up-Scotty moment. She wanted to be away from here. She was meant to rush to the side of the victim to bring solace and comfort. And she'd made a crude, tactless remark. She was a failed loved one.

'You can go over to our father's lady friend's house and talk to him,' said Cathryn.

'Why me?' said Nora.

'Someone has to go if only to find out if all it's true. You have to set a date when we can meet and talk properly. And you have to see this Claire, take notes. What she's like. What her house is like. Then come back and report.'

Nora could see the sense in that. She took down a note of her father's new address, finished her coffee and left.

Dinner with Alex and Claire

The flat was in Shepherd's Bush. The ground floor of a large Victorian house in a small side street. Nora pressed the entryphone, and realised how nervous she was. She did not want to meet this new and glittering woman who had won her father's heart, who had brought this huge upheaval into her life.

A voice that sounded calm and rather pleasant said, 'Yes?'

Nora said, 'I'm Nora, Alex's daughter. I've come to see my dad.'

The voice said, 'Hello, Nora. Come in.'

The door clunked open; Nora stepped into a large tiled hallway. A staircase on the left led to the upper flats; there was a large potted palm in the corner. A woman was standing at an open doorway on the right. 'Nora,' she said. 'It's good to meet you. I've heard all about you. I'm Claire, by the way.'

She wasn't what Nora had been expecting. She was small, middle-aged, wearing black slacks and a blue silk shirt over a black T-shirt. She looked more comfortable than glamorous. Glamour had been in Nora's mind when she envisioned the other woman. Someone young, tall and blonde in tight leopardskin pants and midriff-revealing low-cut lycra top. There was something familiar about this woman that Nora found disturbing. And couldn't figure out.

Alex was in the living room. He greeted Nora with a hug and a kiss. Which surprised her, since they rarely touched. She remembered him once smacking his wet lips on her cheek when she was a child. She'd said, 'Yuck,' and vigorously rubbed the dampness he'd left behind. Maybe she'd deserved not to be touched, she'd put him off.

He was wearing pale chinos and a soft red jersey over a dark blue shirt. Nora was shaken by how fashionable he looked, so when he released her from the hug, instead of telling him how good it was to see him, as she meant to, she said, 'Nice jumper, Dad.'

He looked down at it and agreed. Claire took Nora's coat, told her to take a seat and went to make coffee.

'How's Maisie?' asked Alex.

'Stunned,' said Nora. 'She's sitting in her usual chair surrounded by screwed-up tissues. She's crying and saying she doesn't want to ever see you again.'

Alex said, 'Ah,' and looked at his feet.

Nora nodded. 'I've been sent to set a date for when everyone can meet to talk.'

'You've been sent to have a look at where I'm living. And to suss out Claire.'

Nora said, 'Yes. That's the real reason.'

There was a long, stiff silence. Nora fiddled with the silver ring she always wore. Alex looked at the arm of his chair and tapped his middle finger up and down. Nora thought this was the worst thing she'd ever had to do. She hated this Claire woman for stealing her father away, for causing all this upset.

'Are you going to come home?' she asked.

Alex shook his head.

'This is real, then? You have actually left Mum. This isn't some sort of mid-life crisis?'

'No, Nora. This is me grabbing a little happiness before I die. This is me for once in my life thinking about me. I want to live with Claire. I love her.'

This was too much for Nora. Love? She didn't want to hear about that. 'How long have you been seeing her?'

'About eighteen months,' Alex told her.

'All that time, and you didn't say. You were seeing her at Christmas, and the Christmas before, and you just sat there eating turkey as if everything was OK. How could you?'

Alex said he didn't know, and he sure as hell didn't want to ever do anything like that again. 'Look, Maisie can sue me for divorce. I'll admit adultery with Claire.'

Nora said, 'Right.'

'More information than you need to know?' asked Alex.

'A person doesn't like to think about their dad's sex life.'

'A dad doesn't like to think about his daughter's sex life. But it happens. Maisie can have the house. I'll keep up the mortgage payments. I'll give her a monthly allowance. She won't starve.'

'No,' said Nora. 'But she'll be lonely.'

Right now, across town, Cathryn and Maisie were making plans.

'I can't be alone,' said Maisie. 'Not now. It's not

193

just the silence. It's what's in my head. All the thoughts tumbling about. Him being with that woman, and me sitting here watching television not knowing what was going on. All the wasted years. Round and round it goes. I need someone here.'

'I know,' said Cathryn. 'I'd come. I want to come. But I can't give up my job. Not yet. Another couple of years will look better on my CV, then I can move.'

'I wouldn't dream of you giving up a good job. Oh no, it'll have to be Nora. She has a duty, she has to learn family comes first.'

In the quiet of Claire's living room, Nora, unaware that her future was being sorted out, looked at the dozens of vibrant framed prints on the walls—Cézanne, Gauguin, Degas, Manet. 'It's nice here,' she said.

Alex said, 'Claire loves her prints, she likes a bit of colour.'

That was a familiar phrase. Nora looked at him, wondering if he was being ironic. But no, he seemed to think nothing of it.

She ran her eyes along the records on the shelf at her side, mostly show songs.

'Oh look, *The Sound of Music*. Remember, we used to perform that for you.'

Alex smiled and said he did. This was better. Nora was more comfortable talking about, well, anything other than her father's sex life. She told him she didn't understand. It wasn't just that he had left; he'd left without saying anything. 'You didn't talk to Mum about it.'

'It isn't always easy to talk to Maisie,' Alex said. 'I tried, but she has a knack of taking serious subjects and turning them around in a couple of sentences so you find yourself discussing the weather or what she said to someone she met in the street.'

Alex had often tried to tell Maisie about his affair. He'd said once that there was a reason he was so often late home from work. Maisie had interrupted, telling him that today it was a good job he wasn't home at the proper time. 'I met Mrs Harvester, you know, she lives along the road, her angina's playing up so I fetched a few things from the shops for her, and . . .' Alex had drifted off, not listening. He wondered if he could shut her up by shouting, 'I'm leaving you. I'm having an affair.' But he couldn't. By the time he drifted back and started listening again, Maisie had been talking about something else; he'd completely lost the flow of the conversation. 'So,' she'd been saying, 'I didn't get home till nearly six, but the carnations are lovely.'

Alex said, 'Carnations?'

'Them that Mrs Harvester gave me.' Then she went on to talk about what was on television tonight.

In time, Alex started to go out for a walk in the evening. He'd battle his conscience and work out ways of telling Maisie he was leaving her. He thought the streets pleasant. Sounds of grass being mowed, or sprinklers behind high hedges. Voices drifting from open windows. Smells of meals being prepared. Sometimes a figure would appear at the upstairs window of a house he was passing. It would be just a shape against the light. Someone looking out at the world. Alex liked to imagine the unknown person was battling worries and guilt too.

It helped to think he wasn't the only tormented soul in the world.

It was warm in Claire's flat. Nora hadn't eaten since breakfast, sitting in Brendan and Jen's kitchen, six hundred miles and seven hours away. Now she felt drowsy. 'Does Claire sing?' she asked. 'Is she in an amateur operatic society like Mum used to be?'

Alex shook his head. 'No. She just likes the tunes.'

'Why did Mum stop going to her operatic society? I thought she loved it.'

'She did till she got too old for the lead roles. She said she was only getting offered cameo parts and bit parts. She said they didn't appreciate her talent.'

Nora said, 'Isn't that a bit temperamental of her? I mean, it's not as if she was playing Covent Garden or anything.'

Alex shrugged. 'She said it had taken years of work to get her experience, and they were giving the best parts to youngsters who couldn't carry a tune.'

'But it was an amateur society. It was meant to be fun. People getting together to sing songs. Put on a show for their folks and friends.'

'They take it very seriously,' said Alex. 'At least, Maisie did. She was a bit of a diva.'

'Mum, a diva?' The woman in fluffy fur slippers who doled out tired stews, mournful fruit crumbles, and sat afternoons in her armchair listening to the afternoon play? Nora didn't think so.

Claire bumped the door open with her behind and backed into the room carrying a tray of coffee and cakes. 'Here we are. Have you got everything settled?'

Alex said, 'We are just going to set a date for when we can meet and talk.'

Claire nodded. She gave Nora a cup and offered her a slice of ginger cake. Noticing the relish and size of her first bite, she asked Nora if she was hungry. Nora said she was, she hadn't eaten since she left Edinburgh this morning. She looked across at Claire.

'Well,' said Claire, noticing Nora's glance. 'Don't just give me the swift once-over. Look at me. Here I am. The vamp, the loose woman, the painted hussy who stole your father away from your mother. The hated one.'

Alex smiled.

Nora looked dumbfounded.

'It's a shock, I know,' said Claire. 'But these things happen.'

'Not in our family,' said Nora. 'Until now nothing ever happened in our family.'

'Well it has now,' said Claire. 'It's done. No undoing it. How is everybody taking it?'

'Mum's sobbing her heart out, and when she's not, she is staring fixedly at the bars on the electric fire. Cathryn is whispering in the kitchen with Clive and staring fixedly at the African violet on the windowsill. Clive is staring at the kettle. I haven't had a chance to stare yet, I got dispatched over here to give you the once-over, then report back. Then I might start staring at the wallpaper. It seems the thing to do. The shock has stormed all our minds; we can't think of anything to say, really, so we're staring.'

Claire watched Nora take a second slice of cake

and told her it wasn't good to fill up on sweet things. 'Stay and eat. That way, we can chat, and you can get a look at the kitchen. More to report back. Besides, Alex would love to have you here a little longer.'

Nora looked at him to see if this was true. He was smiling. Urging her to say yes. Something shifted within her, a new emotion. This man liked her. She felt surprise move across her face. She'd never really thought about her father. He went away every morning, he came home at night. Once he'd worn a hat, though not for a few years now. And he had feelings, this was new. Maisie had done all the bringing-up, all the spankings, scoldings, cuddlings. Alex had always been the man who stood in the background, looking on, saying very little. He had just been there.

When she said she'd love to eat with them, Alex stood up, spread his arms and said, 'Excellent. This calls for some wine, I think. That Chablis we bought the other day. Eh, Claire?'

Claire said, 'Why not?'

When Alex had gone to fetch and open the wine, she turned to Nora. 'This is wonderful. This is perfect. Alex so wanted you to come and see him. He speaks about you all the time. He thinks the world of you.'

'Me?' said Nora. Then, unable to hide her astonishment, 'Me?' again.

The shock took her breath away. She didn't know what to say. She hadn't thought anybody really cared for her. She was matter-of-fact about it. It was a simple fact of her life, so ingrained in her she never even thought about it. Her family were the people she'd grown up with, figures who moved through the background of her life. They were there. They never said much about how they felt about one another; expressing emotions had never been part of their many routines.

In the kitchen, sitting in the small dining alcove, Nora watched Claire bustle. Maybe it was the light, or the way her hair fell over her face, or the way she lifted the chicken, crisp and golden, from the oven and crooned to it, 'Oh, look at you. You're just perfect,' but a deep, long-dormant memory was jogged. Nora was five or six years old, back in Maisie's kitchen, the air alive with the smell of roasting bird. Maisie was leaning down, staring into the oven. 'Oh, boy. You're a fine juicy fellow, aren't you? We're going to have a grand time with you.'

Maisie had done that, spoken to the food she was preparing. In those days, routine though they were, the meals she'd served had been happy. The sad food had come along a few years later. Barely edible soups. Soggy fish, lumpen stews. Poor Maisie, thought Nora. Now she'll make sad food for her sad self.

Claire carried the chicken to the table, put it down, leaned over Alex. 'You carve. I'll get the potatoes and the vegetables.' Her head was to one side, her hair hanging across her cheek. She was smiling. And Nora saw it. My God, that was who Claire reminded her of. In the soft light, smiling, she looked like Maisie. Maisie's eyes, lips, cheekbones. Her father had traded in his sad old wife for a happy, sociable, tasteful replica.

For the Best

When Nora arrived home, Clive had left and Maisie and Cathryn were waiting in the living room. They looked at her, a mix of irritation and anxiety. It seemed to Nora they were both in the same position, on the edge of their seat, hands clasped on their lap. Where had she been? What took her so long?

'Talking to Dad. You sent me. Remember?' said Nora.

'You took your time. A ten-minute conversation should have sorted it all out,' said Maisie.

'You can't just turn up at someone's door, discuss what's happening, and go away again after a few minutes. You have to talk. They invited me to supper.'

'Supper? You sit eating supper when we're wondering what's happened to you? I don't believe it. What did you have?'

'Roast chicken. It was very nice. We had wine and everything.'

'Wine?' said Maisie. 'You drank wine at a time like this? Sometimes I think you are completely without common sense.'

Cathryn sighed and asked what Alex had said.

'He says Mum can have the house. He says he's not coming back. He loves Claire.'

'Loves Claire,' said Maisie. 'The man's a pig. I won't have him back.'

'He won't contest a divorce. He'll admit adultery with Claire,' said Nora.

Maisie sobbed and reached into her sleeve for

a tissue.

Cathryn snorted. 'A date, Nora. Did you set a date when we can meet? We have a lot to discuss.'

Nora said, 'Oh, a date. I forgot about that.'

Cathryn looked pained. She pushed her hair back from her forehead. 'But that's why we sent you, to arrange a time and place where we could meet and sort things out.'

'I was sent to give Claire the once-over,' said Nora.

'Yes, that. And to fix a date.' Cathryn spoke slowly, trying to keep a grip on her temper.

'What was she like?' asked Maisie. This interested her far more than any time and place for a meeting.

Nora took off her coat and threw it on the sofa. 'She was OK.'

'Just OK?' said Maisie. 'I was hoping that any woman your father left me for would be more than OK.'

Nora sat down. 'She was nice. I didn't want to like her, but in the end, I did. She's attractive. She wore black trousers and a long silk shirt over a T-shirt.'

'How old is she?' asked Maisie.

'About your age. Maybe a bit younger.' Then she made her lifetime's most tactless remark. 'And thinner.'

Maisie shifted in her seat, turning away from Nora. 'Well. That's just wonderful. No wonder he left me. Attractive, young, thin.'

Cathryn shot Nora a horrified look. Nora shrugged.

'I suppose you didn't ask how much he intended to give Mum every month, or about his estate and his changing his will and his pension; anything at all relevant, now I think about it.'

'Estate?' said Nora. 'What estate? Has Dad got an estate?' Thinking, foolishly, that her father owned a large tract of land with a manor house attached that she hadn't been told about.

'This house is part of his estate. The pension fund he has been contributing to. And stocks and shares he has in the company he works for. His savings. Any bonus he might receive. Did you discuss any of that?'

Nora shook her head. 'Never thought about any of that.'

'No, you wouldn't, would you? Too busy stuffing yourself with roast chicken and wine.'

Nora opened her mouth to protest, but before any words could spill out, Cathryn continued in her best lawyer's manner. 'This woman,' pointing at her mother, 'has given the best years of her life to that man. She has worked to make him the man he is today; she deserves all she can get.'

Nora said, 'Fine. Go for it.'

'And,' said Cathryn, 'you go to see him and you don't even set a date so we can meet and sort out details. Are you totally brainless?'

Nora adopted her adolescent pose, hands in pockets, head to one side. 'Yeah, seems like it. Why didn't you go? You're the brains of the family. You're the lawyer.'

Cathryn and Maisie exchanged a look. They had never been stressed as a family before. They weren't coping. The mood was unsettled, an argument brewing.

'I can't believe you sat down and ate food with these people,' said Maisie. 'After what I've been through.'

Nora said she'd been hungry. She hadn't eaten since leaving Edinburgh. 'I wasn't offered anything here.'

'This is your home, you know where the fridge is,' Cathryn told her.

Nora ignored this. 'Claire's flat's all pale colours. Plain carpets.'

Maisie said, 'I couldn't be doing with that. Plain carpets show the muck. Besides, I like a bit of colour.'

'She's got lots of prints on the walls.'

'Not the same,' said Maisie. 'You want colour you can live with. Move about in, surround yourself with. You don't want to just look at it.'

'She listens to show tunes,' said Nora.

'I used to sing them,' said Maisie. 'On the stage, in front of an audience.'

Cathryn said, 'I know.'

Maisie said, 'So she's not a seventeen-year-old bimbo, then. I could understand that. But she sounds a bit like me. What is the point of that? Swapping me for another me with plain carpets and show tunes she just listens to.'

Nora thought this the most succinct thing her mother had ever said. She'd put it in a nutshell.

'Divorce,' said Maisie. 'I never thought it would happen to me. He gets a new woman. I get this. A lonely house, sleepless nights, shame, silence. A whole empty life.'

Cathryn sighed and said, 'Not really.' She turned to Nora. 'We were talking about things when you were away. We decided you should stay here with Mum. I'll go back to Manchester.'

It took a while for Nora to respond. 'Let me see

if I'm understanding you properly. You are about to swan off back to Manchester. And I am to stay here.'

'Yes,' said Maisie. 'It's for the best, dear. I don't think I'd do very well on my own.'

Ignoring this, Nora said, 'I have to give up my job and my friends and move back here—to live? *I* have to do this?'

'While you were away, we were thinking about what to do so I wouldn't be here on my own, and we decided—'

'You decided,' said Nora. '*You decided.*'

For the next few minutes it seemed as if Nora repeated 'You decided' to the beat of Maisie's 'It's for the best, dear.' In the background of this rhythm, Cathryn, patiently and reasonably, she thought, explained that she was at a crucial point in her life. 'I've got a good job,' she said. 'To give that up now would be foolish. I've worked hard. They're talking about making me a partner. Good money.'

'And I haven't got a good job?' asked Nora.

'Not really, dear,' said Maisie.

'I'll have you know that I am in the middle of a series, "Nadine, Queen of the Trails", and it's going very well. We are getting the best reader reaction we've had in years. Women are writing in to tell me how much they are enjoying it.'

Cathryn said, 'What was that? Nadine?'

' "Nadine, Queen of the Trails". I ride about the country on my bike reporting cycling trails,' said Nora.

'And you think I should give up my job so you can do that?' said Cathryn.

Maisie said, 'But you can't ride a bike.'

'I know that,' said Nora, ignoring Cathryn. 'I just write about it. Cycle routes in the Highlands or in Dorset or the Lake District.'

'You go to all these places?' said Maisie. 'And you never think to drop in on me?'

'No,' said Nora. 'I don't actually go anywhere. I write about them using tourist brochures and the like. I write about riding my bike all over the country.'

Maisie repeated, 'But you can't ride a bike.'

'I know that,' said Nora. 'I never had a bike when I was little. She had.' Pointing at Cathryn. 'A lovely red one with a bell and a wicker basket at the front. She never let me have a go on it.'

'It was mine,' said Cathryn.

'I could have had it when you grew out of it,' said Nora.

'Oh for goodness' sake,' said Maisie. 'You *did* get the bike after Cathryn had finished with it, but you never learned to ride it. You kept falling off. You were covered with cuts and bruises. I gave the thing away before you killed yourself.'

'I always wondered what happened to that bike,' said Cathryn.

'Gave it away to the church sale,' said Maisie. 'It was cluttering up the place.'

There was a small lull in the squabbling. Nora sighed. 'Anyway, that's what I'm doing.'

'Nadine, Queen of the Trails,' said Cathryn slowly. There was sarcasm in her voice. 'You think I should give up my job as a lawyer in a good practice and come to live here, so you can do that?'

'I don't think anybody should do anything. I think you should go back to your job and I should go back to mine and Mum should do whatever she wants to do,' said Nora.

'I don't want to do anything,' said Maisie.

'Not right now,' said Nora. 'But you can do all sorts of things—travel the world, take a job, you could even go to university.'

'Travel the world?' said Maisie. 'You're just wanting rid of me. Packing me off to Alaska or India or darkest Africa so you won't have to bother about me.'

Nora sighed again. 'No. I think you should take control of your life. Do stuff. You shouldn't sit and mope. It isn't good for you.'

'I don't want to do stuff, as you say,' said Maisie.

'No,' said Nora. 'You want to sit in your chair for the rest of your life. And I have to give up *my* life, come here, eat sad food and take some dead-end job to keep you company while you sit in a heap feeling sorry for yourself. You've decided that. Well, I don't think so.'

Cathryn said, 'Perhaps I should have broached the subject more diplomatically. We can talk this through.'

But Nora was on a roll. 'I'm a person. Me. I have thoughts, ambitions. A job I'm starting to enjoy. I have a life and you're not taking it away from me. Anyway, it should be Cathryn who comes home.' She turned to Maisie. 'You prefer her.'

'What makes you think that?'

'You told me. You said why couldn't I be like Cathryn, you preferred her to me.'

Maisie said, 'I never said any such thing.'

'Yes you did, that day when you found out I'd told people you were dying. You said it. I've never forgotten.'

Maisie said, 'Well . . .'

Nora didn't hear the rest. She was furiously shoving on her coat. 'You and the preferred one can stay here. I'm going.'

She walked down the hall, took her bag, still unpacked, and walked out of the house.

She stood a moment, leaning against the front door, heaving chill air into her lungs. Then, hearing someone, Cathryn or Maisie, coming down the hall after her, she hurried down the small paved path. If she spoke to them, she'd give in to them, yield to her longing to have them like her. Think the world of her.

Dark now, streetlights glimmered. She ran. Coat flapping, bag banging against her thigh, she ran. Past the cherry tree, in blossom, at number forty-five, and the collection of leering gnomes at number thirty-nine. Along the pavement she knew by heart, every line and crack, to the corner. Not pausing to look back, filled with anger and confusion, she ran. It would be some time before she passed these things again.

A Given Life, A Chosen Life

The night train took seven hours to get to Edinburgh. It wasn't a good journey. It was packed, noisy and lit inside. Every so often, Nora would see her face reflected in the window. She looked pale, startled and stricken. She pulled her coat round her, but sleep was impossible. A group of businessmen had settled in to a long drinking session that involved many trips to the bar and the toilet, and a deal of raucous laughter, hooting and back-slapping. Travellers round them looked pale and irritated.

Nora's stomach was a turmoil of nerves. She shouldn't have run away. A reasonable person would have quietly talked the matter through, a solution would have been found. She could have come home weekends, phoned Maisie every night, arranged for her to come and visit. It all seemed so easy now she was on the train, hurtling north. But she'd lost her temper, shouted silly things, then left. No, she hadn't just left. She'd bolted at top speed down the street, pushing herself to go as fast as she could, bag banging against her thigh, coat flapping. What must she have looked like? What would Maisie and Cathryn have thought, watching her go?

She decided she'd phone as soon as the train got in. She'd explain, it was the wine, she wasn't used to it, she was tired after travelling south, and going to see her father. She was awash with nerves, guilt and shame. The nerves would in time go away. The guilt and shame would be with her for years.

The train pulled into Waverley station at seven in the morning. Nora walked home through empty streets, Sunday in the city. Perhaps, she thought, it wasn't so bad. Maybe they hadn't actually seen her running away. But she knew they had, and she knew how absurd she'd looked. She could imagine the astonishment on her mother's and Cathryn's faces as they watched her go.

Every time she passed a telephone booth, she thought she might call them. 'I got here safely,' she thought she might say. Then she could say she was sorry, she'd been rude. But then she'd hear their shocked, scolding voices and she'd want to make up with them. They would prod her guilty heart, tell her to come home immediately. Filled with remorse, she'd go back to the tears, tantrums and mansize tissues. It would be bearable for a week or two, but for ever? To live with Maisie's demands for an indefinite period? Nora didn't think so. She didn't phone.

When she arrived at Brendan's house, he was up, in the kitchen, making toast.

'Didn't expect to see you so soon. Everything all right?'

'Fine,' she said, dumping her bag and dropping, sighing, into a chair. 'Absolutely fine. Lots of tears and tissues. And men aren't on my mother's list of favourite things. But she'll live.'

'She'll get over it?' asked Brendan.

'Not really,' said Nora. 'She'll just live. I don't know if she'll get over it. She's devastated, actually.'

The victim was said to be devastated, Nora thought. And is currently at home being comforted by loved ones. Well, loved one. The other loved one escaped, and was no comfort at all.

Jen came in, freshly bathed, smelling of soap, hair still damp. 'Back already. You must have got there, turned straight around.'

'Something like that,' said Nora. She sipped the tea Brendan handed her.

Jen sat opposite her at the table. 'So tell us,' she said.

'I did a terrible thing. I ran away,' said Nora. Though she'd planned not to mention her disgraceful behaviour. 'They wanted me to give up my job and go home to live with my mother. I said

209

I couldn't do that. And I knew if I stuck around they'd persuade me. Pile on the guilt. So I ran away.'

Brendan said, 'Cool.'

Jen shot him a scathing look.

Nora buried her head in her hands. 'I'm a terrible person. My own mother, and I couldn't help her.'

'She shouldn't have made such a demand,' said Jen. 'Still, you have to phone home, sort it all out.'

'I know, but I don't want to,' said Nora. 'I ran away. I literally grabbed my bag and ran. I can't believe I did that. I panicked.'

Jen said, 'Families, I don't know.'

Brendan said they were a bunch of people who shared a corner of your life, who thought they knew all about you, but who you didn't see except at Christmas, weddings, funerals and times of crisis.

'Weird,' said Jen. 'But still you have to phone. Make your peace with them.'

Nora heard the censure in Jen's voice and her shame deepened. She more than respected Jen, she regarded her with a muted awe. Jen was level-headed, sensible, calm, and had the air of someone who always knew exactly what she was doing. In her presence, Nora felt—and she'd thought about this a lot—inferior. It was the only word she could come up with. Nora knew herself to do a trivial job, and think mostly trivial thoughts. She mused, fantasised, speculated, she indulged in imaginings that amused her. Jen was grounded. Jen was worthy, did an important job and was someone who, in Nora's opinion, mattered. She desperately wanted Jen to like her. Now, she was getting waves of disapproval.

For Jen, family was important. She kept in regular touch with her two brothers; she visited her mother and father at least once a week, usually when Nora and Brendan were off poking around record or book shops. When her family called, Jen dropped everything and went.

'You could have phoned Brendan,' said Jen. 'He'd have fixed it for you to get a couple of months' compassionate leave.'

Nora said she hadn't thought of that. She felt stupid. It seemed so obvious.

'Yeah,' said Brendan. 'You could have written Nadine from home and sent it up to us.'

Nora felt even more stupid.

Jen said, 'You'd better phone your mum. Try to sort things out.'

Maisie answered. 'It's you.' Then she handed the phone to Cathryn. 'I don't want to speak to her.'

Cathryn said, 'Hello.'

Nora said, 'It's me. I wondered how you were.'

'How do you think we are?' said Cathryn. 'Mum's been up all night crying. She's exhausted and can hardly speak. She's lost a husband and a daughter. She's just wandering about the house sobbing.'

Nora said, 'I'm sorry.'

'What the hell were you thinking of, running out like that?'

'You wanted me to give up my job. I didn't want to do that.'

'You made that plain enough. Can't you talk? Can't you explain reasonably how you feel? We could have found a way. You behaved like a

211

five-year-old.'

Nora said she knew. She was sorry.

'You've already said that,' said Cathryn. 'Sorry isn't good enough. Sorry doesn't solve anything.'

Nora said she knew that, too. And she was sorry.

'Will you stop saying that,' said Cathryn. 'What you did was unbelievable. Unbelievable. Mum's in a state. I am going to have to give up my job and come here.'

'You could take compassionate leave,' said Nora.

Cathryn said she didn't think so. 'I have no idea how long this is going to take. Mum's ill. She can't be left. She's hitting the sherry.'

'Well, she's in shock,' said Nora.

'She was drunk last night. Drunk and sobbing.'

'Do you want me to come back?'

'No,' said Cathryn. 'I do not. Too late, Mum won't speak to you. She doesn't want to know you. I don't know if she'll ever forgive you for what you did. And I'm not that keen on you either, come to that.'

Nora said, 'Sorry.'

Cathryn said, 'I told you not to say that.'

'Sorry,' Nora said.

Cathryn said, 'Oh for heaven's sake. I don't have anything to say to you. I'll call you when I've calmed down. It may be a while.'

Nora said, 'OK.' Then, 'Sorry.'

Cathryn sighed and rang off. Nora said, 'Sorry,' into the hum of the dead line.

She went back to the kitchen to tell Brendan and Jen about the phone call, but didn't really have to say anything. They'd heard it all.

'My mother won't speak to me and my sister

isn't too keen on me either. She says she'll call when she's calmed down. That may be a while. A year or two. More.'

Jen sighed and said, 'Families.'

Brendan said, 'Your given life.'

'What?' said Nora.

'You have turned your back on your given life, rejected it. The life your mother gave you, had planned for you, you said no to it. Now you have to set about your chosen life.'

Nora said, 'Knowing me, I'll probably screw that up too.'

*   *   *

Claire reached out and took Alex's hand. Nine in the morning and they were lingering over a cooked breakfast and filtered coffee. 'You didn't sleep last night, did you?'

'No. Couldn't,' he said.

He'd spent time staring into the dark, listening to Claire breathing beside him, thinking about the family he'd left behind. The mess he'd made. It all rather surprised him. Of course, he'd known his departure would shock Maisie. But he'd been astounded when Nora had told him that she'd been weeping and wailing, walking about carrying a box of tissues, hardly able to speak. Showing more passion in his absence than she'd ever done in his presence. He hadn't realised she'd cared so much. For years he'd felt taken for granted, just there to fix things, mow the lawn, pay the bills. They'd hardly touched: a small brushing of his lips on her cheek when he left in the morning, and again when he returned at night. In bed, they'd

213

turned away from one another, said goodnight, and slept. They'd long forgotten to be tender.

Leaving had been wonderful. Walking out the door with his suitcase, he'd felt a surge of glee. It lightened his step, made him smile. For years he'd stifled his emotions—no rage, no passion, no howling laughter. Everything had hummed along in a mildly pleasant way. Pleasant, he thought, but boring.

Then he'd met Claire, and there had been thrills again. He'd remembered that life was meant to be fun. Since she'd come into his life, there had been visits to the opera, to the cinema, meals out, day trips here and there. Fun, he thought. Oh, they'd argue, they had worries. But he hadn't laughed so much in years.

He'd gone to her that day. Walking out had been a reaction, something he'd done when he'd found Maisie gone. Too much, he thought. One outburst too many. He'd packed and left, just like that. An outburst, like Maisie's. No wonder she was prone to them. They were indeed cathartic.

'I'm here,' he'd said to Claire when she'd opened the door to him. 'I've left Maisie. I've come to you. If you'll have me.'

She'd opened her arms, said nothing. Just held him. She'd cried. He did, too. A little.

He thought about his daughters. They'd never been part of him like they were part of Maisie. He'd hardly really spoken to them. A bit of a chat now and then, but no deep, revealing conversations. They certainly had never asked his advice about anything. Cathryn was clever. Who wouldn't be proud of her, beautiful and brainy? Fabulous report cards from school. He was sure she was a damn good lawyer. She was smart.

Nora, on the other hand, was dumb. He had to admit it. Not that she wasn't intelligent, she was just dumb with it. She daydreamed. She was gullible. Easily taken in. Prone to believing anything anybody told her. He could imagine her being conned by some smooth-talking lover who'd dupe her out of her money. But then, someone like Nora? She'd never have any money.

This was when thinking got too much for him. He got out of bed, made a cup of tea and fetched some papers from his briefcase. If he was going to think, he'd rather think about work than worry about what might become of his dumb, trusting, naive daughter.

'So,' said Claire now, 'what kept you awake?'

'What do you think? My family. The mess I've made. I've hurt them all.'

'Everybody gets hurt sometimes,' said Claire. She knew about such things.

'I know,' said Alex. 'I just never thought it would be me did the hurting. Why does that happen? All that damage. Why do we end up wounding the ones we love?'

Claire said that seemed to be the way of things. 'Are you worried about Maisie?'

'I'm upset for her. Guilty about what I've done. But it's Cathryn and Nora I'm worried about. Maisie's such a manipulator.'

'What could she do to Cathryn?' asked Claire.

'Not a lot. She's smart. She'll get what she wants in the end. She's always been smart. It's Nora I'm bothered about. She's intelligent, but she's never been smart. Not like Cathryn. Actually, Nora's a bit dumb.'

215

'Oh, Alex. That's cruel.'

'I know. But she was always so easily taken in. You know that thing you do to kids? You tweak their nose, then put your thumb between your fingers and pretend that's the nose.'

'Yes. My uncle used to do it to me. It's an uncle thing.'

'Well, if you did it to Cathryn, she'd look at you with real cynicism and say, "That's your thumb." If you did it to Nora, she'd cry. She thought you'd taken off her nose.'

'How old was she?'

'Three. She was a chubby little thing. Laughed a lot. Maisie played with her all the time. Games of peek-a-boo and the like. If you rubbed your unshaven cheek against hers, she'd squeal. I used to like picking her up, her face next to mine. I loved to hear her breathe. But the nose thing worried me.'

'She'll have grown out of it by now.'

'I don't know about that. Did you see her go last night? She looked thin. She wears funny clothes. She came out of our building and set off down the street the wrong way. We had to knock on the window and point her in the right direction. Wouldn't you worry about her?'

'No,' said Claire. 'But then she's not my child.'

'I don't know what will become of her. She works for some obscure cycling magazine nobody's ever heard of. What future is there in that? She earns a pittance. What the hell is she doing?'

'Her own thing is what I think they call it these days. Let her be,' said Claire.

Alex said something like, 'Ynmph.'

'Send her some money if you're so worried

216

about her. Get in touch. Let her know you care.'

'I don't think I'm going to have any money once Cathryn and her lawyer pals get done with me.'

'Well then,' said Claire. 'You'll have something in common with Nora. You can have a deep and meaningful conversation about poverty with her.' She rolled her eyes at him, stuck out her tongue. Then, 'You're not thinking of going back to Maisie, are you? Worrying about your family all night like that?'

Alex said he doubted she would have him. 'But even if she would, no. I am definitely not going to do that.'

*   *   *

Maisie blew her nose, and gently dabbed at it, sniffing. There had been a lot of nose-blowing recently and it was beginning to hurt. The room was hot, smelled of grief and sherry. Cathryn said she thought it might be a good idea to open the window for a while. 'Just a little. Let some air in.'

Maisie shook her head. 'I don't think so. The cold goes for my chest. I can't risk going down with bronchitis, not right now.'

'Well, I might nip down to the shops. I think we need a few things. Milk. We're running out of tea. Some food might be good. I could get bacon. You need to eat.' And she needed to get out of the house. She was longing for fresh air.

'That Nora,' said Maisie, ignoring Cathryn's remark about food and milk. 'I can't get over it. Running out like that. Just up and away she went. I didn't think she had it in her. That's two gone. Two in just over twenty-four hours. My life in ruins. I can't believe it.'

'I wouldn't be gone long,' said Cathryn. 'Twenty minutes. And I could do with some bacon and eggs. I'm a bit hungry.'

'He betrayed me,' said Maisie. 'He lied and lied. Everything was a lie. A kiss in the evening, just a peck on the cheek, mind, but it was a lie. I'd be here, sitting right here in this chair watching television, thinking he was working late. Thinking what a good man he was, working late for his family. And he was with her. That woman. In her arms, kissing and all such. I'd have his supper keeping warm in the oven. It all goes round and round in my head. I can't stop thinking about it.'

'That's natural,' said Cathryn. 'I could get some biscuits. And some yoghurt. Maybe you could eat some yoghurt. It's easily digested.'

'And Nora. Off she went shouting that she wasn't going to live here. Well, she lived here for long enough. All the cooking and washing and ironing I did for her. Then she ups and away like that. I can tell you, when I make my will, she'll not be in it.'

'Bread,' said Cathryn, standing up. 'We need bread, too. I'll go now.'

'You're not leaving me,' said Maisie. 'I need people round me.'

'I'm going to the shops,' said Cathryn. 'I'll be back very soon. Come with me. It'd do you good to get some air.'

'I'm not going out,' said Maisie. 'I don't want anybody looking at me. They'll all know that my man's been seeing another woman and my daughter's run away. I can't face people.'

'I don't think anybody will know,' said Cathryn.

'They'll know. Bad news is like that. It travels fast. Gossip travels faster.'

'OK,' said Cathryn. 'You stay here. I'll get some food from the shops. Do you want anything?'

'I could do with a wee bottle of sherry,' said Maisie. 'Just to buck up my spirits. It helps the digestion and it's good for the circulation, the doctor says. My last one seems to be almost finished.'

Cathryn said she'd see what she could do.

Talk to Me

'The trouble with us is we don't take ourselves seriously,' said Mona. 'We're a bunch of wasters. We drift along, we don't plan.'

'Plan what?' asked George.

'Our lives. Our careers. Our destinies.'

George said, 'Oh.'

'Have you got a life plan?' asked Mona.

'No. I just wait and see what comes along.'

It was nine in the evening, and they were in Mona's kitchen finishing off a chicken curry George had made. He'd noticed that of late Mona had looked pale and overwrought. A curry would do her good, he'd thought. Something spicy and comforting, not eye-wateringly hot. Something that would soothe her. He thought she needed feeding.

The dishes were still on the table. They sat drinking the wine she'd opened. Joni Mitchell's songs drifted through from the living room. George found kitchens interesting; they said a lot

219

about the people who used them. This one had been planned, built, then ignored. It was blue-grey, elegant glass-fronted cupboards round the walls. Inside the cupboards were arty rows of cups and jugs. On the unit a kettle and an espresso machine. Everything gleamed, but only a little, and not from being regularly wiped, but from idleness. Things had been bought, carefully placed, but were rarely used. Mona lived on toast, ready-prepared meals she had only to heat up, and fruit.

Tonight, she was in her jeans and a pink T-shirt, no shoes. She'd come home, showered and hadn't bothered to put on any make-up. He liked this. He could see the truth about her face. The lines, small wrinkles round her eyes, the slight sag of her cheeks, the marks time, worry and frustration had left. There was something exclusive and personal about this. It made him feel special. She was not afraid to reveal herself, her pale and naked face, to him. It was, he thought, far more intimate than if she'd stripped off her clothes and let him see her nude.

She filled their glasses. 'We have no motivation.'

'We don't pursue self-improvement,' offered George.

'Exactly,' said Mona. 'Do you know, I've been writing fashion and beauty for over fifteen years now. That's fifteen Christmas diets, both lose ten pounds before the big day, and lose that post-Yuletide flab; fifteen spring issues, get into that bikini in time for summer; fifteen summers, shape up for summer; fifteen autumns, get ready to beat the winter blues; then back to Christmas again.'

George said, 'Goodness. There's something a bit depressing about that. It's the way you tell it.'

'I have written about all-protein diets, all-carbohydrate diets, fruit diets, fibre diets and detox diets. Drinking gallons of water to give your skin a glow. I have extolled the virtues of working out. I have written about exercise as a way of feeling sexy and as a way to get rid of depression. I have written about improving your wardrobe, coordinating your wardrobe, revamping your wardrobe. I have told people how to moisturise, shape their eyebrows, make their lips look plumper, and emphasise their cheekbones. I have advised on positive thinking, lateral thinking, and the benefits of a good old-fashioned daydream.'

'You're making me feel inadequate, Mona,' said George.

'I have advised women about fantasising during sex. How to achieve simultaneous orgasm.'

'How do you do that?' said George.

'How the hell do I know?' said Mona. 'I've never achieved it with anyone.'

George said, 'Pity.'

'I have told people to take up aerobics, do step routines, weights, swimming, jogging, yoga and power-walking. I have advised plump women on how to look thinner, thin women on how to look fatter—though I don't think there's many of them—tall women on how to look smaller and small women on how to look taller,' said Mona.

'It's tough being a woman,' said George. 'You're hard on your readers. All that jogging and wanting to be the opposite of what they are.'

Mona ignored this. 'I have told women to use face packs and mud baths. I have told them how to avoid cellulite, and how to get rid of cellulite. I have said what they should wear on the beach if

221

they've got big bums or flabby thighs. George, it goes on and on. Fifteen years of diets, exercise and clothes, and do you know?'

'No,' said George.

'I have done none of it. Jog, me? I don't think so. Step routine? Too sweaty. I moisturise, but not in the way I tell my readers to do it. I eat rubbish. I drink. I stay up late. I love clothes. But really, George, I'm a liar.'

'You've really been thinking about this, haven't you?'

'You bloody bet I have. That photo at the top of my weekly page. It's not even me. It's some girl from accounts years ago who looked like what we thought a beauty editor should look like.'

'I wondered about that. I thought it was you on a good day some years ago, in a good light with a really, really good photographer who had a way with an airbrush.'

'Thank you, George. I don't think I'll fill your glass now.'

He took the bottle and refilled both their glasses. 'I have edited seven books on cats. I don't own a cat. Don't even like them. Prefer dogs. There was someone wrote a motoring column and didn't drive. Didn't even have a licence. Janice Hollies wrote an ask-the-doctor column using a twenty-year-old medical dictionary. What brought all this on, anyway?'

'Gregory's having an affair.'

He couldn't quite understand why she'd be upset by this. She had affairs. Many affairs, as far as he knew. 'Pardon my saying this, but don't you sleep with other people?'

'I have done. But that's different.'

'So it's all right for you to have the odd fling, but not him.'

'Yes.'

They stared at one another across the table.

'My fabulous sex life isn't as fabulous as I've let everyone believe it is,' said Mona.

'It's another of your lies, then.'

'No,' said Mona. 'It's just not as true as people think.'

George said that he was sorry, but he hadn't a clue what she meant.

Mona sighed. 'I admit, I went a bit wild when Gregory first left. I had the notion I could have it all. That's what I wanted—everything. Lovers, and one steady lover who lived far enough away not to know what I was up to.'

George said he could see the attraction of that.

'Doesn't work,' said Mona. 'It's tiring, and you start to dislike yourself. In the end I had two boyfriends. One old and rich, the other young and energetic.'

George said, 'Ah.'

'That doesn't work, either,' Mona told him. 'Really, too much fooling around makes you feel lonely.'

She'd been at a club with her young, energetic boyfriend. The lights were hot, music raged, all round her people danced, a swim of movement, arms waving. She was standing in the midst of that Friday-night frenetic lust for a good time and was dazed by the ripples of strobes that spun over the faces around her. She'd been trying to talk about how moved she'd been by a film she'd seen the night before. But her boyfriend couldn't hear a word she was saying. She'd bawled words,

223

'Wonderful. Moving. Light. Landscape.' He was leaning down, ear next to her mouth. But that made no difference. And it wasn't just that he couldn't hear her. He didn't care about hearing her. He wasn't here to talk. He wanted to drink, to dance, to smile, to show off to the people who were showing off to him.

Mona's throat hurt. Her eyes stung, and they'd be gritty all day tomorrow. The insides of her ears would be hot from the overwhelming blast of music. And she had a vision of where she'd really like to be—at home, the room comfortably dimmed, wearing her old chenille dressing gown, feet up, watching telly and clutching a cup of tea.

'I need to go,' she'd said.

He'd cupped a hand behind one ear. 'What?'

So Mona yelled, 'I'm going. I have to go home.' She felt her throat bruising with the effort. Then she left.

'I've spoken to him on the phone a couple of times, but it's over. It was over the moment I wanted to be out of that club and at home with a cup of tea. I'm entering a new phase in my life. The comfort-over-thrills stage.'

Which would have made her rich man seem ideal. Only, last week he'd proposed to her in a restaurant as they were eating roast monkfish. 'No,' she'd said. Just like that. 'I can't. Sorry.'

'I couldn't believe I said that,' she told George now. 'If the words had come out in a little balloon like they do in comic strips, I'd have plucked it from the air and read it, just to make sure. But I didn't want to marry him. I want Gregory.'

'So go to Gregory and tell him,' said George.

'I can't,' said Mona. 'What if he doesn't want

me?' She put her head in her hands. 'You don't understand. I need to moan right now. I hate how reasonable and logical men can be; they don't understand how a person can have a good whine. They always want to fix things. Whining's good. It helps.'

George said, 'Ah.'

It was true. He didn't understand whining. Though he'd noticed how women enjoyed a good moan. He thought women softer than men, more romantically inclined, more sensitive, but wilder, fiercer, definitely fiercer.

He'd seen Mona through bouts of flu and some painful heavy periods. He'd brought her paracetamol and fruit juice and filled hot water bottles for her. He'd sat with her, made her soup. He'd held her when she cried the day Gregory left. Then watched her, when she returned to work. Briskly walking the corridors as though nothing had happened, make-up on. He marvelled.

'I know I was seeing other men. But only for flattery, comfort, reassurance that I'm still fanciable. I didn't let them into my life. Gregory has let this other woman he's seeing in. Flowers on the windowsill. Fruit yoghurts in his fridge. Ice cream in the freezer. He's got a couple of new cushions, pink and blue stripes. Things he'd never buy. He's made a new life for himself. A life he has chosen, planned. I'm jealous.'

'I'm surprised that you're so surprised. Isn't that what he set out to do?'

'Yes,' said Mona. 'But I didn't think he'd do it. I always thought he'd come back. But he's part of the community. He does accounts for half the district. People call his name in the street and stop him to ask for advice. He's happy. I'm so pissed off about that. And I'm pissed off at myself for being pissed off.'

Last Sunday Mona and Gregory had been sitting at the breakfast table. It was eight o'clock. She slowly buttered a slice of toast, listened to the rain outside, the endless patter. She thought she heard the crunch of footsteps on the gravel path outside. Surely not; it was Sunday morning, after all. The room smelled of coffee. Gregory stood at the stove, back to her. They hadn't spoken much since she arrived yesterday morning. Though Mona could tell from the scent on the pillow that was not hers, and the freesias on the windowsill and the two hideous pink cushions on the sofa that Gregory would never buy for himself, that there was a lot to talk about.

Freesias, she thought, eyeing them. I hate freesias. They're too romantic by far.

'So,' she said, 'the freesias.' The cushions were too awful to mention.

But before Gregory could answer, before the argument that was brewing could start, a face appeared at the window, staring anxiously in.

Mona jumped. 'Who the hell is that? It's eight in the morning, for heaven's sake.'

Gregory turned. 'It's Milly. Milly Stone. Has the antique shop in the village.' He did not move from the stove, but shouted, 'Door's open.'

Milly came in, sat at the table and apologised. 'Sorry to bother you this time of a Sunday, but I got this yesterday morning.' She slapped a tax demand on to the table.

She was a tall woman, wearing jeans and a black turtleneck sweater that looked to be at least two

226

sizes too big for her. The sleeves were pushed up past her elbows. She had ornate chunky jewellery on one wrist, a man's watch on the other. Her hair was fair, crisply cut into a short, no-nonsense style that she brushed from her face often as she spoke. Mona thought her to be in her early fifties; despite that, she was attractive enough. Maybe she was the freesia woman.

'These things terrify me. And when I opened this one, it was diarrhoea time. Been up half the night worrying about it. I don't have the kind of money they're asking for. I imagined myself being declared bankrupt, losing everything. The bailiffs storming the house. So I thought, why get my knickers in a twist when I can pop in here on the way to open up.'

She turned to Mona. 'Always open on Sundays in the season, too many tourists about not to. I'd rather be in the garden, though.'

Mona smiled.

Gregory came over, put a cup of coffee in front of Milly, picked up the tax demand, opened it, considered it briefly and laughed. 'Don't worry about it. It's a mistake or some twelve-year-old tax boy having some fun. If it's diarrhoea time, you could use this to wipe your bum.'

Milly sipped her coffee and laughed. 'Thank God for you.'

Gregory promised to fix everything the following day. 'Really,' he said, 'don't worry. You get a good night's sleep tonight.'

She took his hand, cupped it in both of hers, then kissed it. 'You're a lovely boy.'

When she'd gone, Mona asked Gregory if he often sorted out tax problems at eight in the morning.

'Yes,' he said, 'and at eight at night, and in the pub, and sometimes people just stop me in the street.'

'Will Milly pay you?'

'No. I won't ask her to. It's a favours thing. She'll give me a good deal on anything I want from her shop. Favours. It's how it is.'

Mona said, 'Hmm. You never did favours before.'

'It's how it works here. I like it. I'm happy.'

Happy, she thought. How dare he be happy. I'm not happy. 'So who gave you the freesias?' she said.

'Jools.'

'Is that Jools I smell on the pillow?'

'No. That's Liz. She does my laundry. I pay her. I think one of her kids was spraying the room when she was ironing. That's Liz's perfume on my pillow, but Liz's head has not lain on my pillow. Not while my head's been there, anyway.'

Mona didn't ask any more about Jools, or the freesias, or the cushions. She sipped her coffee and hid from painful things. She left early, drove home heavy of heart. And now, days later, that feeling of despair had not left her. She moved through her days sad-faced, thinking that now she knew how madness was born.

'Oh, George,' she said now, in her kitchen that smelled of curry gone cold, an odour she disliked. 'My mother was right about love. She told me it ruined everything. She said it was best to settle with someone you really, really liked. That way you'd get along just fine.'

George, on his way to the coffee machine, said

228

that there seemed to be some logic in that, 'But in the end, I think I'd rather have love.'

'I've written articles about this,' said Mona. 'What to do when your man cheats on you. I think I mentioned snipping up his clothes and throwing him out of the house. I certainly said to leave him. Now I know what it feels like, and I don't feel like snipping anything. And he's already out of the house. All the stuff I've written down, all the things I've said, and I don't think I've ever spoken in my real voice. And furthermore, I lied. I didn't have affairs because it was fun or because I wanted the sex and the flattery and the reassurance. I did it all because I was lonely.'

George said, 'Sometimes I think everybody is lonely.'

'I'm lonely in the midst of everything, George. Even with my friends I can be lonely. On busy streets, in shops, it's like everyone's speaking and nobody's speaking to me. I'm thinking about him, and I love him. And I'm lonely,' said Mona. She put her head on the wooden table and wept. She reached out. 'Take my hand. Speak to me. Make everything all right.'

'I can't do that,' said George. 'All I can say is I get lonely too.'

Mona leaned over and put her hand over his. 'You're a nice man. I like you. If I listened to my mother, and who does, I'd marry you.'

'On account of the liking rather than the loving,' said George. 'I don't think I'd make you happy. You'd be too much for me.'

'You think?' said Mona. She lifted her head from the table to look at him. Her eyes were red and raw.

Her naked face, thought George. 'Yes,' he said. 'I think you should talk to Gregory.'

At half past seven the next morning, George got out of bed, went to the window, pulled the curtain and looked down into the street. Mona's car was gone. He knew she hadn't gone to work. Away to speak to Gregory in her real voice, he thought.

Now it was his turn to be sad-faced, and to walk among crowds feeling lonely. So what's new? he thought. Don't we all?

Memos

At work, Brendan hid his upset and disappointment at not being confirmed as editor. He carried on, coming and going, briefcase under his arm. 'Mornin', folks,' when he arrived. 'That's me, I'm off,' when he went away. He installed a darts board, and started a championship tournament in the office. When he didn't win, he didn't let his exasperation show.

He joined Nora in writing reviews of the memos Hugh Randall sent.

A wonderful memo, Nora had written, without actually reading it. *Exhilarating, amusing and with all the depth and wit we have come to expect from the master of the memo.* Brendan could not resist. *I wept, I laughed, I was sitting on the edge of my seat. Surely there is no finer memo writer in the land today*. He hadn't read it either.

On account of reviewing memos, and not reading them, the occupants of the office missed two fire drills, and did not know about Hugh

230

Randall's scheme of having people sign in at the main door when they arrived, and sign out again when they left.

'You're not here,' said Hugh to Brendan when they ran into one another in the corridor. 'And you would not seem to have been here for three weeks.'

'I am here,' said Brendan. He spread his arms. 'See. This is me. Here.'

'Our new rule stipulates people sign the book when they get into the office. And sign out on leaving. That way I know who is here and who is not.'

Brendan said it was news to him.

'There was a memo,' said Hugh.

Brendan said, 'Ah, yes. And a very fine memo it was too. I'll make sure everyone signs the book in future.'

The reviewing and non-reading of memos, which were all written on vivid pink paper, continued. But Brendan did see the one that told him that Jason Pierce had been appointed editor in place of Bax. He crumpled it in his fist and threw it into his waste-paper basket.

One bitter Monday morning, Brendan arrived at work and found the office buzzing.

'What's going on?' he asked Mags, the sticky-up girl.

'Jason's first day in charge,' she said. A small cloud of pastry puffed from her mouth as she spoke. She had a Danish and a cup of coffee, and a newspaper was spread out on her drawing board. She arrived at nine o'clock prompt, but didn't start work till half past ten. 'He's says there's going to be changes made.'

In Bax's room, Jason was sitting behind the large walnut desk Brendan had coveted, in front of him a row of telephones. At a smaller desk across from him was his assistant, Marcy, who had, until last week, worked in accounts. Jason claimed he needed someone who had a clear understanding of finances, but, looking at her, anyone could see that this was not her main credential. In fact, she had two credentials that fitted wonderfully into a 36D cup.

In weeks to come, Brendan's envy would deepen when he discovered that Jason had his own headed stationery and business cards, and regular meetings over lunch with writers, agents, artists and advertisers.

'Excellent,' Brendan said to Mags. 'Just what we need around here, changes.'

At home, his cheery resolve crumbled, his bewilderment showed. He complained, he whined. Jen took the brunt of it. Which, in time, annoyed her. Brendan knew he should stop bringing the subject of his disappointment up, but couldn't help it. The upset rattled round and round in his brain, till it burst out. He had to talk about it. Except that now, they no longer discussed the matter, they argued. They quarrelled so often they now had a name for the disagreement: the Brendan-hasn't-got-a-plan argument.

'He had a plan,' said Jen when Brendan asked her how someone could just suddenly achieve the position as head of his own department in the very office, at the very desk, he'd had his eye on. 'A career strategy. He saw an opportunity and went for it.'

Brendan said, 'I suppose.'

'You see an opportunity and walk round it speculating and amusing yourself. When you heard Bax had moved, you didn't go along to management with an outline of how you would take over his job. Oh no. You just wondered if you'd get the job. Then you went off into a daydream about it, and would you have to buy a suit, and what sort of suit, and of course if you got a new suit, you'd have to get shoes too. And how they'd look when you put you feet up on your desk shouting orders at people.'

Brendan held up his hands and said, 'Wait a minute. Wait a minute. Are we having a fight?'

'Yes,' said Jen. 'We're having the old, boring Brendan-hasn't-got-a-plan argument. You know it well. You ought to be able to do it by rote now.' She stopped. Drew her breath, told herself to calm down. 'I've got a plan. I want to head up my own maternity unit. I want it to be the best, most innovative in the country. I go on courses. I read the latest literature. I work at it. You go through life gazing into the middle distance with a slight smile on your face, quite happy with the whimsy in your head.'

Brendan said, 'Well, I don't know about that.'

'You got made deputy editor, and you were delighted. You were on your way, I remember you saying that. But it seemed like you reached some sort of plateau in your life and started to bumble along.'

'Bumble?' said Brendan.

'Yes, bumble. And I'll tell you who's egging you on to even greater heights of bumbling—Nora. She's the biggest bumbler I've ever met.'

Brendan said, 'Nora?'

233

'Haven't you noticed? She drifts and dreams. Her mind's full of trivia. Don't you worry about someone who can endlessly produce dreamy pieces about cycling along thinking about her old loves and moments from her childhood? For crying out loud, Brendan, don't you ever wonder what the hell's going on in her brain?'

'I'll have you know that she gets more letters from readers than anybody else. Women cyclists and non-cyclists write in to tell her what they think about when they're alone. The word genius has been said in the same breath as Nora's name.'

'So we have da Vinci, Shakespeare, Einstein and Nora Marshall.'

'Not exactly,' said Brendan. 'But she has a way of writing about things people notice but don't notice they're noticing.' Then he'd said, 'Are you nagging me?'

'I believe I am. You are hopeless, Brendan. You are letting people at work walk all over you. You should be earning twice what you are getting. Well, I hope you're happy, you and Nora, bumbling about together.'

'We won't be bumbling so much any more. Nora's in love,' Brendan told her.

'Who with?'

'Nathan,' said Brendan. 'We think it's love. Nora says it's an obsession, but there's good sex. We are trying to find a word for it.'

'That's my point. She can't just be in love, and take on everything that means. She distracts herself from feeling it by trying to define it.'

'Don't you try to define your feelings?' said Brendan.

Jen looked at him, surprised. 'No,' she said. 'Of

234

course not. I just feel them and deal with them. What's the point of defining love or hate or jealousy or whatever? Emotions come along, you enjoy them or get upset by them. Where does defining them get you?'

'It helps to let you know exactly what you're feeling.'

By now Jen was shouting. 'Rubbish. I love you, that's it. No ifs, ands or buts. I enjoy it. That's one bit of my life sorted. Now I can get on with the other bits. OK?'

Brendan looked confused. He thought she might be right, and this was painful. He felt a fool not to have pursued the job he wanted. 'I'm cursing myself. I don't need you to make it worse.'

*   *   *

In the months since she'd made her escape from her mother, Nora had come to realise she had to move out of her attic room in Brendan and Jen's house. There was an atmosphere.

It was mostly about Jen's open disapproval of Nora's family situation. She understood why Nora had run away, but not why she did not go home again. Jen was sure that all Nora had to do was turn up on her mother's doorstep and say she was sorry. 'They could sort it out,' she told Brendan. 'Families do in the end.' Seeing Nora make no attempt to make amends with her mother disturbed Jen. 'A phone call is all it would take. They should start talking again.'

In fact, Nora had phoned home several times, but her calls were not welcome. She hadn't been forgiven. 'What do you want?' Cathryn said.

'I wondered how you were.'

'How do you think? Mother is not a happy woman. She hates me leaving the house. She worries something will happen to me. She hardly eats. She's lost weight. She cries every day. She's stunned.'

'Do you want me to come back?' asked Nora.

Cathryn told her not really. Things were bad enough without any more scenes.

So Nora said what she always said, she was sorry. But Jen's disapproval was becoming too hard to bear. Nora knew she'd have to find somewhere else to live.

Mona came to her rescue. The morning after she'd confessed to George that she lived a life of lies and loneliness, she'd driven down to see Gregory.

He'd been surprised to see her. 'Shouldn't you be at work?'

'I took the day off. I wanted to talk to you.'

He put the kettle on and asked what she wanted to talk about.

'Us,' she said. 'I don't think this seeing each other at the weekends is working.'

He told her neither did he.

Mona's heart sank. She thought he wanted to end it. She asked who Jools was. And why she had given him freesias and the hideous pink cushions. One was heart-shaped with 'I love Greg' embroidered on it. Only there was a heart instead of love. I heart Greg. The other, also heart-shaped, but upside down, so it looked like a bum. It was wearing a thong.

'She works at the pub,' he told her. 'Makes cushions to order for the regulars. I helped her with her tax, she made me a couple of cushions to say thanks.'

'Is that all?'

'Yes,' he said. Though it hadn't been all. He'd slept with her, too. But decided not to tell Mona about it. Too risky, he thought. She might go away and not come back.

'Why do you think it isn't working?' she said.

'I hardly see you. By the time we really get together, you have to go away again.' The kettle boiled. He made coffee. 'We're becoming strangers.'

'I miss you,' she said. She had decided on the drive down to tell him everything. How she'd wanted it all. Her two lovers, her rich man and her energetic man. But now she was here, looking at him, she couldn't. What if he couldn't forgive her? What if he told her to go away, he didn't want to see her again? Too risky, she thought. 'I'm lonely without you.'

He told her he missed her too.

Some sugar had spilled on the table top; she drew patterns in it with her finger, didn't look at him. She had never really asked anyone for anything before. 'I could commute,' she said.

'You want to live here?'

She nodded. 'With you, yes.'

They looked at one another, all the things they weren't going to confess niggling in the back of their minds. She wanted to say she loved him, but thought she'd leave that till he told her he wanted her to stay. Or maybe later still, when they were in bed. That would be the moment. She started to lick the sugar from her fingers.

'There's no shops. No cinemas. No clubs. I don't

237

eat out,' he said.

She said she could learn to cook.

He told her please, no. 'I'll cook. You commute.'

She smiled. 'I could get into country life. Grow things in the garden. We could get a dog.'

'Let's just cook and commute at first,' he said. 'What about the flat?'

She said she would rent it out.

He said, 'Best plan. If this commuting doesn't work, you'll need somewhere to stay.'

'Very practical of you,' said Mona. 'So we've sorted out the flat, the commuting, the cooking. Do practical men talk about love?'

He said he'd been saving that till later.

'Yeah,' she said. 'So was I. But as a practical woman, I have to tell you that no way could I live with those cushions. They'll have to go.'

Gregory said he hadn't a problem with that. He didn't like them either. Though he thought them silly and jolly. Their frivolity reminded him of Jools.

'My mother told me that love ruins everything,' said Mona. She was thinking of all she was about to give up: her flat, which she loved; the city where she was happy; her secret boyfriends.

Gregory said, 'I think your mother was right.' He was thinking of his solitary life in this cottage where he kept the door open all day so the scents and sounds of the world outside drifted in, and where he had only himself to please. And he thought, too, about Jools in his bed. The warmth of her, the softness of the inside of her mouth, her willingness. The things they'd done together had been a romp; sensuous, unfettered fun. It had been the closest he'd ever got to uncomplicated sex. He'd miss her.

The next day, Mona asked Nora if she'd like to rent her flat. The day was warm; swallows skimmed the sky above the car park, where they were sitting. Lacking a staff canteen, at lunchtime people, when the weather allowed it, took chairs outside to sit facing the higgledy-piggledy rows of cars, amidst the blossoming weeds, and eat their sandwiches.

Nora and Brendan had a favourite spot by the fence where the briars bloomed and almost squeezed out the nettles. But today Nora was alone. Brendan was taking Jen to lunch. He wanted to talk to her away from the house and tell her that, while he might not look it, or even act it, he was a man of ambition and wit. 'I'm not just air guitars, roast beef and daydreams,' he would say. Jen would say, 'Come off it. You are. I wouldn't want you any other way.'

Mona sat beside Nora in the fold-up canvas chair she kept in her car, her lunchtime chair, which was more stylish and reliable than any other chair in the car park. 'So,' she said, 'what do you think? Your own place.'

She had thought about this a lot. She figured she needed someone she could boss about. Nora fitted the bill.

Nora said that it was a bit expensive. But really, she couldn't refuse. She'd looked at flats in her price range and had been horrified. Dreadful wallpaper she could fix, but sloping floors, damp, and revolting junk shop furniture were all beyond her budget.

'There are conditions,' said Mona. And the

239

conditions were the reason Nora had been selected as a suitable tenant. Mona couldn't think of anyone else who'd agree to them. And she didn't want to advertise and end up with someone she didn't know living in what had been her very precious home.

'One,' said Mona. 'I need your agreement to vacate the flat at any time, should I need it back.'

This seemed reasonable to Nora, who thought that if she owned a flat, she'd want to keep a tight grip on it too. She didn't foresee how inconvenient this might be. She said, 'That's fine.'

'Then,' said Mona, 'I need to be able to stay in it for the odd night. Maybe I won't be able to get back to Gregory's. The road might be blocked with snow. Or be icy. Or I may have been out somewhere and can't face a long drive. I'll want my bed. You can have the sofa.'

Nora said, 'OK.' It was, after all, a very nice flat. She was willing to make concessions to get it.

'Good,' said Mona. She was pleased with herself. She'd found the ideal tenant. 'Last condition. Be nice to George.'

Nora said, 'Excuse me. What do you mean by that?'

'He's a nice bloke. Be nice to him. Chat when he drops by to borrow things. Of course, that means you have to keep a supply of garlic, limes and ginger for him to borrow from you when he doesn't have them himself. That happens a lot. But sometimes, I think, he just turns up for a little conversation. You'll have to supply that, too.'

Nora shrugged and said, 'Whatever.'

Mona clapped her hands. 'Excellent.' She loved it when things went her way. She had it all planned. George would borrow this and that from Nora, and in return he'd bring her food a couple of times a week. That way Mona wouldn't feel so guilty about Nora paying rent that was a little beyond her means. It's love, Mona thought, it gives you a conscience. It makes you soft. Damn love. Then again, Nora might fall for George, who Mona thought far more suitable as a partner than Nathan. Everyone knew Nora and Nathan had had a few dates together.

'How's Nathan?' Mona said.

'Fine,' said Nora. Then, thinking Mona knew a whole lot more about life and love and sex than she did, said, 'Can I ask you something?'

'As your new landlady, feel free to ask me anything,' said Mona.

'What does Nathan see in me? Everything comes to him. He seems to float through life. Do you think it's true that good-looking people don't have to try as hard as those of us who are less gifted facially? You know, that haven't been tenderly assembled. Noses and lips and cheeks that don't quite go together.'

'I hope you don't include me in that,' said Mona.

'No,' said Nora. 'Not really. But me. And most people in the world. The non-handsome ones. We who are aesthetically challenged. But Nathan is beautiful. He expects. He smiles. He gets. He does well in queues. Never has to wait long. He makes it along busy streets without ever being shouldered or banged into, or getting the odd dismissive glance from gorgeous strangers. I never do. I hang about in queues looking glum.'

'Me too,' said Mona. 'But why shouldn't Nathan

241

be attracted to you? You're young, not nearly as bad-looking as you seem to think you are. You're funny, intelligent. Of course he likes you.'

And, of course, Mona wasn't giving Nora the whole truth. She thought Nathan had reached a point in his loneliness when he needed someone in his life. Someone to talk to, be with, sleep with. Someone to fill the void his wife had left. Nora had done what she did best: she'd been there. She was available. And she adored him. Nathan needed that.

Feeling Mona hadn't quite answered her question about Nathan, and what he saw in her, with complete honesty, Nora asked Brendan.

'Um,' she'd said. 'I don't know how to put this without sounding a complete fool, but what does Nathan see in me?'

It was Saturday. In a few days Nora would move out of her attic room and into Mona's flat. She and Brendan had been to the Filmhouse to see an afternoon showing of *Jules et Jim*. She loved that film; every time she saw it, she wanted to live like Jules and Jim and Catherine in a whirlpool of days. And sing, though she could not for the life of her hold a tune like Catherine had in the movie, and have men fall in love with her.

Nora sighed.

Brendan, who was honest, said, 'I don't know what he sees in you either.'

Now they were making their way back across town, late March, five in the evening, and just before dark, the air was the colour of cool water.

Nora loved this time of year. Not because it was spring, and there were early blooms in the gardens she could see from her window, but because

February was well and truly over. She thought February a bitter, dour month, boorishly grey. 'It ought to be banned,' she said.

Brendan didn't think you could ban a month. But if he was given a choice, it would definitely be February.

Really, though, while saying this, they were both thinking about Nathan. How he looked, walking along streets wearing his long black coat that he never fastened no matter the weather; underneath the coat jeans and a plain T-shirt, or softly cut trousers and a dark shirt. He always knew that people were looking at him.

'But he never lets people know he knows they're looking. He doesn't strut or swagger. He just walks boldly, looking neither to the right or the left. And he's the master of scarves. They will be left hanging, long and neatly draped, swinging slightly as he goes. Or he will have them wrapped round his neck in some stylish manner that never comes undone. How does he do that?' said Nora.

'No idea,' said Brendan. 'If he could bottle it, he'd make a fortune. The man is the master of walking down the street.'

Brendan and Nora walked down Kings Stables Road, into the Grassmarket. Lights in the pubs now; in the restaurants the first eaters of the evening were gathered at tables. Nora and Brendan lingered to read the menus displayed outside. Sighed, and moved on.

'Saturday night,' said Brendan.

They walked up Victoria Street, a winding uphill curve. They were a rhythm, their walks. In silence, they'd stop to gaze into the same shop windows every time they passed, no comments, no wish to buy anything. They just looked. They paused at the shop with a never-changing display of ceramic pigs, and at the shop that sold brushes. Stared a little, and moved on, in perfect unison.

'It was magic,' said Nora. 'Put on your lippy and step out filled with hope. Things might happen.'

At the top of Victoria Street, they crossed the road before walking down George IV Bridge. Nora always looked up. The trick with cities, she told Brendan, was to look up. 'Architecture all the way to the sky.'

So walking down George IV Bridge, they always looked up. Till they got to the end, where they'd stand a moment looking across at the pub. Wondering.

Brendan was fond of pubs. They were high on his list of favourite places. He didn't drink, but that didn't matter. He thought them lively. He loved the banter, and to banter among other people who were also bantering filled him with a certain quiet joy. But then he had to get back to the house before Jen, who had been out visiting her mother. Whatever, she'd need a cup of tea and a meal when she got in. Nora just wanted a beer. But if she had one, she'd want another, and then would definitely need a pee when walking the rest of the way home.

So they dallied, looking at the pub, debating the matter of a drink.

'Too many students,' Nora said. 'Chattering and talking nonsense.'

Even from their place on the pavement, across the road, they could hear brays of laughter and bawled conversations.

'Saturday night,' said Brendan.

And Nora agreed. 'It's better to be part of it than an onlooker with an overdraft.'

'It was all anticipation. Maybe tonight I'll have the time of my life.'

'Off you'd go, high heels clicking, into the dark. And all you wanted was a bit of sweat. A snog, a grope, a vodka and orange.'

'Playing,' said Brendan. 'Sometimes it'd turn ugly. Fights, hysterical girls. Sometimes you'd walk long, long streets, carrying tins of beer, looking for the party.'

'Best time of your life,' said Nora. 'Playing at being grown-up. Better to play at it than be it.'

'Yeah,' said Brendan. 'You wouldn't go out in your best shirt, face splashed with Brut, and play at having a mortgage and worrying about work and reminding yourself to pay the gas bill.'

They walked on. 'There are a lot of arrogant people about these days,' said Nora. 'Have you noticed that? People in black who swagger.'

Brendan said he had. 'And there's a thing going on with cuffs. Nobody fastens them. It's all to do with cuffs, haircuts, jackets and certain shoes.'

'I know,' said Nora. 'We're out of step with the times. Left behind in the surge for wealth and power.'

'And us so young,' Brendan added.

'We shall have to try to sort out our images. We'll start with the stride. We'll walk arrogantly to the lamppost after next. Then meekly for a while.'

They strode and slouched alternately till they reached the end of the street. They decided that, though the arrogant walk was healthier, head up to gulp in oxygen, arms swinging to boost circulation, they were both natural slouchers.

'We'll never make it in today's thrusting, upwardly mobile culture,' said Nora. 'We lack the purposeful stride. So what are you doing tonight?'

'I'll make some pasta for Jen. And we'll chat about her mother, who is sixty-seven and has just got back from a fortnight's trekking and white-water rafting in the Rockies. Then we'll have the Brendan-hasn't-got-a-plan argument, watch telly for a bit and go to bed.'

'So you'll have a snog and a grope at least.'

'Oh, yes. You?'

'I'll go down to Nathan's. We'll head for the pub, then an Indian meal, and home to bed.'

'Excellent Saturday night,' said Brendan.

'I think so,' said Nora. 'All this sex is good for my complexion. That's handy, because as of next week when I start paying rent to Mona, I won't be able to afford any creams. Or food, now I think about it.'

'You'll be thin, but glowing,' said Brendan.

'Just the sort of woman Nathan loves,' said Nora.

An Affair

It was wonderful. Nathan phoned her during the week after Nora had returned after running out on her family. 'What about dinner?'

'Sounds good,' Nora had said. She didn't want to sound as enthusiastic as she felt.

They had dined at an upmarket restaurant. Waiters hovered, refilled their wine glasses. Their conversation had been light. Nora didn't mention her mother. Nathan didn't mention his ex-wife. He'd taken her home in a taxi, kissed her pleasantly on the cheek. And that had been that.

'He's posher than me,' Nora said to Brendan. 'Three-course meals with wine. A restaurant with crisp white linen. And only a peck on the cheek at the end of it all. I'm still at the large plate of pasta with a glass of the house red and a full-blown snog, at least.'

Two days later, he'd asked if she'd like to go to the cinema with him. They'd sat in the dark, and all she could think about was the proximity of him in the seat next to hers. His breathing. 'It put me off my tub of vanilla ice cream,' she told Brendan. On that occasion, she also only got a pleasant kiss.

A week later, Nathan invited her to his flat for dinner. 'If I say so myself, I'm a bit of a cook. Peppered steak in marsala sauce?'

'I could eat that,' she said. Keep cool, don't sound enamoured, she told herself.

He turned out not to be quite the cook he imagined himself to be. The steak was burned, the sauce sweet and sticky. 'Trying too hard to please you,' Nathan explained. They'd eaten in the kitchen, and afterwards took a bottle of wine through to his living room, overlooking a small, tangled garden at the back of the flat. They sat on the sofa; the lights were dimmed. They kissed.

When Nora arrived in his kitchen at eleven o'clock next morning, Brendan was rolling a large joint of beef in a soft mixture of mustard powder and flour. 'How was it for you?' he asked.

'The earth moved,' she said. 'Well, something did. How was it for you?'

'Not quite as thrilling as that.'

After that first thrilling night, when something moved, the romance took wings. They saw each other several nights a week. He put his arm round her shoulders as they walked along together. They lingered on the phone. She, though her days of toing and froing from the balloonists had ended, took walks through the building, always going up to the third floor, where she would pass the art department and might just, accidentally, bump into him. Catching a glimpse of him was exciting, too. He'd come visit her at her desk. He'd sit perched on the edge and, gazing at her fondly—there was a lot of fond gazing going on—engage her in witty, flirtatious conversations.

This had to stop when Hugh Randall spotted them and, knowing it was not business they were discussing (the body language said it all), issued a memo saying that all interdepartmental staff communications were to be restricted to business conversations only. Personal matters were to be kept to out-of-office hours. Nora had read it and written that it was *profoundly moving and insightful.*

Evenings, they'd meet after work and eat in small restaurants, huddled into a corner, drinking wine and sharing forkfuls of each other's food. Sometimes they'd walk, take to the hills. Nathan was an enthusiastic hiker. He'd stride along in his walking boots, Nora tripping beside him in her Nike training shoes. He'd top small peaks, stand gazing about him, arms stretched, breathing gulps of pure unleaded air. 'This is it for me. This is my everything.' Heading back to the car, he'd set a more amiable pace, so they could talk. She was aware that she hung on his every word. She thought he knew so much; she wanted to learn. He told her about music, about art, architecture, books. It was a time in her life when Nora was aware of saying, 'Goodness, I didn't know that,' a lot.

Once she'd asked him about love. What did he think of it? Did he think, as Mona thought, that love was a curse? That it cramped your style?

Nathan said, 'Mona would think that. She doesn't like to have her style cramped. She's given up her whole lifestyle to go and live with Gregory.' He'd turned to her, smiled, and swept her into his arms. 'You wouldn't cramp my style, would you? You wouldn't cramp anybody's style.'

A bell rang for Nora. Not a gong or a screaming siren, just a little ring that interrupted her moment in paradise. No, she thought, I wouldn't cramp your style. And that's what you see in me. I'm here. And I don't make many demands. She knew she was in love with him, and a little in awe of him.

It was hard to pinpoint a moment when the affair, with its passion, its wild trembling, its sweet phone calls when neither wanted to put the receiver down, became something more routine. Nora admitted to Brendan, 'He has got over the wild trembling phase, but I'm still wildly trembling.'

She still felt that tremor of joy when she saw him walking towards her. It was as if her face was out of control, she couldn't stop it smiling. And when he smiled back, she felt something physical happen inside her, a thrill, a swift movement of blood surging towards her heart and cheeks. A sighting of Nathan caused Nora no end of emotional upheaval.

For Nathan, the romance was going well. The

flame still burned, but a little less brightly than in the first few passionate months. Now it was something more comfortable, manageable, and this was what he wanted. A relaxed, easy relationship with a woman he slept with.

He was a man, Nora observed, who put his life into boxes. Nobody in one box mixed with anyone in another box. In Nathan's work box he kept his colleagues, people he laughed with, bantered with and drank with in the pub most evenings after work. His ex-wife and daughter were in a sad box that he grieved over and never spoke about, but at least the occupants of the sad box were allowed to meet, now and then, with the people in his box of relatives, which included his mother, brother and sister and all his aunts, uncles and cousins.

Nora knew that she had a box all to herself. She was never invited to the pub Nathan visited with his mates in the art department. She knew nothing about any of his relatives, not even what they were called. Only that they existed. She did know a lot about Nathan's wife, Lorna, and his daughter, Justine. But all that knowledge had come from Mona, Jen and Brendan.

Lorna was tall, beautiful and played the harp professionally.

'A harpist,' Nora said. 'For God's sake. What chance have I against such a person? What an exquisite way to make a living.' She imagined a woman with flowing blonde hair, long fingers, a fey and slightly fussy personality, prone to needing lie-downs at certain times of the day when life got too much for her. A delicate woman, a lady, in fact, who demanded, and got, a lot of attention. She wasn't far wrong.

Justine played the cello well enough to have gained a place in the National Youth Orchestra.

'So what do you do on your days with your daughter?' Nora had asked. 'Go to the zoo? Have burgers and thick shakes together?'

'Last week we went to a Mozart recital,' Nathan told her. 'Then we had sushi. Week before that we listened to some Shostakovich at my place and I made her a cassoulet. Sometimes we catch a French film, or do an art gallery. She's sixteen, vegetarian, except for fish, and has a bit of a crush on Nigel Kennedy.'

Nora said, 'Oh.'

To Brendan she said, 'Well, no wonder Nathan drives that ancient tank of an estate car. He'd need it to tote around the cello and the harp.'

She felt that all the boxes in Nathan's life were beautiful, lacquered and ornate, except hers, which was cardboard and a little cramped. This was the box of one who was kept for restaurants, pubs and sex. The sex was excellent, though. Addictive, and inventive. He'd taught her a lot, naughty things to do together when the doors were closed, the curtains drawn. But it was crossing her mind that he was doing with her all the things that Lorna hadn't agreed to.

Among the things Nora didn't tell Brendan about her affair—and she told him most things, though not the naughty sex or the sweet, silly names Nathan whispered across the pillow—was that often, on a Friday night, after they'd been to the Black Barrel with the gang, and after their Italian meal, but before bed, she'd do Nathan's ironing.

She knew that, unlike the family box or the

251

relative box, there was no clear definition for her box. It may have been the Nora box, she didn't know. They never said what they were to one another. They never mentioned the word love. Though Nora breathed it when Nathan was sleeping. 'I love you,' she'd say, but only when she was sure he wouldn't hear her.

'I don't know what I am to him,' she said to Brendan.

'Lover?' he suggested. 'Girlfriend? Partner? Pal? Mistress?'

'Well, lover,' she admitted. 'But only in terms of making love. None of the sharing things. So that also rules out partner. I don't think he thinks of me as a pal, no banter, no confessing embarrassing moments, or liking for naff things like green lollipops or old Abba songs. I'm not sure about girlfriend; I think that includes giving of gifts and planning a life beyond the girlfriend mode. Mistress? I'm not sure about that either. I think mistresses are more temperamental than me. I'd have to be more demanding, exotic, sulky. I'd have to wear a black basque and stockings.'

Then she'd looked away, blushing slightly. Last Saturday night, she'd done just that.

In the midst of all this, Nora worked. She wrote about her first love. *The thing about your first love is you don't know it's your first love, and you don't know how magical it was till it's over. My first love was Gordon. I was seventeen. When we split up, I hurt. I didn't know I could hurt so much. I dread it happening again.* She was cycling between Inverness and Fort William at the time. It was, she said *exquisitely scenic.* Then she'd mentioned her handlebars, which needed adjusting, and gone on

252

to say, *The tyres hummed on tarmac, the road ahead shimmered in the heat, and I wondered about power. If we are incapable of gaining power for ourselves, do we seek it by attaching ourselves to someone who has it? Do we think that by walking with the powerful, we gain some of their power over others? And if we are not beautiful, do we try to become just a little bit beautiful by attaching ourselves to someone who is?* Then, she'd said, she stopped for a cheese and onion sandwich and had renewed her sunblock.

Jason Pierce read it and threw the magazine in the bin. 'It's about cycling, for heaven's sake. What's this power and beauty crap?' He decided he'd have to do something about all this. 'People don't think when they're cycling. It's about pushing your body to the point of not thinking. Fuck that woman.'

Mona read it and saw the truth. 'The girl's in some sort of pain.'

Brendan agreed.

But Jen said, 'Rubbish. This is her usual bean-brained nonsense. She makes jokes about everything and won't get taken seriously by anybody till she takes herself seriously.'

Nathan said nothing. He didn't read it. He may have worked for Martinetti, produced illustrations for Martinetti. But read one of their publications? Never.

Every Saturday night, he opened his Nora box and let her into his life. He did not know the full extent of the joy this brought her. Did not know the care she took, bathing, dressing, black silky knickers always underneath whatever else she might wear, putting on make-up, doing her hair. Did not know about the lightness of her step as she

253

walked along West Crosscauseway to catch the bus to Princes Street. And how, once off the bus, she'd run down Frederick Street and Queen's Street Gardens and Howe Street, coat flying behind her, smiling all the way. At the corner of Royal Circus, she'd stop, clutching the black railings. She'd slip off her training shoes, drop them into her copious bag, and put on her high heels. The shoes he preferred by far.

Then she'd walk to the gate of his basement flat. Trip down the steps to his front door. Smiling, smiling. And when she saw his face, she always, always felt that same internal upheaval that she didn't want him to know about.

Every time they met, Nora forgot the box in which he kept her separate from the rest of his life, and possibilities opened up to her. Whole vistas of them: anything might happen. He might do more than have sex with her. He might actually love her. She pinned all the hope she had on that *might*.

A Bright One and a Dumb One

Nora still phoned home every so often. Maisie wouldn't speak to her and Cathryn was brusque. 'Oh, it's you,' she'd say. 'What do you want?'

'How are you doing?' Nora would say.

'How do you think we are? Terrible. You're well out of it. Our mother, or rather my mother—she says you're not her daughter any more—is going off her head. She makes a fuss if I have to leave the house, and when I come back she's in a state thinking I've been run over, or mugged.'

254

'Why?' said Nora.

'In one day she lost her husband and a daughter, and she's afraid she'll lose the only person left. Me.'

Nora said, 'Oh, sorry.'

And Cathryn said, 'Don't you say sorry to me. I'm sick of sorry. I'm stuck here and you're up there having a fine time. Don't phone any more, please.'

Nora would agree to that. Then, months later, would find the urge to get in touch irresistible and would once again pick up the phone, dial the number and find Cathryn still brusque and Maisie unforgiving.

'I don't want to know her,' Maisie said. 'A daughter who turns her back on her family doesn't deserve to have a family.' She folded her hands in her lap, tightened her lips and sat staring resolutely ahead. Her eyes, Cathryn noticed, gleamed.

It would have been nice, Cathryn thought, if her mother had taken solace in the care she and Auntie May, who visited every day, bearing cakes and advice, offered. It would have made leaving her job in Manchester worthwhile. But no, it was bitterness that helped Maisie prevail.

Cathryn could not count the times she'd helped a tearful, and rather the worse for alcohol, Maisie to bed, undressed her, settled her under the duvet and held her hand till she slept.

Nights, she would sit with Clive and review her situation. 'I can't leave her. I'm stuck here. I need to get out. I need to find a new job.'

Clive had taken her hand and said, 'I know. I think you're wonderful. Amazing.'

255

'No I'm not. You don't know how angry I am. Sometimes I rage. My heart pounds. I feel so furious with my father and bloody Nora. I'm trapped here and it's all down to their bad behaviour. What have I done to deserve this?'

Cathryn had hated leaving her job in Manchester. She missed it. She missed, too, the life she'd had. Her boss hadn't wanted to let her go. 'Just stay away as long as you need to. We'll keep the position open for you.'

Cathryn had stressed how much she didn't want to go. 'But I can't leave my mother on her own. She's dreadfully ill.' She hadn't gone into the nature of Maisie's ailment. 'And even when she does get better, I'll have to be nearby just in case something happens.'

So she was back in the house she thought she'd left for ever. The heating was on even though it was hot outside. And no matter what she cooked, Maisie would pick at it. No matter what was happening on the news, Maisie would only talk about Alex, and Nora, and how awful they'd been to her. Often, Cathryn would find Maisie sobbing in the spare room. It was, she said, the only place in the house that held no memories for her.

'But your family stayed in here when they visited,' said Cathryn.

'They didn't come very often,' Maisie told her. 'So there's not a lot in this room for me. I can cry here.'

Cathryn felt stifled, frustrated. She walked from room to room, fists clenched so hard her nails bit into her palms.

'It hurts,' Maisie said.

'Of course it hurts. What they did to you was

256

hurtful,' said Cathryn.

'No,' said Maisie, 'you don't understand. I've got pains. In my arm, and in my stomach. I've got some horrible disease. I know it. Not that anybody cares, of course. You'll all just be glad to see the end of me.'

Cathryn said she'd get the doctor to call, and that Maisie was wrong, people did care. She cared.

The doctor came the next day. He declared Maisie to be as healthy as could be expected; she was suffering from stress. She was given tranquillisers and something for her indigestion.

Cathryn put on her coat. 'I'll take your prescription to the chemist's.'

'No,' said Maisie. 'Don't go out. I don't want to be alone in this house. I need you here. What if something happens to you? You could get run over.'

'I've been walking down streets, crossing roads for years without getting mugged or run over. I'll be fine. I'll keep an eye out for suspicious-looking lurkers and speeding cars.'

Maisie agreed. 'I suppose you're right.' She thought it would be good to be alone for a while. She could cry openly, profusely. She could have a little glass of sherry, without Cathryn looking on, disapproving. A little glass of sherry was such a comfort these days.

Cathryn left the house. Stood breathing in the fresh air. Then she walked up the path, out into the street, and ran. She needed movement, she needed to get the heat and despair of her home out of her system. She needed to get away before Maisie summoned her back.

Not long after that, Maisie took to her bed. She

257

claimed to have flu or a bout of chronic bronchitis coming on. 'I'll nip it in the bud,' she said.

She lay, pleasantly removed from the world, and thought that it would be good to stay here, head on pillow, for the rest of her life. Only she'd brought her chaos with her, in her head. She would follow Nora and Alex through their days. They'd be getting up now. Alex in some luxurious bedroom he shared with that woman, Claire. They'd be having breakfast. They'd be leaving for work. In her mind, Alex and Nora in their separate worlds were always smiling; the sun shone on them.

Floating on tranquillisers, she retraced her life. Moments, like coloured snapshots, came to her. Nora at three running across the garden, a chubby child who'd hated wearing Cathryn's hand-me-downs. But what else was there for her to put on? And good clothes couldn't go to waste. She'd been a tomboy, while Cathryn had been a perfect little girl who smiled and smiled in pink dresses. Nora coming home from school, socks round her ankles, tie unknotted, swinging her bag singing, *My girl's a corker, she's a New Yorker* at the top of her voice. What got into her?

'A song,' she'd said. 'We learned it at school.'

Maisie had told her to stop. 'Don't go singing at the top of your voice in the street. It's not nice.'

Nora had asked why. Maisie had told her it was noisy. Nora was like that, prone to outbursts of song. Not that she was much of a singer, but Maisie remembered being impressed the child knew so many lyrics. And poems, Maisie thought. Nora could recite a poem after reading it a couple of times.

Another snapshot memory: Nora, ten years old,

washing the dishes. Evening, the lights were on and it was snowing outside. She was repeating Shakespeare's 'Winter's Song' as she wiped plates and let them sail in the sink. *'When blood is nipp'd and ways be foul, Then nightly sings the staring owl, To-whoo; Tu-whit, to-whoo, a merry note, While Greasy Joan doth keel the pot.'*

A merry note, she'd bobbed her head as she said that. And had sung out the tu-whits to-whoos, then stirred the dishes in the sink and cackled about Greasy Joan.

Maisie had slipped away before Nora became aware of being watched. The girl was a turn when she wanted to be. But there was something about her that she found unsettling. She stopped halfway down the hall to ponder this. It was Nora's lack of desire to communicate. She was perfectly happy to amuse herself with what was going on in her head. Sometimes she'd grin hugely, having thought of something funny, but felt no need to tell anybody what was amusing her. The girl would stare into the distance, lips moving, conducting an internal dialogue, acting out some dreamed-up scenario. Maisie shook her head. She knew what it was disturbed her about Nora. She reminds me of me, she thought. And the one person in the world Maisie truly disliked was herself.

Teachers had said that Nora was quiet. And she hadn't many friends. Her school reports had been dreadful—always dreaming in class, lives in a world of her own, never pays attention. Maisie could hardly remember the girl passing an exam. Dumb, Alex had said. Not stupid. Intelligent, but dumb. Maisie had agreed. They had a bright daughter and a dumb one.

Lying in her bed, visiting her past, Maisie would listen to the world outside. Voices from the street, cars swishing by, a dog barking somewhere. She'd hold her breath, waiting to hear the sound of a car stopping outside, its door banging shut, footsteps on the path. Alex coming back to her. But she never heard anything like that. Slowly, slowly she started to get angry.

Alex took the full brunt of Maisie's wrath. Cathryn had found her a splendid divorce lawyer. She demanded a large sum of money every month from her ex-husband. In addition he had to pay all her household expenses—telephone, gas and electricity bills—and fork out for Cathryn's moving back to London, and buy them a car. He'd offered to give Maisie his own car, but she insisted it held too many memories for her. 'It would make me cry every time I went somewhere in it,' she claimed. She also demanded a new bed. 'I will not sleep on my marital bed any more,' she'd said. She'd wondered about having him buy her a new three-piece suite for the living room, but had decided against it. She would have had to part with her favourite chair, and it was comfortable. 'It likes me,' she'd said. 'It fits me.'

Alex had handed over more than half of their savings, and agreed to let her have half his pension when he retired. Maisie's lawyer had said that it would be impossible for her, at her age, to get work and provide for herself, whereas Alex still had some productive years left.

'I feel ripped apart,' he told Claire. 'As if someone has peeled my very skin from my bones. All I've worked for, gone. I'm poor.'

Claire said, 'No you're not. You're just not

260

particularly rich.' Then she'd smiled. 'Unlike me. I have my savings, that include all my parents left me when they died. I have more than enough for two. If you want.'

He'd smiled, and squeezed her hand. 'You have to hand it to Cathryn, though. She's a good lawyer. I know she didn't exactly handle the case, but I can feel her force behind all this. The whole deal has her mark on it. If it wasn't me she'd fleeced, I'd be proud.'

He didn't recognise that he'd been proposed to. It was too veiled for him. And, anyway, right then, and for some time afterwards, he felt battered, bruised. Cast out by his family. He'd come out of the divorce so badly, he felt bewildered and, somehow, clumsy. A fool. Oh, he knew he'd been the one to start it all. He'd left his wife and his home for another woman. But he was just looking for a bit of calm, and happiness. He hadn't thought he was being brutal. He certainly hadn't known how brutal his wife would be back.

At home, Clive had taken his place. He visited every day, often bringing Maisie flowers. He chatted to her, paid her compliments. He mowed the lawn. And it was he who finally got Maisie out of the house. He invited her and Cathryn out to dinner.

At first, Maisie refused. She had nothing to wear. She'd get in the way. She didn't like fancy food. But Clive was persuasive. 'Of course you've got something to wear. I bet you've got a whole wardrobe full of glitzy gowns and tiaras. A woman with your taste.'

Maisie glowed.

'And we won't go anywhere that serves fancy

food. I'll phone ahead and tell them the fabulous Maisie is coming, and she likes a good plain supper. Steak and chips.'

'I do like steak and chips,' said Maisie. 'But I'm fond of pasta, too.'

In the kitchen, listening to all this, Cathryn rolled her eyes. Maisie liked pasta? This was news to her. She'd always declared it to be greasy and coated with heavy oil.

'And you won't be in the way,' said Clive. 'We'd love to have you come along. We'd have a miserable time sitting in a candlelit restaurant, sipping wine, with all the laughter and chat going on round us, and you sitting alone at home in front of the television with a ham salad on a tray. You must come.'

In the kitchen Cathryn gritted her teeth. A Maisie-free evening alone with Clive in a candlelit restaurant sipping wine was what she needed. But Maisie came along. She ate pasta, drank too much wine and flirted with the waiters.

'Oh,' she said to Cathryn when they got home, and Clive had gone, 'I had a lovely time. He's a good man, your Clive. He'll make a wonderful husband.'

Cathryn said that he hadn't asked her to marry him.

'Ah,' said Maisie. 'But he will.'

Next morning, Maisie was up before Cathryn, rattling pans in the kitchen, cooking breakfast, humming a song from *South Pacific*. She said she felt quite cheered up after a night on the town. And putting a boiled egg and toast on the table said, 'I think you've been hanging about the house for too long, Cathryn. It's time you got

262

yourself a job.'

Cathryn tapped the top of her egg with her spoon, breathing deeply. 'Yes, it is. I've already written to one or two law firms to see if there's an opening for me.'

Maisie said she was glad to hear it. And she was off to the shops. 'I could do with a bit of air after all that wine last night.'

Cathryn waited till Maisie was out of the house before she raised her eyes to the ceiling, spread her palms and screamed a silent scream.

She got replies to her letters enquiring after jobs, had several interviews, and was offered two. One was with Harriet Smith, who ran a tiny one-woman practice in Islington. Cathryn had warmed to her and to her office, which had been comfortable and messy. The other was with a firm of media lawyers in Soho Square who needed someone to look over their libel cases. This office was slick, modern—a lot of glass and chrome—efficient and air-conditioned. Desperate to escape the heat and clutter of the home she shared with Maisie, Cathryn decided this was the place for her. She could come here every day, enjoy the sterility of her surroundings, lose herself in work, and for eight to ten hours forget about her mother.

In a time of jackets and haircuts, she flourished. Though mostly she spent her time boning up on libel laws, she did, from time to time, see producers and directors. All this, and her salary was almost twice what it had been in Manchester. She couldn't believe her luck.

She loved the feel of the new, expensive clothes she bought herself, the soft rustle of her silk shirts, the cut of her charcoal-grey and black jackets, the sound of her high heels as they clicked over the marbled floor of the office reception area. She loved the leather folders, containing letters, memos and contracts for her to sign, that her PA brought her every day at four o'clock, the compact black phone on her black-topped desk, her leather chair, her expense account. What she didn't really love was the job itself. Too much paperwork; she liked dealing with people.

Clive had, by now, become part of the household. He dropped by every evening and no longer rang the bell, opening the door and announcing his presence. 'It's me, anybody home?'

Maisie would shout back, 'Of course there's somebody home for you, Clive.'

He would kiss her cheek, hold her at arm's length, surveying her. 'Looking good, Maisie.'

She would thrill at this, but deny it. 'You're a terrible flatterer. You'd do anything for a cup of tea.'

It was a Wednesday evening when he took Cathryn to The Ivy. He invited Maisie along too, but she refused. She said she didn't want to miss her programme on television—she was an ardent soap follower—and it was time the two of them learned to go out together without her. 'I can't always be looking after you,' she said. And winked at Clive.

It crossed Cathryn's mind that to get a table at The Ivy, Clive must know some awfully influential people, or he must have booked months ago. Still, she went. It was exciting. It was perfect. After their main course, while they were waiting for pudding, Clive said he'd found a flat in Holland Park.

'Holland Park,' said Cathryn. 'Ooh, posh.'

'It's not very big,' he said. 'Lounge and two bedrooms. But airy, good light. Fabulous kitchen and bathroom.'

Cathryn said it sounded wonderful.

'I want to share it with you,' said Clive.

'You want me to live with you?'

Clive said not exactly. He wanted her to marry him.

It was, for Cathryn, a dazzling moment. A fairytale. When Clive reached into his pocket and brought out a velvet-lined box containing a diamond ring that glinted at her, beckoned, *you want me, don't you?*, how could she say no? 'I'd love to marry you,' she said. There were tears in her eyes.

Back home, she told Maisie all about it. Maisie nodded, kissed her and said, 'Good things happen to the good.' Cathryn had the feeling Maisie had known Clive was going to propose. There was no surprise, no squeals of joy, just the slight and worrying undertone of something having been discussed beforehand. It was perturbing, but Cathryn wasn't going to let anything spoil her glittering moment.

She knew she didn't love Clive. She liked him. He was charming, attentive, comforting to be with. And that was what she needed—comfort. There were men at work who found her attractive. They dropped by her tiny office with cups of coffee, they flirted. They asked her out. Cathryn always said no. A date might be exciting, fun—those swift glances, little suggestive statements. She loved all that. But not right now. Clive offered something she was longing for. Contentment.

After Cathryn started work, Maisie was alone all

day. But the rhythm of her life still beat to the regular comings and goings of people who'd left her behind. She still rose to prepare breakfast, even though Cathryn only drank a cup of coffee and ate a carton of fruit yoghurt. She still started to prepare an evening meal at five o'clock, though Cathryn didn't ever get home before seven, if she did come home. She usually went out to eat with Clive after work.

Maisie had thought she could keep herself busy with the wedding arrangements. 'Invitations,' she'd said. 'The reception to book. A cake to order. There's more to a wedding than people think.'

But Cathryn had done it all, she didn't trust Maisie's taste. She wanted a muted, elegant affair. A small ceremony with Mozart playing. A meal in a sophisticated hotel, nouvelle cuisine, chilled champagne. The cake was ordered from a patisserie; it was chocolate, had been soaked in Amaretto and was topped with roasted almonds and glazed cherries.

'Chocolate?' Maisie had said. 'That's never a wedding cake.'

'It's my wedding cake,' said Cathryn. 'I like chocolate. Everybody likes chocolate.'

The wedding went as planned. It was what Cathryn called a floaty day. A small civil ceremony attended by Maisie, Auntie May, Clive's parents and a scattering of his relatives, and one or two friends. The reception was at a small upmarket hotel in Chelsea. The champagne was chilled, the food excellent, and the cake was, for the most part, very well received.

Auntie May had doubts about it. Eating a slice of the cake, a large slice, she had chided Cathryn for not inviting her sister.

'She's up there in Edinburgh breaking her heart. I can't tell you how hurt she is. Coming today would have been a fine moment for you and her to mend your broken bridges. To start talking again. But no, you're too proud.'

'She ran away,' said Cathryn.

'That she did,' said May. 'And a good thing too. Maisie would have crushed her.'

Cathryn couldn't help noticing that when Auntie May got worked up about anything, her voice regained its natural Scottish twang. She bought new shoes and visited her friends and invited people to tea in a soft, but slightly lilting accent. She berated them in broad Scots.

'Aye. And if she hadnae gone off, you wouldnae have come back to London. You wouldnae have that posh job. You wouldnae have married that nice young man of yours. An' you wouldnae be standing here in this grand hotel wi' flunkies in funny suits and white gloves flapping aroon', eatin' this grand cake. Nora should be here eatin' it too. You've a mean streak in you, Cathryn Marshall.'

'That's a horrible thing to say to someone on their wedding day,' said Cathryn.

'Maybe it is, I'll give you that. I'll say no more. Except that one day, you'll be glad you've got a sister. You'll see.'

'You're in touch with Nora?' asked Cathryn.

Auntie May dug her dessert fork deep into her slice of cake, removed a chocolate-layered wedge and put it into her mouth. She shut her eyes, sucked in a selection of flavours, then pointed at the remains on her plate. 'Awful good. Though it's chocolate, and that's not a proper wedding mixture. You want fruit and marzipan. I'm not sure chocolate's lucky.' She moved her head to one side, considering the luckiness of chocolate cake. Then, 'Me and Nora are on the phone every week.'

Cathryn said, 'Oh.' She had nothing to say on the matter of what fortune might befall someone who opted for a non-traditional cake when getting married. She turned away to join her new husband and his family who were standing nearby.

To her retreating back, Auntie May said, 'She's asking after you all the time.' Pointing out that Cathryn hadn't asked after Nora.

Clive and Cathryn honeymooned in the Bahamas. Cathryn's idea; Clive had rather fancied a country house hotel in the Lake District. On the plane, wearing her Armani going-away outfit, sitting in her first-class seat by the window, sipping her umpteenth glass of champagne, Cathryn reviewed her situation. Face it, girl, she told herself, you done good.

Not that she was without worries. She hadn't slept with Clive since her teenage years, and then it had been fumbled and swift. She often said to her friends that sex before marriage was more than important, it was a must. But there had never been a chance for Clive and her to get together physically. Maisie had always been around at home, and often when they went out together, she'd come with them. She hadn't had a chance to find out if he had improved since those sweaty, heated first encounters.

'I'm flying off for a fortnight in the sun with a man I haven't slept with in years' she said.

Clive said he was doing the same thing with a woman. 'We'll be fine.'

'You don't know that,' said Cathryn. 'What if I'm lousy in bed? I mean, we've never done it in a bed.'

'You're not, though, are you?' said Clive.

'Of course not,' she told him. 'I'm fantastic.'

He said he'd thought so, and also, it was somehow very romantic to wait till after they were married before they had sex. 'It makes it so much more perfect. And when we do finally do it again, it will mean a lot, so much more than if we'd been banging away at one another beforehand.'

Cathryn said she supposed so. But she thought that of the two, sex and marriage, sex, right now, was what she needed.

The other thing that bothered her was Harriet Smith, the lawyer who'd offered her a job. More and more, while sitting at her desk, Cathryn had thought about Harriet and Harriet's office with its shiny-leafed potted plants, its old sofas covered with throws, its filing cabinets with half-opened overstuffed drawers, its phones that rang and rang. Cathryn had liked it there. It was her kind of place. Then there was Harriet, warm-hearted, hair turning slightly grey, and a soft, throaty voice. Her laugh burst sexily from somewhere deep inside, and she laughed a lot. Cathryn had never felt so drawn to somebody in her life. She couldn't help thinking about her. She thought she might have loved to work alongside Harriet. 'Ah well,' taking a sip of her chilled wine, 'too late now.'

Thrilling and Glittering
Battersea

Sitting at the kitchen table with George, Nora cried. She didn't want to, but there was nothing she could do about it. He had brought her a plate of pasta with garlic and chillies, one of his favourite meals. Nora had prepared them a salad to go with it. She told him about her sister getting married.

'It was on Saturday, and they didn't invite me,' she said. And the tears, unwanted but persistent, flowed.

George reached into his pocket for his hanky. He'd learned that in relationships with women who were friends rather than lovers, a handkerchief was often required. So he always carried one.

'It's because I ran away. I said terrible things and I'm a terrible person. They hate me.'

'No they don't,' said George. 'They just haven't forgiven you, or more likely don't know how to. Families are like that. A set of people embroiled with memories and misconceptions all caught up with duties and stuff. Probably love, too. I don't know.'

'You think?' said Nora. 'I bet it was a fabulous do.'

She imagined it all. The bride in her flowing dress, the chauffeur-driven Rolls Royce (in fact Cathryn and Clive had gone to the ceremony together in his Audi), and afterwards a reception in a striped marquee. Nora didn't know where this

270

marquee would have been. Certainly not in Maisie's back garden; not enough room and really not a marquee sort of place. She knew, too, that Clive's parents lived in a similar house to the one she'd been brought up in, so not there, either.

Still, there would have been a marquee. There would have been rows of tables heaving with delicious food, witty speeches, a triple-layered cake with bride and groom figures on top, a band playing, people dancing. She imagined laughter, amazing outfits, glittering people, none of whom wanted anything to do with her. She was Nora, the shameful one, the outcast. Nora the selfish. She cried, she was inconsolable.

George did something he never could do with Mona. He hadn't ever thought of her as vulnerable. He came round the table to Nora, pulled her from her seat and took her in his arms. He stroked her hair, and patted her. 'It'll be fine. You'll see. One day you'll all be speaking again, and this won't matter at all.'

Nora sobbed. 'It will matter, it does matter,' she said. 'You don't know my sister. She was the beautiful one, she was clever. She was good. I always wanted to be like her. She used to be my hero.'

George took his hanky from her, wiped her eyes and nose. He told Nora she was beautiful and clever too. And funny. 'And I bet there wasn't a marquee.'

'Oh, there would be,' said Nora. 'Cathryn would have wanted one. And my mother would have definitely wanted one. She's a marquee sort of person.'

After the wedding, Maisie was, for the first time in her life, really alone. She didn't like it at all. Sleeping, she still lay curled into her own side of the bed. She dusted, she hoovered, she still made meals at her set eating times, and washed a single lonely plate afterwards. Sometimes she'd speak out loud and thought how strange and hollow her voice sounded, vanishing into emptiness. 'This is what happens. You give your everything. All you've got. Your whole damn life. And you end up like this, standing in your kitchen, washing a plate, and nobody cares about you. Nobody at all.'

This wasn't true. May and Cathryn called in to see her several times a week. And they both phoned her every day.

A song moved constantly through her head, and she'd sing it slowly, blandly, in a monotone, 'Don't blame me.'

She'd lie in the bath long after the water had gone cold, her fingers wrinkled, and the same song still drifted out into the damp air. She'd stare listlessly up at the ceiling, not thinking. Just sighing. She'd clear a small round area in the steamed mirror and the face that appeared surprised her. It was the same old face, no doubt about that. But now a strange grieving look had developed, especially round her eyes. She had a permanently mournful expression. It's what happens, she told herself, your life starts showing on your face, and there are no creams or potions that can fix it. It's the way your face falls, she thought, the expression it's grown used to. The shock of seeing that suffering face stilled her.

She was listless, fatigued without ever doing anything that would tire her. Some afternoons, the phone would ring and she would stand beside it, listening. She would be removed from the moment, aware of the sound; she'd stare at the thing making it. But standing in front of it, arms hanging limp at her sides, she'd feel too weak to reach out and lift the receiver. And too fragile to talk to anybody.

And she drank. She was ashamed of this. In fact, she'd been drinking for years, but quietly. At first it had been tonic wine. A glass in the late afternoon, to get her over the four o'clock dip. In time, she'd switched to sherry, she preferred the taste. A sherry or two of an afternoon seemed to give her life promise. It raised her hopes, made things seem possible. Once, and none of her family knew about this, after her post-lunch tipple she'd reflected on her recent failure to land the lead part in her amateur dramatic society's production of *Guys and Dolls*. It became clear to her that this had been a mistake. Possibilities turned into actualities. All she had to do was go round to Edith Bennett's house and talk to her. As a producer and director of over ten musicals, Edith would quickly see how right Maisie was for a lead role, and how not casting her in any part at all was an absurd oversight.

She'd had another small glassful, just to see her on her way. Popped a peppermint, put on her best red coat and set off. Chin up, determined eyes on the road ahead, a song, 'Luck Be a Lady', the only thing in her head.

Edith's house turned out to be a lot further away than Maisie remembered. She had been

273

there several times doing early script readings, but had always been driven there by another member of the cast. Walking tired her. She got hot, flushed. Her hair was dishevelled. Edith's house, when she opened the huge iron gate and walked up the long gravel path, seemed to Maisie more formidable than she recalled. It was large, ivy-clad, huge bay windows, a glossy black door ornate with polished brass.

Edith had been surprised to see her on the doorstep. And Maisie's confidence had been undermined when she was not invited in. The conversation she'd imagined taking place in Edith's huge living room, sitting on Edith's plush satin sofa, took place on the doorstep.

'I'll not beat about the bush,' Maisie had said. 'I'll come right to the point. I think you've made a mistake in your casting. I should have one of the leads. I've been playing leads for the past few years, and I put a lot of work into my performances and had good reviews.'

Reviews, for Maisie, had been the opinions of her family, who always came along for first night, and some mild praise in a small paragraph in the local paper.

But she had dreams. She imagined that one day someone, a West End producer perhaps, would sneak, unknown, into the audience, see her perform, be thrilled to discover an amazing new talent, come backstage and sign her up. Of course, she'd have to take small parts, but in time she'd find a chance to shine. It would be hard.

In the first cruel light of morning, when Maisie was alone, clearing up the breakfast dishes, fetching out her dusters, she knew that her dream was nonsense. Childish imaginings. Such things never happened. But after lunch, sitting down with a glass of sherry, her cherished, secret possibilities became real to her again.

'I don't think that would work this time, Maisie,' Edith had said. 'These are difficult parts, not that you haven't done difficult parts, but we have to make them credible. Sarah Brown, for example, is a tricky role; she's determined, full of her own sensibilities and yet beautifully serene. Maisie, dear, you don't do serene.'

'I do too,' Maisie huffed.

'The other is Miss Adelaide, a gangster's moll with a heart of gold. She's vital, but tender. We need someone lively. Someone the audience will give their hearts to.'

'I'm vital. I'm lively,' said Maisie. 'Ask anyone. They'll tell you I'm as vital and lively as you can get.'

'I don't think you'd be quite believable,' said Edith. She'd given Maisie a swift and critical head-to-toe scrutiny. Maisie didn't feel she came out of it very well. She realised how much Edith disliked her.

'Why not? I can sing. I can make audiences love me.'

Edith had sighed and said that she had a lot to be getting on with, and really Maisie shouldn't come knocking on her door questioning her casting. But if Maisie wanted to come along and help with the production, there was scenery to be painted, props to arrange, costumes. 'We are always grateful for an extra pair of hands.'

'It's wrong,' said Maisie. 'I should be in one of the lead parts. I am a dedicated performer.'

'Maisie,' said Edith. 'My dear, you are too old. Please don't come bothering me again.'

And she'd shut the door.

By the time Maisie got back home, after a heated walk, stamping along the pavement, her crazed humiliation had turned to fury. 'Bloody stuck-up cow,' she said. 'Damn, bloody, bloody cheek. They don't need me now. Oh, they wanted me when they needed a lead in *The King and I*, and when nobody could do the solos in *Carousel*.'

She hung up her coat, walked down the hall. 'I'm not old. I'm never old.'

She passed Nora's bedroom. Looked in, saw the scattered juvenile mess. 'This is all I'm good for. Cooking and cleaning up after people. Well, young madam, I'm not cleaning this pig sty.'

And the red mist descended. Rage seethed. She stormed into the room, picked up shoes, socks and a couple of books, rushed, fuming, to the back door and threw it all into the garden. Not enough, her anger hadn't subsided. She made trip after trip. Dropping something, returning to pick it up only served to fuel the tantrum. She emptied the room, emptied the drawers in Nora's chest. The last things to go were the Wellington boots. They'd been standing neatly side by side at the foot of Nora's bed. Maisie scooped them up. But throwing them had been a disappointment. They hadn't travelled very far. In the end, she'd taken them down to the compost heap past the lawn and the small vegetable patch, and dumped them there. 'There, madam, that'll learn you.'

She'd gone back into the kitchen, and started to make scones. Clattering her brown baking bowl on the unit, tossing flour, baking soda and butter into it, then eggs and milk, she beat the mixture wildly, elbows going. 'Cooking is it, then? Well, I'll cook. Here's some scones for you all.'

By the time Nora came home and saw her possessions strewn over the garden, Maisie had calmed down. But no way could she tell a small child what had happened to her. Her shameful confrontation would for ever be a secret. Too proud and embarrassed to apologise, she beat her floury mix and told her daughter that seeing her mess tossed out would learn her. And she never went back to her operatic society again.

Today, sitting in her living room, the gas fire humming, feet up on a small leather stool, the radio playing, Maisie could see everything clearly. It was all her fault, of course it was. It had all started from that furious doorstep scolding, when she'd been told she was too old, and she was not to come bothering Edith again.

'Shouldn't have done it,' Maisie said. She looked ruefully into her glass, swilled the liquid it held, and sniffed.

Before that confrontation, too shamed to leave the house lest she met someone from the society who would have known she had, for the first time, been left out of the cast, she'd feigned an attack of bronchitis. And had sent Nora out to do the family shop, when she'd come home with the mangoes. Which everyone had loved.

'I hated that,' Maisie said. 'Mangoes would never have crossed my mind. I was jealous. Jealous of my own child.' She shook her head. The disgrace of it.

'Face it, Maisie, you're a fool. You told your own daughter you preferred her sister. What sort of mother does something like that? Now look at the mess the girl's in, cycling about the countryside on her own, thinking about loss and rejection. It's all my fault. She could get attacked and killed.'

Recently, much to the local newsagent's surprise, Maisie had been buying a not-at-all-glossy, low-circulation cycling magazine. She came in every week and eagerly picked it up. Once home, she would smuggle it upstairs where neither Cathryn nor May would come across it, and read 'Nadine, Queen of the Trails'.

It was her way of keeping up with Nora. Maisie wasn't at all happy with what seemed to be going on in her daughter's life. Nadine did get around, and Maisie thought that a good thing. 'A person ought to see a bit of the world. But not on their own,' she said to herself. And she thought Nora had a good way with a sandwich. 'If I'd known that, I'd have had her make some for Saturday lunch.' Maisie promised herself she'd try a few of Nadine's sandwich suggestions. The passages about loneliness and rejection bothered her. She wondered if some young man was giving her daughter the runaround.

She couldn't quite accept that Nora didn't actually go to the places she wrote about. In her head was a vision of the girl, as she still thought of Nora, struggling through winds and rain along desolate roads, her heart aching from a broken love affair. 'If some man has done the dirty on her, he'll have me to deal with,' Maisie vowed. Then remembered she had no contact with Nora, and was only speculating about her circumstances. She was taking a possibility and turning it into a reality.

Nora had done the same. Maisie remembered

that once Nora had come home very late from school. 'Where have you been?' she'd asked. 'It's almost six o'clock.'

'The bus got diverted,' said Nora. 'There was a terrible accident. Then on the diversion there was a road up. We had to go all the way to Battersea and back by a funny route.'

'Battersea?' said Maisie. 'That's miles away.'

'I know,' said Nora. 'But it's lovely there. I want to go back. There's fish and chips to eat and a pier with lights and music playing.'

'In Battersea?' said Maisie.

'Yes,' said Nora. Of course she'd never been anywhere near Battersea, she just liked the name. She'd imagined a place near the sea where all the food was served in crispy batter. There would be a pier with glistening, spangly lights. Jingle-jangle music would be playing. And there would be puppies. One thing Nora knew about Battersea was that there was a dogs' home there. So there would definitely be puppies, wriggling round her, wagging their tails. Golden retrievers, she hoped. They were her favourites.

In the course of this conversation, Maisie discovered that Nora thought Primrose Hill was a grassy knoll covered, year in, year out, with primroses. Swiss Cottage was rows and rows of chalets and the streets alive with people in lederhosen, herding goats and yodelling.

'I'm not even going to ask what you think the Isle of Dogs is like,' said Maisie. 'Only you're in for a lot of disappointments when you discover London. It's all streets and noise and buses and shops and people. There are no spangly piers with hundreds of golden retrievers licking your ankles.'

'Yes, there are,' said Nora. 'I've been there on the bus. I saw them.'

Now Maisie sipped and sighed. What was the girl like? She missed her. She thought it was her fault that Nora had gone away the way she did. And her fault that Alex had left. I should have talked to him, she thought. I should have told him about going to Edinburgh before I went. I was a fool.

She sipped some more. She'd only herself to blame. Still, now she could see, as she sipped again, that she could fix everything. Possibilities opened up to her. She only had to go and talk to Alex calmly, tell him everything. Confess about the dreadful visit to Edith Bennett. The fool she'd made of herself. The shame she felt.

He'd understand. She'd tell him that she'd dreamed too much, and had let all that was wonderful slip away. She'd tell him to come back to her. The things they'd do. Trips they'd take. The new life they'd have. He'd come back to her. And this time they'd do it right.

Tenderness

August, and hot; it hadn't rained for weeks. Outside in the car park a swirl of grey dust hung permanently in the air.

Hugh Randall and Jason were having a meeting in Jason's office. It was cooler than Hugh's.

'We want to close it down completely,' said Jason. 'Start up something new in keeping with the times. Cycling's big business.'

'The circulation is up at the moment,' said Hugh. 'There's some enthusiasm for the pieces about bike trails.'

Jason said they'd keep that in as long as it was about trails and not women's thoughts. 'It will be by a cyclist for cyclists. We'll keep some of the staff on. But Nora can go, and Brendan.'

At four o'clock Nathan came to see Nora. He passed Jason's office and saw an important meeting going on. He thought it was funny when you looked into an office and knew decisions were being taken. It was the way people sat, he thought. They didn't slump like they did when they were talking about what was on television last night.

In the office, he tossed a piece of artwork on to Brendan's desk. 'Snow on the lettering.'

Brendan sighed. 'Already?'

'All December issues have snow on the lettering, it's the rule. It's a heatwave outside, but it's Christmas in here.' He came over to Nora's desk. Leaned over. 'How're you doing?'

'I'm hot,' said Nora. 'And so are you.'

He had huge damp patches under his arms.

'I'm getting out of here,' said Nathan.

'Now?' asked Nora. 'Are you planning an escape? Take me with you.'

'Going to my house in the hills,' he told her. 'Little place, great views. Peace. Good bird-watching. Log fires. Wine on the veranda in the evenings.'

'Sounds magic,' said Nora. 'I didn't know you had a holiday house.'

'Oh yes. Want to come?'

'I could do that. I'm due some time off.'

'Right. We leave next Monday. Back the

following Saturday. The simple life. Walks. Good food. Wine. Time to ourselves.' He patted her shoulder. 'This will be great.'

When he'd gone, Brendan said, 'So you're off on holiday with Nathan. A step forward. The romance is flourishing.'

'Yes,' said Nora. 'He's letting me into his life. Then again, he might just want someone to carry the bags.'

A glib remark, but only to hide the thrill she felt.

*   *   *

Maisie always said that if you were going to do something, now was the time. 'No putting off till tomorrow; you never know what tomorrow will bring.'

She would go now to speak to Alex. It was only four o'clock, and he didn't ever get home till after six, but she'd have to get to Shepherd's Bush, and locate the house he shared with Claire.

She sat on the tube, handbag on her knee, and mentally rehearsed what she might say. She'd remind him of their happy times. Picnics in the garden, a cloth spread on the lawn, salmon sandwiches and chocolate cake, the kids sprawling on the grass, she and Alex in striped deckchairs, music from the radio in the kitchen wafting out. Holidays in Cornwall, making sandcastles, and how she and the girls had once buried him on the beach while he snoozed. She had a vague memory of Alex not being very happy about that, and of Cathryn and Nora moaning and whining for most of the six-hour drive to St Ives, 'Are we there yet?

Are we there yet?' But she put that away, and brought out the time Cathryn was born, when he'd held Maisie's hand and told her how proud he was. 'We're a real family, at last,' he'd said. Yes, that was good, she'd remind him of that.

It was after five when she walked down the street where Alex now lived. She stood outside and looked into the front room. She could see a sofa, a large plant, pictures round the walls. Arty-farty, she thought. Not homey at all.

She bobbed about, peering in, trying to see more. But thought, well, I'll see the room proper when I come back and Alex takes me in for a chat. She moved on, fearing she might be spotted by a neighbour and taken for some no-good lurker. She'd come back round about seven o'clock. Give them time to get their coats off and put the kettle on; nobody wanted someone coming to the door when you'd just got in and were needing a cuppa.

She found a small café where she could sit outside, drink coffee and watch the world go past. She sipped from a large plastic cup, wondering if Alex ever came here. Every few minutes she checked her watch. Soon she'd be fighting to win her husband back. Well, ex-husband. But that wouldn't be for long. Her imagination flew, she pictured how Alex might tremble slightly when he saw her. How he'd realise how wrong he'd been. Why, he might even leave Claire there and then. 'I'm sorry, I've made a mistake. It's Maisie I love. I've loved her all along.' He'd fetch his jacket, and together they'd walk away, out of the flat, along the street and home.

At seven o'clock she was standing once again on the street where Alex and Claire lived. From

283

where she stood, across the road, she could see into their living room. It was still light. Claire was sitting on the sofa; Maisie had the perfect view of the top of her head. She drew her breath. Well, here goes. Then Alex came into the room. He was wearing a white shirt, sleeves rolled up, collar undone.

They should be sitting down to a good hot meal, Maisie thought. There was always a plate of something ready for him the minute he stepped through the door when he was with me. I looked after him properly.

Alex said something, and Claire looked round at him and laughed. He stepped further into the room, put his hands on her shoulders, then kissed the top of her head. She turned, reached up and stroked his cheek.

Maisie was halfway across the road when she observed this small intimacy. Her heart stilled. Her hand touched her mouth. She turned and ran away.

In all her years with Alex, she couldn't remember him ever doing anything like that to her. A small passing kiss on the top of the head. The tenderness of it made her gulp. Tears in her eyes, she bustled as fast as she could to the tube station. And home, to shut the door and hide.

A Hut on a Hill

'It was a hut,' said Nora. 'A small wooden hut with a tin roof, rusting. On a hillside. I'd imagined a small but beautiful house, with roses clambering

284

up the walls. Good views, though.'

'What about the famous veranda?' said Brendan.

'Excellent veranda,' said Nora. 'Three chairs round a little table, all wooden and bleached by the weather. I liked it. I would have loved to sit out on it, but the rain put me off. And the midges. Hordes of them, zooming in, sucking blood and zooming out again. We sat there trying to look leisurely, sipping wine, but we were waving our arms about, fending them off. And smacking our cheeks and arms on the bits where they'd landed. It doesn't do a lot for your love life. Do you suppose the birth rate slumps in midge-infested areas, nine months after the season?'

They were in Nora's flat, a few hours after she'd arrived home. He'd brought her some new LPs to listen to. But really, he wanted to chat. He'd missed her, though he wouldn't tell her that. Admitting fondness for one another would ruin everything. They'd find such a thing too embarrassing to cope with.

'What did you do all day?' said Brendan.

'We looked at things and we walked. We walked for miles. Miles and miles. God, we walked.'

'Where did you walk to?'

'I don't know. Sometimes we went out of the hut and walked down the hill and through the village and along the road to the next village, which was eight miles away. Then we'd walk back again. Then sometimes we went up the hill through the woods and over more hills and at some point turned round and walked back again. That was it, really.'

'See,' said Brendan. 'That's holidays for you.

285

You should avoid them. You're looking awful, by the way.'

'Thank you. I know to avoid holidays now. But I didn't a week ago. I also didn't know that Nathan was so serious about things. We didn't just go for a walk; he had to get all geared up—boots, socks, waterproofs. A rucksack with maps, a thermos and spare socks. I just had on jeans, a jumper, training shoes, and a bar of chocolate in my pocket.'

'You're just never going to make a backwoodsman,' said Brendan.

'I know. I ate the chocolate as soon as we left the hut. I didn't keep it for an emergency. Like if one of us fell down a hole and broke a leg and we had to wait to be rescued. He said I knew nothing about survival.'

'He's probably right. Inappropriate footwear and stuffing yourself with chocolate.'

Nora sighed. 'All that passion and it comes to this, screaming at each other in a hut on the side of a mountain.'

'Think positively,' said Brendan. 'You found out it was a city romance, a fling that needed the support of pubs, restaurants and other people, before you made the mistake of moving in together. Or marrying, even.'

Nora said, 'It was the silence that did it. He got mad at me for talking when we walked. He said we shouldn't chat too much, voices frighten away the wildlife, and he needed to breathe properly to conserve his strength. When we first got together, he walked me home. He didn't talk much then either. I thought he was savouring my company. But no, he was just not talking.'

'Seems reasonable,' said Brendan.

286

'That's not reasonable. That's absurd. What's the point of going for a walk if you're not going to have a conversation? That's what we do when we walk—we talk. Walking is a mobile conversation. It's just something to do with your legs while you speak. Nathan just walks. And it's more than a city romance, it's a dry-land romance.'

'What's that?' asked Brendan.

'We hired a boat. A really little boat, now I think about it. And we rowed out to the middle of this loch, then everything went wrong. We started to go round and round in a circle. We had an oar each. He said it was me. I said it was him. So he said I should give him my oar, which meant me moving to the back of the boat. So I stood up and we starting rocking violently and he said I was a clumsy oaf and we were about to drown. I can't remember what I said, but soon we were shouting at each other and somehow the argument shifted from our inability to row a boat together to my being a thoughtless bitch who ran out on her family and him still being in love with his wife.'

'Sounds dramatic,' said Brendan. He was biting his nails.

'It was. Very. Yelling. Being nasty about our guilt and pain and shame. Bringing up our dirt at the top of our voices. And we forgot that sound carries in those remote places. There was quite a crowd lining the shore, watching through binoculars. It was deeply embarrassing when we got back to land.'

It had started well. It had been a long drive north, but they'd played favourite tapes. They stopped for coffee and sandwiches a couple of times, and poked round small villages, looking at

287

tiny art galleries and ceramics shops. Nora bought a couple of mugs. 'One each,' she said.

She admitted a certain surprise when she first saw the hut, a lonely wooden structure on the side of a hill. They'd had to walk to it as the track from the road was too narrow for Nathan's car. Inside, the place was charming. Sea-grass carpeting, a sofa and two armchairs in the living room, positioned round an open fireplace. The kitchen and bathroom were at the back.

'What more could you want?' said Nora, looking round.

'The simple life,' said Nathan. 'Real life.'

They'd eaten the steaks he'd brought, sitting by the fire. They drank red wine and listened to a recording of Mendelssohn's violin concerto.

There had been passion on their first night. The bedroom, with a four-poster bed, a small velvet chair and a chest of drawers, was across the hall from the living room. They slept with the window open, scents of heather and peat drifting in. From the depth of the dark outside, they heard a heron's rasping call. Nora was enraptured. She told Nathan she couldn't remember ever being so happy.

In the morning, he'd gone down to the local shop to buy food for breakfast, leaving Nora alone. She knew she shouldn't do it, but she couldn't resist. She poked and pried, she opened drawers, searched inside. In the chest in the bedroom she found some of Nathan's ex-wife's underwear and nightdresses, flimsy silk things, and a bottle of Dior perfume. Her walking boots were in the wardrobe along with a brown Barbour coat that was obviously too small for Nathan, and a thick

288

woollen polo-neck jersey.

On one of the walls in the living room was a collection of framed family photographs. Nathan, Lorna and Justine standing side by side holding up their catch after a fishing trip; sitting on the veranda outside toasting the camera, in front on them, on the table, a birthday cake. Judging by the amount of candles, Nora figured it to be Lorna's: too many for Justine, too few for Nathan. They were all smiling. There were photos of Justine in this very room, playing her cello, and photos of Lorna playing a violin. Well, thought Nora, she could hardly bring her harp. A photo of Nathan and Lorna standing, arms round one another, on some lonesome mountain track, peaks behind them. They were wearing thick jerseys, jeans and walking boots, and looked beautiful and joyously healthy. And there was a photo of Justine, alone, sitting on the steps outside, wearing shorts and a T-shirt, her hair blowing across her face. She looked shy, delicate and a little like Nathan.

There were other things: sheets of music, books with Justine's name written on the inside page. Nora found a note from Lorna, written on the back of a postcard depicting a Highland scene—shaggy cattle in a field at sunset. *Darling Nate, Have gone out for a walk, taken the binoculars, there's waxwings about. Casserole in the oven, ginger cake in the cupboard—made it this morning. Wine cooling outside at the back. Can't wait to see you. I'll go through the woods, why don't you come and find me? Love L. xxx*

Nora put the note back into the drawer, and shut it. Of course, Nathan could have forgotten it was there, along with the other half-dozen or so

Nora had seen but didn't read. But she thought it more likely that he'd kept them because he couldn't bear to part with them.

When Nathan returned, he cooked bacon and eggs for them both. 'You're very quiet,' he said.

'I'm tired. Big night last night. And all this clean air is going to my head.'

He smiled and told her she'd get used to it.

After that, it was little things that set them apart. Nora turned the radio to a rock station, Nathan turned it back to classical. 'We don't have stuff like that in this house.'

He looked at her in dismay when they were starting out on their first walk. 'Don't you have boots?'

'No.'

'But you knew we were coming here. You should have bought a pair.'

'Didn't think,' she shrugged. 'Never been this far out in the wilds before.' In truth, she couldn't afford to buy a pair of boots.

Little bickerings flared up, but they'd turn away or change the subject before they developed into full-scale arguments. They didn't want to spoil their holiday.

Nora's holiday, however, was spoiled. She felt the presence of Lorna and Justine everywhere in this small place. A mug with an L on it in the kitchen. Lorna's old mascara and lipstick in the bathroom cupboard. It was obviously she who had chosen the duvet cover and curtains in the bedroom. She was everywhere.

Nora found, in the pages of a book she took down from the shelves in the living room, a photograph of Nathan and Justine on the track leading to the hut. She had been a child, maybe two years old. The family had been coming here for years and years, then. Nora felt like an intruder, jostled by memories.

In the end, it was the prawns that did it. On the evening of their disastrous boating trip, Nathan had suggested a meal out at a restaurant not that far away. 'Plain food, but wholesome,' he'd said. He'd ordered chicken, she prawns. She'd mentioned that they tasted peculiar, but Nathan dismissed this. 'You're just not used to really fresh seafood.'

By the time they got back, it was becoming clear that Nora had been right. There had been something peculiar about the prawns. She was ill. She spent a miserable night, mostly in the bathroom, suffering fever, chills, violent retching and diarrhoea.

'I mean,' she said to Brendan now, 'some things must be endured in private. Diarrhoea's one of them.'

'So he saw you, then,' said Brendan. 'Puking, and worse.'

'No, he didn't see me. But it was a tiny hut, thin walls. He heard me. And that's worse.'

'Didn't do a lot for your allure. A sex siren with diarrhoea is not a sex siren at all. What did he do?' asked Brendan.

'Not a lot,' said Nora. 'He said, "Oh dear, not again," every time I leapt out of bed and ran to the loo. In the morning, when I was in bed, pale and wan and looking sweaty and poorly, he made himself a huge breakfast then got kitted out in his walking outfit and went off. He said he needed to stretch his legs. He was away all day.'

'I can see his point. I mean, diarrhoea and all,' said Brendan.

'I wish I hadn't told you now,' said Nora. 'Still, he was sweet when he came back.'

He'd walked. He was getting away from Nora and her vile bout of food poisoning. He knew it wasn't her fault. He should be sympathetic, for, by God, the girl had suffered, but he wasn't. He was appalled. Every time he'd slipped into sleep, he'd been awakened by her jumping out of bed and running from the room, hand clasping her mouth. Lorna, his ex-wife, would never have behaved like this. She'd have taken a couple of blankets and slept on the sofa to allow him some rest.

He was a little ashamed of himself. He felt nothing but disgust at Nora's upset. When Lorna had been ill, and she rarely was, he'd fussed round her, bringing her water and cups of tea. He'd hovered by her sick bed, anxious for her to recover and come out of her fever to talk to him, to be his companion again. He'd always been lonely without her.

So he walked until walking was all he was doing. There was only breathing and movement; he'd stopped thinking. He made his way through forest tracks, and up to high peaks, where he soaked up views. He sat behind a rock, out of the wind, eating a sandwich he'd prepared, drinking tea from his flask. It was hot. He could see for miles and miles, the world spread before him, hills and valleys, a loch simmering. He wished he could stay here. He always wished that. When he was in Edinburgh he thought about this place, his hills, his mountains. He imagined them here, silent and huge, waiting for him.

At last he got up, gathered his things and started back to his hut, hoping that Nora was better. She was. She'd eaten, and kept down, some weak tea and a slice of toast. In bed that night, they'd made love tenderly. He'd held her in the dark and said she was a poor thing and he hoped he wasn't hurting her. She'd told him the bit he was concentrating on wasn't the bit that had given her so much bother. And he wished she could just have said she loved him to touch her.

'So it's still an on-going romance,' said Brendan.

'On-going,' said Nora. 'But we have new points in our undiscussed contract. No music other than classical and jazz. And I don't get to be sick. Or, if I do, I'm on my own.'

They'd driven home on the Saturday morning. Nora had been sorry to leave behind all the scenery, and the soft Highland scents, but hadn't felt the least tinge of sorrow to say goodbye to the hut. She'd felt crowded by memories there.

'You're biting your nails,' she said to Brendan now.

'I know, can't help it. It gives me something to do while I'm worrying.'

She asked what he was worrying about.

'It hasn't been a happy week. Hugh Randall told me the magazine is to be folded. Circulation's too low. It has to go.'

'So what will happen to everybody?'

'They're all staying to work on the new cycling magazine. *Cycling for Cyclists*, Jason says. Except me. I'm going downstairs, to books. I'll have a little room at the end of the corridor. I will spend my days reading through all the non-commissioned submissions. I have been put in charge of the slush pile.'

'Is that a step up, or down?' said Nora. 'Are you getting a raise?'

'Oh yes, I'm getting a small raise,' said Brendan. 'So I comfort myself that it's a step up. But really it's sideways.'

'What about me?' said Nora. 'Do I stay or do I go?'

'You are going upstairs to comics,' said Brendan.

Nora said she hated comics. 'I don't want to do that.'

Brendan shrugged. 'That's the way of it. We go where we are sent.'

'What does Jen think about all this?'

Brendan told her that Jen had written a long and impressive CV and was applying for jobs.

Stalking

Maisie, as she went about her day, dusting, polishing, hoovering, sitting in her armchair, sipping sherry, couldn't help thinking about Alex and Claire. They obsessed her. That relaxed kiss he'd dropped on to the top of her head. The way she'd reached up and touched his cheek. The pang Maisie had felt as she watched had been physical, painful. 'Oh,' she'd said, just before she'd hurried away.

The more she thought about it, the more she wanted to know about the couple. Watching them had been a little bit thrilling. It had made her feel powerful. She knew something they didn't. She knew they were being watched.

She wanted to see more. She *had* to see more. Two nights later, she returned to stand across from their house, and gaze in. She hadn't seen much: the tops of their heads as they sat on the sofa in front of the television. This had pleased her briefly while she was spying, but later, at home, she felt ashamed, pathetic.

A few days later, the obsession returned. It was exciting. She knew that Alex preferred travelling by bus, rather than taking the tube. She could guess at which stop he and Claire would alight, and decided to wait for them there and follow them through the streets.

It was a Friday. To Maisie's joy, as she trailed some way behind them, stopping to look into shop windows while still keeping an eye on the pair ahead, Alex and Claire didn't go straight home. They went to the supermarket.

She went in after them. Now she could do some real detective work. She could find out what they ate. She was also keen to know what sort of washing powder Claire used on Alex's shirts.

She moved through the aisles some way behind them, stopping when they stopped, then pushed her trolley to the place where they'd picked something from the shelves, so that she could take note of their purchase. And maybe put the same thing into her trolley, too. A pack of penne, a bottle of instant tomato and basil sauce, neither of which she'd ever bought before. She watched, fascinated, as they selected bacon, sausages, breakfast cereal. She disapproved of Claire's choice of washing powder, thinking it far inferior to her own favourite brand. Alex pushed the trolley, something he'd never done when he went to the supermarket with her, and he often took things from the shelves, held them for Claire to look at. They seemed to discuss what they wanted to buy.

She remembered shopping with him. She'd pushed the trolley, she'd selected the goods, Alex hadn't said much.

At the wine section, Maisie's heart got broken. She stood at the end of the soft drinks aisle, watching from afar. Alex and Claire parted. He looked at the reds, she the whites. He lifted a bottle from the lowest shelf and brought it over to Claire. 'What do you think of this?' Maisie drew in her breath. She'd actually heard him speak.

'Let's see,' said Claire.

Maisie strained to hear.

But Alex and Claire stood side by side, backs to her, talking, discussing. Claire put on her glasses to read the label. Then she said something. A joke. Because Alex laughed, put his arm round her, and squeezed her shoulders.

Maisie said, 'Oh.' That same pang she'd felt several days ago, outside Alex and Claire's house, when she'd spied the top-of-the-head kiss, returned.

Claire chose a bottle of white.

'Knew you'd go for that,' Maisie heard Alex say.

'Well, I like it,' said Claire.

'So why not take two bottles,' Alex said. 'Treat yourself. You deserve it.'

And pretending to look at bottles of fizzy orangeade and cola, Maisie wept. It just happened. She turned and made her slow, blurry way to the aisle where the giant boxes of tissues were displayed. By the time she'd taken a box, opened it, blown her nose, and got control of herself, Alex and Claire had been through the checkout and were on their way out. They carried their bags to a taxi rank, climbed into a cab, and were driven away. From the door of the supermarket, standing beside the potted plants and the selection of lettuces, Maisie watched them go.

She went back to the wine section, picked up a bottle of Claire's favourite white. *A fresh, crisp Sauvignon Blanc. Flavours of peaches and lemon, excellent with white meat, fish or to be enjoyed on its own*. Maisie bought two bottles.

It became an addiction for her, spying on Alex and Claire. She couldn't help herself. Twice a week she'd go to Shepherd's Bush so she could walk past their house and peek in. She would stand a while across the road looking in their window. She never lingered long. She feared they, or a neighbour, might spot her. On Fridays, she'd wait at the entrance of the supermarket, thumbing through the magazines, till Alex and Claire came in. She'd follow them, taking note of what they bought. It fascinated her.

Every time, when the thrill had waned, she was engulfed with sadness and shame. Found herself, on the bus going home, scratching herself trying to get rid of it. Once back in the house, she'd run a bath and wash herself vigorously, working the foam over her body, cleaning, purging, getting rid of the self-loathing. She'd cry.

The obsession always returned. The need to know what the couple were up to, the desire to glimpse them consumed her. She could think of little else. An afternoon would come when the urge to find out what they were up to got too much for her. She'd put on her coat, and set off. There would be glee in her step, a gleam about her. She felt wicked, powerful, impudent, and loved it.

Everybody Wants to Fly

George Henry missed Mona. He'd quietly watch her across the kitchen table when he brought a dish of something he'd cooked, taking in the movements of her face.

It wasn't a beautiful face. But it was full of all that Mona had experienced—sadness, rejection, hope, loneliness, and more. There was wisdom in that face. George always wanted to know how all that got there.

He'd heard the story of what happened on that morning when Mona had driven to confront her love. How they'd agreed to live together. 'I'll commute. He'll cook,' Mona had told him.

So she moved in. Gregory didn't mind when she rearranged the furniture, and insisted they buy a new sofa. Or when she gutted the kitchen. He thought it just the nature of the woman. He was surprised when she started taking an interest in his garden. He understood her desire to look out of the window and see colourful things growing there, and had thought she would hire someone to do it for her. He was, then, taken aback when he looked out one morning and saw her, in old jeans and boots, digging, weeding, sorting out the brambled tangle he rather liked. In the end, though, the thing that shook him most wasn't that she moved in permanently, commuting to work—a thing she'd vowed she'd never do. It was that she didn't move out again.

He told her he thought she was mellowing. She denied it. She was, she said, simply looking for new ways to express herself.

George noticed a change in her, but couldn't define it. 'It's something that happens to people when they settle down,' he told Nora. 'A look. I see it in their eyes. Maybe it's a kind of calm, or maybe they're not so scared any more. You don't have it.'

'No?' said Nora. 'I look scared?'

'Not scared. Just you haven't got that settled-down calm.'

He liked Nora. At first he'd thought she wasn't as vital as Mona, less noisy. She wore quiet shoes. But then he'd started to enjoy her company. This was a good thing, since they saw a lot of each other. They travelled to work every day in George's car, and they ate together most nights. The way she chatted about, well, anything, she filled the air around them with a stream of gossip, jokes, observations and theories.

'Do you think,' she asked him, 'that plain people attach themselves to beautiful people so that they too might be seen as a little bit beautiful?'

George had said he'd noticed that most beautiful people attached themselves to other beautiful people. 'To double the gorgeousness. But you mean yourself and Nathan, don't you? Not that I think he's beautiful. I'll give him striking. He does turn the ladies' heads. You are an odd couple, though. I used to wonder what he saw in you.'

'Thanks a lot for that,' said Nora. 'I feel all huffy now.'

'You've given him back his self-esteem. He was always a proud man, and breaking up with his wife ruined that. Now he's found you, he's got someone who looks up to him, listens to his every word. He's your mentor.'

'He has taught me a lot. How to eat oysters and artichokes. I've read Sartre and a bit of Freud. I understand a lot more about Mozart and the like. He's broadened my horizons.'

'But that's not what your attraction is about,' said George. He thought that he shouldn't be saying this. 'You know that he will reject you one day.'

Nora stared at him. Her mouth was open.

'That's what you expect from people. You hide yourself behind jokes and self-deprecation. You don't let anyone get really close. You don't let them in, Nora, because you think one day they'll hurt you.'

'I'm close to Brendan,' she protested.

'But that's friendship. He won't break your heart. Besides, the pair of you, all you do is banter and waffle. Both your minds are full of trivial speculations, minute observations. You need someone to help you clear out the debris, all the nonsense that amuses you. You don't love him.'

'No,' said Nora. 'Well, not like that.'

'But Nathan's different. You expect him to reject you, and when he does, it will break your heart. Only somewhere inside you, you'll be thinking that he was right and you were right. He should leave you. It will confirm what you think of yourself, that you are not worth loving. And that everyone will, in the end, reject you.'

Nora didn't say anything. George thought, yes, I

knew it. And he thought, got her. Now for the jokes. He decided he'd give her to the count of five before the first one. This was a two-joke situation.

'Well,' said Nora. 'This is very profound. And it's only quarter to eight in the evening. That was a three-o'clock-in-the-morning remark.'

Joke one had taken till his count of four. The second took longer. Good, George thought, I've made her think.

'So I'm going to have my heart broken,' said Nora. 'Bring on the man-size tissues.'

He smiled, and changed the subject. *'Butch Cassidy and the Sundance Kid* is on tonight. Want to go through and watch it?'

Nora nodded. 'I don't want to have my heart broken,' she said.

'Oh, don't worry,' George told her. 'You won't feel a thing. The fall'll kill ya.'

He put his arm round her as they walked to the living room to watch television. He'd noticed how much he touched Nora. He was a person who reached out to others, but noticed that many of the people he knew were surprised by this, so he kept his hands in his pockets when dealing with colleagues and casual friends.

The business of touching interested him. Brendan touched Jen a lot. Mona touched Gregory. He touched Nora, and she liked it. He felt it in her, a slight movement nearer to him when he did it. He knew she needed the feel of another's hand on her arm, her cheek, her shoulder. He thought that as a child she hadn't been touched enough, and certainly not when she'd needed it.

Reviewing his feelings for the women in his life,

301

Mona and Nora, he knew that he'd been fascinated by the former. As a woman of mystery and intrigue, Mona didn't disappoint. But what he felt for Nora was different. He thought of her tenderly. He liked the way her face lit up every time she saw him; she always had a smile for him. He liked her clothes, the way she dressed, her banter, her absurd observations. He even liked the foolish way she waved hello to him every morning, when he was standing by his car, and she was at the door of the building. Probably five feet away from him. No, he didn't like that, he loved that.

But he couldn't tell her that. For now, all he could do was touch her. And be glad she was a willing guinea pig.

A few weeks ago, he'd met Max Weaver at a dinner party thrown by one of his old school friends. George had been invited along to partner Melanie, a single woman in her thirties, who obviously dismissed him as a loser. But then he dismissed her as a woman with her eye on the main chance. 'Which is not me, that's for sure,' he'd told Nora later.

It was hard to tell how old Max was, though by looking at his face, George thought late forties. He and George were the only people at the table who hadn't bothered to dress up for the occasion. Neither wore a tie. George wore a pair of pale chinos, his favourite denim shirt, sleeves rolled up, a pair of somewhat elderly high-top training shoes on his feet. They were red.

Max was similarly dressed, though his trousers were grey, his shirt pale blue with a designer label on the back. His boots were Italian leather. There was a softness about him, a moneyed ease. He'd

302

been born rich. And from what George knew about him, he'd die rich no matter what absurd financial ventures he embarked on. He had a couple of racehorses, and a yacht. He invested in the stock exchange. He dabbled in this and that. At the moment it was publishing.

He'd set up in a small office in Hamilton Place. The area had everything, he thought—good pubs, decent places to eat within walking distance. And he lived nearby so he didn't have to drive and bother about parking places. 'These things matter,' he said.

His first books had been tourist guides. A look at cities from the inside, places to visit that the established guides didn't mention, and places to avoid that the guides might mention, along with places to absolutely never go because you could leave them in a worse state than you arrived, and, probably, without your wallet. They were books for tourists who didn't want to be seen as tourists. They'd been a success, of sorts.

Talking to George, Max heard possibilities. The guests could hear the raised voices of their host and hostess bellowing in the kitchen. The pudding, a soufflé, wasn't behaving properly.

George spoke about cooking. 'It shouldn't be a hassle,' he'd said. 'It's about lifestyle. How you live. I only use one pot if I can. Coming home at night should be relaxing. You kick off your shoes, put on the radio, or some music on the stereo. You slump on the sofa and flick about the television stations. You shower. You remember that you're hungry. So you want to make something quickly. No stews, nothing marinated. I mean, who is going to wait three hours before they eat? You stare into the fridge scratching yourself, thinking, what can I make? What do I feel like?'

'A diffident cook,' Max said.

George nodded. 'Exactly. Suppose you've got a partner, they want to hang about the kitchen while you cook. It's about chatting. Telling each other your day.'

'Hanging about the kitchen, chatting, making quick meals, using one pot,' said Max.

'So there's hardly any washing-up,' said George.

'That's fantastic,' said Max. 'Could you get fifty or so recipes together?'

George wasn't drunk. He'd just reached the point of alcoholically enhanced confidence. 'No problem. That'd be easy.'

'Could you do a book? *The Diffident Cook*, fifty fifteen-minute meals.'

'Absolutely,' said George.

They met for lunch a week later. A deal had been struck. Within a week, a contract dropped through George's letterbox. He signed. Felt dizzy with joy for a day. Then it struck him, he only knew of a single one-pot meal. He'd six months to come up with another forty-nine. In finding them, experimenting with recipes, Nora was his guinea pig. She was the only person he'd ever come across who didn't mind eating the same thing every day for a week.

'I come from a very inhibited culinary background,' she told him. 'We ate the same thing on the same day week in week out. So I'm used to a lack of variety.'

They were, at the time, on their third day of George's penne and broccoli.

'You cook them in the same pan, then when

they're draining, you use the pan again to mix in some bacon and chillies. Excellent.'

Nora said that yesterday's version had been spicier. Today's was cheesier, 'More Parmesan.' She thought a mix of the two would be best. Then regretted this; it meant she'd have to eat the same dish again tomorrow. And make notes in the small book George provided. *A bit too cheesy*, she wrote today.

'You don't have a girlfriend, George,' Nora said.

'Observant of you,' said George. 'Not at the moment I don't. I used to have. I was engaged, in fact. Beth. Tall girl, liked sports. I spent a lot of time watching people running about with balls either hitting them with a hockey stick or throwing them to one another. She left me. Said I had no ambition.'

Nora asked if that was true. Had he no ambition?

'I used to have a lot. I wanted to rise to the top. I was restless and edgy. I wanted things, success, power and all the trimmings. I just realised that I was so uptight I never enjoyed anything. I was so busy planning for some moment in the future, I stopped enjoying the one I was in. Before that, I went through a phase of wanting to have a lot of hair and no job. That was when I fell out with my family.'

'Have you made up with them?'

'A little. But I still don't want to join the family business. Right now, though, I'm pretty ambitious about my one-pot cookbook.'

'Are you being paid lots?' asked Nora.

'I'm being paid about enough to buy a new set of pots,' George told her. 'But they'll be wonderful pots.'

'Well, that's all that matters,' said Nora. She was having difficulty finishing her one-pot dish. The queasiness that had followed her bout of food poisoning still lingered.

Nora and George dined together every day. He'd come to her flat carrying his one pot, hands encased in a pair of blue oven gloves. They fell into a routine of her putting out plates and cutlery while he put the pot on the hob to heat it through. They moved about the kitchen without getting in each other's way. They chatted easily. Sometimes they drank wine. Nora told him she'd sort of gone off alcohol since her holiday illness. 'In fact,' she said, 'I've gone off all sorts of things. And I've developed a passion for tomatoes.'

George thought it was her body talking. 'Telling you what it needs. Bodies do that. There's probably something in tomatoes that's cleaning out your system.'

Nora thought this a splendid explanation and thought no more about her gastronomic urges. She ate tomatoes.

Two weeks after returning from her holiday with Nathan, the magazine closed down. The staff stayed at their desks and got busy with the new cycling publication. Brendan started work in his tiny room at the end of the corridor in the books department. He sat alone thumbing through typescripts about herbal medicines, astrology, travels in Peru, and other subjects.

Most afternoons, he took a couple of sheets of paper, tucked them under his arm, and went walking the corridors. The papers, he thought, made him appear as if he was on official business, doing something important. He'd visit George because his office had a chair for visitors to sit in, and a kettle so George could make those visitors a cup of tea. Generally, though, Brendan was miserable.

Nora reported to Farrell Greyson, editorial manager of comics, head of the third floor. She hadn't ever seen the man. It was rumoured he knew everything that went on in the building without ever leaving his office.

It was a good office, though. It was carpeted, thick grey Wilton. It felt pleasant underfoot after long working days on lino. From the window she could see across greying Edinburgh rooftops to the Castle, and beyond. Farrell Greyson sat on an old leather chair, behind a desk spread with notes, memos, letters and doodled-on pieces of paper. There were oil paintings dotted around, mostly abstracts which cheered the asylum cream of the walls. All the walls on the third floor were that same bland cream, the innocuous colour often found in mental institutions. Farrell bought his paintings each year at the Edinburgh Art College show, and was rumoured to have a valuable collection at home. Though nobody knew for sure, for nobody had ever been invited there.

He was a tall man, mid-sixties, with a penchant for flamboyant ties.

'Nora Marshall,' he said, welcoming her and waving her towards the chair on the other side of his desk. 'Come in. I asked for you.'

Nora said, 'You asked for me?'

'Yes. I cherry-pick my staff. I picked you. I'm a fan of Nadine. I think anyone who can write a thousand words every week about riding a bike to visit places, when they plainly know nothing about cycling and haven't been to any of the places they mention, has to be worth getting to know.'

'You could tell I can't ride a bike?' said Nora.

'It was becoming obvious. It seems to me you have potential. And you've made enemies, which is to be admired I always think. Nobody's worth a light till they've caused some animosity. I can tell you that neither Hugh Randall nor Jason Pierce is particularly keen on you.'

'Why? I've hardly ever spoken to either of them.'

Farrell shrugged. 'It's the way of things. I think you have the wrong chromosomes for Hugh. He's not one for promoting the careers of those among us who have mammary glands.'

'He doesn't like women?' said Nora.

'Not in the office,' Farrell told her. 'Outside of the office, I'm reliably informed, he's very fond of them. And I'm afraid when it comes to Jason, you have angered him because your column was more popular than his. Success can made you unpopular.'

Nora looked round and said, 'I like your office.'

Farrell asked if she had her eye on it, and Nora said she could have, but suspected that someone with mammary glands and the wrong set of chromosomes had little chance of reaching such dizzying heights in this organisation.

'You're probably right,' said Farrell. He slapped his hands on his desk as he stood up. 'I'll take you along to where you are to work, and introduce you to Captain Colin.'

Captain Colin was a boy wonder who saved the planet every month, flying to distant corners of the

308

earth, performing miraculous feats of strength, but always home for fish and chips and to feed his pet rabbit at five o'clock.

Nora was to work in a small office with Valerie Hyams, who had once been knitting editor of a long-defunct magazine. Valerie had been producing the comic on her own for fifteen years, but was now nearing retirement. It was Farrell's plan that Nora should, when that time came, replace her.

Valerie wrote the scripts for Captain Colin, and did everything needed to produce the comic except draw the strip. It bored her, and she did as little as possible, preferring to spend her time knitting. She sold her wares at county fairs across the country.

'See what you can do with this,' said Farrell. 'It's a bit dated. Put some pep into it.'

Captain Colin was drawn by Monty Redford, who was seventy-five, lived in Devon and was long out of touch with the world. Nora never did meet him. But she had to send him photographs of things he might need to draw—a video recorder, a stereo system, clothes. He didn't keep up much. She also had to check the spelling in the balloons, that Colin always had five fingers on each hand, and that the wallpaper in his living room was the same when he arrived home from one of his adventures as it had been when he left. It often wasn't. Monty wasn't a man who bothered with details. She also had to do the letters page and the feature article that was spread over the centre pages, plus the Captain Colin quiz, which ran on the inside page, and the editor's letter. Valerie knitted.

Spread over a month, the work Nora had to do

wasn't particularly taxing, so she, like Brendan, took to paper-carrying and corridor-wandering. She'd visit Brendan in his tiny room. They discussed the business of superheroes undressing, or if it was comfortable wearing a gaudy outfit under your clothes. They talked about flying and the ideal flying position. One hand raised, the other pressed by your side. 'So you can get the perfect cloak ripple,' said Nora.

'Upstairs,' Nora said, 'everybody flies. There isn't a single comic-book character who doesn't fly.'

'But the actual people are grounded,' said Brendan. 'Like us.'

'Yes, but they want to fly. Flight has occurred to them. Everybody wants to fly.'

'Talking of flight,' Brendan told her, 'Jen's got several job interviews coming up. The big one's in Bristol. I think my wife is heading for the top.'

Wanting to be Cat

A new quiet had entered Cathryn's life. By day she worked. Her time in the office was, at times, hectic; some colleagues were aggressive. It was definitely competitive, but, really, nothing she couldn't cope with. Evenings she spent with Clive. Over dinner they'd chat about their separate days, the future they planned, or, perhaps, exchange gossip they'd picked up. They sometimes ate out, or walked to a nearby pub. It wasn't demanding, but that was what she needed. After the storm, the calm, she thought. And, in the end, she needn't have worried about Clive's sexual performance. He'd definitely moved on from sweating and fumbling. He knew a lot about passion; life was good.

In this stillness, she found time to think, to review the Maisie situation. She started to see her mother anew. Maisie was a woman packed with emotions, too many of them. In a single day she'd visit them all, and never think of holding back. Cathryn doubted Maisie ever considered the word control. 'There's just too much Maisie,' she said to Clive. She had hardly been able to cope.

She was beginning to agree with Nora. She had said that everyone should get on with their lives. Cathryn, also, started to see her father in a new light. He'd been with Maisie for over thirty years, taking the brunt of her expansive personality. A person would either explode, or decide they'd had enough and walk away as her father had done. Cathryn didn't blame him.

She'd phoned Alex and said she wanted to see him. Now they met regularly, either for lunch in town or at his home. Cathryn hadn't wanted to like Claire, but she did. She'd stared at Alex's new partner. Nora had been right. Claire did look like Maisie, only younger, thinner and calmer. It was the only way to describe her.

Over tea one Sunday, Alex told Cathryn how unhappy Nora had been at not being invited to the wedding. 'She was really upset,' he said. 'She thought it must have been lovely, the band, the big marquee, everything.'

'I didn't have a marquee or a band,' said Cathryn. 'It was a quiet affair.'

'Try telling Nora that,' said Alex. 'She has

imagined a marquee filled with glittering people, laughing and drinking champagne. So that's what she missed.'

Cathryn sighed. 'Nora, what's she like?'

'Maisie,' said Alex. 'Only Nora's not over the top like her mother. But same active imagination. It's probably why they don't get on.'

Then Cathryn said, 'You're in touch with her?'

'Oh yes, she phones, or I phone her, once a week, at least.'

'She seems to be worrying about broken hearts at the moment,' said Cathryn.

'You've been buying her cycling magazine,' said Alex.

'Yes, every week. I'm quite addicted to Nadine.'

Alex told her Claire was, too. 'And your Auntie May. It's folding, though. There will be no more Nadine after Christmas.'

'What about Nora?' said Cathryn.

'The magazine is already finished. But there are some issues still to come out. Nora's in a new job on a comic.'

'What will she make of that?' said Cathryn.

'She's doing fine.' Alex said. 'Hated it at first, but she's settled into it. She has left Nadine behind and is now concerned with Captain Colin.'

Cathryn shook her head. 'It's all nonsense.' But she made a note to start buying the comic. 'I'll miss Nadine, though.'

It had taken Cathryn some time to say sorry to her father. It was their third lunch together when she told him she wanted to apologise for directing Maisie towards the lawyer who fleeced him over the divorce. He said there was no need to say sorry. He'd been rather proud of her and had wished she'd been on his side.

In fact, he'd been quite affable about it. 'Made me feel better about leaving her,' Alex said. 'Sort of eased my conscience. It couldn't have been easy for her.'

Cathryn had told him it hadn't been. And still wasn't.

'She isn't obsessing about anything, is she? Because that's what she does. Gets worked into a lather, then blows like a volcano.'

Cathryn shook her head. 'No. She seems calm enough. In fact, last time I saw her, she was the happiest I've seen her in ages.'

Alex said, 'Ah.' He knew Maisie. If she was happy, she'd either got over her trauma, or she had embarked on some hare-brained scheme. He suspected the latter.

Cathryn also visited Maisie regularly. She popped in several times a week and always made time on a Saturday to spend a couple of hours with her mother. This weekend, Cathryn was entertaining, and to give herself time to shop and cook, something that made her nervous, she'd dropped in on Friday night.

The door was locked. Fearing something dire had happened to Maisie, Cathryn let herself in. She wandered from room to room, shouting, 'Hello. Hello.' But the house was empty. Good, she thought, Maisie's on the mend, getting out and about. She decided to wait a while in case her mother came home. It would be interesting to know where she'd been. Perhaps she'd made some new friends.

Waiting wasn't something that came easily to Cathryn. She paced, then sat in Maisie's chair.

Thinking she might watch the television, she looked about for the guide, and discovered the bottle of sherry her mother kept handy on the floor beside her. Cathryn shrugged. Why not? Maisie made no secret of her fondness for a glass of an evening.

Thinking she would make a cup of tea, and perhaps prepare a meal for Maisie for when she returned, Cathryn went into the kitchen. She opened the large cupboard where the cups were stored, and saw, lined neatly on the floor, Maisie's stash of wine, bottles and bottles of Claire's favourite Sauvignon Blanc, along with a fair collection of Alex's favoured Merlot.

Cathryn stared at them. She couldn't remember Maisie ever drinking wine. Weird, she thought. She felt unsettled. She was snooping. If Maisie were to turn up now, Cathryn wouldn't know what to say to her. She hurried from the room, picked up her coat and handbag, and left. She put her car into gear, and hammered away down the street, anxious to get away lest Maisie turn the corner and see her.

Driving home, Cathryn decided to say nothing to Clive about the wine stash. Things weren't going too well between them. Her fault, she thought. She'd married too quickly and for the wrong reasons. She'd been swept off her feet by notions. A flat, a handsome, caring husband, an enviable job. Who wouldn't want all that? But more, she'd married because she'd needed to start a new life for herself. Only, she thought, perhaps she had chosen the wrong life. She needed involvement, people. Before, in Manchester, there had been that feeling almost every day that while she had a diary and appointments and regular clients,

314

something might happen. There was always an element of surprise. She yearned for her days in Manchester. She wanted her old job back.

She hadn't realised how much she'd enjoyed it, till she left it. She'd worked for a busy legal practice, and had a wide-ranging list of clients. There had been messy divorces, a woman fighting her landlord over an illegal eviction, a young man taking on his employers over a wrongful dismissal, a family at odds with their neighbours over the strip of land separating their houses, a seventy-five-year-old charged with shoplifting, an eighteen-year-old caught stealing a bus.

'It was interesting,' she'd told Clive. 'I felt energised. Well, some of the time. You never knew what was going to come up next. Who was going to walk through the door. There was humanity. I was doing some good.'

'And you're not now?' he'd asked.

'Yes. But it's not the same. There are some fascinating, even famous, people, but I don't deal with them. I look out for potential libel actions. I nitpick. The clothes are better, and the coffee is upmarket, no longer instant. My colleagues are urbane and ambitious. The jokes more sophisticated. And there are definitely opportunities I'd never have dreamed of in my last job. But I miss it.'

Clive said he understood. But sometimes you had to give up something to get something else. And what Cathryn had got was a superb pay hike and a classy modern work environment, rather than a shoddy office.

'I know it was shoddy. But I kept plants on the windowsill. I had lovely cushions on the chairs. Till

315

a client stole them. I got a glimpse into people's lives. Things I would never have imagined. There was one old lady came every other month who was convinced her neighbours upstairs were bugging her flat. She said she could hear their voices. She said they hadn't done a proper job of bugging her flat and that's why she could hear them as well as them hearing her.'

'She shouldn't have been in your office, then. There are establishments who deal with people who hear voices,' said Clive.

'Thank goodness they didn't get hold of her. She used to bring us in scones. Anyway, one day my boss said I ought to go round to her flat and see if anything really was going on. So I went. I looked round to see if I could spot any bugging devices, though what they're actually like, I do not know. Then I heard voices. I thought I was going mad. But I traced them. Turns out the block of flats had once been a huge house that belonged to some rich importer. There had been a small lift shaft that had connected the top floor to the kitchen, and when the builders had converted the building they hadn't closed it off. I put the old lady's mind at ease. She wasn't being bugged. She was right, she was hearing voices. I wrote to the people in the flat above and told them about the old lift shaft, and they and the old lady split the cost of having it blocked. I helped.'

'So you want to go back to helping old ladies who give you scones, and teenagers who steal buses and people who are about to get evicted, and probably illegal immigrants, drug addicts, prostitutes and God knows what else?'

'Yes,' she said. 'I do.'

If this surprised Clive, it astonished Cathryn. Only weeks ago, she'd been heady with plans for the life she was going to have. She'd imagined dinner parties, glistening with sophistication, a larger flat. She'd had visions of herself in Dior suits swishing through London streets in a BMW. And now here she was, absurdly nostalgic about an old lady who imagined her flat was bugged, and who baked her scones. And a teenage boy with a baseball cap on the wrong way round and dazzlingly expensive training shoes on his feet who'd stolen a bus.

'Why on earth did you do it?' she'd asked him.

He'd looked at her as if she was brainless. 'It was there,' he said. 'An' the driver had gone off an' left the keys in. I mean, I couldn't not take it, could I? You'd have taken it too, Cat.'

'I don't think so.'

'Come on, if you'd been there, you'd have had to. Admit it, Cat.'

Cat. That was another thing, everyone back then had called her Cat. She *had* been Cat. Only Clive, Maisie and her Aunt May called her Cathryn. She wanted to be Cat again.

She'd known Clive since she'd been at school. She didn't really have a nasty word to say about him. Except that, after a few months of marriage, she knew she didn't love him. He was kind, considerate, he worked hard, and everything he planned, he planned for the both of them. Thing was, his plans didn't match her plans. He wanted to move to the country one day, to a large house with a huge rolling garden. They'd have three or four children. She wanted to move to a town house, small garden, no more than two children.

When choosing a car, he wanted something large and comfortable, good for the motorway. She wanted a car that was easily parked and quite sporty. When buying things for their flat, they'd found they had totally opposing tastes in everything from rugs to cups. He was a considerate man, he let Cathryn have her way, most of the time. Once they'd even discussed buying a dog. She wanted a companionable, reasonably sized pet that didn't need a lot of exercise; he wanted a deerhound. For the moment, they laughed about their differences. Both knew that some day they'd have to face a decision too important for laughter. One of them would have to give in to the desires of the other.

No, she thought, as she drove home from Maisie's house, she would not tell him about the wine stash. He'd want to do something about it right away. She wanted to find out what it was about first.

She feared the worst. Maisie was a shoplifter. Deranged with insecurity and grief over her lost marriage, she'd been going out on stealing sprees, taking anything she could get her hands on. Cathryn remembered dealing with such a case in her last job. The woman had got a six-month suspended sentence. She decided she would quietly sort things out before they got out of hand. Indeed, before Maisie got caught and brought scandal and disgrace upon the family. And most of all, on herself.

*　　　*　　　*

May had eaten, washed her dishes and was settling

down to watch a television quiz show when the doorbell rang. 'Ach,' she said. 'Who's that this time of night?'

It was Alex.

'You,' said May. 'What do you want?'

'I need a word. About Maisie,' he told her.

'What about Maisie?' she said. 'I thought you'd got all that settled.'

'Something's come up,' he said.

She invited him in, barged down the hall ahead of him, telling him she'd just been about to watch one of her programmes. 'This better be good.'

'Oh, this is good,' he said. 'This is excellent.'

'So,' she said, sitting down and slipping a last sad look at her television screen before switching it off. 'Tell me.'

She hadn't yet forgiven Alex for walking out on Maisie. She thought that marriage was for life. You made your bed, you lay on it. But there was a small voice that sneaked into her mind now and then and told her that she couldn't have put up with Maisie for as long as Alex had. Sometimes she didn't blame him at all.

'Maisie is making a nuisance of herself,' said Alex. 'She is stalking me.'

May said she'd never heard anything so ridiculous in her life.

Alex said he could assure her it was true. 'She stands outside the house several nights a week, looking in. Then on Fridays she follows me and Claire round the supermarket.'

May put her hand to her face, rubbed her eyebrow. 'Oh, Maisie,' she said. Then, 'I better put the kettle on.'

She disappeared into the kitchen, then came

back, holding the kettle. 'Are you sure it's Maisie?'

'Am I sure it's Maisie? Come on, May. I was married to the woman for over thirty years. I'd recognise her anywhere. There aren't many people I know who wear a bright red coat. Not *that* red, anyway.'

May smiled. 'She was always fond of a bit of colour. Nobody ever had the nerve to tell her that some bits of colour don't seem that fond of her.'

She disappeared again. Alex heard the kettle being filled, the gas being switched on.

May came back into the room again, waiting for the water to boil. 'I can't believe she put on that red coat to go stalking somebody. You can see it for miles. Did she not think to disguise herself a bit? That's what I'd do if I was going out stalking.'

The kettle boiled; May disappeared again. When she returned, she was carrying a tray, heavy with a teapot, cups, saucers and a plate of walnut cake. 'Tuck in,' she said.

Alex would have told her that he'd just eaten, but he knew that May didn't see that as a reason not to eat some more. Besides, she couldn't mull over problems without something in her mouth. Cake would be consumed.

'Now tell me about it,' she said.

'I told you,' said Alex. 'She appears outside the house, peering. She follows us round the supermarket, buying the same things we buy. She peeks round the end of the aisles watching us. Sometimes I backtrack and follow her. I slip up another aisle and come up behind her. I didn't read *Last of the Mohicans* for nothing. She never notices. Too busy checking on Claire.'

May said, 'Yes. Indeed. Sometimes I think

320

Maisie is the stupidest person I've ever come across. She has no inner life. It's all on show. She just lets rip. Has an idea and follows it through.'

Alex said nothing.

'Of course, she's a lovely person. Underneath all that stuff, the tantrums and moods, there's a lovely person trying to get out.'

Again, Alex said nothing.

'It was all get, get, get with Maisie. She was the youngest. Spoiled. She never understood about giving. You know, giving love to get it back. I don't think she ever learned how to handle her emotions. She just has them, and lets everyone know about it.'

'I'd agree with that,' said Alex. 'She engulfs herself in whatever emotion she's feeling. Then it all comes spewing out. It was like living with a volcano.'

'My favourite volcano,' said May. 'She never ceases to amaze me. You have to hand it to her, she's entertaining.'

'I can think of better ways to be entertained,' said Alex. Then he snorted. 'She stands outside the house, bobbing about, desperate to see in. You can spot the little face moving about out there. She seems shiny and eager.' He laughed.

'It's hard for her. All that time, people coming and going. Then suddenly, nothing. Silence, and nobody to speak to. Time on her hands. You've got to feel for her.'

'I do. But I can't have her following me about.'

'You want me to speak to her,' said May.

'Yes. Of course I do.' He couldn't think of anything else. He could could call the police, but Maisie wasn't really doing any harm. What really bothered him was that Claire wanted to talk to her, to tell her to go away. He had horrible visions of a screaming match in the supermarket. It would be too much to bear. He could never go back there. It was so convenient, too.

'Have you spoken to Nora recently?' he asked.

May told him she had. 'On the phone most weeks. She's fine. Got herself a young man.'

Alex smiled and told her he knew. 'Nathan.' He said he was thinking of going to visit her.

'You should,' said May. 'Doesn't do to let your family slip away.'

'Maisie has let her slip away,' said Alex.

'Never mind Maisie. She'll come round. She's just stubborn.'

When Alex had gone, May switched the television on again. She planned to go and talk to Maisie tomorrow, but remembered she had her ladies' club outing to Brighton. The day after that she had her bridge club. Then there was a talk about Love and Sex in the Novels of Jane Austen at the local library. Can't miss that, May told herself, I like Jane Austen, and I liked a bit of sex when I could get it. Then a trip to a West End show with her friends at the over-sixties swimming club. It would have to wait till next week.

*   *   *

Nora had long mastered the art of walking through city streets alone. She had learned it as a child when she'd wandered, killing time, before she went home. Don't stare at people, unless they are seeking to be stared at. Then you might get away with it. Look up, because buildings are lovely, but

322

keep a keen eye on the ground beneath your feet. Cracks and lines. Mostly, though, always appear as if you know where you are going. Aimless meandering leaves a person open to questions from kindly people asking if you are lost. And to being badgered by beggars, odd strangers with dubious motives, and out-and-out nutcases. A person with their mind on a destination usually gets left alone.

She now followed her street rules instinctively. Today, after work, she'd taken the bus to Princes Street, bought a new pair of shoes, and headed back to her flat on foot. She needed to think.

The Festival was over. But notices, flyers and posters still lingered in shop windows, pasted on to doorways and hoardings. She liked Festival time, the bustle, the throngs. But knew it was a novelty thing. In time, she'd be like other Edinburgh residents, avoiding pubs that were in the heart of the city, taking roundabout routes to keep clear of the extra traffic, but still going to one or two shows. She, Brendan and Jen had gone to some late-night concerts, a few films, and as many free exhibitions as they could fit in.

Making her way up the Mound, past the queuing cars waiting for the traffic lights to change from red, she noticed how many BMWs and Golf GTis there were. And most of them black. Driven by people in black. People who shouted and spoke in braying voices in public. Two of them could come into a bar and seem to fill the place. Braggarts swaggering. A time of swaggarts. There's no humanity, no place for angels here.

She thought she might need an angel. A grim realisation had seeped into her mind yesterday.

She had told Brendan how incredibly well she felt. She was thinking of her wellbeing now. Food poisoning didn't linger for weeks, she was pretty sure of that. You ate something nasty, your body threw it out, one way or another. Then you got better.

And you weren't just sick in the morning. Then relatively fine for the rest of the day. Food poisoning didn't give you sore breasts, put you off alcohol, give you a strange desire to eat tomatoes, and stop your periods. That she knew for a fact. But there was one thing that did all that. She was pregnant.

How had that happened? Well, she knew how. But she was on the pill. She vaguely remembered the doctor at the clinic where she'd gone to get her prescription telling her to take extra precautions if she had a stomach upset, sickness or diarrhoea. But she hadn't paid much attention because she was meeting Brendan. They were going to see *Diva*.

I loved that film, she thought. That huge warehouse-garage-type flat and the young girl skating round it. Jules and the opera singer walking, him with a white umbrella over her head. The aria the woman sang from Catalani's *La Wally*.

She stopped. That's what's wrong with me. I don't concentrate. I drift off. I'm pregnant. Think about that. She worried. The awful thing about pregnancy is it's so inevitable. The thing has to come out, sooner or later.

If she chose sooner, it would have to be very soon. If later, then she'd have six months of hell. She figured she'd done three. There would be a birth. Would Nathan be there? What would he say when she told him? How would she care for a baby? What did babies do? Sleep, eat, shit. There must be more to them than that, she thought. Else people wouldn't have more than one. Many people, she noticed, did.

She'd have to tell other people as well as Nathan. Brendan. Her mother? She didn't know about that. She hurried. Worrying made her walk quickly. Besides, George was making risotto tonight. As he had last night, and the night before. He'd told her that next week she would have to eat at his place. 'I need to get the hang of cooking when there's someone about. That's part of the book, cooking while chatting. Easy recipes to come home to.'

She'd have to tell George, too. She thought she couldn't do it. The whole thing was defeating her already. So she thought about *Diva*, trying to remember the name of the singer of the wonderful aria. It came to her as she hurried along Potter's Row. 'Wilhelmenia Fernandez,' she said out loud. 'Wilhelmenia Fernandez, great name.' She thought she could call her baby this. I'm Nora Marshall and this is my daughter Wilhelmenia Fernandez. She breathed, she told herself to stop being silly. This was serious.

Something Happening
in My Body
Without Me Knowing About It

The first sniff of autumn always made Nora feel melancholy. There was no real reason for this, for it was her favourite season. She liked cool evenings, and by far preferred winter clothes to summer ones. But there it was: a certain sadness welled inside her when she realised the nights were drawing in and it would be getting dark by the time she reached home after work. She thought it might have something to do with her childhood. The days when she returned to school after the freedom of six weeks' holidays. The glum donning of her uniform, pleated skirt, white shirt, striped tie, which she hated. But more than that, it had a lot to do with her feet. The regulation clumpy black lace-up shoes she was forced to wear. They were heavy and cumbersome after months of sandals and no socks. Imprisoning her feet in these loathsome things, tying the black laces, was the final act that meant the inevitable discipline of nine-to-half-past-three routine.

So Nora always wore easy shoes that made her feet happy. Today it was tennis shoes. She and Brendan had been to the antenatal clinic. She thought the nurse had looked a little confused, as the last time she'd been, George had accompanied her.

'They wouldn't have noticed,' said Brendan. 'They see so many preggie woman, you all look the same to them.'

'I don't think that's true. They're very kind.'

'I thought so too. Then, of course, it's easy for them. They're not pregnant.'

Nora said she was going to have to tell people, and was dreading this.

'Don't bother,' said Brendan. 'Everyone already knows. You shouldn't have told Mona.'

'Don't,' said Nora.

'Don't what?'

'Ask about Nathan. You were just about to. He went white when I told him, and when I said the doctor thought I'd left it a little late for an abortion, he went whiter.'

The first person Nora told about her pregnancy was George. She thought this was because he was there. They saw one another every day. He had said, 'That's wonderful.' Then, thinking about the complications she'd be a single mother, how was she going to manage?—had added, 'Isn't it?' Nora had told him she didn't know. She was numb. 'Something happened in my body without me knowing about it.'

After that, she'd told Brendan and Jen, who also congratulated her. Then gave her the same dubious look as George. Mona had dropped by one evening to collect some clothes she'd left behind when she moved, and had stayed to chat. She had put the kettle on and fetched cups from the cupboard, reminding Nora that she was but a sitting tenant, this flat was still Mona's. It was a territorial thing.

Thinking her landlady should know that soon there would be two people living in her property, Nora had told her about the baby.

Mona had come straight to the point. 'How did

that happen? Don't you take precautions?'

Nora told her yes, she was on the pill. 'But I got sick.'

'You're going to keep it then?' said Mona.

Nora nodded. 'I can't face doing something about it. It's more complicated at this stage. Having the baby seems easier.'

Mona thought it wouldn't seem easier when the child was born and Nora faced sleepless nights, feeding, teething and the breakdown of life as she knew it, but said nothing. She gazed round at her kitchen, wondering what it would look like when an infant was being catered for. It wasn't a good prospect.

'Is Nathan pleased?'

'Nathan doesn't know,' said Nora. 'I haven't told him.'

Mona nodded. She could see why Nora hadn't told him. He wouldn't be pleased at all.

He wasn't. It was Saturday. Nora had come to his flat, as always. At the door they'd kissed, as always. He'd led her into the living room; they'd kissed again. He'd slid his arms round her waist and told her she was putting on weight. 'I'll have to tell George to stop feeding you.'

'I'm getting fat,' said Nora. 'And I'm going to get fatter.'

She hadn't needed to say any more. He'd paled, sunk on to the sofa. 'How far on are you?'

'About four months. It was when we were on holiday.'

'You're keeping it, then?'

'It's a bit late to do anything else. So, yes, I'm keeping it.'

Nora watched as he went even paler; he was

328

shaken by this. 'I hoped you'd be pleased,' she said.

He hadn't answered. He knew he should tell Nora it was wonderful she was expecting his child; he should buy her flowers, tell her to put her feet up as he cooked a splendid meal. He should make a fuss of her.

But he couldn't. This was not what he had planned. Over the past few weeks he'd been getting closer to Lorna. It was happening slowly. First he'd been allowed to pick up Justine from the house instead of meeting her in town. Then, when dropping her off, he'd been asked in and offered coffee. Last week, he'd lingered in the kitchen, chatting, and had stayed to eat. The atmosphere had been friendly, he thought. There were signals; at least, he imagined there were signals.

He had decided that if he was right, and Lorna was considering taking him back, he would have to finish his affair with Nora. He was going to do this gently. He had small speeches written in his head. She needed someone who was the same age as she was. He couldn't give her the fun she'd enjoy. He was too old for some of the things she wanted to do. This was a special stage in her life, she shouldn't waste it with someone who wanted a quiet time. Now this. She'd ruined everything. He cursed himself for taking her on holiday with him. He knew it wasn't all her fault. He'd had a big part in the conception. In fact, it wouldn't have happened without him. But still, he blamed Nora. And he didn't want another child.

'So,' he'd said. 'A baby. You just never know what's round the corner, do you?'

Now, Nora told Brendan, 'We don't talk about it

much. We don't talk about names or what we'll do when the baby comes.'

'He's got a child. He probably wasn't planning on another. You shouldn't have waited so long before going to a doctor.'

'I know. I couldn't make up my mind what to do.'

She didn't quite believe herself. She thought she'd dithered because she had secretly wanted the baby, and didn't want to be offered the option of an abortion. Yet not that long ago, she'd been adamant she hadn't wanted a child, ever. But she'd conceived, and hadn't been able to get rid of the baby. She'd stayed pregnant.

'Maybe I just want someone to love,' she suggested to Brendan.

'Don't we all,' said Brendan. 'But I think your way of doing that is a bit extreme. Most folks go clubbing or scour the personal ads.'

'Never thought of that,' said Nora. 'Damn.'

After Nora's appointment at the clinic, they'd headed for the High Street. Without discussing it, they'd walked towards Holyrood Park. The day had started warm, but was turning chilly. Neither of them wore coats, so they went into a coffee shop. Brendan ordered tea, Nora an espresso. 'Though it'll give me indigestion.'

Brendan wanted to know if she was scared.

'Terrified,' she said. 'So I try not to think about it. George doesn't help. He reads all these books and tells me what's happening. As in, it'll have fingernails. Actually, he bought all the books. He's keen on the whole thing. A lot keener than me. He feeds me spinach and broccoli.'

'I'm finding it a bit scary,' said Brendan. 'A baby

will disturb the flow of things.'

'Rubbish. You can push the buggy. I'll chat.'

Brendan smiled. He agreed with Jen, on this, at least. Nora had no idea about having a child. She was under the impression she'd go into hospital, give birth, come home and carry on as before. 'It's going to hit her hard,' Jen had said.

*   *   *

Sitting alone in the evenings, Maisie thought about Nora. She wanted to see her again; she missed her. Several times, she'd phoned. But Nora was never in. Maisie was impressed. Nora must have a wonderful social life. In fact, Nora had been upstairs helping with the cookbook. But how could Maisie know this? Imagining Nora's wild nightlife, Maisie felt shy. Nora was young, surrounded by friends; she was an old lady with a sherry habit who'd been caught stalking. Who would want to know her?

Sitting in her chair watching *Columbo* reruns, Maisie sipped sherry and thought about Alex. It was strange not having him in her bed. She still hadn't got used to it, still hadn't claimed the whole mattress and duvet as her own, still left room for him. She still bought lamb chops, which she knew he liked, and still had problems every Wednesday night when she put her bin out for the rubbish collector in the morning. She thought it was his job.

What did he do on a Saturday? Did he still wash the car? Did he and Claire go out together? Did they have friends round for supper? She had to know. It was an itch, a longing. It wouldn't go

331

away. The more sherry she sipped, the more reasonable it seemed to go to his house. And find out. Why not? She had a right. After all, Alex had, for years and years, been a vital part of her own Saturdays. The lure was irresistible. She *had* to go.

The street was quiet. But Maisie thought it had a Saturday feel about it. It was strange how one day of the week could feel and look different from the rest. You could get up in the morning, look out of the window and know it was Saturday, even though nothing had changed from the day before.

On her first trip past, Maisie paused. Inside she could see the same pale walls and pictures she'd seen before. Someone had left a jacket draped over the back of the sofa. That was interesting. She walked on, and round the block.

The second time she arrived outside the house, she stopped. There seemed to be nobody in. She stood on tiptoe, hoping to get a more satisfactory view of the interior. She saw a coffee table, magazines strewn on its shiny surface. She stared in, and drifted into a balmy little dream, imagining herself inside, sitting on that sofa, reading one of the magazines. She was so entangled in her thoughts, she hardly noticed Alex and Claire coming to the window to stare out at her.

It was probably one of the most humiliating moments of her life, the two of them, side by side, watching her watching them. It was silent. She could see they were not saying anything. But they both had the same expression on their faces, a mix of horror and disapproval. She knew she looked mortified. She knew she should have turned and walked away. But she didn't, she just stood.

The staring only lasted a minute or so, but

whenever Maisie revisited the scene in her head, something she did often in years to come, it seemed like an age. Time stopped. Then Claire said something to Alex. He turned, picked up his jacket.

In the fleeting moments it took for Alex to grab his jacket, collect his car keys and join her outside, things that Maisie had long banished from her memory came back to her. Flashbacks, spinning through her mind, in this moment of losing everything—the man, she realised too late, she loved dearly.

Alex the young man who wore, when he was not in his army uniform, black turtlenecks and soft flannel trousers. He'd liked jazz, Louis Armstrong and Jelly Roll Morton. She'd liked musicals. He'd said, 'Great.' She'd said, 'That's nice.' He'd read the First World War poets, Siegfried Sassoon, Rupert Brooke. She'd read historical romances. He'd wanted to travel, to see a bit of the world before they settled down. She'd just wanted to settle down.

If they went out at night, he wanted to go to small jazz clubs that were down narrow streets, in parts of town she rarely visited. People there would listen, serious-faced, to music that sounded wild and noisy to her. She'd look gaudy in these clubs, wearing her bright floral tight-waisted frocks. She'd sit looking uncomfortable and bored, saying, 'Is that it? Can we go now?' A night out to her was a meal somewhere, a steak, perhaps, or shepherd's pie, followed by lemon meringue pie. Bright shiny nights on the town. And a taxi home. He liked walking the night streets.

When they'd bought furniture, he'd wanted

sparse. A chair, a sofa, a record player and a lamp. She'd wanted a proper three-piece suite, bulky and comfortable.

And how had they ended up? They'd settled down, listened to musicals sitting on their three-piece suite, and from time to time they had the odd shiny night out, with a taxi home.

He'd brought home records, put them on, but she had always curtailed his pleasure. What had happened to all those records? Alex's jazz collection. She remembered, and was shamed. She'd thrown them out. 'We'll not be needing this rubbish,' she told herself, and tossed them away with the garbage.

He'd longed to go to San Francisco. 'To walk where Ginsberg walked. To see it all, even the fog.' She'd been happy with suburban life, suburban weather. His ideas about everything scared her. She'd only ever wanted to be safe.

She had wanted to satisfy her notion of how respectable people lived. She'd desperately wanted the approval of her sister May and her parents. He'd wanted to please himself. Standing here, on the pavement outside Alex's house, she saw it all. He'd abandoned his dreams to please her. Long ago, when they'd been young, those dreams had seemed crazy to her. Now they seemed simple and possible.

Why did we marry? she thought. We had nothing in common. What were we thinking of?

Then he was by her side. 'Get in the car,' he said. 'I'll take you home.'

It was a stiff, awkward journey. They hardly spoke. When he drew up at her front gate, they sat a moment.

'Maisie,' said Alex. 'This won't do.'

She said she was aware of that. It wouldn't happen again. 'I just wanted to know,' she said, 'where you live now. What you do. I think about you.'

'I think about you. And Nora and Cathryn,' he said. 'You don't just live a life then walk away and forget it.'

'You weren't there when I came home that time from seeing Nora. And I hardly saw you again. It just ended.'

He said that really it had ended long before that.

'You live your life,' said Maisie. 'And nothing happens. You just get on with the day-to-day. Peeling potatoes, putting meals on the table, dusting the dresser, washing the kitchen floor. It's all part of the nothing that happens, years and years of it. Then a whole load of things happen, all together. And suddenly. Like there's been a tornado you didn't notice on your doorstep, waiting to sweep you away. And all the things you did through the nothing-happening years were worthless.'

He said he knew.

'I just can't get used to it. I wanted to see you again. I needed to know where you were so I could picture you when I thought of you. I was angry for such a long time. Then it stopped. That's when I needed to know where you were.'

'Well, now you know.' He hated the words that gathered in his mind. Phrases he'd read. Get a life, Maisie. Move on, Maisie. He thought them heartless.

Instead he said, 'You make a crap spy, Maisie.

335

Your stalking techniques are diabolical.'

Maisie smiled, said, 'I was thinking that myself. I think I'll give it up. I had the notion I could talk to you, persuade you to come back.'

'Maisie,' said Alex. 'That won't happen. I'm sorry.'

Maisie said, 'I'm sorry, too. I'm sorry for everything. I'm sorry I threw out your jazz records. I'm sorry.'

She got out of the car, walked up the path, unlocked her front door and went in. She hung her coat on the hall stand. Walked into the living room, switched on the television so the room was filled with Saturday-evening heartiness. But she felt awful. She was beaten down and bruised with shame and humiliation. She hated herself.

It wasn't Alex. He'd been kind, a lot kinder than she deserved. It was Claire that had done it. Just before Alex had arrived at her side, she'd looked at Claire. The expression on her face was shocking. It took Maisie's embarrassment to the depths of howling mortification. Claire's expression had been calm, slightly pained, and pitying. This was what had truly wounded Maisie. She'd seen that Claire was sorry for her.

Two days later, May came round. She bustled down the hall and into the kitchen, sat down, unbuttoned her coat, and said, 'Have you been making a pest of yourself with Alex?'

'I don't know what you mean,' said Maisie.

'You know what I mean all right. Alex came to see me, said you'd been stalking him and Claire.'

'I just walked by their house, taking a wee peek in, as you do, when you pass houses and the curtains are open. I wanted to see where he was

336

living. I've a right after years of marriage. You don't just stop caring, you know.'

May said, 'Stop it. Let him go.'

'Why should I? I cooked and cleaned all those years. I don't know what I did wrong.'

May said, 'Maybe you didn't do anything wrong. Maybe he just changed.'

They said no more about it.

But Maisie felt humiliated. She thought Alex should have come to talk to her, not May. That was all she'd wanted, just to talk to him. Just to say goodbye. By now, she had convinced herself of that.

Rabbit Impersonations

Farrell Greyson had shrugged when Valerie Hyams had mentioned, in one of their rare meetings on the stairs as they were both leaving, that the new girl was pregnant. 'You'll have to be finding someone else,' she'd said.

Farrell said he'd wait and see. And that he rather liked the colour of the jumper Valerie was working on. Her knitting was plainly on view at the top of her bag.

He wasn't surprised, then, when his secretary, Mrs Blackstoke, told him Miss Marshall was wanting a word with him.

'So,' he said, when Nora was shown into his office, 'you wanted to see me.'

Nora said she did. 'About the rabbit,' she said.

'The rabbit? I thought you'd be after maternity leave.'

'That, and the rabbit,' said Nora.

'When are you due?'

'March or early April,' she said. 'I was hoping to work up to the birth, then take a few months after that.'

'A few months seems vague,' he said. 'I think the company policy is three. But we can look at letting you do some work from home.'

Nora said, 'Thank you.'

'How's Nathan taking to the notion of being a father again?'

He really did know everything that went on.

'He seems to be getting over the shock. I think as long as the baby's tasteful and cries melodically we'll be all right.'

Farrell smiled. 'That's Nathan.'

Nora said, 'The rabbit.'

'Ah, yes, the rabbit. What rabbit?'

'Captain Colin has a rabbit. I thought we could do something with him. Only there's a blank page at the end of the comic, and it occurred to me to fill it. The strip always starts and ends with Colin feeding his rabbit. I thought the readers might like to know a bit more about it.'

'A view from the hutch,' said Farrell.

'No,' said Nora. 'Well, the first one would start with the rabbit sort of sniffing and chewing, the way rabbits do.' She gave a demonstration, a sniffing and twitching of her nose.

'Good rabbit impersonation,' said Farrell.

Nora wished she hadn't done it. 'It would be looking sort of blankly at the readers. Then it would say, "Wanna come in? Have a look about?" And it would open the hutch and invite the readers in.'

338

'How would it do that? It's a rabbit.'

'How do blokes in silly, embarrassing outfits fly? They're blokes.'

Farrell smiled. 'You win that one.'

'So we go into the hutch. And it looks small from the outside. But inside it's huge. He opens a door at the back, and there's his real room. It's cool. A huge cupboard thing where he keeps his shoes. That's all the clothes he wears, training shoes.'

'Training shoes?' said Farrell. 'A rabbit with training shoes? And are these training shoes magic, or plain?'

'Magic, I'd thought,' said Nora. 'And he's got a big leather swivel-type chair and a huge stereo with earphones and a wall lined with records. A television, of course. And a phone.'

'He'll get calls on his phone whenever somebody needs a rabbit to avert some national disaster.'

'Yes,' said Nora. 'Or maybe just to help someone in distress.'

'Of course,' said Farrell. 'And does he fly?'

'Everybody on the third floor flies,' said Nora.

'You've noticed that too,' said Farrell. 'So, the rabbit flies and wears shoes. If I went out dressed only in a pair of shoes, young Nora, I'd get arrested.'

'You're not a rabbit,' said Nora. 'Presumably you can't fly either.'

'Well, certainly not unaided. I need an aeroplane. Even then, I'm not that happy about it.'

'So, then,' said Nora, 'the rabbit goes out, walks about the city, where he's lippy and has street cred and does a bit of superhero stuff, and comes home again. It ends up we see him in his hutch, sniffing and chewing.'

'Please do not do the rabbit impersonation again,' said Farrell.

'I wasn't going to,' said Nora. 'I regretted it the first time. I don't think animal imitations do much to give viability to projects you are pushing.'

'I'd noticed that,' Farrell agreed.

'Anyway,' said Nora, 'at the end he always says, "Remember, the rabbit is more than just a rabbit."'

'And,' said Farrell, 'at what point does this rabbit cease to be a pet rodent and develop superpowers?'

'When he puts on the shoes,' said Nora.

'Shoes,' said Farrell. 'They seem to be a big thing with the young these days. I have a grandson who knows more about shoes than I thought there was to know.'

'Shoes are the thing,' said Nora. 'Then, at the bottom of the page, I thought that the rabbit could give us all a piece of advice. Like eating greens, being kind to old ladies, stuff like that. Only it would be funny, hopefully.'

'Well,' said Farrell, 'why don't we give it a go? Do me some scripts.'

Nora gave him the folder she'd been holding. 'The first four. Along with some sketches.'

'Who did you use?'

'Jimmy Keynes. He's got a couple of kids. He speaks the language.'

Farrell smiled. He watched Nora eyeing up his paintings. 'You like?'

'Yes,' she said. 'Very much. Except the orangey one. It's a bit brash. But maybe that's just me. I'm a bit hormonal these days.'

'Yes, it can do that to you. I have five children, five pregnancies. Five times my wife wanted ice cream in the night and drank a worrying amount of tomato juice. She got hormonal too. It passes, you'll be pleased to know.'

Nora said she'd been hoping it would.

He asked her if she'd like to come and see his etchings some time. Nora said, 'Well, I . . .'

'Oh, don't worry about it. I'm not a dirty old man. Well, I may be but I don't do anything about it. Anyway, I may be alone here, but at home I'm crowded out. There's always a child or two hanging about, wanting to be fed. And often a scattering of grandchildren. Not to mention my wife. She wouldn't like it if I didn't mention her. She's very mentionable.'

Nora said she'd be delighted to come and see his etchings and meet his mentionable wife.

'I hope you are eating well,' said Farrell.

'George Henry is feeding me.'

'Ah, you're the guinea pig for his cookbook.'

'You really do know everything,' said Nora.

'I sit here and all the information in the building floats up to me.'

Nora looked at him in awe.

'I have a gossip for a secretary. Specially chosen for that attribute. But don't tell anybody. I like people to think I have some mysterious power.'

'If only you could fly,' said Nora.

'If only,' he said. 'I'd fly away.'

She left his office. Jubilant. Walking back along the corridor, she did a little skip.

When she arrived home that night, there was a letter from her father waiting for her. He was, he said, coming to Scotland for a short holiday and planned to drop in on her. *Unfortunately, by the time you get this letter, Claire and I will be on our way. We are stopping for a night in York. I hope to see you the day after tomorrow. Looking forward to it, haven't seen Edinburgh in years. Best, Alex.*

So, he's coming tomorrow, she thought. And wondered why he'd called himself Alex and not Dad, which was how she thought of him. A shift in the relationship, perhaps. Then again, when she thought about it, it had been a while since he'd done anything dad-like.

'He's quiet,' she told George. He was on to stir fries. 'Never said much. I can hardly recall having a conversation with him.'

'Sad,' said George. 'You've got to finely chop the veg.'

'My mother sulked, raged, was sometimes lovely. She used to sing all day. But Dad was just quiet.'

'There would have been a man inside the quietness,' said George.

Nora stopped chopping. 'That's disturbingly profound.'

'I can do profound from time to time,' he said.

Nora told him about going to see Farrell Greyson. 'He just gave me the go-ahead. Didn't even read the scripts.'

George told her that he wouldn't, Farrell was like that. 'He tends to judge the person, rather than the work.'

'You know him?'

'He used to be in books when I had just started to work there. He got moved upstairs. I liked him.'

'I don't think I made much of an impression. I did an impersonation of a rabbit. It keeps haunting

342

me. I wish I hadn't done it.' All afternoon, when that nose twitch and sniff had come sneaking back into her mind, she had put her hands to her face, and screamed silently. 'Still, he invited me to see his etchings.'

George looked at her, impressed. 'It must have been one hell of a rabbit impersonation.'

Harriet Smith

It was a small advert, tucked at the bottom of the page in *The Guardian. Small, impossibly busy legal practice needs help. Hours atrocious, pay meagre. But work rewarding, stimulating, even. Applicant must have experience of criminal law. Apply to Harriet Smith . . .*

Cathryn read it on the bus on her way to work. The job she'd gone after months ago was still vacant. Or maybe the person who got it had given up. She didn't know. But when she reached her desk, she phoned.

'Um,' she'd said. 'It's about the job. I'd like to apply.'

Harriet said she'd need to do that in writing. 'CV and all that.'

'You already have it,' said Cathryn. 'I applied before and you gave me the job. Now, I'd like to apply again.'

'Are you the woman who went all corporate and got offered lots of money to work in some media place?'

'That's me,' said Cathryn.

Harriet said, 'A change of heart? Or have you

343

been sacked?'

'A change of heart. Or more a finding of heart. I used to do your sort of work, and I miss it.'

Harriet had invited her for an interview. 'Tuesday, six o'clock. I don't do the nine to five.'

It was a small office tucked down an Islington side street. Inside it was light, painted a creamy blue; there were plants everywhere. In fact, the place looked more botanical than legal. There was a huge palm by the door, plants along the windowsills, plants on the receptionist's desk and plants on the table by the sofa where clients sat waiting for their appointments. The sofa was old, a faded red, lined with a natty selection of cushions. Nothing could be more removed from the cool, modern place where she worked. Cathryn liked it as much the second time she saw it as she had the first.

Harriet Smith was a name Cathryn was familiar with long before she'd applied for a job with her. She'd seen it on letters to *The Times* and *The Guardian*. She'd heard Harriet on the radio, seen her on television once or twice. Harriet was a vocal and very passionate woman. Her clients were abused wives, prostitutes, mothers looking for child support, home workers who hadn't been paid—underdogs all. It was Cathryn's type of place.

Harriet was small and had a tumbling mass of black curls that fell over her face. The black in her hair was streaked with grey; she seemed to care little about that. Her clothes were worn for comfort rather than style. She was in her fifties, and when she spoke, a wild rush of words spilled out. She thought too quickly for her lips to keep

344

up. She was pale, only a scrape of make-up on her face. But she had a kindly, calm beauty that Cathryn thought attractive.

'I can't understand why you want to come and work with us,' Harriet said.

'It's what I want to do,' said Cathryn.

'You don't like your present job? I'd have thought it exciting.'

'It has its moments. But I liked my old job better. I miss the people. The clients. Some of them were awful, of course. The hours terrible. The office was rundown. But I liked the job. I was good at it.'

Harriet said she thought they could certainly come up with a few diabolical clients, and they could compete on the hours front. But she thought the office cheery enough. In the reception the phone rang. As soon as it was answered, and the receiver replaced, it rang again.

'In my present job, it's mostly contracts I look at. But in something like this there's more diversity. And a lot of the time it's worthwhile. I'd get to use my training,' said Cathryn.

For forty minutes they discussed the work: 'We deal with an awful lot of clients and cases other people turn down.' How Cathryn might handle different cases. How she'd have to keep up with new legislation. And outside in reception the phone rang and rang and rang.

'So,' said Harriet, 'you can start next month. Once your notice has run out. I'd really like someone to start tomorrow.'

'I can do that,' said Cathryn. 'I handed in my notice over three weeks ago. I can start whenever you want.'

Harriet said, 'Excellent.' Then, 'You're taking quite a pay cut to come here. Can I ask you what your husband thinks of all this?'

Cathryn said, 'He doesn't know. I haven't told him yet.' She knew that Harriet thought she just hadn't told her husband about applying for this job. But it was more than that; she hadn't told Clive she was leaving her last one. The longer she kept this to herself, the harder it became to tell him. She knew only one way out. Lie.

'If he doesn't like it, I don't really care,' she said. 'This is what I want to do.'

*   *   *

In the weeks following her being discovered spying on Alex and Claire, Maisie had hardly left the house. Once a week she'd go, early in the morning to the supermarket. She'd come home, unpack her bags, put her new supplies away, and that would be that till next week. The rest of the time, she hid in the house. She listened to the radio, she cleaned, she read the newspaper, she sat in her chair. Several times she phoned Nora, but only once did she answer. 'Hello, hello.'

Maisie stood holding the receiver, listening. But she couldn't speak. She didn't know what to say. So she put the phone down without saying anything. Often, when she was going through some mindless routine, heating a tin of soup, wiping the sink, Claire's face would loom into her mind. That expression, pity. 'Pity,' Maisie would say. 'Don't pity me. I don't need it.'

At times like this she'd pour a small drink and take it with her, to sip now and then, as she went from room to room with her vacuum cleaner and yellow duster.

Sometimes she'd stop what she was doing, and she'd remember some moment from years ago. She'd stare ahead and let the memory flow. She'd think about days long gone, when she and Alex were not married. They'd gone walking through Princes Street Gardens one Sunday. It was what you did, paraded on a Sunday afternoon in your best clothes. She'd be secretly eyeing the boys. He'd be talking avidly about Duke Ellington or some such person she hadn't heard of. But he'd look at her, see what she was doing. 'Stop that. You're mine. You're never going to get rid of me.'

All that, she thought, and it comes to this. Alone in your house, cleaning things that don't need cleaning, and drinking to cheer yourself up. She thought about when her children were young, and on hot days she'd fill a plastic basin and put it out on the lawn so they could paddle. She'd give them a picnic tea, sandwiches on a cloth spread out on the grass. They'd tie the clothes rope across the garden so Nora and Cathryn could use it as a net and play tennis. She and Alex would sit on striped deckchairs and watch. She hadn't thought, back then, that these days would end. Of course, she knew the girls would grow up, but the reality of it never crossed her mind. 'Lonely, lonely,' she'd say, and take her glass back to the kitchen and fill it up.

It was evening. Early winter, the clocks had gone back. The kitchen window was slightly open; the air coming in was crisp, chill. Air like that brought back memories of when the children came trailing home from school, their faces rosy, hands icy. 'Ooh,' Maisie would say. 'Cold hands, warm

347

heart.' She'd take them in hers, rub some heat into them.

She smiled. Put her chip pan on to heat, put some cold ham from the fridge on to a plate and took a drink. She remembered that. That had happened just before the blackness. She'd come to sitting in her chair; looked around, thinking, how did I get here?

Smoke was billowing in black clouds, swirling from the kitchen. It took her a moment to realise what was happening. The house was on fire. She ran to the cooker. Flames and thick black smoke were gushing from her pan. Sweeping up the wall and across the ceiling.

Panicking, heart pounding, shouting, 'Oh God. Oh God,' she turned off the cooker, soaked a towel and flung it over the burning pot. The flames calmed. She doused what remained with another wet towel, opened the back door to let the room clear of smoke, then slumped into a chair thinking that after all that, she needed a drink. Just a little something to steady her nerves.

She admitted herself it wasn't to her advantage to be discovered sitting at the table, legs apart, face streaked with soot and sweat, pouring a huge amount of sherry into a large glass, surrounded by smoke in a blackened kitchen. But it happened.

Cathryn, putting off the moment she had to tell her husband she'd quit her highly paid job in a classy media law firm to work with a small, vibrantly feminist and fiercely socialist lawyer in Islington for half her previous salary, had stopped by to check on her mother. Cathryn still suspected Maisie of being a shoplifter, and often visited hoping for a chance to rummage through the cupboards for the spoils.

'What the hell is going on?' said Cathryn.

'Only a wee fire. Got it under control,' said Maisie. She saw Cathryn looking at her glass. 'Just a little sherry to steady my nerves.'

'That's hardly a little sherry,' said Cathryn. 'That's a glassful.'

'Well,' said Maisie. 'I like a little drink. No harm.'

'You're drunk,' said Cathryn.

'No I'm not,' said Maisie. 'I never get drunk. I have never been drunk in my life.'

'You're drunk now. Is that what you do? Get drunk and go shoplifting?'

'Shoplifting? Me? Cheek of you. I don't go shoplifting. What makes you think that?'

'All the bottles of wine in the cupboard. The food you've been buying. Not your sort of thing at all. I think you've been stealing it. You're stressed. You go into the supermarket and take things, anything, and you don't pay for them. It's a well-known syndrome. You're drawing attention to yourself to express your loss and grief.'

Maisie said, 'Absolute stuff and nonsense. I just picked up those things when I was shopping in Shepherd's Bush.'

'What the hell were you doing there?'

'I was just checking up on Alex. I wanted to see how he was doing.'

'Stalking,' said Cathryn. She put her head in her hands. 'Please don't tell me you have been stalking Dad.'

A slice of what might happen flashed before her. Maisie in the dock, pleading guilty. She'd probably get a suspended sentence, thought

Cathryn. But Clive would find out, and there he would be, a deeply ambitious man who had his life planned out, who would discover his mother-in-law was a drunk and a stalker, and whose wife was working for a well-known feminist who had once, if Cathryn remembered correctly, appeared on television shouting at Margaret Thatcher. Clive wouldn't like this at all.

'I just wanted to see how he was getting on,' said Maisie.

Cathryn stared at her.

'He saw me at it. I wasn't a very good stalker, if you want to know the truth. But Alex was very nice about it. He was always such a nice man. He took me home and told me to stop it.'

Cathryn still stared. She couldn't believe this.

'Don't just stare,' said Maisie. 'I hate that.'

But Cathryn ignored her. 'How much do you drink?' she asked.

'I have a wee one at lunchtime. Another in the afternoon. And one more at night. Three glasses a day.'

In her head, Cathryn doubled this. And still she felt she'd got it wrong. 'How many bottles a week?'

'Two,' said Maisie. 'Two and a bit, sometimes.'

Cathryn said, 'It's more than that, isn't it?'

Maisie shifted in her seat, wiped her grime-streaked cheek and said, 'Maybe. I don't know.'

Cathryn stared.

And Maisie couldn't stand it. 'All right. I was drunk. I put on the pan for the chips and passed out. I woke up in the chair. I don't remember going there. I don't remember anything. Just blackness. I nearly burned the house down.'

It was more than Cathryn could grasp in a

moment. Yet there it was in front of her—Maisie, sweaty, dishevelled, black smoke streaks on her arms, clutching a tumbler of sherry. She could see it was true. All she could say was, 'Why?'

'I don't know,' said Maisie. 'Why does anybody drink? It helps. I'm lonely, lonely, lonely. So I have a wee drink to cheer myself up. And then another. And when I've had a few, everything seems not so bad. I feel cheery. There are possibilities again.'

'What possibilities?' said Cathryn.

'It becomes possible that Alex might come back. Though I know he won't. Or Nora, I might see Nora. I might be happy again.'

Cathryn put her hand over Maisie's. 'What are we going to do with you? How long has this been going on?'

Maisie said she didn't know. 'Years it's been going on. Started as a little secret. It was my secret, I loved that. Seemed harmless enough. I just couldn't resist. I got happy. Not drunk, happy.'

Cathryn said she didn't remember Maisie being happy.

'No,' said Maisie. 'I used to think. Too much thinking and not enough doing. I'd think about things I'd done wrong, choices I'd made. And a drink made me feel I could do something about it all, fix things. Or it would make me feel like nothing really mattered anyway. But by the time you and Nora got home from school, the happiness would be wearing off, and the things I thought I could do seemed impossible again.'

Cathryn said, 'Oh, Mum.'

Maisie said, 'I've been getting through a bottle a day. At least.'

Cathryn said, 'You've got to stop. You could

die.'

'I can't stop,' said Maisie. 'I need it.'

Cathryn took her mother's hand. For a while, they didn't speak. The room smelled of old fat, the walls were black, and it was cold. The door was still open.

'It's strange to think about us all. This family. We were so ordinary. It's all gone wrong. I do believe you could call us dysfunctional,' said Cathryn.

Maisie said, 'We're never that. We were all fine, getting along. Then we all started to think. It's thinking that's done it. If we hadn't done that, we'd be getting along still.'

Cathryn said, 'But you have to think about things. It's how you sort out your life. You decide what's not right, and you set about making it right.'

'That's what I'm doing now. Making it right. All the stupid things I've done were because I drank.'

'It has to stop. Now. Before you destroy yourself.'

Maisie said she'd been thinking that herself.

'We'll have to get you some help. We should go and see the doctor.'

'No doctor,' said Maisie. 'I'm not having him know about this.'

'But . . .' said Cathryn.

'I'm an alcoholic,' said Maisie. The word seemed almost to drift out of her soft lipstick-pink mouth. She said it so gently, it sounded poetic. 'There you go, I said it. And if I'm not an alcoholic, I'm well on my way.'

Cathryn looked at her mother's hands. The things these hands had done. Buttons sewed on, cuts cleaned and bandaged, puddings baked, floors wiped. How strange that it was only now that she thought them wonderful.

There were things Nora had said about their mother. 'Our Maisie's quite the star of the butcher's queue.' 'My mother is fond of a good illness.' Cathryn had laughed. Only now did she realise that such attributes were signs of some deep shyness and unhappiness.

'I've always been a bit scared,' said Maisie. 'But after a couple of glasses I knew what to do and say. I was cleverer, brighter. I stopped thinking I was only me. But really I'm ashamed of myself. Shame. Shame. Shame. It's an awful thing. I hate it.'

Cathryn thought about Maisie. The arms that had held her, the knee she'd once sat upon, the face that had looked down at her night after night before she fell asleep. She thought that before she'd gone off into her world of Coca-Cola and boys and school and studying and marriage and work, before all that, Maisie had been everything to her.

'OK,' she said. 'If you want to finish it, then finish it.' She took the glass from her mother's hand, poured it down the sink. 'I think the rule is that when you want to stop, that's when you stop.' She turned to Maisie. 'Where do you keep your stash?'

'There's a bottle by my chair,' said Maisie. 'One under the bed. One behind the bucket under the sink and one in the vegetable basket.' She didn't mention the one at the bottom of the wardrobe in the spare room. She thought that giving up the drink would be hard; she might need that.

Pretend We're Normal People

Calm light, calm evening, not quite dark but the streetlights were on. The sky was paling, a yellowness there. A glow on the rooftops. Birds on the telephone lines, huddled. They looked like they were waiting for some weather.

'I think it's going to rain,' said Nora.

George agreed. 'Looks like it. Open the wine, would you?'

Nora thought that anyone noticing her standing with her head against the window pane, gazing down into the street below, would know the turmoil she was in. Every time a car pulled into the street, she'd crane to see if it was her father and Claire.

If she didn't feel so anxious, she thought this would be quite placidly domestic. She and George had both left work early to prepare a meal and get things ready for her visitors. While he cooked, she cleaned up and changed the bed. Now he was still cooking, and she was hanging about, moving between the window and the kitchen.

'How long does it take to drive up here from York?'

'About four or five hours,' George told her.

'So why aren't they here yet? If they left at ten o'clock they'd have been here about two.'

'You don't know when they left,' said George.

'I'm making a shrewd guess,' said Nora. 'If I was leaving York to come here, that's when I'd set off, ten o'clock.'

He told her to stop fussing.

'Do you think he'll notice I'm pregnant?' she asked.

'I think it's likely. You're five months gone. It is a little obvious. I take that to mean you haven't told him.'

'I haven't told any of my family,' said Nora. 'I just couldn't find the words. It just never seemed right to blurt it out.'

She phoned her father regularly, but hadn't mentioned the baby. And once a week, usually on Sunday mornings, she phoned her Aunt May. They spoke about May's swimming club, the talks at the library she'd been to, her bridge club, all her activities, in fact, and Nora's work. Somehow, in the middle of this Nora never found an appropriate moment to say, 'By the way, I'm going to have a baby.' So May knew that Nora had been moved to the third floor, and that she was writing a strip about a rabbit in trainers, but not that she was going to be a great-aunt. Meantime, Nora knew all about May's friends and her busy life, but had no idea about what was happening to her mother. May could never find an appropriate moment either.

In the street below, Nora saw a car stop. Claire got out and looked around. A few seconds later, Alex did the same. He reached into the back and brought out a bag and his jacket.

'Oh God,' said Nora. 'They're here. I don't want to do this. I don't want them to see me. You answer the door, George. Tell them I'm not here. I've moved away and you don't know where I am.'

George said he wouldn't do that.

'Well, we have to put on a show. Pretend we're normal people,' said Nora.

'We are normal people,' said George.

'Yes, but pretend we're normal people like them, and not normal people like us.'

George said, 'Christ, Nora. Months ago I wouldn't have known what you meant by that. But now I know you, I do know what you mean. What are you doing to me?'

When Nora opened the door to her father and Claire, there were cries of hello, and we made it at last, thought we'd never get here. They kissed and hugged a little. Nora introduced George, but made no mention of the nature of their friendship. She did not even say he lived downstairs. 'This is George,' she said. And to George, 'This is my dad and Claire.'

Alex sat on the sofa and considered the room. 'Nice place you've got here.'

Claire sat beside Alex and she, too, admired the room. 'You're very lucky to have found a flat like this.'

Nora agreed, indeed she was.

Alex fished about in his bag and brought out a bottle of wine, and a gift, a teapot. 'For the home,' he said.

'It's lovely,' said Nora. It was shiny dark blue. 'It's the first teapot I've ever owned.'

They spoke about the route Alex and Claire had taken to get here, the traffic situation in Edinburgh, how beautiful York was, the weather— it looked like rain. Nora brought them both a glass of wine. She had orange juice. Nobody mentioned the pregnancy.

Alex didn't know how exactly to approach the subject, and was hoping Nora might bring it up. But at last, when the small talk began to taper into small, stiff silences, he said, 'So, I suppose congratulations are in order.'

Nora stroked her bump. 'Thank you. Due late March, early April. You'll be a grandfather.'

He said a long, slow yes. He hadn't, till this moment, thought of that. He liked the idea, but didn't think he'd see much of the child. 'What does your mother think?'

'She doesn't know. We don't speak. Haven't since the night I ran away.'

Alex said that he'd wondered why Cathryn hadn't mentioned it.

'You see Cathryn?' said Nora.

'Yes. We have lunch from time to time. She didn't have a marquee, by the way.'

Nora said, 'Oh.'

'You're on your own, then?' said Alex.

'No. I've got lots of people. I'm just not related to any of them. Brendan and Jen, Mona, George, of course. Nathan.'

It was understandable, considering the way Nora had put it, that Alex would think George was the father.

'Well,' he said, 'are you two thinking of getting married? Though I know people don't these days.'

'George isn't the father,' said Nora. She turned to look at George.

'No. No,' said George. 'Not guilty. I live downstairs. We're friends, that's all.'

'Nathan's the father,' said Nora.

'And where is Nathan? I'd like to meet him.'

Good question, Nora thought. Where is Nathan?

Nora said, 'Nathan can't come. He's head of the art department and had some meeting he couldn't

357

get out of. He sends his regards, though. You'd like him.'

Alex said he was sure he would. 'I'll meet him soon enough.'

'Oh, yes,' said Nora. Though she doubted it. She looked at George, who raised his eyebrows. Nathan's important meeting was news to him. He'd seen Nathan leaving work, and it looked very much as if he was heading for the pub.

At dinner they praised George's cooking and discussed the book he was doing. Claire wanted to know Nora's plans for after the baby was born. Nora told her she would take some time off, then go back to work. 'I'll have to.'

'Isn't Nathan going to look after you?' said Alex. He was shocked. 'In my day that's what you did. You accepted your responsibilities.'

Nora said, 'Oh, he'll do his bit. In fact he wanted me to stop working, he said he'd look after me and the baby.' She was lying. 'But I think it's best I go on with my job. I have to think of the future. Once you stop, it's hard to get back on the ladder.' A phrase she'd overheard in the pub a while ago.

Everyone round the table nodded and agreed. Though they thought, what ladder are you talking about, Nora? And Nora thought she sounded like a fool.

Alex and Claire stayed the night, sleeping in Nora's bed. Nora took the sofa.

'You should have told us,' said Claire. 'You shouldn't be on the sofa. Not with a baby on the way.'

Nora said she sometimes took the sofa when Mona came to town. 'This is her flat.'

'You don't have a proper lease?' said Claire.

'Oh yes. Only it's in the contract that Mona can stay when she needs to. And she can have the flat back if she wants to come back to live in town.'

'You don't think all that is a bit precarious?' said Claire.

Nora said, 'I don't ever think about it.'

Claire thought, no, you wouldn't.

In the morning, Nora had to go to work. Before she left, she knocked on the bedroom door and stuck her head into the room. It was strange to see Claire's head on the pillow next to Alex's. She paused, staring and thinking about Maisie. She often thought about her mother these days. She wondered how Maisie was, and if she was coping.

There had been a time, when Nora was five and had just started school, when Maisie had been the centre of her world. Fresh from life at her mother's side, she knew every bit of her day. Mondays, the washing, changing the sheets on one of the beds, and polishing the lino surrounding the living-room carpet. Tuesdays, ironing. She knew almost minute by minute what Maisie would be doing. At ten o'clock, she stopped her chores and made herself a cup of tea.

Nora would sit, three days a schoolgirl and already bored with her education, and think about Maisie, willing her mother to think about her.

'Did you hear me thinking about you?' Nora would ask when she got home.

'Yes, I did,' Maisie would say. 'I heard it clear as anything in the kitchen. I was making a cup of tea.'

'That's right.' Nora would be overjoyed about this. 'Ten o'clock.'

Nora thought herself terrible to have forgotten

this. Her mother had smelled of eau de Cologne, her lips were always painted red. She had been vivacious and strikingly pretty. How could she have forgotten all that?

Claire sat up. 'Have you time for a quick cup of coffee before you go?'

Nora said she had.

They sat in the kitchen, behind them, cluttered into the sink, the debris left after last night's meal.

'Don't worry about all that,' said Claire. 'We'll clear it up before we go.'

'It's been lovely to see you,' said Nora.

'We enjoyed it,' Claire told her. 'I'm so excited about the baby. It's a great excuse to shop for little clothes and shoes and things.' She stopped, remembering she wasn't officially related to Nora. She wouldn't be a real grandmother. 'I hope you don't mind.'

Nora shook her head. 'Go ahead. All contributions welcome.'

'I'll be an unofficial granny,' said Claire. She looked pleased at the thought. 'So, what are you doing at work?'

Nora told her about the rabbit. Waited for the usual dubious response. A rabbit with trainers?

Claire said, 'How wonderful. I'll look out for it. I'm going to start ordering *Captain Colin* from the newsagent so I can see how you're getting along.'

'It's a bit boring,' said Nora. 'I keep having to send the artist photographs of things from the modern world so he knows what they look like. He doesn't get out much. His cars are the automobiles of yesteryear.'

Claire laughed. 'I think it's wonderful.' She nearly said she didn't understand why Alex wasn't proud of her. 'I'll be watching you from afar. You don't mind if I phone you now and then, to see how you're getting on?'

Nora said, 'Feel free. Sorry I can't phone you much. I can't afford the bills.' Thinking this sounded a little nonchalant, she said, 'I'd like that.'

When she got home from work, after kicking off her shoes and putting on her favourite tape, a Brendan selection of radio moments, Nora looked round. The flat had been cleaned; it smelled of polish and air freshener. Just like home, she thought. There was a bunch of flowers on the coffee table, and a note. *Just to say thank you for a wonderful evening. We're off on our travels round Scotland. Alex thought this might come in handy. You never know. Love Alex and Claire.*

There was a cheque for two thousand pounds. The note was in Claire's handwriting. The cheque was signed by Alex. Nora looked at it, and imagined Claire had urged Alex to give her some money.

She was right.

'I can't give her a cheque. She hardly knows me. She probably still thinks of me as the woman who broke up her family. But you can. You're her father.'

Alex had hesitated.

'I'll refund you if you want. But you gave Cathryn money to move, and money for a car. Nora got nothing. She needs something now.'

Alex said, 'When you put it like that . . .' And wrote the cheque.

'Two thousand pounds, two thousand pounds.' Nora couldn't believe it. It was more money than she'd ever had in her life. In fact, she'd never really

361

seen such a sum written down before.

She took it downstairs to show George. 'What am I to do with it?'

'Put it in the bank? Buy some baby things. A cot. Nappies. All the piles of stuff.'

Nora supposed so.

George said, 'Well, my solvent friend, back to one-pot meals. Fancy an omelette?'

A Saturday Afternoon in January

A Saturday afternoon in January. Brendan and Nora had gone to the Modern Art Gallery. Beyond the windows of the café, winter was falling. A wind-driven wet mix of rain and hail.

'It's raining slush,' said Nora.

Brendan agreed. It was good weather for the mood he was in.

Nora said that she thought the carrot cake complex and reflecting a modern urban urge to find something beyond the elaborate infrastructures of relationships, routine travel and work. 'It cries out for the rustic.'

Brendan said that the walnut and coffee cake was much the same. 'Yet it makes a definite statement about our need to find an inner meaning to our own existence. This cake, while modern, takes risks with our leaning towards nostalgia. Times past.

'So,' said Brendan, 'how did it go with your dad?'

'Fine. It was quite jolly. Only Nathan wasn't there. He refuses to meet my family.'

'Why?' said Brendan. 'Your family sound admirably nutty.'

'You know why,' said Nora. 'He's happy to see me, to fuck me. Meeting my family is an intimacy too far.'

Brendan said, 'Yeah, well, meeting your girlfriend's dad when you've got the girlfriend up the duff can be tricky.'

Nora sniffed, and looked out of the window. 'He'll never meet my family. You know that, I know that. I still see him on Saturday nights, that's all. We eat together, go round to the pub. But I can tell he's just being kind to me. I hate that.' Her eyes glazed with tears, and she rubbed her nose violently to stop them. 'You want a taste of my carrot cake?'

'Definitely,' said Brendan. 'Never mind about Nathan. Wait till he sees the baby. Nobody can resist a baby.'

'I'm trying not to mind. But it's hard,' said Nora. 'I don't know about nobody being able to resist a baby. They don't do much for me.'

'Ah,' said Brendan. 'When it's your own, you don't notice the baldness, the lack of teeth and the incontinence. Funny, that.' He reached over and took a forkful of carrot cake. 'This is better than mine. I should have ordered this instead.'

'I've always had better taste than you,' said Nora.

'True, true,' said Brendan. 'Except for music, books, films and . . .' He'd been about to say men. But thought, perhaps not.

She took a piece of his walnut cake. 'Yes, mine is better.'

They ate. Watched the weather.

'So,' said Nora. 'Jen's interview. Sounds important.'

'She'll be heading up her own maternity unit in Bristol. It's what she's always wanted.'

'If she gets it,' said Nora.

'If she gets it,' agreed Brendan.

Nora hung on to that if. There was a sliver of hope. But at last she said, 'She'll get it, won't she?'

Brendan said, 'Yes. She deserves it.'

'I feel awful, really,' said Nora. 'She's worked hard. She wants this. I like her a lot. In fact I'm sort of in awe of her. But deep inside me I hope she doesn't get the job.'

Brendan said, 'I know. I'm vaguely hoping too. And if she doesn't get it, I'll feel bad for feeling secretly glad. Christ, Nora, I'm starting to sound like you.'

'It's a gift I have. I infect people with my verbal confusion. You want me to get you a slice of carrot cake? I'll pay. I'm rich as anything.'

Brendan said he would like a slice but she shouldn't go throwing her cash around.

'Nothing to me,' said Nora. 'The cakes are on me.'

When she came back from the counter, she said, 'You'll go with her, won't you?'

'What else can I do? Stay here? I sit sifting through that slush pile all day. I hate it. It's not me, you know that.'

'I know,' said Nora. 'But . . .' She wanted to tell him she didn't want him to go. What would she do without him? Who would she chat to? She sniffed again.

'May not happen,' said Brendan. 'She might not get it. You don't know what the competition

364

is like.'

'They'd hardly pay for her to go all the way to Bristol if they weren't interested in her. If it was just an ordinary interview, she'd have had to pay her own fare, surely.'

Brendan said, 'There's that. Maybe she'll blow the interview. She might be nervous and babble rubbish.'

Nora shot him a look. 'Jen? I don't think so. I wish I'd had apple cake instead of another slice of carrot. The apple looked good, and healthy.'

'You can't beat a slice of healthy cake,' said Brendan.

Nora sighed. Her Saturday companion was leaving her. She indulged in imagining a lonely life, walking the streets they'd moved along alone. And hugely pregnant.

'If Jen goes,' Brendan said, 'I have to go too. Why would I stay here without her?'

Me, thought Nora. You can stay for me. Then smiled slightly, thinking of Brendan telling Jen he wasn't going with her. 'I'm staying here so I can thumb through records with Nora, and eat cake at the art gallery, and walk about town talking about sweets from my childhood and the best films to eat popcorn to and how it's awful when someone sees you when all you're wearing is socks. It's goodbye, Jen.' She gathered up a few stray crumbs on her finger and put them into her mouth.

'It'll do you good to get away. Fresh start. New job. And Jen'll be really happy. Though Bristol's a helluva way for us all to come for roast beef on a Sunday.'

Brendan said, 'True. I'll post a sandwich up to you instead. Save the fare.'

Nora thought that an excellent solution.

He looked at his watch. Half past three, time to go. Jen's train got in at four. They'd come to the gallery by car because of the weather. Driving to the station, he thought that Nora was right, it was time to move on. Though he'd miss this life. He'd miss Nora. But he loved Jen, was looking forward to seeing her. More, he admired her. And the thing that he admired most in her was that she'd never once objected to his friendship with Nora. The woman's mature, he thought.

Once Jen had said that she didn't know what to make of the two of them. 'Everybody likes pleasant things, but you two are addicted to pleasantness. I can't think of a word for what you are. You're both ambitious, but do nothing about it. You'd both rather loaf around and amuse yourselves, giggling and making stupid remarks.' She'd told Brendan she thought he and Nora were Saturday-afternoon castaways caught up in a reverie, masters of the sacred art of idling. 'Like teenagers,' she'd said. 'It'll end one day. Life, kids, mortgages, work and other calamities will catch up with you.'

Brendan always thought that life caught up with him on that rainy Saturday afternoon in January standing on Platform 17 with Nora watching Jen step off the train.

As soon as she saw him, she waved wildly. She glowed. She shouted, her voice clear over the babble of other passengers pouring out into the day, hauling cases and backpacks, and the thrum of trains, doors banging, 'I got it. I got it.' She glowed. She jumped, punching the air, as she saw Brendan shoving through the throng to get to her. When he took her to him, and kissed her, he knew she was leaving town, and he would be leaving with her.

Seeing Daisies, And A Golden Array Of Butternut Squash

Cathryn moved in with Maisie. Clive wasn't happy about it. He wondered what was the point of them being married if she was going to up and leave, just like that.

'I'm not leaving you,' said Cathryn. 'I'm just looking after my mother for a while. Auntie May is going to see to her when I'm at work.'

He offered to pay for Maisie to go into rehab.

Cathryn said she didn't think so. 'She's been through enough. All she needs is company.'

'You prefer her to me,' said Clive.

Cathryn told him not to be silly, of course she didn't.

'What am I to think?' he said. 'You go and change your job without telling me. I'm your husband, we're meant to discuss these things.'

Cathryn said she knew that. 'But I was afraid you'd talk me out of it. I love working with Harriet, it's what I want to do. It's who I am.' She said she was sorry, she should have talked to him, but she wasn't used to discussing her life decisions. She was used to doing what she wanted to do.

Clive asked if it was also what she wanted, to abandon him for her mother.

'No, it's not what I want. It's what I must do,' said Cathryn. 'Though abandon is a bit strong, isn't it? She's ill, she needs help.'

'Why is it you that has to help?'

'Who else is there?' said Cathryn. 'Do you think I want to do this? I'm furious with my mother. Furious that she should be so self-absorbed and weak that she has started drinking. And I'm sad for her, how lonely she must have been. And most of all, I feel guilty about her. I hate that—guilt.'

Clive asked if she didn't feel guilty about him.

'Yes,' she said. 'And that's something to worry about. I don't think I should. I'm up to my eyes in guilt. Guilt. Guilt. Guilt. It's all I feel. Don't ply me with any more, I can't take it.'

He didn't say any more. He let her go.

It was a long commute, morning and evening, but coming home to Maisie and a cooked meal was more pleasant than she'd imagined. Often she had to bring work home, and she'd sit at the table, papers in front of her, trying to ignore the flicker and blare of the television set.

Maisie chattered. It amazed Cathryn that her mother could make the doings of her day sound so interesting. After all, Cathryn had found an abused woman a place in a refuge, talked to the local member of Parliament about an immigrant who'd been living illegally in the country for five years and wanted nationality, helped Harriet prepare a speech to give to a women's group in Birmingham. How could someone make doing the washing and visiting the shops with her sister sound more fascinating than that?

But Maisie could. Recently she had re-emerged into the world, mostly because Cathryn and May had insisted she should. Her first sorties had been small, timid. She thought she blinked a lot. In time she travelled farther and farther, visiting shops and libraries. She found the world an attractive and fascinating place full of strangers to talk to, mostly on buses, and things to see. Today, she'd seen a long white limousine, a man in purple trousers, a couple of boys with orange Mohican haircuts—the state of them—and a dog with no back legs, just a trundler thing, on wheels. 'Did the trick,' said Maisie.

Nora could do that, thought Cathryn. She remembered Nora talking avidly about standing alone in the back garden. Not interesting at all, thought Cathryn. But Nora had said that if she stared and stared at a daisy, then shut her eyes, she could still see daisies. It had been related with such infectious passion, Cathryn had gone out and tried it.

'I wonder how Nora is,' she said to Maisie.

'She's writing a story about a rabbit,' said Maisie. 'May told me.'

Cathryn said, 'Oh. That's nice.'

Then Maisie said, 'Things they have in the supermarket, butternut squash. Isn't that a lovely thing to be called? Butternut squash. Lord knows what you do with it. I'll have to get a book at the library tomorrow. It'll keep till then, won't it?'

Cathryn said she thought so, and prepared herself for the tale of Maisie's discovery of butternut squash. The golden array she saw before her at the fruit and veg in the supermarket, and the smell of it, and the clatter round her. And the look on the checkout girl's face when it slid along the conveyer belt. Anticipating this, she said, 'You haven't been drinking, have you?'

'Oh, no,' said Maisie. 'I think about it. But I know it's no good. I can never get hold of the moment. You know, that moment, before you go too far, when things are wonderful. It's trying to make the moment last that gets you.'

Thinking back to her student days, Cathryn said she knew the moment well.

Nights, Cathryn would sit beside Maisie, drinking tea. Listening to her stories. Her dance-hall days. 'We were out every Saturday night, me and May,' said Maisie. 'Dancing. Big glitter ball twirling, and a band playing. You'd wait round the edge of the floor, hoping to catch someone's eye. But you had to look like you didn't care. Proper dancing, too. Foxtrots and waltzes. Your father never did like to dance like that. He liked jazz. Dim cellars, smoke and music that floated towards you. Though I always loved musicals. People in musicals can be walking along a street, and they start singing, and everyone joins in. I always wanted things like that to happen.'

Cathryn said she would, too.

Cathryn thought it was time and companionship that helped her mother recover. Maisie said it was wildlife programmes on the telly. She'd watched some penguins standing over their eggs, waiting for their mates to come and take over so they might go back to the sea and feed. 'Amazing,' said Maisie, 'standing bolt upright in the snow and wind, waiting. Not thinking, not making a fuss. See, I can understand that. It's how we were brought up.'

'What?' said Cathryn. 'To be like penguins and stand bolt upright in a blizzard?'

'No,' said Maisie. 'To stick things out. To be good. Not to make a fuss. Seeing those penguins reminds me of what things were like. How we stood in queues, and did what was expected of us, and never questioned things.'

Cathryn said she'd hate that.

'No,' said Maisie. 'I can see the point. With the penguins, it's all nurturing. When it's done, they all go their own way. And anyway, I like a bit of weather.'

One evening, when Maisie was sleeping, Cathryn went to see her Aunt May. 'Tell me about my mother,' she said. 'What was *her* mother like?'

'Quiet,' said May. 'She died when Maisie was seventeen. She was tired out, I always think. All us children to look after. She never stopped. Up in the morning to cook and clean, and back then it was all elbow grease, no miracle sprays or the like. Then at night, she'd sit in her chair mending, darning, sewing on buttons. When the family grew up and she had more time, she read. Not romances; she liked Dickens and the Brontës and biographies. She had brains, but back then it didn't do for women to be brainy. You take after her.'

Cathryn nodded. 'I don't think I'll ever be sitting mending and darning in the evening.'

'No,' said May. 'But you have the same goodness about you. And a lot of guilt. You should watch that. Guilt's a bugger when it gets you in its grip.'

Cathryn said she knew that.

'Maisie's more like her dad,' said May. 'He was a dreamer. Nights, he used to tell stories. No television then. We made our own entertainment. He'd start a story off, and we all had to add a bit, so it grew and grew. Maisie used to love that. Her stories were always full of people singing and dancing in the street. She hated sad endings.'

Cathryn said she'd noticed.

'She was a beauty, though, your mum. All the boys were after her. She could have had her pick, but she chose Alex. He was besotted. Wrote her love letters, sent her cards and flowers. Then Maisie married him. The house was sad after your grandmother died, sad and gloomy. None of us realised how much we needed her till she went. I think your mother married your dad to get out of the house. I think the getting-out-of-the-house thing runs in your family.'

Cathryn nodded.

'Nora takes after your grandad and Maisie. Makes up stories. Runs away from things in her head. Only she's making something of it. She'll be fine. Maisie and Alex used to think she was dumb, bright but dumb. She's not, really. It's Maisie that's dumb. She was spoiled rotten. The youngest, pretty, got anything she wanted. She was always being picked up and twirled around and tickled and loved. She never learned that you have to love people back. She thought it would always come to her in bucketloads.'

Cathryn said she supposed.

May put down her knitting and went into the kitchen to put on the kettle. She bustled, fetching cups from the cupboard, warming the pot, putting slices of fruit cake on a plate.

'It makes me want to cry for her,' she said. 'I think it was all our fault. The family, we treated her like a lovely puppy. What must it be like to realise one day that you're too old, too big to be picked up and twirled round and tickled and loved. To find yourself sitting alone in a room with everybody you thought loved you gone. Well, we know. She took to drink.'

'I know,' said Cathryn.

'I feel guilty about her,' said May, pouring the tea. 'But I'll never let her know that, she'd take advantage.' She put down the pot, turned to Cathryn, wagging her finger. 'Here's something you must know about Maisie. She will never love you, or anybody, as much as you love her. Never. She was taught to love herself. She knows nothing about devotion or real commitment or even guilt. And for that, you have to feel sad for her, she's missing a lot.' The finger-wagging speeded up. 'And you mustn't lose your husband or your job or anything because of her. You just do what you can, then get out of the house. You should be able to do that, it's in your blood.'

And Cathryn laughed.

Afternoons, if May was at one of her clubs, Maisie walked. She cruised the streets that, years ago, Nora had wandered when she didn't want to go home. As she walked, Maisie would think about penguins and how cold they must feel, and all they had was instinct. And she'd think about Nora, the one that got away, she thought. That was instinct, too.

She passed a charity shop with a notice in the window, *Volunteers wanted.* She read it, walked on, then turned, went back to the shop and read the notice again.

When Cathryn came home that night, Maisie told her she had a job. 'Well, not a proper job. I don't get paid. But a job, something to do.'

She'd gone in, and told the woman behind the counter that she had come about the notice in the window. She wasn't nervous, because this was an impulse, a whim. She was good at whims. Nerves struck when the woman behind the counter said she'd fetch the manager. Formalities hadn't occurred to Maisie. She'd thought if she was volunteering, she'd be immediately welcomed with open arms.

'I mean,' she told Cathryn, 'I'm offering to give up my time for nothing. There's not many would do that.'

But the interview had gone well. Maisie claimed to have shop experience, though that had been thirty years ago. Still, she was good with numbers and had an eye for colour. 'I could do something with your window display,' she said. 'You need something more striking. Make people stop in their tracks.'

Cathryn thought Maisie's colour combinations could certainly do that.

'I was asked what times suited me. I told them any time. My children were grown up and away from home and my man had left me. So I had no commitments. Turns out Patricia's husband had left her too. Only he left for a woman half his age. Mine went for a woman only five years younger. So I have that to comfort me.'

Cathryn agreed. Though she thought it more understandable for a man to leave his wife for a much younger woman.

'There's checks to be done. But, all going well, I'll start in a couple of weeks.'

In time, though Cathryn's professional life was busy, working with Harriet on a high-profile court case involving a woman accused of murdering an infant son she claimed had died from cot death, her home conversations involved the lives of

Patricia, Nancy and Joan, Maisie's colleagues. And there were tales of the junk that appeared overnight at the shop door. 'The rubbish people dump. We have to get rid of it. And there are folk don't bother to iron the clothes they hand in. Lazy beggars.'

Maisie's wardrobe began to include bits and pieces she'd bought from the shop. A red and black silk shirt, a pair of chinos, a luminously pink sweater. Cathryn thought her mother was beginning to look like she was dressed by the charity shop.

A Gauguin print appeared on the wall. Alone in a quiet room, it would have been striking. In Maisie's home, it had to fight to be noticed. The blaze of fevered hues made Cathryn blink, as if the sun was glaring into her eyes. 'I like a bit of colour,' Maisie said.

Cathryn knew it was time to go home. For some time, she'd been shifting between her own flat and Maisie's house. She lived with Clive on Saturdays and Sundays, and a couple of nights during the week. The rest of the time she kept Maisie company.

But there was a rift between Clive and Cathryn, they both knew it. Cathryn defined it as them both wanting different versions of the same thing.

One night, after they'd both worked late, Harriet invited Cathryn home for supper. 'Nothing much, there never is much food in the house, and I'm no cook. But it will save you cooking when you get home.'

Harriet's flat entranced Cathryn. She wanted to move in. It was small, three cluttered rooms. A mix of plain walls and patterns on the floor rugs and on the throws over the sofas. There were books, papers and plants, and a piano.

'You play?' asked Cathryn.

'Only badly, but sometimes when I've friends round we sing.'

Singing with friends; Cathryn was impressed. The only time she'd sung with friends was when, as a student, she'd got drunk on an Abba night, and they'd bawled out 'Dancing Queen'.

They ate a warm chicken salad. Drank white wine. When Harriet asked her what she wanted, Cathryn could only say she didn't know, really. 'I only know what I don't want. And that's what I've got. My flat is beautiful. If I were an interior designer, it's what I would design. Then I'd come home to this. You could live here.'

'You can't live where you are at the moment?'

'No. Not actually live. Kick off your shoes, sprawl on the sofa, that sort of thing. Clive loves it. But I only love it to look at. I like some clutter. We're discovering the differences between us. He wants lots of children and a move to the country. I want a child, but to stay in town. He likes all sport. I only like tennis. He loves opera. I like some opera and lots of other things. And on and on, like that.'

Harriet said, 'Hmm.' She'd been married once. It had lasted three months. 'We were great friends and lovers, but married we fought like cat and dog. It's a wonder we survived.'

'Clive is on his way to wealth. He invests, he manages his money. I've discovered, recently, that money doesn't interest me. I'd like to be solvent, of course. But I want to be good.'

'Good?' said Harriet. 'Good? What do you

376

mean? A good person?'

'Naturally,' said Cathryn. 'But more than that. I want to be good at what I do. I want to do some good.'

'If you carry on with that ambition, you'll get tears, frustration, the occasional high, a lot of banging your head against the wall, hours and hours of hard work. You'll come across as atrocious, and make a few good friends.'

Cathryn said, 'That's what I reckoned.'

More Than Just Roast Beef

'It will be the end of everything,' said Nora. 'No more rambling conversations and walks. No more exchanging radio moments. Friday night at the pub won't be the same.'

'When's Brendan going?' said Nathan.

'Handing in his notice on Monday. Then at the weekend he and Jen are going down to Bristol to look for a place to rent. Once they're living there, they'll look for something to buy.'

They were in Nathan's living room, side by side on the sofa, feet up in front of them on the coffee table, which was strewn with the remains of an Indian takeaway. Nora had her hands folded over her stomach, which seemed to have a life of its own. It moved, jumped from boot blows on the inside.

'Lively, isn't it?' he said.

'Probably likes curries,' said Nora. She shifted. 'It's not natural, being pregnant. I think scientists should come up with another way to bring new people into the world. This foetal position business is a lie. Unborn babies jump about, kick you in the bladder and they lean on your ribs. I'm not going to have another, that's for sure.'

They were watching a film on television. Two men were fighting in a bar.

'They haven't smashed through the window yet,' said Nora. 'They always do that. It amazes me that American glass companies don't complain to Hollywood about how their products are presented to the world. People smash through windows very easily and don't get cut.'

Nathan said he supposed so. 'You're not quitting work when the baby comes along, then?'

'No,' said Nora. 'I already told you I can't.'

He said he could hardly wait to see the baby. 'It'll be wonderful. Girl or boy?'

Nora said, 'Yeah, wonderful. I don't know if it's a girl or boy. It'll be one of those for sure.'

'Have you been looking at nurseries?'

'Not yet. I haven't got round to it.'

'Well, have you thought of any names?'

'Nah,' said Nora. 'One will come to me when I need it.'

'You're in denial, aren't you?' said Nathan. 'You haven't admitted to yourself that this is happening.'

'I'm in denial as much as anyone can be in denial when they've got a huge bump to carry about, and they're getting kicked in the bladder and head-butted in the ribs and have indigestion and need to pee every five minutes.'

'You have to face up to this. You have to get ready,' said Nathan.

'I know,' said Nora. 'I will when the time comes.'

'You bother me,' he said. 'This is my baby, too.'

Nora said she was aware of that and he'd never seemed bothered before.

'I am,' Nathan told her. 'I've been thinking about it.'

One man on the television punched his opponent hard enough to send him sprawling into a swimming pool. The winner crunched his knuckles and shook his hand.

'That guy who's floating in the pool is going to get even and win in the end,' said Nora. 'The one who gets beat at the beginning of a film is always the one who wins in the end.'

'Hardly any point watching it, then,' said Nathan.

'We have to know how he does it, how he outwits the bad guys. And there's the cars and the clothes to look at,' said Nora.

'Is this what you and Brendan do?' said Nathan. 'Comment on how the film's going to end, and who has the best car?'

'Different films star different things,' Nora told him. '*Diva* had a fantastic flat. There was one film we saw starred an old Coca-Cola machine. Sometimes it's a dog, or a room, often it's a car. But I won't be going to the movies with Brendan any more. It's the end of everything. The end of roast beef Sundays.'

Nathan said, 'I can cook roast beef.'

She turned to look at him. 'Hidden talents. I didn't know that.'

'Oh yes,' he said.

She took it to mean he was talking about more than that. She thought he was offering her a Sunday lunch, and all that it meant. Perhaps it was

379

the place of roast beef in the scheme of things, it was a traditional meal, a family meal, but Nora had the idea that Nathan was offering her a more permanent place in his life.

If he'd asked her to move in with him, she'd have said yes. But she considered a place at his Sunday lunch table to be nearly the next best thing. Sunday was special to him; it was the day he spent with his daughter. So Nora comforted herself that maybe some part of her life was ending, but something else was beginning. But that was Nora. A man she thought she knew well made a simple remark about roast beef, and she made up a story.

*   *   *

At work, on Monday, Brendan went upstairs to see Nora. He told her he'd handed in his notice. 'Leaving in two weeks,' he said. 'Should be a month, but I've got holidays due.' He sighed.

'Big sigh,' said Nora.

Brendan shrugged. 'I've gone off the whole thing.'

Saturday night had been Jen's night. It had been filled with her plans, her dreams, her triumph at finally getting a chance to do the job she'd wanted for years. She paced the living room, too exhilarated to sit still. Her face was flushed, eyes aglow; she couldn't stop smiling. She kept repeating, 'I can't believe it. I got it. I got it.'

It had been intoxicating. Brendan had been enraptured by the thrill she felt. But, later, when they made love and Jen had shouted, 'Yes! Yes!' he'd had the impression her cry of joy had more to do with her own achievement than any effort he was making.

On Sunday, he'd cooked lunch as always. The fire was lit, music played and everyone arrived bearing gifts and cards for Jen. Nora had spread the news. The atmosphere had been jolly, as near to a Pickwickian Christmas as anything Brendan had ever experienced, even though it was now January.

The gloom, a dense black cloud of it, descended at about nine o'clock at night. Everyone had gone; he'd told Jen to put her feet up and watch the film on telly, he'd clear up. He was standing at the sink, sleeves rolled up, hands deep in water, watching a plate sail the soapy seas. He and Jen had been making plans. They'd go to Bristol at the weekend to find somewhere to rent. In three weeks' time they'd move down, taking some basic belongings but leaving the house as it was because it would be easier to sell furnished. Jen would start her new job immediately, so he'd have to look for somewhere to buy. And once this house was sold, he would have to arrange for everything to be transported to the new house.

Jen had said, 'When we buy a new house, you'll be able to sort it out. Do any decorating and gardening and whatever, because you won't be working. You'll have time to do things.'

He wouldn't have a job. He was going to do nothing. He'd be free to paint walls, fix things, cook and clean. As he wiped a plate, it floated into his mind that in days to come he'd be doing this rather a lot.

'What am I going to do?' he said to Nora. 'Nothing. No job, no future. Nothing.'

'That's what's so great about it,' said Nora.

'Nothing's wonderful. You'll be the new guy in town. Like the gunslinger in westerns who rides in slowly, not lookin' for trouble, but ready should it come along. You'll be moseying along taking each day as it comes, not knowing what tomorrow might bring.'

Brendan said he hadn't thought of it like that. 'I will find a job. I must.'

Nora enthused, 'You'll be like the Lone Ranger galloping up to the saloon, knowing that there's nothing you can't handle. People will step aside for you. Who is that guy without a jacket? Don't you know, why it's—'

'Shut up, Nora,' said Brendan.

'No, really,' said Nora. 'It's wonderful to be able to just go somewhere and make a new life for yourself. There are bound to be opportunities, and it's not as if you don't have experience. You can do anything.'

He smiled. She'd made him feel better. But, considering the Lone Ranger analogy, he thought he was going to be more of a Tonto.

Winter Gets You Down

In the time she'd been staying with Gregory, Mona had kept herself busy. She had planted a garden, painted the kitchen, made jam, which, neatly labelled, lined a shelf in the cupboard. Neither of them had eaten any of it. 'Well, we're not jam people,' said Mona.

'So why make it?' said Gregory.

Mona couldn't answer that. Except to say she'd

enjoyed the process, watching fruit melt into sugar, smelling the strawberryness of it all. Summer in the country had its merits. They'd sat in the garden, had long evening walks in the woods behind the house. Nights they'd slept with the windows and front door open, letting the smells of the world drift in. Summer in the country was fine.

Winter got Mona down. It was dark when she left for work, and dark when she got home. She had to drive slowly; icy roads scared her. When it rained, the track leading to the house turned to mud, and it often rained. She said to Gregory that she couldn't remember a time when there was so much weather about. 'I'm sure we don't have this much in the city.'

He was sure they did. She just hadn't noticed it.

She said she'd never been so affected by it. 'In the city, life just carries on the same as ever. Only in winter you wear a coat and use taxis or public transport more so you won't get wet.'

They watched a lot of television. And Mona complained about that. 'It's rubbish,' she said, squirming. She read, she worked. Weekends, she tramped the woods and fields, not, she said, because she wanted to, but because clean air was good for her skin. Besides, there was nothing else to do. Brown fields and bare trees had a certain aesthetic appeal, she said, but really she'd prefer to be flanked by shops, lit and laden with good things to look at and, hopefully, buy. In bed, she told Gregory that the only temptations of country life were carnal. There was nothing else to do. 'No wonder people get pregnant. Well, there's eating, I'll give you that. Either way, you get fat. Winter gets you down.'

The first signs of spring brought a gladdening of her heart she'd never felt so intensely before. She said she knew, at last, what the old poets she'd read at school were on about: there was pleasure in snowdrops and longer days and the first tiny buds. When she arrived home from work, blackbirds sang in the hedges surrounding their garden. 'I have survived,' she told herself. Not without a small amount of shame. It was not as if she'd been living in vile discomfort. She'd been warm, fed, and had a comfortable bed to sleep in. All she'd endured was a season, some dark weeks, of cold and wet. But still, she rejoiced to see the back of it.

The silence alarmed her. Monday morning, a new week, and she was looking forward to driving into the city. There was still a rush at seeing paved streets, traffic, shops, people. But today, no birds sang outside; the bedroom was lit strangely, grey-blue. She got out of bed, crossed the room and opened the curtains. Snow.

A monstrous dumping of the stuff had come driving in from the east overnight. There was no doubt that it had turned the world beyond her window exquisite. For a moment the glisten of it took her breath away, and then she realised she might be snowed in.

She went to open the front door, to check exactly how deep it was. An iced drift, packed hard and waist high, stopped her going out. Not that she would have, anyway; she was only wearing a silk nightdress, and there wasn't a lot of that to cover her. A blast of freezing chill made her gasp, and she slammed the door shut.

'We're fucking snowed in,' she called. 'There's a

bloody heap of snow blocking the front door. I thought it was spring.'

Gregory came through, still groggy, still coming to. The cold and silence had made him sleep deeply. 'It's January. That's not spring.'

'But it was sunny the other day,' said Mona. As if, somehow, this sudden change in the weather was his fault.

He shrugged and said, 'It happens.'

Mona dressed. Cocooned in jeans, T-shirt, sweater and Gregory's parka, she walked, snow crunching underfoot, to check the state of the road to town. Her car was buried under a white, frosted heap. A snow plough had not long swept past, but had left a five-foot mound of cleared snow across the entrance of the track to the cottage. They'd have to dig their way out.

The storm had brought down the electricity line, and for two days they lit the cottage with candles and cooked on the wood-burning stove, beans mostly. The light outside was exquisite. Mona rubbed a peephole in the steamed window and peered out. She had never known such stillness, the whole world reshaped and sculpted white overnight, trees stark against a thick sky, the occasional refugee bird, crouched, cold and definitely grumpy, in their branches. She said it would be romantic, if it wasn't so awful. 'A person needs electricity.'

Every so often, one of them would click a switch on and off, on and off, checking to see if they'd been reconnected. But no. At least twice a day, they would pull on their outdoor clothes and stamp down the track to see if the wall of snow left by the plough had cleared, or melted. But no.

It was after four; the light was turning grey, granular. Soon it would be dark. Mona and Gregory trudged, in silence, towards the road. 'I don't know why you keep doing this,' said Gregory. 'The snow won't have cleared. You'll have to wait for the thaw.'

Mona said, 'And when's that coming?'

'I don't know. I don't have any control over the weather.'

Mona was in jeans and boots. She wore a fur-lined leather jacket open over a thick, high-necked black sweater and a long blue-and-red-striped scarf. She didn't like to zip her jacket; it looked better open, she thought. The cold bit her face, stung her ears. She felt something soft trickle past her cheek, and looked up. Blinking. Above her, the air was filled with millions of flakes drifting down. It was beautiful. But at that moment, not to Mona. 'It's snowing again. This isn't right. I can't have things like snow in my life.'

Gregory said he was sorry she'd been so meteorologically inconvenienced.

'This is what you get when you love somebody. You move away from bars and cafés and, well, life to be with them. You give up everything, your friends, your lovers, and it snows.'

'Lovers?' said Gregory.

'Yes,' said Mona. 'Lovers. I had lovers. I thought I had it all. I had you and a couple of guys I saw. And don't tell me you didn't have a lover or two. I won't believe you.'

He shrugged.

'Knew it,' said Mona.

Gregory said that what he got when he gave up his lover—'Only one. Not like you, with two'—was a new kitchen he didn't want, a new sofa, and rows and rows of jam on the shelves.

They glared at one another. Snow falling on them, landing in their hair.

'Talk about the weather being inconvenient. Love's inconvenient. It spoils your plans,' said Mona.

'You think I don't know that,' said Gregory. 'I tried. But in the morning all I ever thought about was you. I'd imagine you back at the flat, getting up, making that hideous fruit mush you drink in the Magimix, standing in that robe thing, and I'd want to be there too.'

Mona said, 'Did you? You never said.'

'I thought you wanted the life you had,' he told her.

'I did,' said Mona. 'I really did. I tried. But it didn't work. I only wanted you. You can't have everything.'

Gregory said, 'You can. It's just you come to realise that your everything isn't what you thought it was. It comes down to one person.'

They started back to the cottage, tramping slowly at first. Snow crunching underfoot. Then they began to run, a cumbersome, almost leaden trot, hampered by the thick covering underfoot. They panted, their breath spilling, steaming, into the frosted air. Mona took off her jacket. Gregory took off his Barbour. Into the cottage, and she was peeling off her sweater. Lumps of iced snow, trailed in by their feet, lay on the carpet. In the bedroom they both sat on the bed and fumbled with frozen fingers to unlace their boots.

'Bloody clothes,' said Mona. 'This'll be why there's a low birth rate in cold climates. Nobody can get their kit off.'

Naked, they climbed, shivering now, into bed, and clung to one another. 'Bloody love and bloody weather,' said Mona. 'Things you can't control.'

Gregory said he knew.

It rained overnight. The snow turned grey and slushy. Gregory said the road would be open, and it would be easy to clear away the heap blocking the drive. Mona, still in bed, enjoying the heat and lazy from love, said, 'Stuff it. I'll phone work and tell them I'm still snowed in.'

Over breakfast, Mona lamented the melting snow. 'I forgot to enjoy it when it was here.'

Gregory said that you didn't know what you'd got till it was gone. 'But never mind, it'll come again next year.'

Mona said she didn't want to think about that. 'I love it here in summer. But winter is hell.'

'So,' said Gregory, 'we could live in the flat in winter. I'll commute, so you don't have to drive. We could stay here in the summer. You commute.'

'You'd do that?'

'Said I would. That way there's a flat or a cottage vacant should either of us need it. But you're going to have to evict your heavily pregnant tenant.'

Mona said she'd give Nora till next October to find somewhere new to live. 'I'm not that evil a landlord.'

$$*\qquad*\qquad*$$

In George's kitchen, Nora listed her problems. 'One, heartburn, which I hate. Two, I've run out of milk, which means drinking coffee black, which

388

will increase my heartburn. Three, I can't get into my favourite shoes. Look.' She held out her feet for George to examine. 'They're all swollen.'

George said, 'That's what you're worrying about.'

'Yes, and I have an inkling Nathan's seeing his wife again. I'm about to be booted out of my flat, and Brendan's leaving.'

'But you'd rather worry about the other things,' said George.

'The other things are immediate.'

'But temporary,' said George.

'I don't think I can do anything about Nathan; besides, it's only an inkling. She phoned the other day when I was at his flat. It could have been anything, of course, but there was something in the gentle way he spoke to her.'

'You're imagining it. You imagine something, then, somehow, I don't know how, it becomes real in your head,' said George.

'Perhaps,' said Nora. 'But sometimes what I imagine is right.'

George said, 'Let's talk about the flat problem.'

Nora said she didn't want to, and she'd miss Brendan. But, of course, she couldn't tell him that.

'Why not?' asked George.

'It's not the way of things with Brendan and me. We don't talk like that. It'd embarrass him. We never talk about us.'

'Just life's absurdities,' said George.

'Yes,' said Nora. 'Like when you were a kid, going somewhere in the back of your dad's car with your face breathing on the window, you'd imagine yourself on a white horse riding through the landscape you were passing, jumping hedges and fences and keeping up with the car.'

George said, 'Yeah, I used to do that. Only my horse was black.'

Nora said, 'Really? Brendan's was like Champion the Wonder Horse.'

George said, 'Nora. Nora. Nora. We have to talk about your problems. Not imaginary horses.' He took her hand and led her from the kitchen to his living room, sat her on the sofa.

'Perhaps you'd feel better if you just mentioned to Brendan how much you're going to miss him.'

'Nope,' said Nora. 'It isn't like that.'

'Do you love him?' said George.

'Good heavens, no,' said Nora. 'Whatever gave you that idea? We're just mates.'

Nora and Brendan had rarely spoken about their friendship. Giving it a definition, speaking about it out loud might have spoiled it. But once she had asked him whether, if they'd met at a different time, under different circumstances, they would have 'You know,' she'd said. 'Got together.'

They had been in her flat at the time. Brendan had been instructing her in the art of tea-making. Warming the pot, number of spoonfuls of tea leaves. She had been, for the first time, using the teapot her father had given her.

He had looked at her closely. 'Nah. Don't fancy you.'

'Well, thanks for that. Suppose we kissed, just to check. Nothing meant by it. Nothing physical to follow, just to see what would happen.'

He'd looked at her critically. 'Don't think so.'

'Go on,' she said. 'Just to see.'

But they couldn't do it. They'd put their faces close. Breathed expectantly. And backed off.

'Nah,' they'd said. 'Won't work. It's a chat thing.'

'It was just a chat thing,' Nora told George now. 'Nothing more.'

'I was just checking,' said George. 'Let's talk about your flat situation. We will have to find you somewhere to live.'

Nora said, 'We?'

'Yes, Nora, we. You and me. Us. We will find you a new flat.'

Nora said, 'Oh.'

'You don't think in terms of we, do you?' said George. 'But you're soon to be a we. There will be two of you. I get the impression you have accepted being pregnant, but not what's going to follow. It's not a permanent state, pregnancy.'

Nora said, 'You're right.'

George fetched the morning paper and turned to the property page.

'You're going to start looking now,' said Nora.

'Now,' he told her. 'I'm a now person.'

'I'm a put-it-off-till-tomorrow person,' said Nora. 'I'd rather talk about imaginary horses.'

George had finished and delivered his cookbook. His publisher suggested a series, *The Diffident Cook Goes Italian*, then French, American, Thai and Chinese. George suggested *The Diffident Cook in Love*. Meals you can concoct to show off to your girlfriend. He was given an advance, and was euphoric. He quit his job. Then worried.

'What if nobody buys them? And I lose everything and end up living in a doorway in the Grassmarket, begging for money for a cup of coffee?'

'You'd have to ask for enough for a decent

cappuccino. Any old coffee wouldn't do you,' said Nora. She told him not to worry, he could come and live with her. 'In my new flat that *we* are going to find. You can cook for me.'

Brendan and Jen finally left for Bristol. They had found a flat to rent, and had put their house on the market. When it sold, they'd buy a place of their own.

Nora and George went to say goodbye. Nora had bought Brendan a new teapot. 'For your new house,' she said. 'So you'll think of me whenever you brew a pot. Which will be often.'

He told her she shouldn't have. 'You should hold on to your cash.'

But she said what was the point of cash if you didn't squander some on your pals? 'And I bought you this.' She handed him a gift-wrapped parcel. 'Don't open it till you get there.'

Now, saying goodbye, Brendan shook George's hand. 'Thanks for coming to see me off.' He put his arm round Nora, which was, if she thought about it, the only time they really touched. He told her to take care of herself.

She had hugged and kissed Jen, told her she'd miss them both. Then said, 'Go, please go, before I start crying.'

Brendan and Jen had driven off, tooting the horn of the car, arms out of the windows, waving. Nora cried.

'I promised myself I wouldn't do this.'

George gave her a hanky. 'Knew you would.'

In his car, driving back to their building, Nora said, 'Everything changes. It's not the same without Brendan.'

'He's only been gone five minutes,' said George.

'I know. But you can feel it. The streets, the houses, the buildings. It's all different now he's gone. Why do things change?'

George told her not to ask silly questions. 'Things have to change. We grow up. We get older. Very soon you won't be the same old Nora we all know and love. A baby changes everything.'

Nora said she supposed. And she also supposed she should think of a name. She asked George what his favourite name was.

He thought, Nora. But told her Luke. 'I always liked that name. When I was a kid I used to imagine I was Luke de Grand. I put on an old red tablecloth for a cape and carried a wooden sword, and I used to hide in a huge rhododendron bush in the park near my home, and jump out at people. "I am Luke de Grand, the avenger. Prepare to meet your doom."'

'Really?' said Nora. 'What did people say?'

'They just laughed,' said George.

*　　　*　　　*

Three hours later, after Brendan and Jen had crossed the border, and were headed south, they stopped by the side of the road. They poured tea from a thermos, and took in the view. Brendan opened the parcel Nora had given him. It was a junior Lone Ranger outfit.

'Why did she give you that?' said Jen.

He told her. 'I was a bit low, worried about not having a job. She said I could do anything. I'd ride into town, up to the saloon, like the Lone Ranger. There would be nothing I couldn't handle.'

Jen said, 'I always preferred Tonto.'

Farrell Greyson's Etchings and Lorna's Plan

When, a couple of days later, she went to see Farrell Greyson's etchings, Nora was drawn, briefly, into the movement, banter and bustle of a large family. He had a big town house in Herriot Row, bought, he told her, in the days before parking was a bugger and property prices went silly. 'Couldn't afford to buy the place now.'

The stairwell was lined with paintings, which Farrell said saved a lot on redecorating. 'Hides the paintwork,' he said. There were more pictures in every room. Farrell had been collecting for years.

Nora found the hum of this family's life attractive. When she went home, she was struck by how lonely she felt. Standing in her own flat, alone for a moment in its silence before she switched on her radio, she was aware of herself being a solitary figure in a place where all the rooms, except for the one she was standing in, were empty. She knew she was missing a lot.

In Farrell's house there had been voices, music. His youngest son hadn't yet left home, and one of his daughters was back with the family after a love affair had ended badly. There had been banter and jokes at the table. Farrell and his wife, Pauline, had discussed their grandchildren, the mischief they'd got up to, their cleverness, who they took after.

Nora had felt a pang of grief and guilt when listening to all that. She thought she had little to offer a child. At the dinner table there had been a brief silence when she'd said she had no contact with her mother.

'Who is going to look after the baby when you're at work?' said Pauline.

Nora said she'd been looking into nurseries.

'But you'll need someone after the baby's born. To help. To just come round and be there. You can't be alone at a time like that.'

Nora said she had Nathan. He was all she needed. But she only saw him at weekends, and sometimes for dinner during the week, and they hadn't actually spoken about changing that situation. Mona was involved with Gregory and not living in town; Brendan was gone. She only had George, and actually, now she thought about it, she really needed him.

'Well,' said Pauline, 'babies can make you isolated. I'm glad you've got someone.'

As Nora was leaving, Pauline gave her some baby clothes, a changing mat, a cot duvet and other baby things. 'All grown out of,' she said. 'Save you buying them.'

Looking at them now, seeing the space they took up in her living room, the truth of her situation hit Nora. She emerged from the denial she'd been in. Throughout her pregnancy, she had gone through the check-ups, the weighings, the taking of her blood pressure, everything, and not quite let herself realise the absolute inevitability of what was happening to her. She was having a baby. If asked what names she was considering, Nora would joke, 'Salmonella. This is a child of food poisoning.'

But she couldn't call someone that. She slumped on to the sofa, stroked her belly. Stared, glazed, at the pile of clothes and equipment she'd been given. It was happening, she was going to have a baby, and when she thought about it, she had nothing at all to offer it.

*   *   *

In the dining room of the house he'd once lived in with Lorna, Nathan finished the last of the paella she'd cooked for supper, and drained his glass. He'd taken Justine to see a French double bill at the Filmhouse, and would have taken her to dinner, but Lorna had suggested they both come home for a meal. He told her the food had been fabulous.

The room was painted dark red, with pale cream cornices; a fire glowed in the grate. The curtains, thick red velvet, were drawn. The table glistened: fruit on a huge glass platter, cheeses, an antique decanter filled with vintage port. The only light came from candles, about thirty of them, placed in thoughtful groups on the mantelpiece, the table and bookcase. Nathan had the feeling he was being wooed, and didn't care to wonder why. He was enjoying it too much.

'Can I take this as a good sign?' he asked.

'A good sign of what?' Lorna said.

'That you might take me back. I'm forgiven. Though you're the one who had an affair.'

'Only because I was lonely. You were never here, Nathan.' Lorna was wearing a dark blue silk shirt, tight black jeans and a lot of jewellery. Mostly silver. Her hair was pulled back from her face and tied loosely with a velvet band. She was barefoot, toenails painted scarlet. Nathan thought she looked breathtaking.

Justine had gone out to visit a friend. 'To chill,' she'd told her mother. 'Hang out, listen to some music.' There was no music playing in this room, though. Lorna hated when it was played in the background, insisting it should be listened to and was too important to be merely a sound to ease conversation or provide atmosphere. Still, for the next few hours, Nathan and Lorna would have the house to themselves.

He said he knew he'd left her on her own too often. He was sorry. 'I just got caught up.'

'You got caught up with your work friends, going to the pub, staying late at the office, going to galleries on your own, going walking on your own. You should have been caught up with me,' she said. 'Of course I had an affair. Someone came along and told me I was beautiful and he wanted me. I needed that.'

He told her, of course she did. 'And you are beautiful. You are the most beautiful woman I've ever known.' He had to hand it to her. She'd had an affair, but he was the one apologising. Lorna had that effect on him.

She put a few grapes and a sliver of Brie on her plate, 'You can hardly criticise me for having an affair, when you had one too. Besides, I didn't get pregnant.'

Nathan told her that the baby wasn't his fault. 'Nora was on the pill. She got sick. She should have known to take extra precautions.'

'But she didn't,' said Lorna. 'And now there's a baby to think about. Is she prepared for it?'

He had over the past weeks been lingering longer and longer when he delivered Justine home after their outings. In time, he'd told her about

397

Nora, and then, a little later, about the baby. Lorna had looked at him in horror when he'd confessed he was about to become a father again, and had told him to leave.

But the next week she again invited him in, and asked about Nora. Who was she? Where did she live? What did she look like? Was she musical? Clever? Artistic in any way? Nora fascinated her. And one evening, when Nora was in his flat, Lorna had phoned inviting him to dinner.

'She wasn't prepared the last time I saw her. That was over two weeks ago. I can't just break up with her, not at the moment. I have to let her down gently,' said Nathan.

Lorna nodded. 'Of course.'

'Actually,' Nathan said, 'I don't think anybody's thinking about this child. Nora's in complete denial. She hasn't thought of any names. Nothing.'

'Well, you are the father, Nathan. It's your responsibility too. You could look at nurseries. You could come up with names. Actually, I've been thinking about it,' said Lorna. 'A lot.'

She fetched a pot of coffee from the kitchen, poured each of them a cup, and filled a glass with port for Nathan. She only drank wine. He took this as a very good sign indeed. If he drank too much, he wouldn't be able to drive home. He decided he would drink too much, but not as much as might impair any getting-back-together activities.

'I've been thinking that *if* I have you back, we should take the baby.'

Nathan swallowed. 'You'd do that?'

'Yes. It would be good for us. Besides, the child exists. What has happened has happened. We shouldn't ignore it. And think what we could offer.

Music, books, a good home. An excellent school when the time comes. Security. Children need that.'

Nathan nodded. 'You really have been thinking about this.'

'What can Nora offer? She has nothing. She has an interesting way of dressing, I must say.'

'You've seen her?' said Nathan.

'Of course I have. I wanted to know what she looked like. I've been outside the flat she lives in. I've watched her come home with that chap who drives her to and from work.'

Lorna had parked her car opposite the entrance of Nora's building and seen Nora heave herself from George's Beetle, then disappear inside with him. It wasn't enough, though. On quizzing Nathan further, she'd found out that Nora often went to the Modern Art Gallery with Brendan on Saturday afternoons. She had gone on three consecutive Saturdays before the pair of them had turned up, and she'd followed them round as they took in the paintings, listening to their comments. Then, in the café downstairs, she had sat close by, watching as Nora ate carrot cake and chatted to Brendan.

'You've been spying on her,' said Nathan.

'If that's how you want to put it. I call it curiosity.'

Nathan imagined Lorna hanging about in doorways wearing a dark scarf on her head and impenetrable Dior sunglasses. She looked exotically glamorous in his vision. He was also beginning to remember why he had spent so much time out of the house. Lorna was a driven woman.

She sought perfection in everything—house,

husband, daughter, music. The house was decorated in dark colours with a lot of velvet to be seen. The impression Lorna was after was artistic, intellectual, rather than plain old stylish. Justine was a precious, precocious child. Fed the best balanced diet Lorna could devise, enrolled in the best Edinburgh school two days after her birth. Sent to tennis lessons, music lessons, riding lessons and dance classes. Thus limiting any free time she might have, and restricting the number of unsuitable friends she might make. Lorna had devised Nathan's wardrobe and haircut, making him the man she wanted to be seen with. Nathan hadn't minded, because that had made him the sort of man a lot of other women wanted to be seen with too.

Music was the only thing that had defeated Lorna. Her love for it had reduced her to tears many times. But what really made her cry, well, wail and sob, was that, despite hours and hours of daily practice, she had come to realise she was merely good. Not enough. She wanted to be great.

Still, she was a stunning woman. The sort of good looks that overcame everything. No matter what Lorna was doing, she was beautiful. Beautiful to Nathan when he came across her waxing her upper lip, beautiful when she got horribly drunk one New Year and was sick over the back of the sofa. This event was never discussed in the household. Lorna had even been beautiful when she came round in a hospital bed after her hysterectomy. She'd had cancer.

'I had Hugh Randall and his wife over for dinner last week, and he gave me the lowdown on Nora,' Lorna continued.

'You did?' said Nathan.

He hadn't known Lorna's lover, Howard. But a friend did, and had told him about it. Howard had been wildly in love at first, but in the end had been worn down by Lorna's demands. It was whispered, though, that Lorna had thrown Howard out because he wore his socks in bed. This had made Nathan smile. It probably wasn't true. But if Howard had been foolish enough to slip under the duvet with Lorna wearing only his socks, this was, indeed, how she would have reacted.

'Hugh told me all about her. Nora's a Londoner. Overly imaginative, dreamy, prone to going her own way. Not many friends. Lives in a flat that Mona owns. Not much contact with her mother. Interestingly, Hugh didn't want to employ her but William Martinetti did. She spends a lot of time with her friend Brendan. Scribbles stupid comments on Hugh's memos and wrote Nadine, Queen of the Trails. Hugh sent me some back copies. I think it was the best thing in the magazine. I enjoyed it.'

Nathan didn't know what to say.

So Lorna continued. 'All in all, Nora sounds fine. But hardly a candidate for motherhood.'

Nathan said he'd have to ask Nora about all this. He didn't know what she'd say.

Lorna smiled. 'I imagine she'll miss the baby. But deep down she'll be relieved.' She refilled Nathan's glass with vintage port. 'You must put it to her sensibly.' She sighed. 'Nathan, I want a baby. I'd prefer it to be yours. I can't have one. After you come back to live with me, this will be the only opportunity I'll get.'

'What about Justine?' said Nathan. 'How will

she take to another child in the house?'

'She's delighted. She'd love a little brother or sister.'

'You've discussed this with her?' Nathan couldn't believe this.

'Of course, she lives here. A baby will be part of her life too.'

Nathan ran his finger round the top of his glass, trying to take in all Lorna had said.

Watching him, Lorna repeated, 'Nathan, I want a baby.' Then, 'It's almost half past eight. We have two hours before Justine comes home. What would you like to do?'

As if she had to ask.

* * *

In the weeks since she'd last seen Nathan, Nora's imagination flew. Something had happened to him, he was ill. Maybe she should go and see him? She had phoned several times, but he was never in. She'd left messages on his machine. 'Hi, it's me. Just wondering how you were. I'm doing fine. Both of me.'

Perhaps he was just overloaded with work. Perhaps he'd gone off to his holiday hut. Perhaps he just needed a break from her. Perhaps. Perhaps. Perhaps.

Late on Nathan's third Saturday without getting in touch, Nora asked George if he would lend her his car so she could drive down to his flat. 'Just to see him. I need to know what's going on.'

George gave her the key. 'Just don't drive it fast. It's old and feeble.'

Nathan wasn't in, Nora could see that as soon as

she looked down into his basement flat from the street. But she lumbered down the steps to his door and rang the bell anyway. There was no reply; no lights were on. The pub, she thought. She drove round to Hamilton Place, crawled along, staring at faces, hoping to see his. She imagined finding him, and he would wave to her, come strutting up to her, enfold her, and say, 'Sorry. I've been missing you.'

She parked. She stood at the door of his drinking haunt, scanning the people there. There was no Nathan. She did the same at other pubs she knew he liked. Then at the Indian restaurant he'd often taken her to. Still no Nathan. She drove up The Bridges to his favourite Italian. She stepped inside, looked round at the faces looking at her. No Nathan. She went back to the car. All the time, as she drove along, she searched the crowds. He wouldn't be hard to spot. That way of walking he had, a slight swagger, knowing people looked at him. He stuck out in a crowd.

Then, remembering that inkling of weeks ago, with a sinking heart Nora drove to where she secretly knew he was. She stopped across the street from the house he'd once shared with Lorna. The curtains were shut. His old tank of a dark red car was in the driveway. She sat staring at it for an hour. She didn't move, didn't cry. She'd stopped thinking, speculating. She knew he'd left her.

She drove home. Knocked on George's door, to hand him back his keys.

'Did you find Nathan?' he asked.

'Oh yes,' said Nora. 'I did. He's at his wife's house.'

'What's he doing there?'

403

'At one in the morning, with all the lights out? What do you think?'

'They could be in a back room, talking,' said George.

Nora said, 'I don't think so. He's gone back to her. Knew he would, really. Bring on the Leonard Cohen records and the man-size tissues; my heart has been broken.'

'Do you have to make a joke of everything?'

'Yes,' said Nora. 'Definitely yes. I've been told to get out of my flat. I'm hugely pregnant, bloated, swollen ankles, waddling about. I haven't thought about the baby at all, really. And the man I lost my heart to, the father of my child, has left me for his ex-wife. I think a joke is called for, don't you?' Her face crumpled, tears came. 'In fact,' she said, 'I think I'm it.'

Luke

At eight o'clock on the thirtieth of March, Nora went into labour. It was a Sunday night. Though she had been told what to expect, she was still taken by surprise. The sudden gush of water. She'd been in the kitchen, standing beside the kettle, waiting for it to boil, when it happened. She'd stared down at the floor, felt the wetness between her legs, and thought, what the hell is that?

There was a terrible feeling of blood draining, stomach turning over when she realised it was the baby coming. This is it. She wanted to run away. But where to? And, after all, how could she? When, obviously, the thing she was running away from would come with her.

The first contractions were mild. A pang, she thought. What's the fuss about? This is nothing. Three hours later she was pacing, thinking, oh my God, this is hell. George was out. He'd gone to a convention for cookery writers in Birmingham. Mona was far away; besides, they didn't see much of each other these days. There was a strong desire to phone her mother. But what could she say to her? 'Hello, Mum, I'm having a baby.' She didn't think so. For the same reason, she didn't get in touch with Aunt May.

She phoned Brendan. 'I'm in labour,' she said.

'Well done,' he said.

Nora heard Jen in the background asking Brendan who he was speaking to. 'Nora,' he said. 'She's in labour.'

'Where is she?' asked Jen.

'Where are you?' Brendan asked Nora.

'At home,' said Nora. She heard Jen in the background asking how far apart her contractions were.

'Twenty minutes,' she told Brendan.

Jen took the phone from Brendan. 'Get to hospital,' she said. 'Get Nathan to take you.'

Nora said Nathan wasn't there, and that George was out too.

'Well for God's sake call a taxi. Get into hospital, now.'

Nora put the phone down, then rang the hospital and told them she was coming in. Then she phoned for a taxi. She thought the driver rather put his foot down as they hurtled through the streets. A wet Edinburgh night, Nora thought. I like this city in the rain. She wondered if the taxi driver was anxious to get her to the hospital, or if he just wanted to get her out of his cab.

Waddling up to reception, Nora was aware of how absurd she looked. She had the palm of her left hand on her lower back. She thought her hair was on end. She was pale and sweaty. 'I'm having a baby,' she said. As if it hadn't been utterly obvious why she was there.

At six in the morning, Nora gave birth to a boy. 'And what are we to call him?' the midwife asked.

'Luke,' said Nora. The name slipped out as if she'd been planning it all along.

Two hours after arriving in the ward, Nora was still stunned. Luke lay in his crib, sleeping, and she wished she could hold him, but wasn't sure if she was allowed. She climbed carefully from bed, went to the public phones in the corridor. And dialled Brendan's number.

'It's a boy,' she said. 'Luke.'

'Fantastic,' said Brendan. 'Knew you could do it.'

'He's little, and has black hair. Not bald at all. No teeth, though.'

'Ask for your money back,' said Brendan.

'He's got brown eyes and doesn't look like anybody I know,' said Nora.

'Maybe you've got the wrong one,' said Brendan.

'No, this is him. I haven't let him out of my sight. I've come over all mumsy and seriously hormonal. I want to cry.'

'Please don't,' said Brendan.

'OK, I won't. Still, I wish you could see him. You'd be awestruck, dazzled by his beauty.' Then she started to cry. 'I wish someone would come so

I could show him off. I want to see somebody.'

Brendan said, 'Don't worry. You'll get visitors soon enough. So the baby isn't like you, then?'

'No,' said Nora. 'He sucks his fingers already. A sign of great intelligence. Not at all like me.'

At two o'clock George appeared. He stood at the entrance of the ward holding a huge bunch of flowers, looking round trying to spot her.

Nora waved wildly, shouting his name, and as he approached, opened her arms to welcome him. They hugged. She kissed his cheek. 'It's wonderful to see you. Thanks for coming.'

George told her he wanted to come.

'I've had a baby,' Nora told him.

George said he knew. Then looked round. 'So has everybody else in here. Must be catching.'

He sat on the edge of the bed. Nora took his hand. 'I called him Luke. He's beautiful. He's got fingers and everything.'

George went to look at him. 'Hello, Luke. Good name.'

The child was tiny, pink, swaddled in a blanket His eyes were closed, his fists clenched, tight beside his cheeks. His mouth moved softly, sucking. George peered down at him.

'You're right, he has got fingers. Amazing thing, a baby.'

'I know,' said Nora. She wondered how he knew she was here.

'Where else would you be?' he said. 'Anyway, Jen phoned. She phoned everybody.'

He'd brought her some flowers and a train set.

'Luke's only hours old,' said Nora. 'He won't be playing with it for a while.'

'Everybody should have a train set when they're

407

little,' said George. 'We can set it up in your living room.'

Nora pointed out that her living room wouldn't be her living room soon enough.

'Well, we can set it up in my living room, and you two can come over to play,' said George.

He looked down at the baby again. 'Pretty scary, though,' he said.

Nora said it was the scariest thing in the world.

George looked at her. 'Are you all right?'

Nora said she was fine. 'Really fine.'

Nathan came that evening, brought her half a dozen roses. He lifted his son, declared him to be beautiful, kissed him, and told Nora that nothing smelled better than a baby.

Nora looked at him and said it really depended which end you were at.

He put Luke back in his crib, came to sit on the bed by Nora, took her hand. 'There are things we need to talk about.'

'No need,' said Nora. 'I know you've gone back to Lorna.'

'How did you know that?'

'I guessed,' she said. 'You haven't been near me for three weeks; you had to be somewhere.'

'Do you mind?' he asked.

'I'm in no state to answer that,' said Nora. 'I just had a baby. I'm not thinking at the moment, I'm cruising on hormones.'

'I want to talk about Luke,' said Nathan. 'His future. We'll wait till you get home. I'll come round and we can have a chat.'

Thinking Nathan was going to come up with a financial arrangement, Nora said, 'OK.'

He said he had to go. There was someone

waiting for him in the car.

Nora said, 'Lorna?'

Nathan nodded. 'Would you mind if she came up and saw the baby?'

Nora said she would. 'I'd mind a lot.' Then, 'I'm fine, by the way, thanks for asking. I'm going home tomorrow, George will drive me.'

Nathan nodded again and told her he'd see her soon.

The following morning, George took Nora and Luke home. His car was filled with things he'd bought for the small bundle in Nora's arms who was named after his childhood alter ego.

He watched while the baby fed and asked Nora if she'd like a cup of tea. When she said she would, he still stood, watching. 'A baby,' he said. 'It's amazing. Who'd have thought that was inside you?'

'What did you think was inside me? A sack of potatoes? The Seaforth Highlanders?'

'No,' said George. 'It's just when you see a baby, it's amazing.'

'So you said,' Nora told him. She finished feeding Luke.

And George reached down to take him from her. He held him, looking down. 'Amazing,' he said, watching as Luke's tiny fingers gripped his pinkie. 'Amazing.' He rocked back and forward.

'You're quite motherly,' said Nora.

'Brendan once said that. It's not a term I'd use to describe myself. It's just I like babies.'

'When did you discover that?' asked Nora.

'About five minutes ago,' he said. 'I've never actually met one before. You make the tea, I can't. I'm holding the baby.'

She settled, slowly, into a milky life. She was in a haze of guilt, hormones, sore breasts and sweat. She forced herself into a round of feeding, bathing Luke and washing his clothes, and wondered if she'd ever see the outside world again. But there was always a time, every day, when she would sit on the sofa, holding Luke, watching him breathe. She would stroke his head, his cheeks, hold his fingers between hers, and think: you are mine. She wore the same clothes a lot. Neglected herself a lot. Slept when she could, and spent time with George. Most days, she would go and see him. He'd be sitting at his kitchen table, notebooks in front of him, as he worked out recipes for his new book, *The Diffident Cook in Love*. As soon as Nora arrived, he would abandon his work and take Luke from her. He'd peer down at the child, saying, 'Hello. How are you?' And, 'Who's a big boy, then?'

Nora said, 'I didn't know you were such a softy, George.'

He said there was a lot she didn't know about him.

Sometimes he'd take care of Luke when Nora went out to the shops, but usually they went out together. Nora took the baby, he carried the shopping. He fussed, he took her arm when she crossed the road. Hardly surprising, then, that all the people they came into contact with took them for a couple.

'I'll have to go back to work soon,' Nora said one day. 'I don't want to. But I need the money.'

410

'You don't get paid on maternity leave?' said George.

'Not full pay. Not at this stage,' Nora told him. 'I've got the cash my dad gave me, but I don't want to use it all up. I'll need something for the deposit on a new flat. That's another thing. I need to look for somewhere to live. I think my baby idyll is ending. I have to get on with life.'

Time slipped by. In the narrowness of her world, Nora changed. She noticed that when the baby wasn't pressed against her, she felt empty. She was loath to put him down, and sat in the evenings just holding him. She called him secret nicknames. She grew to know him. The sounds he made, the expressions on his little face; she could read his silences. She watched him sleep. Afternoons, she bundled him into his carrier and walked with him, chatting, for that was her favourite thing to do, even if Luke could not join in. She thought it must be love. 'Weird,' she told him, 'because you're incontinent, dribble, puke a lot and conversationally you're a non-starter. But there you go.'

She loved the quiet way he took in the world. She loved his face, and the way he now smiled whenever he saw her. She thought she could get used to not working, strolling the streets she'd once walked with Brendan; she touched happiness.

The Best Mess

There were good days, and bad days. It was a Saturday, and a bad day. Luke cried all morning, and Nora didn't know why. She walked the floor with him on her shoulder, she patted his back, she winded him. And he howled. Howled more if she put him down. The flat was overflowing with baby clothes, draped over chairs and on the sofa. There was a bottle filled with boiled water on the coffee table, along with a row of empty tea cups Nora had left because she hadn't the time to clear up. Dirty nappies in the bathroom, dishes piled in the sink. And Luke howled. He was sick on her T-shirt. This was baby hell.

That was the day Nathan came to see Nora. He sat on the edge of the sofa, and refused a cup of coffee.

'Long time no see,' said Nora.

He said he was sorry. 'There's something I need to talk to you about. Luke.'

'He'll be fine. You can see him whenever you want. If you want.'

'I want more than that,' said Nathan. 'I want him. Lorna and I want him to come and live with us. We want to bring him up.'

Nora said, 'I don't believe what I'm hearing.'

'We've discussed it. Lorna thinks we can give Luke a good life. Education, a stable home. A child needs that.'

Nora said, 'Lorna thinks? What has my child got to do with Lorna?'

'He's my child too,' said Nathan. 'Lorna is my

wife. Or will be again very soon.'

Nora said, 'Congratulations.' She didn't mean it, though. And that was how it sounded.

Nathan looked at her. Nora shrugged.

Nathan said they should both be thinking about Luke. 'His life. His future.'

'His future is with me,' said Nora. 'I'll look after him. I'll see he is educated.'

'You don't look like you're coping,' said Nathan.

'So, the baby's been howling all day. It happens. There's sick on my clothes, dirty nappies to clear up, mess everywhere. This is what coping looks like. It would look the same in your house.'

Nathan said, 'Nora, you have to give this a little thought.'

'Get out.'

'Think about the life he'd have with Lorna and me.'

'Get out.'

'I could take you to court. I have a right, I'm his father. You are a single mother. You have nothing. You can give Luke nothing.'

'Take me to court? You're bluffing,' said Nora.

Nathan looked at his feet. He was.

'You'll get thrown out, you know that. Nathan, you have shown no interest in Luke. You have offered me no financial support. You have no chance of winning a legal battle. My sister is a lawyer, an extremely good one. She'll eat you alive in court. You'll emerge in shreds, laughed at and a whole lot poorer.' Nora took hold of the arms of her chair to hide how much she was shaking. She had no idea why she had mentioned her sister. Cathryn was not licensed to practise law in Scotland. She hoped Nathan wouldn't realise that.

413

Then again it had been some time since she and Cathryn had even spoken to one another. And she hadn't even been invited to Cathryn's wedding. But there it was. If she had to go grovelling to someone she was sure disliked her to keep her son, she'd do it.

Nathan stared at her. Was this Nora? She seemed oddly sane, grounded and sure of herself. Motherhood, he thought, did that.

'Lorna wants a baby,' Nathan said.

'Well, she can use the same method I did. She's had one already, I'm sure she knows how it's done.'

'She had a hysterectomy a few years back. She can't have a child by the method we used.'

'I'm sorry to hear that,' said Nora. 'But if Lorna wants a baby, she's going to have to go after someone else's. She's not getting mine.'

'Can't you see how good this would be for Luke? The things we can offer him,' said Nathan.

'Get out,' said Nora.

Nathan said, 'Nora . . .'

And Nora said, 'Get out.'

He stood up, sighed. 'Lorna said I'd left it too late. She said you'd have bonded with him by now. I should have spoken to you about all this as soon as he was born. Actually I couldn't do it. I couldn't face seeing you again. I'm sorry.'

Nora said, 'It was too late the second Luke was born. I didn't know how much I'd love him. Please get out. That's all I'm going to say, get out.'

After Nathan left, Nora went to see George. 'You'll never guess what happened. Nathan came to see me. He and his wife want to bring up Luke. They want to keep him.'

George took Luke from her. 'You're not going to agree to this, are you?'

'Of course not. I just can't believe it. He hasn't been near me since Luke was born, then he comes along and that's what he wants. I told him to get out.'

George said, 'I should think so too.' He crooned to the baby, 'Nobody's going to take you away.'

'George,' said Nora, 'don't get too attached to Luke. We'll be moving away. I'll have to start looking for a new flat soon.'

'I am attached to him,' said George. 'How could I not be? I know you have to find a new place. I've been thinking about it.'

That night, Nora phoned her Auntie May. She waited till Luke was sleeping. She fooled herself this was because she'd get peace to chat, and nothing at all to do with the awkward questions she'd have to answer if May heard a baby crying.

Nora knew about Maisie's job. Recently May had told her that Cathryn had left Clive.

'They've hardly been married,' Nora said.

'I know. But it's good they found out their differences now. Before any babies came along. It's all very amicable, as they say. If such things can be amicable. Cathryn's found a flat in Islington, near her work. She's with some feminist lawyer now. Doing criminal cases. She had a woman accused of stealing pork chops last week. Stuck them down her knickers. The woman, not Cathryn. But she seems happy. Cathryn, not the woman.'

Nora said she was glad.

Auntie May spoke at some length about knowing the marriage was doomed when she'd seen the cake. 'It's not lucky, chocolate cake at a

415

wedding.'

Nora said she hadn't known that, and if she ever got married she'd bear it in mind. Luke, sleeping on the sofa beside her, stirred. Nora said, 'Ssshhh.'

'Who are you ssshhing,' said May.

'Nobody,' said Nora. 'So is Mum enjoying her job?'

'You'd think she was running that charity shop to hear her. She's become an expert on starving nations.'

Luke let out a small cry. Nora scooped him up, rocked him. But the movement disturbed him, and he protested.

'Is that a baby?' said May.

Nora told her it was Luke.

'Who is Luke?' said May. 'He sounds like a baby to me.'

'He is a baby,' said Nora.

'Whose?' said May.

'He's mine,' Nora told her.

She thought it was the longest telephone silence of her life. She looked down at Luke, and fiddled with the satin edge of the blanket he was wrapped in.

On the other end of the phone, May wrestled with the news. The clock on the sideboard ticked; outside, somewhere, a dog barked; across the room, on the television, people in a pub were drinking and laughing.

'What do you mean? Your baby?' she said.

'I had a baby,' said Nora.

'And you didn't tell me?'

'No,' said Nora. 'I couldn't find a moment. There never seemed to be an appropriate space in our conversations for me to say, "I'm pregnant."'

416

'You can't just go and have a baby and not tell anybody,' said May. 'Did you think we'd all disapprove? It's not the Middle Ages. These things happen.'

Nora said she knew that.

'Did you think we'd come up to see you, meddling and interfering? Maybe we could have helped. Who's the father? Is he with you? I just can't believe this.'

Nora told her as near to everything as she was prepared to admit. She and Nathan had split up.

She didn't mention sitting alone, heartbroken, in George's car, staring at drawn curtains in Lorna's house. Nor did she tell May about Nathan's visit.

'So you're on your own,' said May.

Nora said she was, but she was fine.

'But there was someone with you at the birth?' said May.

'The midwife, a couple of nurses. It went well enough. No complications.'

May said, 'Oh, Nora. So how old is Luke now?'

'Eight weeks,' said Nora.

'All that time and you didn't say. You've been in some messes in your time, but this is the best one.'

Nora put the phone down. 'This has been a shitty day,' she told Luke. 'And you caused it. Can you say that? Shitty day.'

*   *   *

'Maisie let May in. 'What brings you here this time of night? It's past nine o'clock.' She led the way into the living room. 'You'll have to excuse the mess. I haven't hoovered. Couldn't be bothered

417

when I got in from work.'

May thought the room looked exactly as it always did. 'I had to come as soon as I found out,' she said. 'I thought you'd need to know. It's Nora.'

Maisie paled. Dreading she was about to hear of her daughter's tragic death, she said, 'What? She's had an accident. Don't tell me.'

'She's had a baby,' said May.

'Nora? She can't have,' said Maisie. 'When?'

May told her all she knew.

'A baby,' said Maisie. 'A boy, and I never knew. All that time, I never knew.' She sank into a chair. Said, 'A baby,' again. Then, 'Nora. Goodness' sakes. The things your children get up to.'

May put the kettle on.

'If I'd been asked who in the world was least likely to have a baby, I'd have said Nora,' said Maisie. 'You wonder if she'll know what to do with it.'

'She'll be fine,' said May. 'Nobody knows what to do with a baby at first. But it soon lets you know if anything's wrong.'

'I've got a grandson,' said Maisie. 'I'm a granny. I've got to go and see them.'

'No you don't,' said May. 'Running away up there, arriving on Nora's doorstep out of the blue. You can't do that.'

'Why not?' said Maisie.

'Give Nora a chance to get ready. Phone her or write to her. Let her know you want to see her. Make your peace first.'

Maisie sighed. 'But I want to see my grandson. I want to see him now.'

'Well you can't,' said May. 'That's you, isn't it? You get an idea in your head and off you charge, no thought in your head about other people. You phone Nora and tell her you want to see her. And you tell her you're sorry.'

Maisie said she had nothing to be sorry about. 'It was all her, running away like that.'

'Oh, come on,' said May. 'You planned to have her come home and live with you, without consulting her. You did all sorts.'

'So did she,' said Maisie.

'She was a little girl,' said May. 'And sometimes I think so were you. You phone her, you learn to say sorry. Even if you're not.'

Together

George was lonely. At first, after quitting his job, he'd enjoyed a new freedom. He lay in bed on icy mornings, listening to life going on in the street below. Car doors slamming, footsteps, voices, people out in the wind and sleet, going to work. It doubled the pleasure of a warm bed. Excellent, he'd think.

He'd cook a leisurely breakfast, and became familiar with radio programmes he never knew about because from half past eight to six o'clock he'd always been out of the house. He pottered, and tried to ignore the gnawing anxiety that he had another cookbook to write. Food to impress someone you love, recipes that people who don't want to cook would make, he thought. What the hell would they be?

He drifted towards Nora. Being with her staved off his worry. He learned the ways of the baby. He fed Luke when Nora started bottle-feeding. He did baths. He put on Luke's going-out clothes, manoeuvring small arms into small sleeves. He drew the line at nappies.

Together, Nora and George searched second-hand shops for old books with recipes he could adapt. When Nora took Luke out for an afternoon stroll, George came too. 'Just to get out of the house,' he said. 'Spot of fresh air.' In the evenings, they'd cook and eat in Nora's kitchen. It was nonsense, he said, for them both to prepare a meal alone. 'Two's as cheap as one.' This wasn't the whole truth. He wanted to spend time with Nora. When he wasn't with Nora, he thought about her and not about his work. He was falling in love with her. He thought if he didn't do something about it, it might ruin his career.

One day, George said, 'You still got some of that money left?'

Nora said she had a bit. 'Not a couple of grand, though. I've been dipping into it. Baby stuff.'

'Only,' said George, 'I've got about four grand saved. I was thinking of buying a house.'

'Good idea,' said Nora.

'If you kicked in your money, we'd have a better deposit.'

'You'd own a lot more house than me,' said Nora. 'I'd only have a cupboard compared to your four rooms.' She didn't take this seriously.

'Thing is,' he said, 'I couldn't get a mortgage. I've just left work, haven't got any proof of regular income. You've got a job. Together, we've got a deposit and your pay slips.'

'You think?' said Nora.

'I think,' said George. 'But I don't know.'

Two days later they met with a finance manager at a building society. It went well, except that Mr Barnes, the man they met, assumed they were an unmarried couple with a child.

'Well,' he said, 'I can see you have made one commitment to one another anyway.' He nodded to Luke, on Nora's knee. 'I can assume that while George gets on with his writing contracts, you, Nora, will continue to earn. So there's no problem with thinking you might give up working to look after the baby. That happens all the time.'

Nora said, 'Um.' Then, 'No. No problem at all. We've discussed it.'

George nodded. 'Nora will pay the mortgage, and my advances will cover bills and day-to-day living expenses.'

They weren't offered much of a loan. But they found a ground-floor flat not far from Leith Links, four rooms, a small garden, and a lot of redecorating to be done. They borrowed some extra money to put in a kitchen for George, and to make a nursery for Luke. Nora would have a daily journey across town to work, but George said she could have the car.

'When it goes,' said Nora. 'And when I can afford the petrol. And there is the small problem of us having no furniture.'

George said most of the things in his flat were his, so they'd have somewhere to sit, and what more could they want?

Nora said she'd feel happier if they hadn't lied to the building society about their relationship.

George said, 'Like they're going to send round inspectors to see if we're sleeping together. We didn't lie. They assumed.'

421

Really, though, they were pleased with themselves.

*   *   *

Nora knew May would have told Maisie about the baby. And that Maisie found infants irresistible. She never could pass a pram without cooing into it. 'Oh, they're grand when they're that age,' she'd say. 'It's when they're a bit bigger that they're trouble. The older they get, the worse it is.' Young mothers, complete strangers, would smile, nod and agree, eager to get away. Nora remembered standing apart, looking embarrassed and pretending that this eagerly doting woman, her mother, was not with her.

So she wasn't surprised when Maisie phoned. It was a shock, though, to hear that familiar voice again.

'It's your mother,' said Maisie.

Nora said she knew, she recognised the voice.

'You've had a baby,' said Maisie. It seemed like a reasonable place to start a new dialogue with her daughter. She never was one for how-are-yous.

Nora agreed, indeed she had. 'Luke,' she said.

'And you didn't tell anybody. Were you going to tell us?'

Nora said probably, at some time, when she'd figured out how.

'That's not right,' said Maisie. 'You've no reason to deny me my grandson. Or him me. We might get along fine.'

Nora said, 'Yes, you might. If you want to see him, he's here.'

Maisie said, 'Fine. I'll come next week.

422

Wednesday. I'll get on the overnight train.'

Nora said, 'Excellent.'

It was all a bit tense. Sharp tones, hidden resentments.

'You don't sound like you mean that,' said Maisie. 'Well, I don't blame you. May says I should say sorry to you. I shouldn't have made plans for you without asking you first. She's right, of course. So, I'm sorry.'

Sitting by the phone, Maisie stretched out her left leg as she spoke and considered her foot. Conversations that went beyond the mundane unnerved her. Exposing or examining her feelings out loud, and sober, made her squirm.

Nora sighed. 'I'm sorry, too. Always have been.'

'Actually,' said Maisie, 'I miss you. I think about you all the time.'

'I was going to phone,' said Nora. 'I just didn't know what to say.'

'Not knowing what to say can be a problem,' said Maisie. 'Though in my case it's always a matter of knowing what to say and not keeping my mouth shut. The thing I know to say is always the wrong thing.'

'I could agree with that,' Nora said.

'Fine,' said Maisie. 'That's that. No more apologies. We don't need to discuss it any further.' That was it, she thought, no more deep talk, no explanations, shame or regret. It was over; what was done was done. No need to speak about it. There was too much analysing things these days, she thought. Too much soul-searching; young people in newspapers, magazines, on television looking fraught, blaming their mothers and their upbringing for their bad behaviour. No, she didn't

423

like any of that. 'I'll see you and Luke next week.'
She rang off.

Nora went into the kitchen where George was
draining pasta.

'My mother's coming to see us next week.'

George noted the us, and said, 'Wonderful, I've
always wanted to meet your mother.'

Nora asked why.

'She brought you up. I wondered if you were
anything like her.'

'I'm not,' said Nora.

Services No Longer Required

If she thought about her marriage, and she tried
not to, Cathryn only had an image of two people in
expensive clothes standing upright in an unused
room, looking at one another and saying, 'What
are we doing here?'

It had started with a whimper, and ended with a
whimper. With not much more in between. When
she and Clive had finally parted, it had been by
mutual agreement. After all, there had been no
affairs, no violent fights, nothing except a huge
disappointment, in themselves, in each other.

When they spoke, it was about routine domestic
matters. Have you paid the phone bill? We're
running out of milk. Would you like a cup of
coffee? Their voices always sounded flat, empty
against a tasteful background.

In the end, Cathryn had said, 'This isn't
working, is it?'

Clive had agreed. He didn't know why, only they

had nothing to say to each other.

Cathryn told Harriet that she and Clive wanted different things. 'He wants the best. Clothes, home, car. If we had children, they'd have to go to the best schools, mingle with the best teachers and scholars and grow up to be the best in society. I just think the best of people sometimes come from the worst of homes, and bringing up children takes more than money. Though I'll admit, it helps.'

Through it all, Cathryn and Clive still made love, though not as regularly or as heatedly as when they first married. Well, thought Cathryn, our libidos are still working. Nothing else is.

She was, she knew, a little in love with Harriet. She more than admired the woman, and wanted to be like her. She imagined herself twenty years from now, her hair greying, wearing a long, unflattering but practical cardigan and carrying a huge pile of files. It wasn't a vision she relished. Still, she had a role model. Travelling on the bus to work, she decided everyone needed one. That was what was wrong with Maisie: no heroes, nobody she wanted to emulate. Well, except for Doris Day. Perhaps Maisie should have opted for somebody nearer, more accessible. Then Cathryn had said, 'Oh dammit. What the hell does it matter anyway?'

People had turned, stared at her briefly before returning to their own musings.

Clive had said, 'Why? I don't understand why you would want to do that job. It's so . . .' He'd flailed his arms, searching for a word. 'Grubby and naff.'

'Not it's not. It's fascinating. And the people are lively and funny and atrocious, sometimes. Human, though. I love it, is all.'

425

Maisie said, 'It's the way you are, Cathryn. You have always felt guilty about something or other. You were guilty about me. Guilt, that's what made you come and stay with me. Now you've started to feel guilty about your clients. You think you can save them all.'

Cathryn said, 'Do I?'

'You and Nora, you don't know yourselves at all, do you?'

Cathryn supposed they didn't.

On the day she finally left Clive, Cathryn had locked the door for the last time, walked down the steps to the pavement and looked round. It was a wide street, trees, cars parked, hardly a soul to be seen. She'd looked up at the window of her flat, and couldn't decide if at this moment of leaving she was filled with sorrow or elation. Both, she thought. But as weeks passed, and time distanced her from that last time she'd shut the door of the home she'd shared with Clive, the only thing she felt was guilt. Breaking up had been her fault.

'You want to do something about that,' said Harriet.

'I can't,' said Cathryn. 'I'm to blame. I was never honest with him.'

'Probably you weren't. But you should stop beating yourself up about it,' Harriet told her. Nine o'clock in the evening, they were sitting in a small Italian restaurant not far from their office. They'd both been working late, and Harriet suggested they go for a meal together. 'I can't be bothered cooking. And it's nice to have someone to eat with.' Cathryn agreed. It was balmy outside; the door was wide open, sounds of the streets drifted in.

'Well,' said Harriet, 'you should have discussed leaving your job. But if it was your decision, you shouldn't feel guilty. You are the guiltiest person I've ever met.'

Cathryn said she knew. 'It's a habit. I can't help it.'

'So you've always felt guilty?' said Harriet.

Cathryn nodded. 'It's part of me. I don't know how to stop it.'

'Every time it strikes me, I buy a pair of shoes.' Harriet held out her foot, encased in an expensive strappy black patent high heel.

'Very nice,' said Cathryn.

'I'd advise you to take up a vice of some sort. Shoes are mine. A bit of indulgence helps. But I'm not as bad as you. If you bought shoes every time you feel guilty, you'd have too many pairs to fit in your flat. And you'd be facing bankruptcy. I'd avoid chocolate, too. The amount you'd get through, you'd lose your looks and your figure.'

Cathryn looked into her glass.

'You even feel guilty about your looks,' said Harriet. 'Interesting.'

Cathryn shrugged.

'I've long had a theory that beauty is a disadvantage in life. Good looks are fine, but beauty is hard. Is it because nobody takes you seriously? Or do people stare too much?'

'No,' said Cathryn. 'I've worked hard enough to be taken seriously.'

'Are you all beautiful in your family?' asked Harriet.

Cathryn shook her head. 'No. My mother was very pretty in her youth. My dad is normal when it comes to looks, and my sister is average, I suppose.

427

When we were young, I got all the attention. Visitors would ooh and ahh over me, say I was gorgeous. Then they'd look at Nora and obviously be stumped for some compliment to pay her.'

Harriet wanted to know what Cathryn's sister had done about that.

'She'd make a face, cross her eyes, stick out her tongue.' Cathryn made the face. 'And say she was the geeky little sister. She got by being the family clown, until . . .'

'Until what?' said Harriet.

'Questions, questions, questions,' said Cathryn. 'I thought we were here for a quiet meal and a chat.'

'We've had a quiet meal, this is the chat. It's fascinating. I love to hear about people's families.'

'Until one day my mother told my sister, Nora, that she preferred me.'

'You were there, in the room, when she said that?'

'I was at the top of the stairs. I could hardly miss hearing it. My mother isn't known for speaking quietly. I had a moment of thrill. I was the one she loved most. Then when I came down the stairs, there was Nora sitting alone in the little box room that was her bedroom, staring at the wall, looking desolate. I thought how awful she must be feeling, and what a dreadful thing it was my mother had said.'

'This must have been some time ago. You never discussed it?'

'Good heavens, no, my family never discussed things. We lived our separate lives and met at five o'clock at the table to eat my mother's appalling meals.'

'You did nothing about it, then?' said Harriet.

'I punished myself,' said Cathryn.

She'd started to eat only what she needed to keep herself alive. She gave away her most precious possessions, 'My Beatles records, a Mary Quant dress I loved.' Every week, she had put her pocket money in an envelope and donated it to the church. At the time, Auntie May had been a regular Sunday worshipper and had heard about her niece's generosity. She'd told Maisie, who declared Cathryn, now pale and worryingly thin, to be a saint. 'So good,' she'd said. 'And beautiful, and clever.'

'It didn't do Nora a lot of good. I was Saint Cathryn and she was still the family scruff, untidy, messy and hopeless at school.'

Harriet said, 'Oh, Cathryn. And where is Nora now?'

'In Edinburgh.' She told Harriet about her father leaving her mother, and Nora being sent over to see him in his new home. 'We'd asked her to set a date when we could meet to discuss details, maintenance for my mother and the like. Only she forgot to do it. She stayed for dinner and came home reeking of wine.'

Harriet laughed.

'While she was out, my mother and I decided it would be the best plan for everybody if Nora gave up her job and came back to live at home. Only when Nora heard that, she freaked. She picked up her bag, and ran. She ran out of the house and down the street. I haven't seen her since.'

Harriet said, 'Well, good for Nora.'

Cathryn said, 'Yes, that's what I've come to think.'

She looked at Harriet, bit her lip, put her hand over her mouth. 'She just ran,' she said. 'I didn't know she could move so fast.' She started to laugh. 'I never thought it was funny, till now. I've had too much wine.' And she asked Harriet if they should order another bottle.

Harriet said, 'I've got some at home. Let's go and get drunk and you can tell me more about your family.'

Next day, Harriet put a parcel on Cathryn's desk. In it were several early Beatles LPs and Patti Smith's *Horses*.

Cathryn thanked her. 'This is so kind of you.' Then, holding up the Patti Smith, 'I never had this.'

'The Beatles are to replace the ones you gave away. The other is a get-over-it present. It says, move on. For heaven's sake, Cat, all that stuff happened years ago. Forget about it.'

*   *   *

The letter arrived the day before Maisie was due to visit, two weeks before Nora and George were to take possession of their new flat. Nora opened it and read. And read again. It said that due to certain disclosures about her behaviour, her services would no longer be required at Martinetti and McBride.

She picked up Luke, and went to see George.

'I've been sacked,' she said. And gave him the letter.

'Jesus, so you have. Why?'

Nora said she didn't know. 'I haven't done anything.'

'Is it because you've had a baby without being married?'

'Could be, but I don't think you can be fired for that these days.'

George said, 'You've got to phone and find out what's going on.'

'The man who knows everything,' said Nora.

Farrell Greyson sounded pleased to hear from her. 'How are you? And how's the little one? You must bring him round to visit us. Pauline would be upset if you didn't.'

'I'd love to,' said Nora. 'Um, did you know I've been sacked?'

'Of course I know,' said Farrell. 'Couldn't do anything to stop it.'

'But why?'

'Your memos. The things you wrote on them. You are meant to sign them and hand them back to whoever sent them, so they know you've read them. You, apparently, were writing reviews of them, and throwing them in the waste-paper basket. So your office missed fire drills, didn't know about signing in and out again, and many other things.'

Nora said, 'But . . .'

Farrell told her that Jason Pierce had been removing the memos from the waste basket and handing them over to Hugh Randall. 'I did tell you that you've made enemies.'

'Why now?' said Nora.

'A rare act of compassion on Hugh's part. He didn't want to worry you when you were expecting a baby. And he waited till I was on holiday before taking the memos to Martinetti and demanding you be fired. Like I said, I couldn't stop it.'

'But what am I to do?' said Nora.

'Let's have lunch and talk about that. The Vintners, next Wednesday, one o'clock.'

Nora said, 'Fine.' But she didn't see what good a lunch would do. 'Well, it's a meal, I suppose. Handy for someone who can't afford to eat.'

She put down the receiver, turned to George. 'What are we going to do? Can we cancel the house purchase?'

He told her not to do that. 'Something will turn up.'

'Not for me, George. Nothing ever turns up.'

Saved By the Rabbit

Seven in the morning, Nora saw her mother emerge from the overnight train. Maisie, a gaudy figure, tricked out by the charity shop in bright lemon slacks, blue jacket and red T-shirt, stood looking around, a nervousness about her movements. Nora found some comfort in seeing her mother was as unsure about this reunion as she was. Then Maisie saw her and came surging past her fellow travellers, calling her name, 'Nora, Nora. There you are.' It was then that Nora realised her mother was as shy as she was. Only she dealt with it by using hearty bluff, talking loudly, making a display of herself, and not by tiptoeing into rooms and speaking quietly.

'I didn't see you at first,' said Maisie, coming up to her. They hugged. Maisie pulled away, gripped Nora, holding her at arm's length. 'Let's take a look at you.' She stood back, taking in her daughter. 'You look fine. There's a new bit of oldness round your eyes. But it suits you.' There was a firmness in her expression. I'm the mother, we'll do what I say, we're not going to mention the past.

Nora thought her mother had aged. She was thinner; her expression, beneath the make-up and the smiles, was anxious, tired. She moved heavily, slowly.

Maisie noticed, no baby. 'Where's my boy?'

'At home with George.'

'And who's George?'

'A friend.'

Maisie said, 'Ah.'

Nora said, 'No, not ah. He's just a friend.'

Maisie said, 'Right. I'll believe you, hundreds wouldn't. We'll say no more. Now, tell me what you've been up to. When are you going back to work? Who is going to look after Luke? I'm keen to see that flat of yours.'

They were making their way across the station to where Nora had parked. Maisie was dealing with any potential awkwardness by talking too much.

'It's grand sleeping on a train,' she said. 'I'm definitely going to do that again. All snug in your wee room, as you travel through the night. You can't see a thing outside, because of the dark. But they bring you breakfast.' Then, 'Is that your car?'

'George's. I don't have a car.'

'It's a bit past it,' said Maisie. 'I mean, look at the rust. Is that legal, a car with all that rust? Can we have the roof down? I've always wanted a go in a convertible.'

Nora could tell it was going to be a long day.

'May sends her love, and Cathryn. Have you heard about Cathryn? Left Clive, gone to work in some do-goody lawyer's place. She was always a bit do-goody, Cathryn.'

Nora said, 'Was she?'

'Oh yes, always on about starving people and the like. Gave her pocket money to church.'

Nora said, 'Did she?' She'd always thought Cathryn spent her pocket money on the jukebox in the café, Coca-Cola and lipstick.

'Oh, yes,' said Maisie.

When Nora put the roof of the car down, Maisie looked about and declared it to be grand. 'You can see all about.' But as the car turned left out of the station and up the Mound, Maisie complained about the draught. 'Bit windy in here.'

For a second, a twinkling, before he gathered his senses, shock showed on George's face when Maisie entered the flat. It wasn't the outfit, which was gaudy, but not garish. It was her face, which had a luminescence about it. Make-up, a lot of blue eye shadow, but more it was her eagerness. She glowed a longing to be liked. Women like that always made George cower.

Maisie swept Luke from George's arms and crooned to him about how gorgeous he was and how she was his granny come to see him, and did he want to see the things she'd brought. 'Presents from everybody. Your Auntie Cathryn and Auntie May. Even Patricia in the shop sent you a little something.'

In the afternoon they went down to look at the new flat. They couldn't go in as they didn't yet have the keys. Maisie thought it looked fine. 'Good big windows. Lots of sun, you need that.

434

And a park nearby. It's terraced, though. I like detached myself. You should be able to walk round your own house.'

When they got back, Maisie and Nora chatted while George cooked.

'You've got a good one there,' said Maisie. 'Your father never lifted a finger in the kitchen.'

Nora said, 'We're just friends.'

And Maisie said, 'Oh, yes, right. I forgot. And you're buying a flat together. I don't know, my daughters. One leaving her man and taking up with that lawyer woman.'

Nora said, 'Has she?'

Maisie said, 'I think so. I phoned her the other night and she wasn't in. Next day when I got hold of her she said she'd slept at Harriet's.'

Nora said, 'Oh.'

'Then there's you A baby by one man, now off to live with another. You and Cathryn, what are you like? The way the pair of you behave, you'd think you had a dreadful mother.'

Nora said nothing.

Maisie turned to George. 'But I did my best for them. They had the best of everything. Good food on the table. I don't know how they ended up the way they are. People these days are too quick to blame the parents for how young folk turn out. But I don't. I think young folk just up and do what they want. It's got nothing to do with the way they're brought up. Not my two, anyway.'

Behind her back, Nora pulled an exasperated face.

'Oh,' said Maisie, 'we had lovely times. Singing. Putting on shows for their dad. Happy days.'

Nora rolled her eyes. Spread her palms. She

thought, same old Maisie, rewriting her history. Then she thought, why not? Having a selective memory was, perhaps, the best way to survive the past.

Maisie gossiped about her new job, the people she worked with, the beautiful things and the rubbish that was brought in for the shop to sell. She didn't mention her battle with sherry, her kitchen fire, or being caught stalking her ex-husband. Nora told Maisie about the Rabbit, and dinner with Farrell, and how she missed Brendan. She didn't mention getting sacked.

In the evening, Nora drove her mother back to the station to catch the nine o'clock train.

'So,' said Maisie, 'you and George are just friends?'

'Yes,' said Nora.

'You spend a lot of time together.'

Nora said they'd drifted into it.

'Well, if you don't mind my saying, he should get a new car. I don't like to think of you and my boy, Luke, going about in this thing. It's not safe. If you had an accident, goodness knows what injuries you'd have. It'll worry me when I get home.'

That was the only sign of affection Maisie showed, but it was enough to let Nora know she cared.

Nora said she'd mention it to George.

When she got home, George asked Nora if her mother was on something. 'Was she always like that?'

'I think she's calmed down a lot,' said Nora. 'She seems more at peace with herself.'

*　　　*　　　*

436

Farrell was already at a table when Nora arrived at the restaurant. 'How's the disgraced one?' he said.

'Fine,' said Nora, taking a seat opposite him. 'Shocked, worried, but fine.'

'The Rabbit's doing well,' said Farrell.

'Good,' said Nora.

'Had a very positive response from the first few strips. Very positive. We're going to give it more space. Two strips at the front of the comic. One more at the end. Plus a letters page where it answers readers' questions. This time next year, it'll have its own comic.'

'Quite a spread, then,' said Nora.

Two months after the Rabbit first appeared, Farrell had been driving home. Heading into town along Queensferry Road, he'd got stuck in a traffic jam behind a car with a sticker in the back, *This Rabbit is More than Just a Rabbit*, it read. A couple of days later, he'd seen another. Then, in the pub not far from his home, he'd seen a student with a T-shirt bearing the same statement.

He'd gone into work the next day, got hold of William Martinetti and the merchandising department. 'T-shirts, socks, pyjamas, duvet covers and probably underpants. Wallpaper, lampshades and toothbrushes later,' he told Nora. 'Not to mention games and toy rabbits, of course.'

Nora said, 'Goodness.'

'We're in talks with a television company about an animated version,' said Farrell.

'Already?' said Nora.

'People move fast these days. You get a sniff of a hit, you have to cash in on the moment. Push it along a little.'

'Do I get anything out of this? It was my idea.'

'Your idea, but not your character. We own the copyright.'

Nora said, 'Ah.'

The food arrived.

'Of course,' said Farrell, 'our biggest deal is with the training shoe people. And the adverts they'll be doing. Only we've got a problem.'

Nora took a mouthful of crab cake and said, 'Oh?'

'We got the Rabbit. We got the deals. We don't got a writer. The training shoe people and the television people want you.'

Nora said, 'Ah.'

'There's something about the way you have the Rabbit invite the readers into his hutch. The way he keeps saying, "Wicked." And chats to us, "Should I walk? Or should I fly?"' he said. Doing his Rabbit impersonation.

Diners at the table opposite stopped eating to eavesdrop. A woman from the group leaned towards Farrell. 'Fly,' she said. 'Definitely fly. If I could, I would.'

'See,' said Farrell. 'It's captured imaginations.'

'So you're going to give me my job back,' said Nora.

Farrell put down his fork and said, 'Nora, you don't want your job back. Why do you think I brought you here and didn't ask you into the office? You got us by the balls, girl.'

'Do I?'

'You come back to work and you're on the same pay. You don't come back to work and write the Rabbit, you get script fees. Then you get paid by the advertising company. And, probably, by the

438

television company. Why do you think I let them fire you? Randall has no right to demand that, you don't work for him any more. You're mine.'

'I could be rich,' said Nora.

'You could have a more relaxed attitude to solvency,' said Farrell. 'Go for that. When Martinetti approaches you, you tell him you'd love to come back. But you've got a baby now and you can't leave him all day.'

Nora agreed to that. Farrell gave her the name of an agent. 'And you never saw me. I didn't tell you anything. We're not here having this conversation.'

Nora said, 'OK, I never saw you. I'm not here. You're not here. This is my sort of thing.'

They ate and chatted about their lives.

Nora said, 'The Rabbit hasn't got a name.'

'Yes it has. We had a competition. Name the Rabbit and win a hundred pounds.'

There had been a fair number of entries. Certainly more than Farrell had thought there would be. Valerie Hyams had opened them. But Farrell had insisted they be brought to him. He would pick the winner. He spent a couple of days reading suggested names, then at last, thinking it would not be there, and that he'd have to forge an entry, he found what he wanted. A girl in Glasgow thought the Rabbit should be named after her grandfather, who bred rabbits and who had flown aeroplanes in the war.

'We called the Rabbit Hugh,' he told Nora. 'Randall didn't come up. Besides, it's a little obvious.'

The Hiss Inside

Before they moved into their new flat, a new kitchen was installed. It was a large room, with a walk-in cupboard that meant they only needed one wall to be lined with units. They'd bought a huge cooker, and found an expansive table, big enough for George to write at one end, and for food to be served at the other.

George sanded and sealed the wooden floors, and painted the living room white. But still, when they finally started to live in there, it looked sparse. George's furniture looked small and lost in the living room. They only had one bed, which Nora used. George camped on the sofa. Neither of them had much money.

Nora said that the good thing about the bed situation was it staved off overnight visitors.

They worked together, painting mostly. Evenings, when Luke was sleeping, they'd sit and watch television, and sleep, her head on his shoulder, till it was time to go to bed. They'd go their separate ways, Nora to the bedroom, George to put a sheet and duvet on the sofa, and they'd sleep some more.

Their voices echoed in the empty rooms. Footsteps rattled the old floorboards. An intimacy had developed; they'd stand admiring a newly painted patch of wall and congratulate one another. They'd examine paint charts, material swatches as they ate. When Nora cut her finger opening a tin, George bandaged it, and made her coffee. He'd put his arm round her whilst they

440

stood waiting for the kettle to boil.

They didn't really mention the one-bed situation, except that Nora promised to buy one as soon as her first cheque arrived. She had been in touch with the agent Farrell suggested. And when she'd received a letter offering to take her back into the Martinetti organisation, she'd replied politely, saying she'd love to return, but was reluctant to put her child into a nursery. She said she was in the market for freelance work, and gave the name of her new agent. Now a deal was being worked out. But she was broke.

She and George planned what they'd do with their money. George's book would be published soon. An advance was in the offing. Nora thought they lived well together. They cooked, cleaned, decorated; they shared baby duties. They did it all, except sex.

And sex was on her mind. It was a longing, a hiss inside her. She was emerging from the numbness she'd felt after Nathan left her, and the shock of being fired. She was coming back into the world, and wanted something more from her relationship with George. She wanted things to get physical. Only she didn't want to spoil everything by talking about it. 'Sex will ruin the best of friendships,' Mona had once told her. Now, Nora could see what she meant. If she approached George, in any way at all, and he rejected her, how would they carry on? How could she be in the same room as him without feeling humiliated?

They exchanged what seemed to Nora, anyway, long, lustful looks. They touched one another a lot. They hugged over small triumphs, a wall finally painted, a window that had been stuck being

441

prised open. And they lingered in the hug, longer than the small triumph warranted. But still neither made a move to take things further.

In the end it wasn't a sudden kiss or the long, lusting looks that brought them together. It was guilt. Nora had gone to bed, slipped into the voluminous T-shirt she slept in, and decided she'd like some hot chocolate. Heading back to her bedroom from the kitchen, cup in hand, she'd seen George crammed on to the sofa, legs drawn up, because he was too long for it. His feet stuck out over the arm, and usually got chilled. His head was wedged against a pillow; one hand dangled over the edge.

'You don't look very comfortable,' Nora said.

'I'm fine,' George said.

Nora stood watching him wrestle with his duvet, lie flat, heave himself up, punch his pillow and lie flat again. She began to feel awful about her own nights, spread out, warm and comfortable, on a proper mattress. 'Oh, for God's sake, George, come to bed.'

He told her again that he was fine.

Nora said, 'George, I'm about to spoil everything. I want you to come to bed. I want you to sleep with me.'

He didn't need to be asked again. He padded after her to the bedroom, where he asked her which side of the bed she liked to sleep on. She told him the right, but she didn't really mind.

They climbed in, Nora sitting up, holding her cup. Trying to hide the heat she felt now they were in bed together.

'You going to drink that?' said George.

She told him she'd gone off it now. And

switched off the light. They lay, side by side, staring, through the black, at the ceiling. Under the covers, he took her hand. She turned to him. They kissed. And kissed again, touching inner mouths and tongues. Passion, urgency took hold of both of them; they struggled out of their sleeping outfits, desperate for the feel of skin on skin.

Afterwards, they lay clinging to one another. George said, 'You don't know how long I've wanted to do that.'

'Me too,' said Nora. 'You should have said.'

George told her he hadn't mentioned it in case she rejected him. 'Then how would we have carried on?'

'I know,' said Nora. 'Same with me.' Then she said, 'This is what I need. Someone to cling to.'

George said, 'Yeah, a bit of clinging helps.'

Later, when Nora got up to go to the loo, she asked George if he wanted a cup of tea. But comfortable at last, in the bed that was, after all, his own, George was sleeping.

It was a week before Nora plucked up the courage to remark that they'd done it all backwards. 'Baby, house, then sex,' she'd said. 'Most people do sex, house, then baby.'

George could have pointed out that the baby wasn't his, but he could see what she meant. So he took her to him, kissed her and said that this backwards approach had something to it. 'We got the frightening bits over first. Makes it easier to enjoy the fun bits.'

Nora put her hands on his face. 'No, sex helps with the frightening bits. Takes your mind off things. Eases the pain. I should have kissed you sooner.'

'Yes, you should,' he agreed. 'But later is better than never.'

*   *   *

Nora and Brendan had, in the time since he left, spoken often on the phone. At first it had been every other day. Then it was every week or so. But there was something about a phone relationship that didn't work for them. It was too intimate. Just voices down the line that shut out other voices—Jen's, George's—and nothing going on around them, street life, music, bar conversations, to widen the range of their chat.

'Do you ever hear from Nathan?' Brendan asked her.

'No. He and Lorna wanted to take Luke. But after I told him no, he kind of slipped away. I don't think of him that often.'

Brendan said, 'Really?'

'Really,' said Nora. 'At first I thought about him all the time. Then I was so busy with Luke, I thought about him some of the time. He would appear in my mind every hour or so. Then it was every day or so. Then me and George moved here, and I got busy doing house stuff, and I started to think about George every hour or so. Then, well, you know. Now I only think about George.'

'So, you and George,' said Brendan.

'Me and George. Who'd have thought it?'

'Well,' said Brendan. 'Just about everybody except you and George. It was on the ten o'clock news, discussed in the press, there was even a notice in the window of my local shop asking if you'd got together yet. Mona definitely thought you and George would make a pair. She told him to feed you, hoping it would do the trick.'

'Did she?' said Nora. 'She should have told him to sleep with me. It would have saved a lot of longing looks and painful wondering.'

Brendan said that longing looks and painful wondering were a fantastic part of getting together. 'It's so wistful. And sort of itchy.' He sighed. 'So, is this you settled down at last?'

'Meet a mortgagee,' said Nora. 'You bet I've settled down. I have even bought a pair of fluffy slippers.'

'That I don't believe,' said Brendan.

'Well, I'm thinking of buying a pair. It would make my feet as happy as the rest of me.'

In time, when Nora got in touch, it was Jen she usually spoke to. And Brendan would chat to George.

Soon it would all be reduced to a yearly exchange of Christmas cards. Still, it sometimes happened. Brendan would phone, George would be out with Luke and, with no distractions, they'd talk. They'd discuss music they were listening to, films they'd seen, favourite adverts, small observations about the times they were living through.

It was late afternoon, George had gone to the delicatessen to shop. Luke, now eighteen months, was with him. Nora knew they'd be away for a while. They were both ponderers and starers. Luke preferred buses and lorries. George liked the windows of shops selling fruit or cheeses.

It was autumn. The air smelled slightly chill and Nora was happy. She was sitting at the kitchen table, working. They were going to make the back bedroom into a small study for her, but hadn't got round to it. Still, the house was starting to look like the home they'd planned.

Autumn, and Nora always thought about her mother. 'Ah,' Maisie would say, when she found she had to switch on a light at five o'clock, 'the nights are drawing in. Now we can get down to things, get back to normal.'

What things they were supposed to get down to, Nora didn't know. In fact, little changed, except the heating was switched on and the blankets were removed from their summer quarters at the bottom of the wardrobe in the spare room and put on the beds. Sometimes, celebrating the anticipation of cold weather, Maisie would cook a stodgy pudding, an apple sponge perhaps, or she'd make a huge pot of ham and lentil soup that would feed the family for days. These were dishes Nora loved to eat, warming and filling; they promised the full wonder of frost and fog and rain to come.

She was thinking of all this, and imagining George pushing Luke in his pushchair across the links, coming home, when the phone rang. It was Brendan.

'Hi, it's me.'

'Hello, you,' said Nora. 'How's things?'

'Excellent,' he said. 'Got a new job. Roving reporter with a small newspaper. I get to rove.'

'That sounds like your sort of job,' said Nora.

He asked her what she was doing.

'Working,' she said.

'Rabbiting?' he said.

'Yes, rabbiting. So tell me about the job.'

'I've got to report on things. Means council meetings and football matches, of course. But other stuff. Man grows giant leek. Woman, seventy-five, fights off vandals. I love it. But mostly because of the roving.'

'Are you roving at the moment?' Nora asked.

'Nah. I'm in the office, writing up some copy. But I'll be off roving tomorrow. I get to drive about. I can listen to the radio. Or play tapes. This is the job for me. The roving rather than the writing.'

'This is good,' said Nora. 'I once wrote about roving. But I had to stay in the office. I only wrote. A bit of roving would have been cheering.'

Brendan asked after George, and were they thinking of getting married?

'Don't think so,' said Nora. 'It would disrupt the flow. We had the baby, well, I had the baby, then bought the flat, then had sex. It ought to have been the other way round. I don't know where marriage fits in it all. But in the scheme of things, marriage I'd say comes between the sex and the house. Though my mother would say house, marriage then sex. Perhaps it would be bad luck to get married now.'

'True,' said Brendan. 'Heard any good music?'

'Mostly, at the moment, we are listening to the soundtrack of *The Jungle Book*. I have a child, I am in a cultural void. I'm looking for a way out. You?'

'Oh, yes. I hear some good stuff when I'm roving. I'll do you a tape. You know something? I'm really happy.'

'You once told me that I sounded like a village idiot when I said I was happy. You said nobody was happy,' said Nora.

'Yeah, well. I'm happy some of the time, then. Are you happy?'

'I'm happy,' said Nora. 'I have my moments.'

'You and George,' he said.

'Me and George,' said Nora. 'We're still new to all this domesticity. It's taken us by surprise. At nights we cling. We do a lot of clinging.'

'Clinging's good,' said Brendan. 'I cling, too.'

Then he said he had to go. His boss was coming down the corridor. 'See you later.'

'Yes,' said Nora. 'See you.'

Swamped by Maisie

In the summer of the following year, Nora, George and Luke went to London. They stayed with Maisie, but on their second day had lunch with Alex and Claire.

On their way back to Maisie's house, George had said, 'That was blissfully normal.'

They'd had lunch; Alex and Claire had played with Luke. They'd chatted, had a cup of tea, then at four, they'd left.

'I think you need a Claire in your life,' George told Nora.

'Oh yes,' she said. 'But not as much as Alex does.'

'Have you noticed how much Claire looks like Maisie?' said George.

'First time I met her, I thought that. I wondered if she and Maisie were just the physical type he went for. Now I think Maisie's what he goes for. So he got himself a tamed one. But I think he truly loves her.'

George sighed. They were walking down the

street towards the house. Same street, same houses and gardens that Nora always remembered. Same lines and cracks in the pavement.

As he opened the front gate, George said, 'I have to steel myself for the carpet.'

'Ah, yes,' said Nora, 'the carpet. I should have warned you about that.'

It must have been when she was eleven. Nora was late getting home. She always was. She would have shouted that she was home, but didn't. This place didn't look like home any more. It had changed. It had never, ever been tasteful. But now it was hideous.

In the hours since Nora had left home after her lunch, someone had removed the old hall runner and laid a fitted carpet. It stretched all the way through to the living room.

It was hard to say what colour it was, because it had so many colours. It did have a blue background. But it wasn't a pretty blue, not like the sky or the ocean or the tall blue flowers in Mrs Brecon's garden, five doors along. It was more the blue of the veins that stuck out in her teacher's, Mrs Timson's, legs. Nora could stare at Mrs Timson's legs for hours. She would talk about capitals of the world, or long division, and Nora wouldn't hear a word she was saying, the legs were so fascinating, those jutting, angry crisscross veins.

The pattern on the carpet was a mix of tropical jungle and oak trees. There were branches, some brown, some green, some yellow, some covered with creeping vines. There were leaves, green, yellow, rust and pink. There were flowers, yellow, blue, red, pink and off-white. Every now and then the pattern was interrupted by a strange eye-like

449

thing. It made Nora feel dizzy. The hall, always narrow, looked really, really narrow.

She walked on it. Soft under her feet, but exhausting to look at. She walked on it all the way down the hall to the living room, where more carpet covered every inch of the floor, wall to wall. Here, where the room was wide enough for the whole design to unfold, Nora could see what the eye-like thing was—a peacock with its tail fanned out, amidst the forest and jungle creepers and flowers. She gasped.

Maisie was there, standing by the fireplace, looking triumphant. She saw Nora's face, wide-eyed with shock, which she mistook for delight. 'Ta-ra,' she said.

'What's all this?' said Nora.

'Fitted carpets,' said Maisie.

'But . . .' said Nora.

'We went and chose them a couple of weeks ago. Me, Cathryn and your dad. Then the man came and measured the room and the hall. And here we are.'

Chose them? Two weeks ago? Nobody had mentioned anything about all this to her.

'Nobody told me,' said Nora.

'Well, you're never here. Always away at Karen McClusky's house.'

'But,' said Nora, 'fitted carpets.' Until now she'd never known such a thing existed. But her mother, father and Cathryn had. What else did they know that they hadn't told her about? And they'd all gone to choose them and hadn't even mentioned it to her. She felt left out.

'Isn't it beautiful?' asked Maisie.

Nora didn't know what to say. She knew it

wasn't beautiful, and was disturbed that her mother thought it was. Beautiful was standing on an evening pier with the sea swishing nearby.

A beautiful house might be the Ponderosa in *Bonanza*. Though she didn't know what sort of carpet it had. It certainly wouldn't be something like this.

'I think it's beautiful,' said Maisie. 'All those colours.'

'Yes,' said Nora. 'It's got a lot of colours.'

'Oh,' said Maisie. 'I always wanted fitted carpets. No more polishing the lino. Just carpet. Carpet all the way from the front door to the fireplace. What more could you want? It's luxury.'

Nora gazed at the jungle whorls and peacocks beneath her feet. If this was beautiful, then she was wrong about beautiful. She thought it horrible, and now home wasn't home any more. It was the place with the vile carpet. Her shock and confusion showed on her face.

'You don't like it, do you?' said Maisie.

'I didn't say that,' said Nora.

'No need to say anything. It shows on your face.'

'It's a bit much,' said Nora.

'No it's not. It's lovely. I know. I have very good taste.'

But Maisie had seen her beautiful carpet through Nora's eyes—the mass of colours, the jungle pattern—and for a moment she doubted herself. Maybe it *was* a bit much.

She and Nora had, briefly, looked at each other. It was the instant they'd realised they had different taste, different opinions, different needs, dreams, ambitions. The business of buying mangoes, and of throwing out Nora's things had caused a rift. This

451

was when they stopped communicating.

Now, walking up the front path, Nora said, 'Don't you dare mock the carpet. Maisie loves it.'

'Wouldn't dare,' said George.

When they walked through the door, Maisie came charging to see them. 'Come away in, Cathryn and Harriet's here. We'll get the dinner on.'

Cathryn and Harriet were on the sofa. Maisie introduced them. 'This is Nora and George and Luke and Cathryn. And Harriet, Cathryn's . . . um . . . What about a glass of wine?' She bustled off to the kitchen. 'May's coming later on.'

She returned with five glasses on a tray adorned with a picture of the Leaning Tower of Pisa. Everyone took a glass. Maisie suggested they take them outside. 'Except you two,' nodding towards Nora and Cathryn. 'You can make the dinner.'

The two of them looked into the fridge.

'Has she got any food?' said Cathryn.

'Only stuff for a no-cooking day. Cold ham, salad things and the like,' Nora told her. 'I suppose we could do some pasta and stick the ham through it.'

'No way, not on a no-cooking day. Cold ham salad and tinned peaches with cream to follow, and instant coffee.' Cathryn was adamant.

'Eating nostalgia,' said Nora.

They stood looking out into the garden. George and Harriet sat on striped deckchairs, chatting; Maisie played with Luke.

She was chasing him at toddling pace, arms raised. She was being a monster. Every time she caught him, she picked him up, whirled him in the air. Then she'd put him down, and the whole thing would start up again.

'She used to do that to us,' said Nora. 'I'd forgotten.'

'She'd dress up as a witch with a sheet as a cloak and a black hat,' said Cathryn.

'Yes, she loved dressing up,' said Nora.

'We used to have picnics out there,' Cathryn remembered. 'A tablecloth on the grass, sandwiches and lemonade.'

'And fruit cake. We played at being in an Enid Blyton book. Mum would make up stories about the neighbours being smugglers.'

'Yes,' said Cathryn. 'The shows, remember them? In the living room, dressed up and singing for Dad.'

'She was a demanding director,' said Nora. 'We had to make grand entrances from out in the hall. Sweeping into the room, singing.'

'Yes,' said Cathryn. 'Funny how you forget.'

Nora said, 'You and Harriet? Are you, you know?'

Cathryn said, 'Isn't it funny how you can't really talk about sex in this house? You come over all funny and nod and nudge and say you know.'

'I know,' said Nora. 'It give you this undertone of naughtiness. You want to say something disgustingly rude. Still, you and Harriet?'

'We don't live together, if that's what you're asking. Otherwise, yes we are. She makes me happy.'

Nora said, 'What did Mum say when you told her? Tell me. I've got to know.'

'Well,' said Cathryn, 'she went very quiet. Then she asked if we were sure. Only since I'd been married I could be wrong. She said we didn't look

453

like—um—women like that. Women like that always wore dungarees. Then Harriet laughed so much she had to leave the room. She pretended she needed the loo. We could hear her laughing as we sat in the living room. By the time she came back Maisie had got over the shock. She said if we were . . . ums . . . then she'd have to get used to it. She loves Harriet. Calls her my um. And I'm Harriet's um. According to Maisie, me and Harriet are ums.'

Nora said, 'Still, that's the most interesting thing you've ever done.' Cathryn said, 'Do you and George do it in the sacred spare room?'

Nora said, 'Oh yes. Only for the naughtiness factor, though. It's not easy having sex with Maisie across the hall. But we try.'

Later, Nora and George were in bed in the guest room.

'I was never allowed in here when I was little,' said Nora. 'It was forbidden territory. I might have messed it up.'

Across the room, in a cot Maisie had bought, Luke was sleeping.

Nora asked George what he and Harriet had been talking about as they sat in the garden.

'Cookbooks,' said George. 'She collects them. I'm going to send her mine.'

'That all?'

'She was telling me she once played the lead in a school play and wanted to go on the stage, but thought better of it when she got to eighteen.'

Nora said, 'Pity. She's kind of forceful. She'd have been a good Mary Poppins. Bossy but likeable.'

'Hardly,' said George. 'I like her.'

They lay in silence. They were tired.

George said, 'Is it me, or do you think Harriet looks a bit like Maisie? Not as obviously as Claire. But in certain lights, if you screw up your eyes.'

'A little,' said Nora.

'What's up with your family?'

'It's Maisie. Once in love with Maisie . . .' said Nora.

'Always in love with Maisie?'

'Always looking for the Maisie you fell in love with. I was watching her with Luke, and I suddenly remembered how I worshipped her when I was little. That's what she wants, adoration.'

George said he'd noticed.

'But then she doesn't really know how to love people back. She just soaks up all the love and attention you give her, can't get enough. She loved it when Cathryn and me were little. We adored her, but when you're small, your mother is all you want. She hated it when we grew up and started having lives outside the house. She wanted us to come home to her and listen to her stories about little things that she turned into dramas.'

Nora told him about coming home from school and finding the house in a state of upheaval. 'She'd lifted rugs, taken down the curtains, yanked out drawers. She'd been spring-cleaning and got fed up. And stopped. Cathryn and me had to put it all back.'

Maisie had made a huge joke of it. 'Silly me,' she'd said.

'Actually, now I think about it, I'm sure she'd been drinking. That was my mother.'

'Does she still drink?' asked George.

'Cathryn thinks so. But not so much. Someone

like Maisie, who gets high, is bound to get low.'

George said, 'But—'

Nora, lying on her stomach, draped over him, put her hand on his mouth. 'There are no buts with Maisie. She never accepts bad things. She rewrites everything in her head. She's not a drunk; she just likes a little sherry of an evening. She didn't nearly burn down the house; it was a little accident that happened when she was very tired. She didn't admit to being an alcoholic to Cathryn; she just said something a bit silly when she was in shock. She was always fond of a good illness, but that's not the one. She'd prefer something like consumption, where she'd fade away gracefully, singing a beautiful song. That's my mother. But I think my father and Cathryn were so swamped by her, they both went out and found modified versions. Not that Claire and Harriet aren't lovely. I think Harriet is wonderful. But I was lucky,' said Nora. 'My mother set me free.'

'She told you she preferred Cathryn,' said George.

'Broke my heart. Best thing that ever happened to me.' She took George's hand. 'I didn't realise it till this afternoon, watching her with Luke. I remember adoring her. I'd run home to her. She filled my world. And then she said that. It only took a moment. Probably in those few minutes she did prefer Cathryn. But after that I was free. I got out of the house.'

George said, pulling her to him, 'I don't prefer Cathryn.'

Nora said she wouldn't blame him if he did.

Now, she turned to him. 'I'm fine. I know because, George, in no way, no way at all, do you

456

resemble Maisie.'

He kissed her. 'That's the nicest thing anybody's ever said to me.'

Nora said, 'Do you want to, you know, be naughty in the sacred spare room, as the Rabbit might say?'

'The Rabbit never said any such thing,' said George.

'He might one day. Well, do you?'

George leaned over her, resting on his elbows. 'I don't think I can. There's something about the decor. It kind of leaves you limp.'

Nora sighed. Then she said, 'OK. Let's throw everything in here out into the garden. The sheets, the duvet, that fluffy turquoise rug, the shepherdess ornament, all of it. Then we'll run away home.'

George said, 'You couldn't do that. You'd break your mother's heart. I think you secretly love the old bat.'

'Love? I dunno,' said Nora. 'I love her most when I'm in Edinburgh and she's here, in London. I love the distance.' She sighed. 'I couldn't really be involved with her. Not now. Too difficult. She rewrites too much. You say something to her, and maybe even years later, it comes bounding back to you in a different context. Like I said, she doesn't know how to love back. But she tries. And she's full of life, and she sees the world the way she wants to see it. I could love her for that.'

George said, 'Once in love with Maisie . . .'

The words ran round Nora's head. Once in love with Maisie. Wasn't that a song? A tune sprang up. 'Damn,' she said. 'That'll be rattling round my brain for weeks now. I'll never get rid of it.'

The Thereness of Brendan

Luke grew into a quiet child, fond of drawing, comic books, dinosaurs, silly jokes and books about wizards and monsters. He also liked facts, which he would quote whenever he got the chance. 'Did you know that Hannibal had an army of ninety thousand soldiers, twelve thousand cavalrymen and thirty-seven elephants, and he took them over the Alps?' People would say that they didn't, which was usually true.

By the time he was seven, he'd often visited his family in London, though he preferred to stay with Cathryn and Harriet or Alex and Claire, who fussed over him, bought him toys and took him on outings to the British Museum and Kew Gardens. His favourite person was Harriet. Together they'd make up scary stories which they'd tell with the lights turned off. She'd take him to specialist comic shops, and collect jokes from her clients to send to him, if they were clean enough.

Luke refused to stay with Maisie, and had to be persuaded to go for supper or lunch.

'I hate it there. There's a horrible carpet and Grandma's always kissing me.'

Nora would say, 'It's only for an afternoon. And you know how much she loves you.'

Maisie was, in fact, quite glad that Nora, George and Luke didn't stay with her when they came south. She was, she said, too old for all the fuss of visitors. 'Old, and not very well,' she'd say.

But in reality, she'd settled into a routine that she hated to be disrupted. She worked two days a week at the charity shop, and the rest of the time she pottered in her house in the morning, watched television or read in the afternoon. In the evening, after an easily prepared supper, she'd watch more television or do a crossword. Sometimes she visited May round the corner, and sometimes May visited her. They'd bicker mildly about whose turn it was to walk the small distance between their homes. Still, Maisie said she was happy, the lazy life suited her. 'Born to be idle, me. Just as well with all my illnesses.'

Nobody could tell how well, or ill, Maisie actually was. She'd started collecting maladies. Bronchitis was her favourite, but she had cystitis, bursitis, a grumbling appendix, headaches, angina and dodgy knees among other things. Cathryn and Harriet visited regularly, bringing food, books, magazines, fruit juice and anything else Maisie wanted.

'You'll be glad when I'm gone and you don't have to come all this way to see me,' Maisie would say.

Cathryn once told her father that Maisie was convinced she was dying.

'I don't think so,' he said. 'She's having too much fun. She loves the attention everybody's giving her. She'll just be wishing she'd thought of all this sooner.'

He was right, of course. Maisie spent a lot of time in bed reading her old medical dictionary, and often discovered something she was convinced she was suffering from. Nora said her mother should abandon her job at the charity shop and concentrate on a full-time career as a hypochondriac.

Once or twice a year, though, Maisie would really get ill. It was, of course, sherry-induced. She never could give it up, claiming it was good for the circulation. She'd sweat, shake, have foul dreams. Nora would come and look after her. She'd bathe her mother, comb her hair, tidy up her bed and sit with her, holding her hand. But when she heard wails and cries in the night, she'd pull the duvet over her head and try to hide from them.

She told Auntie May about her mother's black visions. 'She's your mother,' May said. 'You just have to live with it. There's a lovely person in there somewhere. It's sad she never discovered her.'

One morning, Nora brought Maisie a cup of tea. Maisie was still mildly delirious. Nora helped her sit up, wiped sweat from her face, and held the cup to her lips so she could drink.

'Oh, it's you,' Maisie said. 'I was hoping it would be Cathryn. She was always so good. She gave her pocket money to the church, you know. I always preferred her to you.'

Nora said, 'I know. I prefer her too.'

Maisie said, 'At least we agree on something.'

The next day, Nora went home. At night, in bed, she told George what Maisie had said.

'Never mind,' he told her. 'I love you.'

'I know you do,' Nora said.

'Do you love me?'

'You know I do,' said Nora.

'Only you never say it. Not once have you said it. I sometimes think you're afraid to commit.'

'Don't be silly,' said Nora. 'I'm here. I'm not going anywhere. You're the one I want.'

'Still,' said George, 'it would be good to hear you tell me you love me. A person needs that.'

An evening in October. It was cold outside, a wind blowing. George, Nora and Luke were in the kitchen, George was typing up some notes, Luke was reading *The Guinness Book of Records*, out loud. The news was on the radio. The phone rang, and Nora answered.

'It's Jen.'

'Hello, Jen, how're you?' said Nora.

'I'm phoning about Brendan. He's dead.'

Nora paled. 'No. When?'

'This morning,' said Jen.

George stood up. 'What's wrong?'

Nora put her hand over the receiver. 'Brendan's dead.'

Luke stopped reading and watched. He'd never seen bad news come into the house before.

Nora returned to speaking to Jen. 'What happened?'

'He was driving, as he always does, the stupid bastard, up a one-way street. The wrong way. You know, he always said if you were local these things didn't apply. I don't know why he did that. He took his eyes off the road, apparently, adjusting the radio. Probably some song he loved. And hit a lorry thundering towards him.'

Nora said, 'Oh, Jen.'

She said, 'I know. He was an idiot in a car. He was always thinking about something else. Not about the road.'

Nora said she remembered.

'Anyway, I'll let you know when the funeral's to be.'

461

Nora said they'd come down.

'No. No,' said Jen. 'It'll be in Edinburgh. He always missed it. He said he wanted to be buried there. He wanted his ashes to be fired out of the one o'clock gun from the Castle, so he'd get one last look at the skyline. I don't see me getting permission, though.'

Nora agreed. 'But it's a good idea.'

'So it'll be at Warrender Crematorium. Two o'clock. Thing is,' said Jen, 'we need somewhere to meet afterwards. A few sandwiches, stuff like that. Can we come to your place?'

'Of course,' said Nora. 'No problem. In fact, I'd be hurt if you went anywhere else.'

Jen said she had to ring off, she had other people to phone. 'This is awful. Telling people.'

Nora replaced the receiver and sat down. She held her hand over her mouth, eyes wide. Shocked. 'I can't believe it. Brendan, dead. He was my best friend. Always there. I think I really loved him.'

On Tuesday, two weeks later, at two, they gathered in the hush of the crematorium, all of Brendan's relatives, and all the people Nora knew but hadn't seen for a while.

An organist slowly played 'And It Stoned Me', always one of Brendan's favourite tracks. It sounded absurdly prim and religious. For the first few bars, Nora didn't recognise it. She thought if he was somewhere up there, watching, Brendan would be laughing.

She sat numbly staring at the coffin, thinking, Brendan's in there. The ceremony passed, Nora was dazed. Every time the congregation was asked to stand, George nudged her; she hadn't heard a thing.

462

Coming out into the afternoon chill, Nora was crying. 'God, I'll miss him.'

'You hardly ever saw him,' said George.

'But I have memories. And I always thought of him as my best friend.'

Late in the afternoon, when people had drifted away, and most of the food had been eaten, the old gang were left sitting in Nora's living room. Gregory had come along. Not because he'd known Brendan, more to keep Mona company.

Mona asked Jen what she was going to do.

'Back to work on Monday,' said Jen. 'I don't want to sit about the house thinking.'

'Best to keep busy,' said Mona.

Jen smiled and remarked on how well Mona looked.

'It's the lavender and camomile face balm. I'll send you some. It's relaxing.'

Four years ago, Mona had quit her job and started producing a range of face and hand creams made from herbs grown in her garden. The scheme had gone well. She and Gregory had bought land close to their cottage to grow more herbs, mostly lemon balm, verbena, lavender and camomile. At first Mona had made her concoctions in her kitchen. Now she had a small factory employing a dozen or so people. In time, her creams, all beautifully packaged, had been taken up by a leading chain store and recommended in several glossy magazines. Now Mona was on the verge of being rich.

Gregory said, 'I hate to say it, but she's right. The night cream smells fantastic.'

'You use it?' said George.

Gregory nodded.

'Well, you're looking pretty good too. I must try it.'

Nora said, 'Gosh, Mona, you're a high-powered businesswoman.'

Mona said she just made face creams. 'But we're moving into oatmeal and honey body scrubs, and looking at green tea shampoo.'

Everyone nodded.

Mona said, 'Green tea's the coming thing.'

Luke came in with bowls of olives and nuts. He asked if anyone wanted their wine topped up.

Nathan held out his glass, smiling. 'You're a fine boy.' He'd seen Luke a few times, watched from afar as he grew up. He was secretly proud of him.

Luke ignored this and asked Nathan if he knew that La Paz was the highest city in the world. Nathan said he did.

'Well, did you know that bees talk to other bees by dancing?'

'As a matter of fact, I did,' said Nathan.

'Well, did you know that an elephant's brain is sixteen times bigger than a human's?'

Nathan said he didn't know that.

Luke said, 'Well, there you go.' And went to the kitchen to fetch himself a glass of Coke.

Nora followed. 'Why did you tell Nathan that about elephants' brains? It's not true.'

Luke said he knew that. 'He speaks to me as if I was seven years old.'

'You are seven years old.'

'That's no reason to speak to me as if I were. Nobody else speaks to me like that.'

Nora thought he'd been getting lessons on arguing from Cathryn and Harriet.

'He's your father,' said Nora. 'You know that.'

'Yes. But he's not my real father. That's George. And George is my friend. I don't like Nathan, I decided not to give him one of my good facts.'

Nora smiled. When she went back to the living room, Jen said, 'Luke's lovely. You must be proud. Brendan always wanted a baby, I wanted to wait. Now look. No Brendan, no baby. You shouldn't wait,' she said.

'You weren't to know,' said Nora.

Outside, it had started to rain.

'I always loved it in the pub when it was raining outside,' said Mona. 'Remember we used to analyse Brendan's dreams.'

It was always a Friday-evening treat to sit in the pub with the gang, that everybody thought of as a gang but hadn't the courage to say was a gang, and chat. But when the cold weather came, the pleasure intensified. It was blissful to sit by the fire, slightly too hot and slightly flushed from the surfeit of alcohol, listening to the wind rattling the window panes, buffeting down the chimney, and ardently discuss sex, work and Brendan's dreams, which everyone thought had a lot to do with sex and work.

He'd fallen asleep while watching television and dreamed he was standing on his head waiting for Jen to iron a parachute.

Mona had berated him. 'It shows what you secretly think of women that you'd have them doing housework while you're idling about standing on your head. Why can't you iron your own parachute?'

Brendan said that he didn't actually have a parachute to iron, and that it was a dream. He'd no control over it, he didn't think women should be relegated to doing housework when he was awake.

'Ah, but it's your thoughts while sleeping that reveal the true you,' said Mona. She lifted her glass, tilted it towards him, took a swig and grinned.

'It has nothing to do with his attitude towards women,' said Nora. 'It reveals his insecurity. He feels his world has been turned upside down, and he doesn't know where he stands since being put in charge of the slush pile. He is looking to Jen to save him, only she's taking her time about it. And the ironing of the parachute shows he knows that Jen thinks he'd have been made an editor if he wasn't so scruffy. If he wore a jacket, for example.'

Nathan had stared at her. 'That's it,' he said. 'That's definitely it.'

Now, he poured some wine and said he remembered that. Nora had been pregnant at the time. He glanced at Luke again. Wondering if the boy resembled him in any way.

George caught the look, and shifted in his seat.

Nora saw George looking at Nathan and Nathan looking at Luke, and sensed a certain charging of the atmosphere. 'I'm going to make coffee,' she said. 'Anybody want some?'

In the kitchen she put on the kettle, fetched the cafetiere from the cupboard and was laying out cups. She felt she was being watched, turned. Nathan was leaning against the door post.

'He's a lovely boy.'

'Of course he is,' said Nora.

'Do you forgive me?' he asked.

'What for?'

'Leaving you. You can't blame me for wanting Luke. Who wouldn't?'

466

'I don't think about it any more,' said Nora. 'Yes, I forgive you. If that's what you want.'

'I do,' he said.

Nora shrugged and said, 'People do what people do. Bad decisions, panic, guilt, survival, I don't know why. But they do. We should have had a wild affair, broken up and cried a little. That would have done the trick for me.'

'Sounds good,' said Nathan. 'You regret having a baby?'

'I didn't want a baby. Then I had a baby. Now I can't bear to think that I didn't want him, and didn't plan for him. I figure you just can't win with babies. And now my baby isn't a baby. He's Luke and I love him more than I can tell you.'

Nathan asked her if she was rich. 'The Rabbit's doing well.'

She told him not to be silly. 'I just have a more relaxed attitude to solvency.'

'We had some good times,' said Nathan.

Nora said, 'We did.' She thought about how she'd run along Royal Circus on Saturday nights, breathless and alive with the need to see him.

'Funny how things turn out,' said Nathan.

Voices rippled through from the living room.

Nora made the coffee, put it and the cups on a tray and carried it through. Nathan followed.

'Do you know,' said Mona. 'We should have had roast beef and mugs of tea. Not wine and salmon.'

'Yes,' said George. 'We should have a commemorative roast beef Sunday for Brendan.'

They all thought that a wonderful idea, and planned when it might happen. But they all knew it never would. Still, it was pleasant to plan.

'I went back to our pub once,' said Mona.

467

'There was a new gang there. In our seats, at our table, drinking beer and talking about sex and work.'

'Never be as good as us, though,' said Nora. She turned to Jen. 'Did Brendan bring home waifs after you moved?'

'Oh yes,' said Jen. 'He was always one for bringing waifs into our kitchen and feeding them.'

'I was a waif,' said Nora.

'You were the waifiest of waifs,' said Mona. 'That shy walk. You spoke so quietly nobody could hear you.'

Nora said, 'I know. Brendan rescued me.' Then she said, 'I forgot the milk. I'll go get it.'

A moment she had shared with Brendan, that had been long buried in the depth of her mind, floated up.

Jen had seen the sudden flicker of grief and followed Nora out of the room. 'Anything wrong?'

Nora said, 'No. Just remembering Brendan and me, and the things we did.'

'Did you ever . . .? You spent so much time together.'

'No,' said Nora. 'Never. It wasn't like that. We were like school chums. We knew if we touched each other, we'd ruin everything. Once, I asked him to kiss me. Just to see if there was anything more. We couldn't. He wouldn't. He loved you. I was someone he talked to. Not even that, really. We daydreamed, speculated, observed. No deep conversations. He'd say, "Favourite song," and I'd tell him, " 'Georgia On My Mind', Ray Charles."'

'Favourite song?' said Brendan.

'"Georgia On My Mind", Ray Charles,' said Nora. 'Favourite film?'

'Changes. Right now *Diva*. But I saw *The Incredible Journey* when I was little. I cried. Haven't watched it again. I suspect I'd be disappointed. Favourite band?'

'REM,' said Nora. 'You?'

'The Stones when I was seventeen. Favourite times?'

'Now,' said Nora. 'Right now.'

They'd been walking up Dundas Street, heading for Princes Street, cars whisking past them. He had turned, looking round him. Walking backwards, he could see over the skyline to the river. 'Yeah,' he'd said. 'Now.'

*   *   *

By seven o'clock everyone except Jen, who was staying overnight, had gone home. Luke had taken Jen to his room to show her his comic collection, and to tell her some facts and jokes. Nora found George sitting in the kitchen. Head in hands.

'What's wrong?'

'Just feeling sad,' he said.

'About Brendan?'

'Yes, but really you have made me sad, Nora.'

'Why?'

George didn't answer that. 'What were you and Nathan talking about when you were making coffee?'

She shrugged. 'Nothing. He was saying how much he liked Luke. Asked if I'd forgiven him for leaving me. That sort of thing.'

'And what did you tell him?'

'I said I'd forgiven him. I didn't think about all that stuff much any more.'

'I don't like him talking to you. And I don't like the way he looks at Luke.'

'George,' said Nora. 'You're jealous.'

'You bet I am. Do you want somebody who wouldn't be? I'm jealous of Brendan, and that's terrible because he's dead. But after Jen phoned to tell us about him, you said you loved him. You've never said that to me, Nora. All the things we've been through, all the passion, and the times you've cried and the hankies I've given you, you've never said it. What's up with you? Are you scared I'll leave you? Do you think I'm going to hurt you?'

She shook her head. 'No.'

'And Nathan, I bet you told him you loved him.'

'Well, yes, but only when he wasn't listening.'

'Don't make jokes,' said George. He went out into the hall, put on his coat. 'I'm going out.'

Nora said that hadn't been a joke. But George was already gone.

Nora started to put on her coat. Jen appeared from Luke's room. 'I love the joke collection.' Then, 'Are you going out?'

'Yes,' said Nora. 'George has gone out. I need to tell him something.'

'What?' said Jen.

'We need something from the shops,' said Nora.

Jen offered to go. 'What is it you need?'

'Cheese,' said Nora. 'Brussels sprouts, tea, curry powder. Something.'

'I always say milk, at times like this. Milk sounds sensible.'

'Yes,' said Nora. 'Milk, we need milk. Definitely. I have to catch up with George and tell him about the milk.'

Jen said, 'Of course.'

Nora ran to the door.

'You running out of the house again?' said Jen.

'No, just have something to say to George. I'll be back in a tick.'

She ran down the path. Out of the gate and along the street. Dark now; a small teenage gang on the corner whistled as she hurtled past. 'Run, Granny, run.'

Nora stopped. 'I am not a grandmother. You cheeky bastards.'

Then she took off again, saw George in the distance and called, 'George. George . . .'

He stopped and watched her flying towards him, coat flapping.

'George,' she called, 'wait for me.'

CHIVERS
LARGE
PRINT
−direct−

If you have enjoyed this Large Print book
and would like to build up your own
collection of Large Print books, please
contact

Chivers Large Print Direct

Chivers Large Print Direct offers you
a full service:

• Prompt mail order service

• Easy-to-read type

• The very best authors

• Special low prices

For further details either call
Customer Services on (01225) 336552
or write to us at Chivers Large Print Direct,
FREEPOST, Bath BA1 3ZZ

Telephone Orders:
FREEPHONE 08081 72 74 75